laws of the land

what is an *Omegaverse?*

An **Omegaverse** is an alternate universe wherein humans have evolved a biological hierarchy based on three individual designations: **alphas, betas, and omegas**. In an Omegaverse, every person falls into one of those three categories (or "designations") by the time they reach adulthood. Their **designation** then determines certain elements of their physiology, psychology, and physical appearance. The humans in this Omegaverse are not shifters.

Alphas are large, strong, dominant, possessive, and territorial. While civilized, they often struggle with the urge to use force or exert their dominance over others; particularly fellow alphas. Optimized anatomy makes them physically superior in many ways, including reproduction.

Male alphas have a "knot" at the base of their penises. This **knot**, much like the penis itself, becomes engorged when they are aroused and expands to its full size upon completion, "locking" an alpha into his partner. Female alphas have a "lock" inside their vaginas that perform a similar locking maneuver on their partners.

Alphas are biologically compelled to find compatible partners based on individual scents. They also tend to form **packs** with others. Omegas often become the center of packs because they are the only designation capable of creating **bonds** between others. There is rarely more than one omega in a pack. Once a pack bonds with an omega, all of their scents alter subtly. This shift helps protect bonded omegas from unwanted advances.

Betas remain the most similar to everyday humans. They do not have intense scents or the same biological compulsions that alphas and omegas share. Many beta-beta relationships resemble traditional monogamous partnerships. Because they cannot bond among themselves, they often choose to marry instead.

Omegas are smaller and softer in stature, naturally submissive, wary of violence, fearful, emotional, empathetic, and magnetically attractive. Omegas' bodies are built to endure the demands of an entire pack of partners, emotionally and physically.

Omega biology draws alphas in. When omegas are aroused, their bodies send nearby alphas a signal by **perfuming**. Omega perfume is a concentrated hit of their specific scent, intended to lure an alpha to their aid.

Alphas and omegas each have distinctive scents. Their bodies produce these scents at all times, but they are particularly strong when the individual is sexually aroused or emotionally distressed. Alphas and omegas can have very intense, all-consuming physical and emotional reactions to each other's scents. While uncommon, the phenomenon is called **scent-sensitivity**.

Scent-sensitive alphas and omegas are referred to as **mates**. By some twist of fate or biology, they are near-irresistible to one another. Separating from their scent-sensitive mates would cause an omega extreme pain and distress.

Omegas experience **heat cycles**. These "heats" are spurred by the biological imperative to mate/bond with an alpha (or group of alphas) who will provide for and protect them. When an omega goes into heat, he/she will experience intense physical pain unless they are knotted by their alphas regularly. Heats send omegas into a state of limited lucidity that is known as a **heat haze**. This haze makes them extremely vulnerable and unstable.

Omegas can take **suppressants** to lower their hormone levels.

A WHY-CHOOSE
fairytale reimagining

ARI WRIGHT

Published and formatted by Blue-Eyed Books

Once Upon A Pack, Royalverse Book 1

ebook ISBN: 9798991446464

ISBN: 9798991446457

cover art: Sonia Garrigoux

graphic design: Blue-Eyed Books

To the ones who wish on eyelashes,
dandelions, and stars.
The universe hears you.
xx

Suppressants help make the pain of heats tolerable for omegas who do not have alphas. Unfortunately, over time, suppressants become less effective.

Unbonded alphas who encounter an unbonded omega can experience **rut**. Rut is a condition wherein an alpha loses his/her mental faculties and gives in to the biological imperative to knot/lock an omega. Rut is often dangerous for omegas.

Omegas **nest** in order to feel secure. An omega's nest should be a soft, round place that feels low to the ground and dark. Omegas take great pride in building their nests to their individual tastes and their alphas' approval. It is their alphas' duty to provide this space and the resources to outfit it.

Courting is the process by which alphas can press their suits with an omega of their choosing. It is generally a task undertaken by the entire pack in pursuit of their one chosen omega.

A note about scents: While they do not have scents of their own, betas may occasionally be able to catch the scents of alphas and omegas (based on the aroma's strength). In this Omegaverse, an alpha or omega's true scent is not apparent until the individual fully designates. Suppressed or unbalanced hormones lead to stunted scents and limit the ability of others to smell them. An alpha or omega's scenting abilities are also not at full capacity until they designate properly.

by royal decree...

CONTENT & TRIGGERS

I'm so glad you're here!

Once Upon A Pack is the first installment in Ari Wright's Royalverse and it is intended to be read as a *complete standalone*!

This is a why-choose Omegaverse romance. It includes lots of knots, tons of spice, and absolutely no choosing!

If you don't like grumpy alphas, swoony mates, and group sex scenes (including packmates lending each other a hand), this may not be the HEA for you <3

Warning: the following content/trigger warnings *do contain spoilers.*

Content/trigger warnings: health/medical anxiety, childhood bullying (not between MCs), financial abuse, loss of a parent, gaslighting, domestic abuse (off page, not between MCs), violence, past promiscuity, rejection, blackmail/manipulation, health abuse, food tampering, oral sex, anal sex, hand-necklaces, DP/DVP.

A LITTLE NOTE ABOUT OUR ROYALVERSE!

His/Her Highness: a prince or princess
His/Her Majesty: a king or queen
His/Her Grace: a duke or duchess
Lord/Lady: any other noble title (like our baron)

As a pack, the men in this book are collectively referred to as "the princes" because their highest-ranking member/pack alpha is the Crown Prince. Individually, they can be referred to by their birthright titles (baron/Lord Burns and the duke/His Grace).

It's important to know that this is a complete work of fiction! The "rules" and structure of existing societies and monarchies do not apply to this one - we're starting a brand new world!

once upon a pack playlist

ivy — Taylor Swift
Manifest — RUBII
Sailor Song — Gigi Perez
Kings & Queens — Ava Max
Enchanted (Taylor's Version) — Taylor Swift
War Of Hearts (Violin) — Dramatic Violin
Lovers — Anna of the North
The Scientist — SKAAR
Never Let Me Go — Florence + The Machine
Gayageum — minlee
Achilles Come Down — Gang of Youths
Love Story - Indila (Slowed) — Penguin Piano
halo — adore
Do You Want Me — PINES
somewhere only we know (slowed + reverb) — ghostly echos, creamy, 11:11 Music Group
ALWAYS BEEN YOU — Chris Grey
Locked Eyes — Casual Sex
champagne problems — Taylor Swift
Royalty — Egzod, Maestro Chives, Neoni
Fetish — dreamsoda
Savage — Bahari
A Dream Is a Wish Your Heart Makes — Hem
Everywhere (I wanna be with you) — Lyrah

prologue

TWELVE SUMMERS AGO

"NOW, YOU KNOW YOU NEED MORE THAN *THAT*."

The duckling puffs its downy feathers out in a stubborn sort of way. I cock my head at him, frowning as sternly as I can. "Listen, you won't be able to grow big and strong without food. How about some of Mama's sourdough? You liked that last week."

When he blinks back, I giggle to myself and reach for my tote bag. The loaves inside are warm—and not because they're fresh. Mama only lets me take the stale ones for my friends, but the summer sunshine does a decent job of reheating them. Pinching my fingers, I sprinkle sourdough crumbs on the sun-warmed marble beneath our feet.

Well, *my* feet.

His… webs?

Do ducks have a special word for their feet? I should ask Mama. Or maybe Mr. Montrose. He's a groundskeeper, so surely he would…

My newest friend sets to work, gathering his breakfast. I turn my head, looking for the rest of his family. I haven't seen them in a few days and I'm worried he's somehow been left behind.

My eyes prick while I watch him eat, wondering what will become of him if he's really all alone. Mama warned me not to touch ducklings, because it upsets their mothers… *but maybe, if this one is on his own…*

Boyish jeers ring across the yard. I flinch, ducking low to hide before it occurs that no one over there can see me. I'm hidden by the garden's hedges, crouched between a wall of fat pink peonies and the smallest of the castle's six fountains—one that looks like some sort of princess, petting a swan.

Not a very realistic image, I've learned. Swans are quite persnickety creatures; I have a scar on my left forearm to prove it. Still, I suppose I like the bubbling statue well enough—this has been my preferred hiding spot all summer.

During the school year, I spend my days in class and at the public school's aftercare center. But, during vacation, Mama asked permission to bring me to the castle with her.

She said the housekeeper agreed, so long as I "behave like a lady." Which, I've been told, does not include tracking mud inside or feeding any of the mice that totally live in the cellar.

I keep that to myself; who knows what the grown-ups would do to them?!

I'm well-acquainted with the way adults treat creatures they consider to be "underfoot."

Not just adults, actually.

The sneering boys grow closer, and my duckling friend—*he looks like a Bartholomew*, I decide—scurries toward the fountain for sanctuary.

I slap my crumb-dusted palm to my face, whispering, "You're

meant to be in the *lake*, Bartholomew! No wonder your mama lost track of you."

He ignores me, of course. After watching him hop in place for a long moment, my heart hurts. With a sigh, I nudge a nearby bag of mulch toward the edge of the basin and he scurries up the sack, quacking happily.

"Wait."

The unexpected voice is so close, I jump and squeak, wheeling around to find—

The prince.

Asher Leopold Everhart.

The Fifth.

Biscuits.

Mama is going to be *mad*.

That was the king's one rule. The housekeeper wanted me to behave like a lady, but His Majesty decreed that none of the employees' children should "fraternize" with the prince. Which I guess means I'm supposed to leave him alone.

Does it count as "fraternizing" if *he* talks to *me*, though? It's not as if I'll ever have the nerve to actually *speak back*...

I shrink away, heart leaping as he strides toward me, the fountain, and Bartholomew with a mighty frown. Probably because I'm in the royal family's private gardens instead of out on the lawn with the other servants' kids.

They're mostly boys, though. And older. And *mean*.

Last week, one of them tried to *hit a snake* with a stick. And *recorded* it.

I shudder at the memory, but my motion stops the prince in his tracks. There's a long, breathless moment of pause where I feel his eyes on my face but don't dare glance back. Then, slowly, he lifts his hands, showing me his palms.

"I didn't mean to scare you," he explains, his voice deeper than I expect. "But the duck can't get into the fountain. The filter will suck him into the plumbing."

That mental picture is so horrifying, my eyes instantly leap up to the royal's face, aghast. Behind square tortoiseshell glasses, his hazel gaze is calm and calculating. It drops to the bag of mulch.

With a hard swallow, I step back, letting him slide the sack—and Bartholomew—off to the side, near the hedge. When my little friend hops into the mulch and goes right for a thicket of thorns, the prince gently blocks the path with his foot, scowling harder.

"Not that way," he mutters, shooing the little bird with the toe of his Oxfords. "Daft thing."

My stomach twists at the insult, even though it's wry. I kneel in the dirt, carefully guiding the duckling's path and doing my best to keep the prince's toe away from him.

"You aren't *daft*, are you, Bartholomew?" I whisper. "You're just *lost*."

The prince goes so still, I find myself turning to look up at him again. His eyes flicker directly to mine for the first time.

"Bartholomew?"

Oh dear. I did say that out loud, didn't I?

See? This is why none of the other kids at school—or my own cousins, for that matter—can stand me.

My throat sticks as I stammer, "Y-yes. Bartholomew Waddlesworth."

Dear Lord. Maybe *I'm* daft.

The prince's expression jumps in surprise. Reminding me that—*oh, right*—this is *the future king* I'm talking to. Not the stablehand's stick-wielding son or the chauffeur's snobby nephew.

The. Prince.

"Y-your Highness," I add, lashes fluttering as I rise, squeezing my hands together and dropping my head for a very belated curtsy.

I wait for a rebuke. Or, maybe, he won't bother with me and he'll just tell his parents. Then I'll be stuck back at my mother and aunt's flat, dealing with Caitlin and Claire for the rest of the summer.

If I'm there, who will feed Bartholomew?

A quiet laugh has me raising my face, blinking in shock. The prince's eyes crease slightly while he chuckles at me.

He's older, I realize. Only by a few years, but still bigger than me. More mature-looking. And... beautiful? With flawless skin and a head of thick, unruly brown hair the same color as my favorite chocolate tarts from the manor's kitchen. Not to mention the unique green-and-gold of his eyes.

Those irises sparkle as he raises one thick brow at me. "Bartholomew *Waddlesworth*? Is that his official title?"

Yes, by the way, I am daft for sure. Because I simply bumble, "His official title is 'Bartholomew Waddlesworth, of the Maytown Manor Ducks.'"

The corner of the prince's mouth ticks up, but he nods, straightening to hold the book dangling from his left hand behind his back. "Naturally," he agrees, somehow teasing me without making a joke. "And what about the squirrels? Are they all 'of the Maytown Manor Squirrels'?"

"No," I giggle. "There are a *bunch* of different squirrel families on the grounds. They're named by their home *tree*."

Prince Asher is known for being quiet. It's true, even when he laughs in earnest, flashing rows of perfect, white teeth.

Like most beautiful things, his laughter doesn't last very long. The humor falls from his face as he watches Bartholomew totter toward the lake situated east of the manor. "Neither of you should be in this garden, you know."

His gaze slides to mine, briefly, even though it doesn't belong there. We aren't supposed to look the royals in the eye unless addressed by name.

It occurs to me, a second too late, that he's trying to *ask* what to call me. Maybe so I *can* look at him? I swallow again, brushing my hands against my navy leggings. "Ivy," I tell him. "My mom is your—is *Her Majesty's* tailor."

Prince Asher nods again, the motion slow and considering to match the glide of his gaze over my face.

"Ivy," he repeats. "I'm Asher." A mild grimace cracks his

handsome features. "You already knew that," he adds, rambling. "I mean, I *assume* you already knew that."

My head bobs, strangely weightless. Some distant part of my mind wonders what he's *doing* out here. Talking to *me*.

Shouldn't he be, like, at an elite boarding school? Or in a war room?

Do they make princes walk around with dictionaries balanced on their heads, or is that just for "ladies"?

Prince Asher is known for having many texts to choose from. "His Nerdiness," some very mean websites dubbed him after a photo from his bedroom leaked to tabloids.

Luckily, he wasn't in it.

But about four hundred books were.

And some unfortunate star-patterned sheets that are—*okay*—maybe a *teensy bit* nerdy.

Figuring it would be best to distract him from his earlier line of conversation—and any thoughts of my broken rules—I gesture a fluttering hand at the text trapped in his clutches. "D-did you come outside to read, Your Highness?"

That's odd, actually. It's blazing hot out here. Why would he read in this heat? He could be in any room of the manor he wishes...

When his jaw hardens and his throat works, I realize I've accidentally asked a question that *embarrasses* him. And, since I'm not even supposed to *speak* to him, I'm guessing that's also... a blunder.

"Yes," he finally replies, blowing out a breath. "I'm... studying."

I nod, not quite quelling the rude urge to peek at the book trapped in his clutches. *How To—something?*

But the voices I heard laughing interrupt us from the other side of the hedge.

"—total *fucking dweeb*."

I gasp, covering my gaping mouth with my hand. Mama would be appalled if I ever said that word. We heard a valet use it once, and she muttered about it under her breath the whole way home.

A scoff answers the curse. "I know, right? Next time I see him out here, I'm going to kick his ass."

"You will *not*," another kid snorts. "Because then you'd be thrown in the dungeon."

"This place doesn't have a *dungeon*, shithead. And besides, you think the king would care if I tried to toughen up his sissy son? I bet he'd *thank* me. Maybe I'll get knighted."

They're... talking about beating up Asher? Prince *Asher? What on* Earth*?! How* dare *they?! Why* would *they?!*

Fear bolts through my belly, but I start to step toward the hedge anyway, intending to chase them off the way I did when they harmed that innocent snake.

Long, cool fingers grasp my wrist. I whip my head around, finding the prince much closer than he was before. The book in question hangs from one of his hands while the other squeezes softly at my hammering pulse. His hazel eyes are solemn, his mouth a thin line while he shakes his head.

Telling me to stay here. And be silent.

Before I can decide if it's wrong to obey him, the boys start up again.

"I feel bad for the king," one says airily. "He only has one heir and the guy's a *wuss*. I bet he won't even be an alpha. I bet he's a delicate little omega like his mommy."

"Ha!" the other barks. "Even she isn't as much of a pussy as that loser."

The prince's jaw sets. His hand at my wrist twitches.

But the horrible moment isn't over yet. Because the first boy speaks again. "He asked if he could go into town with us; last week when we were meeting up with those girls from the gym?" He snorts. "I told him he needed balls to get laid."

The atrociously rude joke sinks in at the same second every speck of color drains from Prince Asher's face. When his eyes drop to the stones under our feet, I realize just how mortifying this is for him.

Even in front of a nobody like me... he's a *prince*. And they mock him openly. *Gleefully*. Almost for *sport*.

He was seeking their approval when he asked to go somewhere with them. And now he knows that I know just how pathetic they found that.

Hurt blooms behind my sternum. A thick, throat-clogging cloud.

I watch his eyes lose focus, blinking at the ground. He seems to have forgotten he's holding my arm. I note the way his posture changes, hunching in...

And I—*daft, underfoot Ivy Addison*—

I reach over to touch him.

My fingertips graze his starched sleeve. It occurs to me that he must be terribly hot and uncomfortable out here. The aching sensation smoldering in my chest kicks up higher, overpowering the prick of fear I feel when his head turns sharply, that gold-green gaze regaining its focus and flying to where I've accidentally stroked the skin of his wrist.

He stares for a long moment. So long that the boys wander off, unwittingly leaving us on the other side of the hedge, a world away from where we started.

Asher examines our hands and I watch, holding my breath. Bracing.

My aunt usually corrects my social *faux pas* with a sound whack to the back of my head when Mama has hers turned. Surely the prince wouldn't *hurt* me, though. He might tell his father and have me formally reprimanded... or try to get my mom fired or—

His eyes slowly rise back to mine. "I apologize that you had to hear that. It wasn't appropriate for a young lady."

I half-swallow a relieved, nervous giggle. "That's okay, Your Highness. My cousins watch a lot of YouTube, and some of the videos they've put on are—"

"Ivy?"

I cut myself off, gulping. Opening my mouth, hoping the words—the *right* words—are sitting on my tongue.

Yes, Your Highness?

My apologies, Prince Asher.

I beg your pardon.

Before I manage any of them, he tilts his head slightly and holds up his book. Solving the mystery of its title once and for all.

How To Ballroom Dance for Morons.

The fingers wrapped around my wrist twitch again as he blows out a deep breath, scowling seriously. "Do you, by any chance, know how to dance?"

ONE

PRESENT DAY

Five.

Four.

Three, two—

A crash of crystal ricochets through the princes' private dining chamber, echoing into the vaulted corridor on the other side of the double doors. I round my shoulders, cringing with my whole body as the staid dinner I've been eavesdropping on comes to its inevitable conclusion:

Whichever famously beautiful, oh-so-eligible omega the advisers lined up for tonight? Has had *enough.*

As evidenced by the scrape of a heavy, antique dining chair and the sharp *clack* of high heels.

Heading right toward me.

Uh-oh.

I look around for a place to hide—which is silly, because this hallway is literally a tunnel of pale robin-egg wallpaper and patinaed gold wainscoting.

Which, by the way, is *not* easy to clean.

There's only one place to go—so I wind up flattening myself into the space beside the doors, praying to disappear.

The clacking draws closer. My eyes widen, flitting across the opulent hall to land, for half a second, on my friend's.

Before I can speak or scramble, Gracie snaps herself to her full alpha height and brushes at the front of her tasteful navy work dress. Manicured fingers curl around the tablet pressed against her chest, tight knuckles the only outward indication of any strain by the time the high heels—and their owner—burst through the high, arched doorway.

I duck to the floor, doing what I do best—remaining absolutely undetectable.

If any of the staff find out that Gracie let me listen in on this catastrophe, we'll both be toast.

I just barely catch the wince on my friend's dark features before the heiress *de jour* bursts out of the room with a parting, "*Hmph*!"

Ever the professional, Gracie steps forward, smiling blandly. "Ready to depart, my lady?"

From my place halfway behind the door, I get a glimpse of the beautiful omega. She is elegance itself, her long black hair swept into some artful updo. As a beta, her chocolatey scent is just a subtle glimmer for me, but it seems perfectly fine—and the curves of her body are as lovely as her emerald cocktail dress.

Perfect, I think, the word wistful. *She's perfect for them.*

Well. Sort of.

"How you work for this *pack of mongrels* is beyond me," the heiress—*or maybe this one is a princess?*—snaps. "Have my car brought around *immediately*."

"Of course, my lady." Gracie nods, expression devoid of any emotion. "Right this way."

She thrusts out a hand, gesturing in the opposite direction. To keep the woman from turning toward *me*.

Bless her.

As if I don't already owe Gracie everything. She helped me get this job as a housekeeper in Maytown Manor and vouched for me when they reduced the staff to a skeleton crew six months ago.

According to her, the royal family decided to limit themselves to essential, trusted personnel when the princes temporarily moved to the royal family's country house to embark on their search for a princess. With the national media clamoring for details about the "Crown Pack's" prospects, Queen Selene also went out of her way to ensure that the maid assigned to her son's pack's private quarters was a beta—and "the sole of discretion."

Namely, me.

A decision that seems more prudent each time I find myself cleaning their sheets.

Or tidying the remains of these disastrous dinners.

Gracie had the Maytown housekeeper place me with the prince and his packmates specifically because she *knows* I would never betray her by telling a soul what I witness here.

Of course, I didn't disclose that this is *far* from my first summer here... or just how painful it's been for me, watching the alpha I used to know date every eligible omega in the universe.

Or, more specifically, every *beautiful, titled* omega in the universe.

Which is somehow worse?

When all of this began, half of me was sure Prince Asher would recognize me the first time our eyes met. And all of me *hoped* he might.

That was stupid—because, of course, if he had, I would have

been fired. The Crown Prince's parting instructions for me were very clear: I wasn't supposed to come back.

I didn't really have a choice, but once I knew he didn't realize who I am, I made myself a promise. I like to think I've kept it—and done my best never to take advantage of everything I see and know about the prince's pack.

But, I have to admit, I may have developed a *bit* of an eaves-dropping habit since they arrived six months ago...

Does it help that I feel really, really guilty about it?

Either way, it's too late to turn back tonight; I heard the whole debacle. And, honestly? I didn't even *need* to overhear to know what happened.

He happened.

Dair.

I pinch the naughty voice whispering the duke's nickname and prepare to step out from behind the thick wooden slab. A deep, tortured groan interrupts me.

"Jesus, Dair," a lower, steadier voice growls. "*Again?*"

Shuffling inside the dining room has me ducking back behind the door. God forbid one of them notices me here. *Especially* Dair.

I mean, *His Grace.*

That's what I'm meant to call him, until their pack takes an omega to bond them and *officially* turns the others into princes—and I *did* call him that, even in my head.

Until that strange, cold night four months ago.

Shh, little dove.

Would you really say no to a duke?

The warmth of his body, the scent of his rich tartness, all tangled in the thorns of some expensive liquor. A dark shimmer shifting in his even darker eyes. And the toe-curling rasp of his American accent—roughing up words he never should have said. Most especially to *me.*

I don't even have to see him to know the pack's infamous

playboy now wears his signature snarl, replying, "You were going to fuck *her*? With what? A paper bag over her head?"

I grimace again. *Dear Lord*. If he thought that gorgeous woman wasn't appealing, I can't fathom what he wanted with *me*.

Compared to her, I might as well be an end-table. Or an umbrella.

A third voice answers in a mutter—and I know it must be Sebastian, the charming one. "*I* thought she was quite attractive. Nine out of ten."

"*Of course* she was attractive," the first—and most powerful—alpha spits back. "She was *selected* by a *team* of people who are *paid* to keep our optics pristine."

I know that's true. Gracie is on that team.

Dair doesn't seem deterred by this information. He sounds indolent as he replies, "Well, find a new team, then."

Sebastian sighs. "We're running out of time, Dair. If we don't choose an omega soon, Asher's father will choose one *for* us."

The king—Asher Leopold Everhart the Fourth—is the latest in a long line of Everhart kings and rumored to be the most dominant alpha in their family line... though not the most prolific. He and his omega only have one child.

Asher.

Ash.

Seriously, someone needs to come get this voice in my head. She's lost it.

Anyway. Everhart alphas have ruled without forming packs for the last three generations, so it was shocking to most when Prince Asher made a pack with his two closest friends from the Royal Academy: our oh-so-charming Baron Sebastian Burns... and Dairragh Vreeland, the notorious Duke of McAffry.

It's unusual, these days, for a *pack* to inherit the crown. It used to happen all the time in the olden days, when scent-matched alphas and omegas were considered the Holy Grail for royal procreation. Now, it's more common for politics to make these sorts of decisions—and keeping track of one crown prince is a lot easier than having *three.*

Which, we technically *won't*, until they're bonded. Thanks to whichever lucky—or, perhaps, *unlucky*—omega they choose.

If they ever make it through one of these courting dinners.

I have faith in them. They may be a bit chaotic right now, but it should be better once they're a true unit.

And three knots are better than one?

Or so they say.

I certainly don't say that.

I don't even have a way to *know* that.

I'm a beta, for one. But even if I could take a knot like an omega, the extent of my carnal knowledge consists of a handful of dorm room fumbles, whatever I've gleaned from listening to my cousins, and the nonsense I deal with cleaning up after the princes.

When I first started working in this section of the manor, I admit I was shocked. I'd never really been around single men before, so I wasn't prepared for the way they spoke to each other. Nor was I prepared for what *tidying up* after them would entail.

I mean, the sheer number of condom wrappers *alone...*

My cheeks heat as my stomach drops and rolls around the bottom of my abdomen like a marble in a bowl. The spinning sensation isn't new—it's been happening for the last few months—but the strength of it has become somewhat concerning.

It isn't real, I coach internally. *Just medical anxiety. There's nothing wrong with you.*

To distract myself, I try to guess what the duke will say next. A small smile curls my lips when he proves me correct, gritting, "I don't even *want* an omega."

"Not this again." Sebastian groans, the sound alarmingly passionate and masculine and—*no, Ivy.*

Asher's alpha power slices through the bickering. His voice follows, back to its usual even keel. "Enough. Dair, you knew we would have to bond an omega. And no one is buying your blustering about not wanting one. Bast, you'll have to arrange an apology for the girl. Send flowers or plan a tea or something."

I hear the prince stand, shoving back from the table and clipping across the floor. He tends to do that, now. Striding with purpose and rarely ever slowing down.

He's different. So different from—

"Now that our evening is *officially* ruined, I'll be summoned any moment," Asher sighs. "You two better make yourselves scarce."

There's a pang in my breast. I've heard the king go off on the crown prince too many times to count, but ever since this search process started, it's been a lot worse.

My hands wring under my apron as a tide of anxiety engulfs my stomach. *He must feel twice as sick as I do at the thought. I wonder if there's anything I can do to help...*

His steady footfall rounds the corner. I know, even before he notices me, that he'll pretend he hasn't.

That's his way. I catch him every time—perhaps because I know better than most how quick his mind is. I don't expect his expression to flicker. But his eyes... he never could keep them from wandering wherever they wanted to go. To whatever piqued his endless curiosity.

A mind for science, my mother used to murmur with a sad smile. *What a pity he's a prince.*

I think those words in that same tone each time I find him holed up in his study, greeting the dawn after a sleepless night. Or pacing the grounds after a fight with his father.

Or... moments like these. Where he looks at me for just the smallest part of a second.

And I think maybe—*maybe*—this will be the time he *sees* me.

But then he turns away. Strides on. Off to slay the next dragon.

What a pity he's a prince.

two

"Where have you been?"

My aunt sounds as tired as I feel. Which is really saying something, because I've been up since five a.m. and these thrifted Doc Martins finally bit a blister into the back of my heel on my four-mile walk home.

Not to mention the nice slice through the center of my palm. Courtesy of the smashed crystal I cleaned off the princes' dining room floor.

Oh, and that last errand Dair sent me out on after he spotted me crouched under the antique table, scraping shards into my dustpan.

I'm trying my best *not* to recall the look on his face when I turned my head and saw him—looming on the threshold to the rest of their wing, leaning on the arched opening with a hard smirk and flashing black eyes.

"I have special guests coming," he'd said, all loose shoulders and smug amusement. *"But it seems I'm all out of the necessary protection. You wouldn't mind running up to the market in town and fetching more for me, would you, little dove?"*

I tried not to notice the way his signature black vest hung open around his lanky frame. Or how he'd unfastened one too many pearly buttons on his collared shirt. And *especially* not the way the silk fabric was juuuuust thin enough to hint at the black ink painted across his pecs...

No wonder I wound up agreeing to his horribly rude, completely inappropriate request. Despite my torn-up feet.

As humiliating and painful as that task was, the worst part about Dair and his rude demands always comes later. When I find myself thinking about them all the way home.

Four miles is a fair bit of time to mull. Or, really, try to talk myself *out* of mulling.

Still, it's impossible not to wonder: *Who are these women? Where does he meet them? What does he do to them?*

And why on Earth did he come on to me that night if he has better options at his beck and call?

All my curiosities are... embarrassing, but fine. Annoying, but not hurtful.

No.

Hurtful is wondering about Ash.

If he gets women from the same circles. How he sneaks them in and out without anyone noticing. Why he's so meticulous about cleaning up after himself in this one regard.

As stupid as it is (truly very stupid), I hate to consider it.

Which is why I often fling my thoughts over to the baron as quickly as I can.

Not that it's a chore. Lord Sebastian Burns is, undoubtedly, the most attractive man in the country. Possibly the world.

And that isn't just me romanticizing. He's actually won *contests.* Been published at the top of international Hottest Men Alive lists.

I never need to wonder where *he* meets the women he entertains. Sebastian is easily the most social alpha in their pack—he attends every event, looks gorgeous in any attire, and plays every gentleman's sport imaginable, to boot.

Thinking about the way he looks in his polo gear, fresh off a victory high—his blond hair sweat-misted and perfect lips spread in a grin—makes my lower abdomen all quivery.

Even now.

Even *here.*

I wince at myself, focusing on the small twin bed beside mine. Months ago, it belonged to my mother. It was where she languished for years, drifting in and out of consciousness while her health deteriorated.

My father died when I was too young to remember him. As an omega, losing her alpha mate was the worst thing that could have happened to Mama. It's still hard for me to understand since I'm a beta and I don't experience the same biological impulses; but many doctors over the years tried to explain it to me.

The bond sickness my mother battled is almost always fatal. It usually isn't so tragic, as most omegas who lose their bonded alpha mates tend to be elderly. My poor mother, though, dealt with steadily diminished health for nearly two decades before she finally found peace.

About five years ago, things got so bad she started needing help with her work. Two years after that, she had to stop working entirely.

That all happened during my final year of college. I dropped out and moved home to replace her income at the manor with my own. My aunt, Matilda, used to make the majority of our money—but the worse Mama got, the more help she required. Aunt Matilda eventually wound up staying home, too.

It left me paying the rent, but I never minded hard work and keeping busy.

The final year of Mama's illness was the worst. She barely ever woke up, and when she did, she usually mumbled incoherently for my father. Those were the times I most wished I'd had a chance to know him, even for a little while—any story I could have told my mother might have helped.

In the end, her death felt like a mercy. She so clearly *needed* to be with him... I'd been praying she would find her way to peace for a long time, wishing on stars that my parents might make their way back to each other in some other realm.

I may have breathed a sigh of relief to know my mother wasn't suffering anymore, but it was short-lived. Years of advanced medical care created quite a mountain of bills—and when my mother passed, they all fell to me.

Matilda still isn't happy I've gone from paying all the rent to only being able to afford half. She comes to stand in the doorway of my bedroom, throwing her hands on her hips. "I thought you said you were working late tonight."

Considering most of the other maids finish before five and it's nearly eleven p.m., I did. Instead of arguing, I mumble something about earning time-and-a-half all week. Gracie texted a few hours ago to tell me the king and queen have decided to throw a big party and they'll need extra help leading up to it.

Matilda harrumphs, somewhat mollified. "Between that and the mending your mother's former clients dropped off this week, you should be able to cover our rent *and* your medical bills this month. By the way, the receipt for your portion of the groceries is on the counter. And I left a smoothie for you in the fridge."

My aunt believes in nothing so much as she believes in the healing power of a green smoothie. She's been making them every day, for everyone in the house, for as long as I can remember.

Extra protein for my scrawny self. Green tea and ginger to

keep my cousins trim. We're all betas so, according to my aunt, we "need all the help we can get" attracting suitors.

Well, I don't really *want* any suitors. And the idea of drinking liquefied kale isn't necessarily my *favorite.* But it's food I don't have to prepare or clean up, and it's healthy.

I thank her and nod, keeping my eyes down. Out of my periphery, I catch her gray eyes glinting as they sweep over the one piece of furniture in my room—a worn dresser with Mama's urn on it. Aunt Matilda blinks, her drawn features narrowing.

Before she can speak again, her daughters trounce into the apartment, mid-argument.

"It was fucking pathetic," Caitlin sneers. "You could have at least pretended you have some dignity."

"He won't know it was me calling him," Claire flings back, her face every bit as angular as her mother and sister's, especially while twisted in amusement. "Didn't you notice I used *your* phone?"

Caitlin screeches. "You little bitch!"

"Girls, girls," Matilda chuckles as if their bickering is endearing, somehow. To her, I suppose it might be. They all have the same cutting sense of humor—one I'm not quite sharp enough to keep up with.

"We only came home to change," Claire announces. "We're meeting some guys at the pub."

They don't invite me, but that's fine; I can barely keep myself upright at this point. Still, after my cousins saunter to their room and emerge looking like glamorous twenty-somethings, watching them leave has silly tears rising in my throat.

Matilda waves them out, then turns to me with a new gleam in her gaze. "I'm also going out to meet a gentleman friend," she announces. Something sly slides into her expression. "I was wondering if I might be able to borrow your necklace. You know—the heart one?"

My hand automatically flies to my chest, where the locket sits under my work uniform. Instead of grabbing it, I force myself to lay my palm flat against my sternum, hoping I haven't given too much away.

"W-why?"

I might not be as cunning and calculated as my aunt or her daughters, but I *have* noticed that all of my mother's jewelry has steadily gone missing over the past few years. Every piece but the one she gifted me on my sixteenth birthday. A necklace my father once gave to her.

...and the same one Asher untangled from my hair the day he kissed me for the first time.

It's the one and only item I've managed to save for myself. I suspect Matilda sold everything else of value—not that the thin silver chain and slender locket would fetch much money. They have far more sentimental value than anything else.

Matilda notices the way I guard the chain around my neck, her gray eyes gleaming with avarice. "I just think it would look good with my outfit."

Her red dress seems fancier than my simple locket, but I find myself starting to unclasp the necklace anyway. A pound at the door startles us both, and she gasps, whirling to look at herself in the mirror she keeps hanging in the hallway.

"I haven't even finished my hair," she snaps, bustling out of my room. Relief bursts the bubble of panic strangling me when she scoops up her purse and pauses to clip her dirty-blonde hair back.

The man waiting for her looks like her type—dressed in a suit, smiling widely.

Wearing a wedding band.

She likes married men, she once told me after half a bottle of wine, because they're always the most willing to pay handsomely for a woman's silence. Since she's made dating advantageously into a career of sorts, the preference for guys who need to keep her quiet about their extracurricular activities makes a horrible sort of sense.

As the front door slams shut, a sob sneaks into my throat.

Then another. Until I'm standing in our dark, empty hallway, fisting the charm around my neck and crying for no reason.

But it doesn't matter how tired I am or how shaky I've felt all day. Aunt Matilda was right—the mending needs to be done if I want to pay our rent this month.

Besides, I doubt I'll be sleeping well tonight, anyway. No matter how depleted my body feels, as soon as I lie down and close my eyes, Dair's dark smirk will float to the top of my brain.

Followed by Sebastian's friendly, oblivious grin when I got back with the duke's "protection." How he waved to me from their couch, utterly unbothered by the noises coming from Dair's bedroom as he watched me hang the bag of condoms on the polished brass handle, knock briskly, and scurry off as fast as I could.

And even if—*if*—I can somehow stop cringing over *all of that*... it won't matter. Because my last thought will always be Asher.

Ash.

And tonight? I won't be able to stop reliving the way he had to march off to face his father.

Like a man walking to the gallows.

Remembering the hollow, grim look on his face, I turn on the oven and hunt for a pincushion. *I'll keep myself busy*, I decide. *And do everything I can to help where I'm able.*

Slumping into the old metal chair under the galley kitchen's only window, I turn to look down at the street. Our neighborhood used to be ramshackle in a charming sort of way—but as the years go on, the signs of disrepair have slowly overtaken whatever historic ambiance the worn brick roads and stooped row houses once had.

Now, it all looks as exhausted as the rest of us.

I feel it in my *bones* today. A familiar slither of fear snakes around my stomach, tickling the base of my lungs until they pinch. A hard tremble judders through me, leaving my fingers too shaky to thread Mama's needle.

Shutting my eyes, I exhale slowly, repeating what every one of the village's free clinic doctors have told me for years.

Just health anxiety.

Perfect specimen of a beta.

Extremely fit and resilient.

And, my favorite: *The only thing that's wrong with you is your head, girl.*

Well, I can't exactly argue with that. Talking to birds and rodents is my favorite hobby, and I routinely fantasize about a guy who doesn't even remember spending three summers with me a million years ago.

Who's also, you know.

The literal *prince.*

With another wince, I force a hard exhale and ignore the seethe in my middle. The lightness that spins through the back of my skull and the spots that dance across my vision.

I'm fine. There's nothing wrong with me. This is just anxiety, and it will pass.

Needing a distraction, I lift my chin and peer up at the inky sky. My gaze snags on the first star it stumbles over—a low, shining pinprick in the dark velvet fabric overhead.

I stare, imagining there really is a vast universe of light stretched beyond that one small speck of brightness. Focusing on the way it seems to wink at me and how the blurs dotting my vision fade away the longer I look.

Remembering far too much.

"Did you make a wish," he'd asked, closer than he normally stood.

"No, silly!" I laughed softly. "You can only make a wish on the first star you see. Otherwise, it's bad luck."

Ash's mouth softened into a warm curve that matched his gold-green eyes. "Says who, goose?"

I'd waved my hands at the heavens with an eye-roll. "You know —the universe!"

That earned me one of his secret smiles—where his eyes shim-

mered with mirth while his lips somehow got sterner. “Mm. Well. If the universe says so.”

And his... his hand, so very tentative as it settled under my elbow. When I didn’t move—didn’t dare even breathe, *for fear he would stop—he stepped closer. Almost flush against my back.*

Bending to put us cheek-to-cheek, scanning the sky. “Which one did you spot first? We’ll both wish on it.”

I shook slightly as his deep murmur sank into my shoulders, stammering a reply. “B-but then you’ll *have bad luck.”*

“Your *wish will come true, though,” he’d hummed, earnest as ever. “So it will be worth it.”*

What did I wish for that day? Whatever it was, I’m sure it didn’t come true.

But is that any reason not to try again?

Mama would’ve said no, so I let my eyes fall shut for one more moment. And wish all over again.

three

THE MECHANICS OF SOUND ARE VERY FAMILIAR TO ME.

Decibels, reverberations. It's a simple sort of science I've understood since I was a small child.

The louder a sound, the larger its amplitude. The thicker the substance it runs into, the less momentum it has.

The doors of Maytown Manor are hundreds of years old. Solid and well-fitted. With heavy locks.

The rugs are thick, too. Perfect for absorbing noise.

Which is how I know Dair is being an absolute ass on purpose.

Across our circular common room, the door from the

southern hallway snicks open and Bast steps over the threshold, dripping sweat. He's been working out since dawn, as is his habit before a day of scheduled appearances.

Even after two hours in the gym, the sweat-darkened blond hair swept loose over his crown and faint dark circles under his eyes are the only things out of place. We're opposites in that way—my oldest friend isn't meticulous about anything, apart from his appearance. Which is the only subject I truly couldn't care less about.

Dair might be worse than I am, actually. Then again, as the sheer volume coming from his room would indicate, he doesn't care about much of anything at all.

I fight off a wince, imagining the state of his bedroom. Thinking of the poor maid who will have to contend with it later.

The pretty, blonde beta with messy bangs and unpolished fingernails. They're always covered in pin-pricks. Does she sew? For us?

It's the one bit of curiosity I've allowed myself where she's concerned. Because if I let myself truly think about her at all, I would likely notice just how lovely she seems.

And that would be unacceptable.

Ever since the day they introduced us to our private staff, I've done everything in my power not to notice *any* of the women. Tuning out any mention of their names—the maid's is something with an A, I think—and averting my eyes every time one of them raises their face from a task, rushing past whenever I can get away with it.

Still, I pity the woman who deals with our personal quarters.

Dair is the messiest of the three of us. And he's been at this for *hours*.

Bast pauses just inside the entrance. His brows tweak up in true astonishment. God love him; no matter how much any of us fuck up, he's always surprised.

"Still?" he asks, incredulous. "Again?"

I drop the first of three daily newspapers on the coffee table and reach for the second. My Alpha growls, the aggressive sound vibrating my lungs before I manage to stop it. Bast only flinches a little, huffing out an annoyed breath that coordinates well with his expression.

"He's doing this on purpose," he grumbles, dropping into a nearby armchair.

I snap my paper open. "So it would seem."

A particularly high-pitched wail rends the air. Then another —just as loud but distinctly different.

"Jesus," Bast curses, his blue eyes bulging. "He has *two* of them in there?"

"Mm," I hum, just as another woman's screams join the cacophony. "Three, by my count."

My packmate balks, then frowns, considering. "Seems like a hell of a lot of work," he mutters.

Despite my black mood, I smirk slightly. "You know Dair. Never one to slack when there's a statement to be made."

"Just every other hour of the day," Bast replies, pouting as he digs his phone out of his joggers. "Speaking of—he better finish up soon. We both have fittings at ten. And I am *not* covering for him with *Maman* again."

The mention of my mother brings a reluctant smile to my face. "He's her favorite. You know that."

"Yeah," Bast snaps back, "and it's utter *shite*, considering what a useless prick His Grumpiness is and how charming I am in comparison."

I lift a shoulder to shrug. "She likes an underdog."

Bast rolls his eyes to the ceiling. "Oh yes. Dairragh Vreeland, Duke of McAffry. Heir to a veritable fortune and—apparently— in possession of a dick that can run through three women at once. The poor dear."

I have to swallow an actual laugh that time. "I doubt he's used his dick all three times."

My packmate harrumphs and mutters more about "His Grumpiness."

Sebastian is easily the funniest of us, but he's also, normally, the most upbeat. All this sniping and complaining isn't like him. I lower the corner of my newspaper, lifting an eyebrow in silent question.

He sighs, deflating. "Sorry. My Alpha is *raging* this morning. I had a guest of my own last night, and it did *nothing*. I thought maybe a morning on the lake—but I rowed for two hours and, again, nothing."

His eyes drop to the silver breakfast tray on the table between us, and he bends forward. "Fuck it. Guess I'll try food."

I lift my foot from where my ankle sits crossed over my knee and shove the toe of my Oxford at his incoming fingers, intercepting them before they pluck up the last piece of banana bread. Glaring, I hold back another growl. "That's mine."

And, hell, I must be more on edge than usual, too, because his answering glower makes my insides lurch. The urge to bark and flex my dominance rears high and surges out.

All over food?

Fucking hell.

As if I've ever been hungry.

I spend hours every week working on the urban homelessness issue in Crenmore's cities, so I know every statistic there is. Tens of thousands are actually starving under our rule. People I do everything I can to help, despite Parliament's desire to divert funding to every godforsaken military endeavor and land entitlement they can come up with.

Evil, selfish politicians with weak characters. Their existence is the one reason I've allowed this courting farce to go on—we *need* an omega to bond and ascend the throne.

Once we do? I'm changing *everything*.

Bast feels my simmering rage and curves a brow right back at me. "Apologies, *Your Highness*," he jokes. "Feeling territorial today?"

That's an unsettling notion. What would my Alpha be possessive of? Banana bread?

It's true; I do love it. And our Michelin-star chef only lowers himself to bake it whenever my father and I have one of our infamous shouting matches. Word travels fast among the staff, I suppose, because the morning after a big fight, I always find a small loaf of banana bread on my breakfast tray.

I frown at it, now, pondering what has my blood racing thicker and hotter than usual. "Maybe that omega from last night merits a second look," I muse. "If she has us all so..."

I nod over at Dair's closed doors and the squeals within. Bast grimaces.

"Amped?" he finishes. "Yeah, I thought the same thing. But, to be honest, her scent didn't do much for me."

Me, neither. It was a thick, white-chocolate aroma. Sweet enough to tempt, but also overwhelmingly rich. By the end of the salad course, I felt like I needed a glass of something bitter and ten minutes on the terrace to clean my lungs out.

"Besides, Dair hated her, and the feeling seemed mutual," Bast adds. "So I doubt this show has anything to do with last night. Who knows what the fuck his problem is?"

I still don't. Even after ten years as a pack.

"One of his moods, no doubt," I murmur, hoping Bast finds me more convincing than I find myself.

The baron nods, plucking a bowl of fruit from my tray and tossing a blueberry into his mouth while he sprawls back in his chair, hiking one knee over the armrest. Blue eyes scan the side of my face for a long moment.

"What did His Majesty have to say last night?"

It's my turn to flinch, but I hold steady, turning the page of my newspaper as calmly as I can. "More of the same."

I know Bast can sense my lie. We've been friends since high school and he knows me well.

Still, I don't know how to tell him—or Dair—about my father's most recent tirade. Or how I suspect the man who loves to berate me may actually have a point this time.

Was it a mistake for me to take a pack? I'm the first Everhart

Crown Prince to do it in centuries—and I'm starting to understand why. Sure, it's less work for me individually, but it also means contending with three opinions on every single decision.

The guys seem content to let me take the lead in matters of state—Bast because he knows I'm better-bred for it and Dair, I suspect, because he doesn't give a shit.

But now? When it comes to finding a future queen?

We all have to agree. Anything short of that wouldn't be fair to the two of them. Or the omega.

Maybe my father's blustering actually makes sense. Would all of this be easier if I didn't have Dair and Bast to consider?

The omega we met last night is practically an *empress*. She was born to rule. She could expand our diplomatic relations in the East...

She did nothing to unite my pack, though. If anything, we're more fragmented this morning than we were yesterday.

It's ironic. I thought having them here would help. I knew I wouldn't have strong feelings for any of these prospective queens, so I hoped one of my packmates would. Or both of them, ideally.

Since I never will.

My reluctance doesn't surprise the others. I'm known for being emotionless. Practical. Duty-bound and more content when I don't have to manage others' feelings.

They never expected me to have romantic notions, because I've never shown any.

Little do they know; logic and duty aren't the reason I won't ever find my match.

They're the reason I already lost her.

four

It's happening.

I've snapped.

The world has been waiting for this day—when, finally, the goddamned Duke of McAffry would lose his mind.

Or, at the very least, *admit* he's lost his mind.

My mind.

Jesus.

The hallway smells like whatever Asher ate for breakfast. Muffins or something sweet enough to cloy. It isn't like him. He's usually a poached-eggs, dry-toast, served-with-a-side-of-sadness sort of guy.

And don't even get me started on Bast. That motherfucker eats *egg whites*. With *vegetables*.

Why not just scrape bird shit off the castle windows with a leaf and put some salt on that?

As if he can read my mind, Bast shoots me a dark look as we pass one another in the entryway to Maman's suite. "You're late."

Yes. And?

I don't think I've ever actually been on time for anything. He knows that. I return his glower with one of my own. "I had guests to see to."

"You could have at least showered," he comments, dropping his dark blue eyes to my rumpled white shirt and open vest. "Or buttoned your shirt all the way."

Asher's mother won't be surprised that I'm a mess. Queen Selene may have perfected her role, but my reluctance toward mine amuses her to no end. And always, regardless of how poorly I perform, she treats me like her own son.

She even likes me better than Bast. A fact that irks him to no end.

Maybe that's why he's dressed like a total tool. The cashmere sweater tied around his shoulders matches his spotless white pants. I glare at them, wishing I could smear something into the fabric.

I've been chasing that itch—the need to destroy pristine things—my whole life. All in all, I've done pretty well. Ruined my family's proud lineage. My own reputation. And now, I'm slowly poisoning our pack, too.

It's a wonder any of them put up with me. Let alone... *care.*

God.

Can you imagine?

Ignoring the way my stomach pitches, I shrug and give a lazy nod toward Maman's open fitting room. "How bad is it this time? Does she have us all dressed as matching show ponies?"

Bast snorts. "And ruin your carefully crafted pirate aesthetic? Never."

That merits a slight smirk. "Good. Ash is in there?"

He nods. "Finishing up. He's sending me out to have tea with the omega from last night. Apparently, your constant litany of insults poses a risk to national security and he needs me to make sure her military doesn't try to nuke us like a microwave burrito."

Oh right. That.

Better Bast than me.

Especially today.

My Alpha has been on a *rampage* ever since that dinner last night. So it may have been short-sighted of me to scare the polished, chocolatey omega off. Based on the way my impulses have been prowling just under my skin ever since?

No.

I won't let myself consider the possibility that any of these stuck-up bitches belong to us.

Maybe the other guys. But not *me*.

"Have fun with that," I taunt, strolling past him.

"Yeah, yeah," he grumbles, but leaves all the same. Off to do The Crown's bidding, like the good pup he is.

Makes you wonder how the fuck a feral wolverine like me got in here.

Truth is, my whole life is some half-assed boarding school plot that got away from me. When this whole fucking mess started, I had no designs on the *throne*. The title, the castle, this pack.

Well, okay.

So I *did*.

But not *really*.

I didn't slither my way into Asher's pack to become a *king*. I had my own reasons—selfish, immature ones that I still totally stand behind.

And either way, it worked out, didn't it? I got to piss off all the people I hated most; and Asher stopped getting his ass kicked every damn day.

Now, when I step into the queen's sumptuous dressing room,

I see no traces of the cornered, dorky prince with fear lurking behind his glasses.

Nope. Our little Asher is all grown up. Looking like a goddamn nutcracker in whatever formal suit Maman's selected this time.

Good God. Why is it white?

The creamy color matches the plush, over-stuffed room around us. And so do the polished brass buttons.

I swear, if she tries to stick me in something like that...

Queen Selene smiles knowingly at her phone screen, not bothering to glance up. As an omega, she can sense our scents, even before she sees who's entered the room.

"Come in, *cherie*," she calls, wagging her manicured fingers at me. "I've almost finished torturing *mon petit*."

Her little love. She only calls Asher that, and I suspect he secretly likes it, because he never balks at the endearment. While I internally cringe every time she uses mine.

Hailing from France, *Maman* has one for each of us. Mine —*cherie*—means darling. And Bast's—*petit chou*—literally translates to "little cabbage."

It's possible he has a point about being Maman's least favorite.

Asher looks over his shoulder, shooting me a black look. Probably in retaliation for my entertainment this morning.

Maman stands and meets me beside the fitting pedestal the prince is standing on. She brushes at my shoulders. "Are you sober?"

I manage a half-smile. "Unfortunately."

Her pursed lips nearly wobble into a smirk. "Hm. Well, you smell like the bottom of a bottle."

"At least a bottle of something good, I hope."

"Cheap wine," Asher drawls, tugging at the tails of his tuxedo. "The boxed kind."

Maman's mouth finally curls up, her eyes flashing affectionately to her son. "As if you've *ever* had boxed wine."

Anyone who saw them would immediately note their similarities, especially when they smile. Apart from his height and his alpha designation, Asher got most of his looks from Selene. He has her dark wavy hair and hazel eyes. He's pale like her, too. Not quite as fair as me, but several shades off Bast's tanned complexion, at least.

Asher ignores the punch I lob into his arm, absorbing it easily and raising his brows at his mother. "Control your beast, won't you? I have a meeting with Portugal."

I grunt, flipping him the bird as Maman grins, waving me toward the seat next to hers and the lunch service on the table beside it.

Slouching into the beige damask fabric, I put on my very best impression of Asher's posh accent and sarcastically repeat the latest news headline, "*His Highness has declared that there is to be a royal ball.*"

Asher grumbles. "His *Majesty* has declared," he corrects. "Spurning Princess Ahmad was the last straw for him. He wants us to select an omega from those in attendance this week, or he's going to go ahead with the marriage contract he and Shah Ahmad made up for his daughter's hand."

I snort. No way in hell are we bonding with someone because Asher's *daddy* says so. "Her *hand*?" I spit, "Or her—"

Maman swats the back of my head, silencing me. Asher scowls, adjusting the sleeves of his suit. "The fact is, we've taken too long to decide. He wants the matter settled within the week."

They're not his words; they're the king's. But I see a glimpse of my packmate's true feelings when his eyes drop to his feet.

"I want no part of this whole thing," he mutters. "It's a huge distraction from my actual work. And, despite your many claims that I have a computer where my heart should be, I don't relish the thought of marrying a total stranger I didn't even choose. Plus, I find the entire concept of a party to choose a mate utterly ridiculous."

That tracks. He hates parties almost as much as I do.

Which is a fuck-ton.

Watching him pout satisfies my chaotic streak enough to allow for a goading grin. Because, really, this is a *joke.* There's no way we'll find a mate at this thing—and I'm not about to be trapped in an arranged marriage, either. This isn't the fucking Dark Ages.

"What's the theme this time?" I ask, "Butterflies? True love?"

Asher cuts me a more severe glare. Without his usual reading glasses, he actually manages to look halfway imposing. For a second, I think I've truly pissed him off, but then he speaks. And the reason for his rage is acutely clear.

"A masquerade."

Oh FUCK no.

Mouth gaping, I turn to Maman. She cackles. "It's *traditional.* And an oh-so-delightful way for me to torture you."

I have to stab an answering growl. "Traditional?"

An older beta woman who tailors our suits starts to carefully peel pinned layers off Asher as he sighs. "Back when all royal alphas formed packs and looked for scent-matched omegas," he explains, "masquerades were popular ways to search for mates. The idea being, without people's faces in view, alphas and omegas were more likely to be attracted to each other on scent alone."

When I full-on snarl, Maman rolls her eyes at me. "It's meant to be romantic, *cherie.*"

Christ. Gag me.

"I know," Asher agrees darkly. "Trust me, I argued against the whole mess. Strenuously."

Judging by the look on his face, I actually believe him. Which means I'm forced to direct my outrage at his mother.

Queen Selene laughs merrily at my betrayed anger, hemming and hawing while Asher changes into his regular suit and the seamstress wrestles me out of my shirt and vest.

"Yes, yes," Maman tuts, holding up a midnight-blue tuxedo jacket with a frown. "You have to go to a party with every beautiful, rich, single omega in the continent. Poor baby."

When she puts it like *that*...

I scowl, taking the second suit jacket from her. It's black—and the way she snorts to herself when I put it on tells me she knew I'd choose it.

What did Bast call this? My pirate aesthetic?

It makes sense when I see the others' suits back on their mannequins, all in a row. White for Asher and a medium, cloudy color for Bast. Almost the same shade of dove gray the maids wear.

Shh, little dove.

The words I wish I dreamed float through my mind. Along with a sting of regret and another, even worse recollection.

Would you really say no to a duke?

Turns out, she would. And *did*.

Despite me spilling my miserable guts to her. Telling her things I never should have *thought*, let alone said out loud... Addison did, in fact, say no.

Ivy Addison.

No idea why the girl decided to go by her last name, but that detail annoys me. Along with pretty much every other thing about her.

I can't stand the way she flinches and trembles like a nervous dog. I hate watching her work, having her in our space. Especially after nights like last night.

Mostly, though, I really can't stand how damn *nice* she is.

I mean, what's *wrong* with her? After what I pulled? She should have run to every tabloid in town.

She could have made *millions* selling that story. Or gone viral posting it herself. Instead, she just... moved on with her life? Kept all my secrets? For *no reason*?

What the hell is her game?

It kills me, not knowing.

But I'll watch her until I figure it out.

Asher storms off to go deal with whatever bullshit he thinks is actually important, and Maman forces me to button my vest. A new tray appears, laden with tea, and the server who scurries off has my glare lodged in his back as he retreats.

"That one steals silver, you know," I mutter, popping a piece of shortbread into my mouth.

Maman nods, brushing off my shoulders. "Yes, but he's the fastest runner we have and only takes two place settings a month."

He's also using the money to pay for his kid's braces, which is the reason I didn't tell Asher or Mrs. Kemp. Maman is like me—she sees everything and knows everyone a little better than they think she does.

The king is a sledgehammer, but our queen is a scalpel. There's a precision and an elegance to how she wields her power. His Majesty is lucky he wound up with someone so much better than his sorry ass.

Maman reads my mind again, patting my arms. "Don't you think," she says quietly, "that just maybe, you could meet someone perfect for you? All three of you?"

I don't. Because I'm not the kind of person that people love easily. If at all.

And the ones who do?

Learn better eventually.

five

My first act as a king?

Outlawing white pants.

Mumbling obscenities, I brush the front of my colorless trousers, scowling at the spot of black lint that won't budge. Because it is, in fact, a stain of some kind.

See?

Damn things are a *scourge*.

Although, they look good with this new sweater. And it *is* summer. For a few more days, at least.

In case there was any doubt, the second I step into the garden, a wall of humid heat slams into me. *Great*, I think, shaking my head. *Because taking tea with what's-her-face wasn't already going to be a pain in the ass. Now I get to sweat some more while I do it.*

My Alpha—the absolute lunatic that he is today—snarls at the thought. I ignore him, still preoccupied with my pants as I round the first hedge—

And stop short.

There's an angel in our garden.

Down on her knees, between the faded white stone of the swan fountain and a row of pink peonies. Dappled sunlight peeks through the nearest wall of greenery, gilding her bangs and the wisps of cool-blonde hair hanging loose around her slender neck.

The skirt of her soft gray work dress pools around her, but scuffed Doc Martins poke out, their clasps pressed into the cobblestones underneath. When she shifts, the movement betrays a run up the back of her stockings.

In profile, I only see certain features. The downward tilt of a pointed chin. Lips that pull into a small, fond smile. The hollows under her eyes and cheeks. Lashes long enough to catch the light.

After a breathless second, she turns. I recognize her and all the air in my chest heaves out on a relieved exhale.

I smile. "Addison!"

Thank God.

Internally, I shake my head. What's with all this *relief*? It's not like I was looking for her. Our suite will be cleaned by the time I get back from tea with Princess Fake Lips—and there's literally no other reason for me to trouble our housekeeper.

Maid, my mind corrects.

Because, really, she isn't even our housekeeper. Mrs. Kemp manages Maytown Manor's cleaning staff, and she runs an impossibly tight ship. It's a wonder she hasn't pulled all her hair out, having Dair here.

If the manor is a tight ship, my packmate is an iceberg.

Oblivious to my inner turmoil, Addison turns to offer a smile. The thin, silver chain at her neck gleams slightly with the movement. Pure innocence and kindness shine in her blue eyes—much lighter and prettier than my own.

She remembers herself too soon, bowing her head and dropping her gaze back to the ground. "Good morning, my lord."

I sigh. "Addison, we've been over this."

Since I said her name, she's free to glance up at me. The small twitch of her petal-pink lips betrays her amusement. "*Lord* Burns," she scolds, flashing a look that somehow manages to be impish and submissive all at once. "You know I can't call you by your first name."

My blood thumps, resurrecting my aching cock. *Fuck*. I went at it all night and it did nothing. Except maybe make me hornier?

Seriously, what the *hell*?

Maybe it's Addison. The way she's looking at me—like a perfect angel, begging me to play with her—is exactly what I like.

I lock the thought down, even as my dick twitches in my starched pants. Addison is our employee—and she works harder than anyone I've ever met.

I know just how hard her life is from the numerous little conversations I've finessed her into. The last thing she needs is trouble from the likes of me.

But, damn.

She *is* pretty...

"Heaven forbid," I tease, rolling my eyes and crossing my arms over my navy button-down. The pristine sweater slung over my shoulders shifts as I shrug. "I forgot the *entire* monarchy would fall if you dared to call me Sebastian. Let alone a *nickname* like Bast. My apologies, dear Miss Addison. You're right, of course."

She gives a chiding shake of her head, averting those sparkling eyes as the corners of her lips pull higher. "Lord Burns," she says again, trying for sternness she does not achieve. "You'll get us both into trouble."

I won't tell if you won't.

The words nearly come out, but I stop myself. It isn't fair for me to flirt with her, even if I genuinely like her.

I'm on my way to court some random royal omega *right now.* Not to mention the announcement His Majesty made this morning, hosting a ball for us to find a match *once and for all.*

This sweet beta woman doesn't need me messing with her head. In fact, as I stand there, watching her swallow the last of her smile, I get the familiar instinct that she needs a *friend.*

I'm not the best with serious topics. I'm the charmer—the one who smooths all the feathers Dair and Asher ruffle. So it takes concerted effort for me to drop my flirtatious posture and fight the discomfort roiling through my middle as I ask, "How is your mom doing?"

It's been a long time since we first discussed her mother's health. I make a habit of getting to know everyone who works for us—and, well, *everyone* in general. But, from the very beginning of our stay here, Addison was especially easy to talk to.

She answered my curious questions about where she was from (just here, in town) and how she came to work at Maytown Manor (her mother was some sort of dress designer for *Maman*) and why she wasn't off at school like most people her age (her mom's untimely illness).

As the months went on—while Dair death-glared at her and Asher avoided her—I found myself chatting with Addison whenever I got the chance.

Though, somehow, it wasn't like my polite chit-chat with Mrs. Kemp or the cook who makes my post-workout protein shakes. Or even the ass-kissing flattery I offer most debutantes.

Talking to Addison always felt *effortless*. Refreshing.

She laughed easily and shared about her life without any hesitation. Never asking me anything personal in return, of course. But suffering my inquires like she truly didn't mind them. Or maybe even liked them.

That was my first clue that she probably doesn't have many people to talk to. Her work here is solitary—and she hardly ever leaves. When she's home, she's told me, she spends most nights by her mother's side to give her aunt a break.

Does she ever go anywhere for fun? Does she have someone to tell her how beautiful she looks in the sunshine? Or kiss her until she can't breathe?

Oh, for fuck's sake.

Down, boy, I snarl at my Alpha. *This woman is not for us. She's our* friend.

The fact that I haven't checked in on her mother's condition since she shared it with me sends a sudden bolt of shame to the base of my throat. Especially when Addison's chin trembles slightly.

"She... passed on, my lord. Five months ago."

My throat dries as everything in my chest lurches. "Addi. Damn it. I'm *sorry*."

She tries to smile, which is somehow worse than letting herself cry. "It's all right, my lord. She suffered for a long time. I'm glad she isn't anymore."

I'm about to ask if there's some way we could help her—though I have no idea *how* or *why*—but a small squeak sends me back a step, nearly tripping over my loafers and the polished stone underfoot. Some small rodent-like creature darts to the left while Addison startles, sending a cloud of dry dust puffing up around her.

And my white pants.

I'm telling you, once I have the power to make laws, it's off with their heads.

Er, legs.

All my thoughts screech to a stop when Addison hums—a soft, warm sound that does *nothing* for the unfortunate state of my knot. "Nigel," she says, "There you are."

Nigel? As in, the *squirrel* she's currently feeding from the small bag of crumbs beside her?

It's too full to be the remnants of a meal. It almost looks as if someone took one of Asher's beloved loaves of banana bread and crumbled the whole thing up. Smells that way, too.

The sweet, buttery aroma wafts into the humid air, reminding me how hungry I am. I swallow a sudden rush of saliva and shake my head to clear it out.

Jesus, man. Get yourself together.

My Alpha doesn't listen. He only gets more insistent. *Shoving* me toward...

The bag of crumbs?

Seriously?

Calm down, I think. *We're going to have tea with Princess Stick-Up-Her-Snatch. No reason to lose it on me over a bag of breadcrumbs.*

Still, *I have to* stoop and pick them up. It's the dumbest, smallest thing I could possibly do for her in this moment—and Addison seems as confused as I feel, blinking at me until I stupidly hand them to her. She accepts the bag from me with a bemused look.

"I... thank you." She remembers her manners and adds, "My lord."

For a member of the manor's staff, she's actually pretty terrible with formalities. I've noticed it's a little too easy to lure her into conversation—and she has an adorable habit of eavesdropping. That might bother me, if she wasn't also the single nicest person I've ever met.

No. Seriously.

She works here seven days a week, busting her ass to pay her mom's medical bills. And the one time I asked what her hobbies were, she looked at me like I'd started speaking a foreign language before admitting she enjoys "making friends with animals."

I can't even *imagine* her gossiping.

And since we moved in here six months ago? There hasn't been one single security leak.

The thought of her listening in on us simply to satisfy her own innocent curiosity makes me smile wider. "Is this an acquaintance of yours?" I ask, smirking at the squirrel nibbling crumbs from the cobblestones.

Addison flushes pink, grimacing but telling me the truth all the same. "This is my friend. Nigel."

Okay. Well. That's... fucking adorable.

Am I just supposed to go on with my life? Like knowing there's a squirrel named Nigel wandering our grounds hasn't made my entire year?

"Nigel," I repeat.

And, goddamn it, the little bastard actually pokes his head up. I laugh before I can help myself, raising a brow at him. "Any chance you'd fancy a picnic, mate? I know of one in desperate need of sabotage."

The furry guy chitters at Addison, and she sighs, her mortification melting into fondness. "Yes," she coos to him. "I know. I promised."

She casts me a quick, cringing glance, sprinkling more crumbs onto the ground. "Nigel likes banana bread, so I... found some for him."

I'll have to remember to tell Asher he has the same taste as his manor's squirrels. Then again, he would hate knowing one of the staff members was feeding "rodents." Especially out *here*.

For some reason, he's always been weird about keeping the staff out of his family's garden. I don't want Addison to get in trouble.

"You should probably stay low," I mutter, thinking of all the busybodies milling around. "I won't tell, but no one is supposed to be in here except for the royal family."

She nods, dropping her eyes again. My heart twinges at the chastened expression slamming shut over her features. "Yes, my lord. I only—I was given permission, once. I suppose that doesn't matter now, though. I won't come back out here."

I wonder who gave her permission. I wonder if *I* could grant her the same latitude. Hell, it's worth a shot. After everything she's been going through, I can't let this angelic woman get kicked out of such a peaceful spot. She seems *happy*... how could I take that away from her?

"No," I decide, straightening. "You stay. If anyone asks, tell them I said it was okay." I toss in a grin. "And *please* send them to interrupt my tea if they have any questions."

Addison's answering smile is almost a grimace. "You seem to be... looking forward to it."

I kick my shiny toe at a nearby stone, chuckling humorlessly. "I think I'd rather stay here with Nigel."

She beams at him, then up at me. "He is *excellent* company, my lord. You could do worse."

I'm struck by the sudden feeling that, really, I couldn't do much *better* than this woman and her kindness. Her soft, strong spirit. Her friendship—the way she looks at me and waits. Listens. Here if I wanted to talk.

Always here. Someone we rely on for a hundred things and never thank. Someone who never complains or contempts.

She's lovely. And I hate that I've *noticed*. Because now I have to walk away. And stay away.

"I'll have to take my chances," I reply.

I turn to go—and, for the first time in as long as I can remember, can't seem to force a smile.

six

SOMETIMES, IT'S BETTER NOT TO ASK.

That's one lesson I've learned when it comes to cleaning up after other people.

It's best not to look too closely when I'm tidying for the princes. After all, it's none of my business how many condom wrappers line the bottom of the waste basket. Or the number of crumpled water bottles are mixed in.

Or why there's also an empty canister of whipped cream?

I mean, really. A *whole canister* seems excessive, but...

At least I can pretend that's the sole reason for the white-streaked sheets.

Maybe I ought to ask for hazard pay. Or a Hazmat suit.

Or, at minimum, better insurance. Because by the time I finish restoring the duke's bedroom to its stoic, gray glory, I'm distinctly lightheaded.

He must have had candles burning in here last night during his... date. There's a new scent wound through all of his linens. Something tart and fresh, with a clean edge. It blends well with whatever bitter, citrusy tea one of them spilled on their common room's couch.

That's a bit of a mystery, actually. Not the tea—Prince Asher is known to love his breakfast tea. Or even the spillage—I remember from childhood how exceptionally unobservant the prince can be when he's reading. But it's more the fact that someone bothered to try to clean it up.

By the time I got to it, only the scent lingered. There wasn't even a stain.

I assume he tossed whatever rags he used to clean up after himself in his bedroom. I'm forbidden to go in there; everyone on the staff is. So, I suppose I'll have to see if the cloth ends up coming down his laundry chute later this week.

Sebastian's door is the only one that perpetually hangs open. It's very like him not to care who sees the socks balled up under his bed or the alarming array of skincare products displayed on his desk. Right beside the latest treatise he's working on—which is sort of the whole appeal of Lord Sebastian Burns. He's as smart as he is beautiful.

Friendly, too. He's never gotten my name quite right, but he continually asks how I am and apologizes for their messes. Compared to Dair's lethal glares and Asher's utter apathy, the baron's jovial comments about the weather are practically swoon-worthy.

His new cologne isn't bad, either. I took note of it earlier when he caught me in the garden and—kindly—left me in peace. He smelled sweeter than whatever neutralizing fragrance he usually wears.

His room does, too. This new scent is warm and sugared, with a uniquely delicious thread of burned bitterness.

Once I finish in Dair's room, I might go back to Sebastian's and see if I can't spot a new bottle mixed into his others...

But by the time I finish fluffing the duke's clean bedding and collecting his laundry, my dizziness is so bad, I have no choice but to sit on the edge of his mattress and put my head between my knees.

Every sharp inhale feels like snorting a cold burst of wooziness. The more I try to breathe, the harder it is to stay upright. Until my whole mind dissolves into a tumbling fog of scents and sensations that don't make sense.

I'm making this up. It's just anxiety, I remind myself. *There's nothing wrong with you. The doctors said so. "Perfect beta woman." In "excellent health." Just "an overactive imagination" and a "low pain tolerance."*

Which explains why this sudden abdominal cramp feels like a *stab—*

"*What* are you doing?"

Oh. Crap.

It's the duke himself, paused halfway over the threshold to his bedroom. Staring at me through a mask of horrorstruck rage.

Which is fair.

Because he's naked.

Not fully. But his shirt hangs open and his pants do, too. I immediately turn my face away, stuttering as my cheeks flame. "I—I beg your pardon, Your Grace. I was tidying your bed and I felt faint."

An alpha growl vibrates low in his chest—the wide, chiseled expanse full of black ink patterns and sinuous lines. When he clocks the way my blurred vision locks onto those designs—*a skull wearing a crown, a butterfly with flames for wings, a candle melting into a puddle of midnight*—his snarl deepens.

"You're supposed to be *out* of our wing before noon," he grits.

Nodding is a mistake—as soon as I bob my head, the whole

room tilts sharply. "I usually am," I mumble, blinking to clear my bleary eyes and swallowing the nausea inspired by my gut's latest tweak.

Just anxiety. Overactive imagination. Low pain tolerance.

"I only—Lord Burns stopped me this morning in the garden a-and your room was s-so—"

Those cold black eyes snag mine, ending all coherent thought. Memories and fantasies blend into a blurry mess. Things that happened—that *happened*, right?!—things I wished for.

Shh, little dove.

Don't leave me. Please.

As if he can hear my recollections, Dair snaps up to his full height with a hard jerk. Feral menace flickers through his gaze. "Get. Out."

I nod again, faster, the room rotating another thirty degrees. "Uh-of course. Your Grace. Sir. I'll just—"

It's all in my head. An overactive imagination. Silly fear that makes no sense.

So I stand up.

Take six steps. Or maybe just one.

Then I hear his voice. Closer and rougher. "*For fuck's sake.*"

Two tattooed hands fly out. And I'm not sure if they're pushing me into oblivion or trying to pull me out. But everything goes black either way.

THE FIRST THING I SEE WHEN MY EYES OPEN IS A chandelier. It's one of my least favorites—the one with a thousand crystal baubles that take ages to shine individually.

As soon as I see it, I know we're in the princes' meeting rooms. Just down the central hall from their living quarters—this space is rarely used for anything apart from PR pow-wows and party planning. Their *real* business happens on the other side of the manor, in the king's study. Or back in the capital, at their *palace*.

I stare up at the gold-foiled ceiling, turning my head slowly. My neck is stiff. Likely because I've been slumped in this rolling chair for...

Oh dear.

Outside the nearest window, the sun glows gold. Too near to the western horizon for my taste.

Last I knew, it was just after noon and—

Oh.

Oh *no.*

With a groan, I jolt upright and scrub both palms over my face. "No, no, no!"

A dry harrumph answers from the other side of the long, antique table. "Oh yes," Gracie retorts, glancing up from her laptop to give me side-eye. "You passed out in *Dairragh Vreeland's* room. Don't worry—I'm all but certain this isn't a first for him."

My stomach heaves as horror washes through me. "Did he—did I—"

Gracie closes her MacBook and offers a sympathetic frown. "He wasn't as terrible as I would have expected. Carried you in here himself, actually. And only snarled at me a few times while he explained. "

He... carried me?

Mortification swarms my middle. "W-what did he *say*?"

Gracie shrugs her shoulder, shifting her berry-red blazer. "That you were in his room, cleaning, and you fainted. I don't know how he knew where to find me, but he didn't mention that at all. Just said I should call for help if you didn't wake up soon."

My thoughts lurch, trying to understand. "And you didn't think me being passed out all afternoon was a problem?!"

Gracie raises one of her black brows. "I *thought* you wouldn't want to be hauled out of here on a stretcher in front of everyone. Or lose however many days' wages it would take to get you back out of the hospital."

Her painted lips quirk up. "Besides, your pulse was strong, and you were breathing. I figured you had been pulling your usual no-sleep, no-food routine and just needed some rest. Here."

She pushes a tray down the length of the table, past piles of party linens and different china patterns. It's a platter of charcuterie, all arranged by the manor's cook. He must have sent it up for Gracie.

My stomach is tender, but it gurgles insistently. Reminding me that I did, in fact, forget to eat last night. And this morning.

"Fine, fine," I sigh, picking around the cured ham and rolling a piece of cheese around an apple slice. As soon as I crunch into it, my friend visibly relaxes.

"You know what I'm going say," she mumbles, leveling me with a wry look as she passes me a silver pitcher of water and a glass.

I nod. "I know."

Her expression softens. "I worry about you, babe. When's the last time you took a night off?"

I squirm in my seat, gulping down the last of the apple slice. "What do you mean? I almost never work nights. Unless the princes have one of their courting dinners."

Gracie watches me for a long beat before gently replying, "I didn't mean a night off from work. I meant a night off from *everything*. Have you gone out *at all* this summer? Even just for dinner? Or a drink?"

At my cringe, she nods knowingly. "I think you should," she

suggests. "Just for one night. You can tell your aunt you're working one of those dinners."

Imagining the lie, I automatically wince, but ask, "Where would we actually go?"

My best friend gestures around at the party stuff strewn everywhere—all the makings of… the princes' *ball*.

Uh-oh.

Gracie grins. "I'm so glad you asked."

SEVEN

RAIN SPLATTERS ONTO THE STONE COURTYARD, THE deluge punishing and purifying.

I stand in the middle of the garden, letting it sink into my bones. A certain lightness expands through my chest with each droplet—the giddy knowledge that I've never done anything like this. Never allowed myself to stand in the rain and not care.

Let it ruin my hair, my clothes, my phone.

I don't care about anything except the girl in the white T-shirt, spinning circles under the storm.

She laughs up at the heavens, as if all of this weather is some sort of inside joke between them. Rain soaks the fabric of her top until it sticks to her body... and turns entirely see-through.

I'd be lying if I claimed that isn't part of why I step out from the alcove carved into the side of the manor. Because, as much as I hate the fact that the girl who has become my best friend looks more and more like a woman *by the day... I also love it.*

Things are different this summer. Last year, we still felt like kids. Childhood friends.

Now, all the ways she's transformed into a young woman make me feel more like a man—protective and possessive. Wanting to shield her beauty by hiding it away for myself. Wishing to be the only one who will ever see it... or touch it.

Some magnetic force draws me closer, tugging at my middle. I'm an alpha, but she's recently designated as a beta. There should be no pull between us. It isn't possible...

Unless maybe this isn't chemical at all.

Maybe I just... love her.

How could I not? It would be like not appreciating sunsets or springtime or the stars she likes to wish on.

This girl is an undeniable thing of beauty.

And I can't stay away.

When I find myself at her side, she stops her breathless giggling and spins to face me. Her thick, wavy hair is dark from the rain, a large swath of it tangled in the silver locket at her throat. My fingers reach for it without thought—because her joy has somehow turned off the part of my brain that constantly analyzes and overthinks.

Now, there's just silence.

Peace.

The rain.

And her.

Her hair sliding through my fingers. The warm skin between her collarbones. The drops clinging to her lashes as her lips part around my name.

There's only her. And me.

Until suddenly, in the space of half an instant, there's us.

THE DREAM KEEPS ME IN A HEADLOCK AS I STAND under a stream of water. It burns, but that's the way I like it. Scalding. Especially at this hour, after a night of restless remembering.

Shifting under the shower head, I glare down the front of my body. At my dick. And knot.

Both of which have decided we've had enough of this courting horseshit.

My disdain for the process may not be new, but the thick heat swarming my veins is. We've been looking for an omega to suit all three of us since we left university—and I've never had an issue like *this*.

Hard day and night. With no solution apart from—

No.

No.

I won't go back to random women and the spiral of self-loathing that followed every one of my hook-ups.

Because they weren't right.

They weren't *her*.

And even though I knew I'd never see the girl I sent away again, it still felt like a betrayal every time I loaned out everything that ought to have been *hers*.

Hot water pelts my back, but, for once, the burning stream isn't enough to shut my mind off.

What will I do if this godforsaken ball doesn't produce the mate we need?

What will I do if it *does*?

Will it still feel wrong to think about another person if that person is our *mate*? And, if it does, how will I manage to produce the heirs my parents are so desperate for?

I guess Dair could always handle that part.

But, surely, any omega we bond with will expect an explanation for why I don't allow anyone in my bed. Or my heart.

I somehow make it through my shower without succumbing to all my insane urges. The insistent hum of need gets harder to ignore in my silent room, though.

I find myself hurrying to shove myself into clothes, hunting for a distraction.

There's always work. Plenty of it.

When I realize how impossible sitting at a desk feels, I turn to my bedroom's library, scanning for anything unread. *Maybe the latest study on particle physics. And a walk.*

It's masochistic to pause by my window and look below. At the garden.

Which sits empty. Because I basically *decreed* it should always be empty.

Perhaps that was childish. At the time, I only knew Ivy was gone. And all I had left was the blank space where she should have been.

Soft rain patters over the cobblestone path carved between the hedges. I watch moisture soak into the rocks, lost in involuntary memories.

Last night's dream wasn't the first of its kind. Anytime the weather turns gloomy, I wind up right back in the garden below, reliving the day I kissed Ivy for the first time.

But recalling the feel of her lips on mine and her body heat radiating through our wet clothes doesn't steal my breath. It's the image of her dancing under the deluge, smiling at the sky.

Now I know. That was the moment I fell in love.

Young and clueless, but true.

And permanent, apparently.

Because watching the rain drench the garden still puts a hard swell of regret in my gullet. I choke it down, turning away from the window and the mirror on the adjacent wall. Not wanting to see the ink branded into my chest.

Fucking hell. *That* will be impossible to explain to whoever we pick tonight.

It's only eight a.m., but I'm already on-edge. So staggering out of my room and nearly tripping over our maid is decidedly *irritating*.

She squeaks, dropping her dirty cloth and straightening on her knees to bow her head. "Your Highness. Apologies. I was only—"

Something in my middle *snaps*.

A strong current ripples under my skin. I step over her with a growl. "Your duties don't interest me. Be mindful of blocking doorways."

Christ, I sound like an asshole.

What I really want to do is sink to my knees and make sure the door didn't hit her when I burst out of it. Look her in the eye, for once. Ask her name again, since I made a careful effort not to remember it the first time.

I remember that day with an odd clarity that's always irked me. Wasn't it hard enough—this young woman in our intimate spaces? Did she have to be so damn *beautiful*?

I only let myself look that initial day, when I saw her from across the main ballroom downstairs. It was our first time coming to Maytown as a pack and my first summer back since university. One of our assistants scurried through the manor at our heels, introducing the staff. But when we got to the ballroom and I saw that our personal housekeeper was exactly my type...

No.

Enough.

I can't let myself think of the maid that way. I don't let myself think of *any* woman that way.

There was a time when I did. I might have been the tamest alpha in my pack and the calmest royal in my family, but I was still a *man*. For years, I pushed through the guilt and wrongness, driven by carnal need.

But every time I found myself back home, alone in my bed… I saw her face.

It didn't matter how many other women I tried on; that shame always found me.

Because even *pretending* to like other women was an awful betrayal of the girl I sent away.

As I stride off, my stomach hardens into a wad of lead. It drops, rolling around in my abdomen, striking nerves that send painful charges to my lungs. I ignore them, focusing on all the things that usually make me feel better.

I had to.

It was for her own good.

She would have been miserable with me.

I would have ruined her.

She wasn't my mate—couldn't have been—so there must be someone else waiting for me.

It's logical. And *true*.

So why does it all feel like a lie?

eight

"Um, wow."

Gracie leans back, brows arched in surprise. Behind her, one of the manor's only omega employees smiles broadly.

Tanya works in the stables as an apprentice for the royal horse trainer.

Yes.

The *royal horse trainer*.

I'm not one hundred percent sure, but it seems like my best friend might have a little crush. Usually, when she dates someone new, I hear *all* about it. But today, when Gracie yanked me down to the staff quarters and took me to Tanya's room to get ready for the ball, I found out they've already been out twice.

If the giggly goo-goo eyes they exchange aren't suspicious enough, their scents definitely are.

I'm a *beta*. I'm not even supposed to be able to pick up on these things. So you know they must be pretty attracted to one another.

In fact, their pheromones are sort of making me woozy.

Or maybe that's just whatever insanity came over me the other day.

"What?" I fret, turning to Tanya's narrow, full-length mirror. "Do I look ridiculous?"

It's sort of a rhetorical question. *Of course* I look ridiculous. My face is all made up, even though it's, apparently, going to be hidden under some sort of mask?

Gracie neglected to mention that until I got here. When I took my carefully rolled-up evening gown out of my bag and shook the wrinkles loose, she grimaced.

I thought she was reacting to the fact that the thing is clearly older than me—one of my mother's handmade pieces. Something the queen probably wore when she was my age and then gave to Mama when she didn't want it anymore.

I took care to change a few things, hoping to disguise it just in case Her Majesty actually notices, somehow. But the boxy cut and rosy hue are here to stay.

And they do not match the mask Gracie whips out.

Nothing ever could. The light-blue silk garment surely has no equal. From the thin silver filaments outlining its curves to the delicate pearls sewn into its icy lace overlay—it feels too beautiful to touch, let alone wear on my face.

"This is the only one I could find on short notice," she tells me. "It was donated."

Who in their right mind would get *rid* of something so lovely? There's nothing wrong with it at all! It's almost as perfect as the dress hanging on the closet door.

Actually, the two pieces match. I wonder if whoever didn't want my borrowed mask also gave Tanya her dress. One of the wealthy omegas here to court the princes, maybe?

Though, I'm not sure why they would give their fancy hand-me-downs to our staff. Perhaps as an attempt to win over the princes with acts of generosity?

I swallow the lump that accompanies that thought, turning back to the mirror and lightly touching my sleek, blow-dried bangs. Tanya is a wizard with hair and makeup—I barely recognize my own blonde locks now that they've been styled to perfection.

"Here." Tanya smiles, whipping the lovely dress I've been admiring off its hanger. "This one is for you."

A very unladylike sound sticks in my throat as I wave my hands. "Um, no."

Gracie rolls her big brown eyes. "Ivy, your dress is thirty years old, and moths have eaten the slip."

A hot wash of embarrassment rolls through me. "Still. I can't take Tanya's dress!"

The omega shakes her head with a happy smile. "This one isn't mine! The omega princess giving away dresses had a bunch. I grabbed a red one for myself, but I thought this blue would be pretty with your light hair! Plus, it goes with the mask."

Honestly, what sort of woman travels with multiple masquerade outfit options...?

A princess, I suppose.

Plucking up the hem of my mother's dress, I stare at the nibbled edges, worrying my lower lip. Gracie *does* have a point... Besides, it's not as if anyone will be looking at *me*. Whichever wealthy, titled omega donated these clothes likely won't care I'm wearing one of them if she has so many, she was literally handing them out.

I sigh, silently admitting defeat and shuffling into Tanya's tiny attached bathroom. When I finally finish wrestling myself into the powder-blue fabric, I peer into the small mirror over her sink and guffaw.

"I look ridiculous," I announce, stepping back into the small bedroom.

Telling silence greets me. Gracie glances at Tanya and back at me, eyes widening. "You don't look *ridiculous*," she says. "You look—"

Tanya snorts a laugh from her spot on the floor, where she waves her curling iron in my direction. "*Hot*," she finishes. "Super hot, Ivy."

I normally wouldn't believe them—but the fact that Gracie felt uncomfy saying what she thought in front of the girl she likes makes it feel too real. I turn to the bedroom's larger mirror, trying to see what they do.

I guess I look all right? My eyes feel funny with these lashes stuck on them. And the blush seems a bit much. But Tanya really did a lovely job styling my hair in a half-up style.

Big bows are in, they assured me, so that's what I have. A silver satin bow to match the trim on the blue-and-silver mask.

Now that I know they planned to foist this beautiful dress on me all along, the rest of their choices makes more sense. The smoky gray eyeshadow, the crystal-clear heels that look like they're made of glass.

My fingers skim along the thin, silky fabric of the light-blue gown, tracing the slit sliced up the left thigh.

The material is shimmery. Cut to hug someone's upper body, with thin, pearl-lined straps and a bit of silver-blue lace peeking along the cups.

And it *isn't mine.*

"I told you," Gracie huffs, adjusting her own fake eyelashes. "No one will care about the dress."

I open my mouth to protest, but as I pull the skirt out to examine it, Tanya wrinkles her nose. She mumbles something under her breath about the fabric "reeking like the princes," which I take to mean the previous omega owner didn't want to keep it because she had already worn it for the guys.

It still feels wrong to be in someone else's dress. Hopefully, with any luck at all, no one will notice me. Especially not *them*.

Especially not *Asher*.

He was so mad today when I got underfoot. And watching him do everything he could to avoid glancing at me bruised my heart in a way nothing else ever has.

I have to blink the burn out of my eyes to keep from ruining Tanya's careful work. With a hard swallow, I lower myself onto the small twin-sized bed behind me and slip my borrowed shoes on.

Gracie's new girlfriend pauses, her lips pursing as she stares at my chest. "Okay, don't hate me, but... I think the outfit might look better without that necklace."

Startled, I look down and remember—*oh, right*—I have my locket on. The one piece of jewelry I own is basically part of me, at this point. I haven't taken it off more than a handful of times over the last eight years, and the thought of removing it now makes me wince.

Then again, I don't want anyone to recognize it...

Well. I don't want one person in particular to recognize it.

With a nod, I unclasp the silver heart strung over my sternum. Some insane part of me balks at the idea of simply leaving it in Tanya's room, so instead, I silently slip it into my strapless bra, where I can keep it close and know it's safe.

I'm sure the dizziness that rolls over me while I tug the cups of the gown higher is only my imagination. Again. And I'm sure the nauseous roll in my middle is just me feeling sorry for myself...

I'll be fine.

It's all in my head. I have an overactive imagination and a low pain tolerance.

Whoever this dress's previous owner was, she smelled divine. Something fresh and sweet and bitter and tart all at once. I surreptitiously sniff the lace lining the bust before shaking my head.

I am losing it.

And I *can't afford* to lose it.

Quite literally.

I need this job. *My family* needs this job.

But before I can open my mouth and talk my way out of this insanity, Gracie glowers. "I see that look on your face Ivy Addison; and the answer is no. We are going to this party, and we're going to have fun! The champagne alone is three-hundred-dollars per bottle. It would be a crime not to enjoy ourselves."

Tanya pats my arm reassuringly. "I'm sure no one will even recognize us, Ivy. With the masks and everyone so focused on the princes? Besides, compared to what the royal women will have on, we'll seem boring."

Oddly, that comforts me. She has a point, anyway. Back when my mother made Her Majesty's dresses, it boggled my mind how intricate and luxurious they were. The hand-stitching and exotic feathers and real gemstones—I'll look downright dull beside all *that*.

Sighing, I pick up my mask. As Gracie ties the piece around my face, expertly hiding the strings under my half-up hair, a little thrill trills up my spine.

I may be nervous... but it *is* exciting, knowing no one will recognize me. And I *do* love dancing...

It's *just a party*.

Nothing's going to happen.

nine

THE OMEGA STANDING ACROSS FROM ME HAS SPINACH in her teeth.

The fact that she will be mortified beyond compare once she finally stops assaulting my eardrums and moves on to someone else is the only reason I'm able to keep a placid smile-adjacent expression on my face.

Over her shoulder, Asher glances up from the one he's speaking to. His harried look loudly proclaims what I already know—

This is a *nightmare.*

We've been here, what? Ten minutes? I've already lost track of all the girls. Cooing and giggling, pointing and whispering. Swirls of tulle and sparkles and every type of mask on this whole godforsaken planet.

Catlike ones and peacock ones and—*oh God*—is that supposed to look like Medusa?

If Asher is already flagging, I don't have a prayer.

Lord only knows where the fuck Dair is.

Wait. There.

The close cut of his black suit stands out among the other tuxedos. He stands beside one of the marble pillars propping up the ballroom's staircase. A group of girls approaches, but the look he gives sends them reeling back.

I have *got* to ask him to teach me that.

The omega across from me reaches over to brush my forearm. Her eyes slant my way, implying she's just said something suggestive.

I tweak my smile higher, wondering why I'm not interested. Why I'm not *anything*. Except...

Then I feel it, unfurling in my lungs like the first deep breath after a long stretch underwater—

Relief.

Not because any of these omegas smell right.

But because they all smell *wrong*.

The party's scent-neutralizers have been carefully calibrated to give us the barest edge of every omega we encounter. According to the experts, if one of their scents jumps over that hurdle... well.

But, so far? Nothing.

Why does that make me *happy*?

Up high, a twirl of shimmery blue catches my eye. Standing on the landing for the second floor—or near it, at least, hovering at the threshold to a hallway.

Doesn't that one go to the northern wing and staff quarters? What's one of our eligible omegas doing up *there*?

It's hard for me to ponder for long. Impossible, actually, to think about anything except *her*.

That dress looks familiar, but I know I've never seen the woman in it before. Because the way my Alpha shoves at me?

I'd *remember* that.

Then again, the last time he did this, it was over a bag of breadcrumbs.

That felt like a fluke, though.

And this? This feels like...

I stop myself from thinking the word, tuning out the woman who's still babbling at me and squinting to get a clearer picture of the mystery omega in blue.

Because, yes, even from here, I can tell she's an omega. All finely turned ankles, elegant collarbones, and the sort of angelic features that call to me on a visceral level.

At least, the ones I can see. Most of her face is covered by a simple mask. The silver and ice complement her cool-blonde waves and the wispy bangs brushing her forehead.

She has no jewelry. And, goddamn it, that's *wrong*. She should be dripping in diamonds and aquamarines. My omega should always—

Whoa.

WHOA.

Wait.

What?

My body doesn't want to wait, though. I'm already in motion, gritting my teeth as I pluck my current companion's hand from my sleeve and mumble, "Excuse me."

She sputters something indignant, and the edge of her fruity scent sours. Suddenly, I *can't stand it*. My insides heave and flip, desperate to get *away*.

Get to *her*.

The girl who's turned her pretty blonde head to speak to someone behind her.

Another alpha.

A growl crouches low in my lungs as the tall woman appears behind my blue angel. The sweet omega bites her glossy lip and darts a timid look at the landing situated between both sets of curved stairs.

Because she doesn't want everyone to look at her when she steps out into the light?

Why does that make my heart *hurt*?

The woman with her isn't having it. With a nudge, she pushes the omega out of the shadows, sending her staggering slightly as she approaches the gilded railing. Her plain, unpainted fingers curl around the lustrous balcony, and she straightens, lifting her head. The ballroom's lights reflect off her skin and hair, glowing.

And holy shit.

Holy. Shit.

That's our mate.

THIS FEELING REMINDS ME OF BEING A LITTLE KID AT the beach. Standing next to the ocean, turning my back for one second too long—

And getting clobbered by a wave.

It drags me under, blotting out the ballroom whirling in my periphery. Muting the cacophony of voices and music and clanking crystal. Blurring all the gold and grandiosity into a white fog.

Just like being swallowed by the sea—once I get over the initial shock of having my legs swept from under me, it's almost peaceful.

I float in a weightless moment of awe, not even feeling my feet as they carry me to the stairs. Someone's shoulder connects with mine. There's a flurry of apologies and bowing. I'm not sure I manage so much as a glance in their direction, but the jolt is enough to bring me back to reality.

The string quartet's whine fills my ears as the room reappears. I stop below the bottom step, blinking. Pivoting to look around.

Because there's no way I'm the only one who feels this.

Turns out, I'm right.

Asher is exactly where I left him. It's hard to tell what he's thinking with his gold mask covering his eyes, but his body is so utterly, eerily still, angled in the same direction mine is...

I know he sees her, too.

Whipping my head the other way, I scan for Dair...

And sure enough, he's frozen, too. Still leaning against that pillar—but all casual pretense has abandoned him. Instead of looking indolent, he seems dumbfounded.

Unlike Asher's stoic stillness, Dair's body is slack. His mouth hangs wide for several seconds before the features visible under his simple, black mask twist in *absolute horror*.

Does he recognize her?

Why is he staring like *that*?

Lord, I am fucked. Because while I'm curious, I actually don't *care* what his excuse is.

The need to protect rises hard and high inside me. And I don't give a shit why he looks like that—I will kill him if he makes her feel uncomfortable for even half a second.

It's an insane impulse. That's my *packmate*. And I don't even know this girl's *name*.

But—oh. She's looking at me.

Normally, I would be pleased. My appearance is one of my primary draws. And even though I have a slate mask over my face, I know this gray tux is setting off my blond hair.

Only, she isn't gazing the way other girls do. Under the shade of her own mask, the whites of her eyes flash, betraying her balk before she steps back.

Like she's about to run away?

The female alpha I wanted to rip to shreds moments ago turns out to be my savior. She halts the omega before she can flee, turning her to the nearest set of stairs with two firm hands on the angel's bare, flawless shoulders.

They exchange a few words before the alpha gives a bossy nod, all but pushing the omega down the steps.

I *hate* it.

But it means the blonde angel I'm desperate to meet has no choice but to float down to me.

I'm there, waiting. Watching her stare at her own feet as she navigates her descent. As if she's not used to the heels strapped over her unpolished toes—or the long, divided skirt of her gown.

Her trepidation is cute as hell, honestly. Every other woman in the room has been flouncing around like they own the place. This one acts like she's not even sure she's allowed to touch the handrail.

By the time she hits the last step, I'm grinning. My hand reaches over automatically, hovering. Waiting.

She finally glances up from her feet and finds my open palm. With a blink, crystalline eyes flutter up to meet mine.

There's a long, breathless pause. Another moment where I swear the room around us ceases to exist. And it's just me. Just her.

Just this.

Us.

Me and my mate.

My scent must be overpowering, because her lashes flutter again, those blue irises taking on a distinct glossiness while her pupils bloom. The visible reaction leaves me winded. I suck in a deep breath, inhaling *absolute heaven*.

And it smells like shortbread.

ten

It's Ivy.

Addison.

Whatever the fuck her name is.

Our maid is here. In a gown.

Our *maid* is here in a *gown*?

And, Jesus. She is *beautiful.*

This isn't news to me. I noticed the first day I met her. I've noticed every damn day since. And that night.

Shh, little dove.

Would you really say no to a duke?

I loathe the memory of what I said, but recalling her reaction is always worse. She was *scared.* And then, when I grabbed her wrist...

Don't leave me. Please.

I hate that I begged.

I hate that I would do it again.

Now, it all makes horrible, perfect sense.

She sways slightly, reaching for Bast's offered hand to steady herself as she steps onto the marble floor. Those gathered nearby turn to watch, no doubt taking note of the way she's captured Bast's complete focus.

And Asher's.

And *mine.*

God fucking damn it.

No, I argue with my Alpha, though it sort of sounds like a plea. *No. It can't be* her. *Because that would mean—*

That would mean I've already fucked this whole thing to hell and back.

Yeah, he snorts, like I am the biggest idiot on Earth. *Exactly, dipshit. The fuck did you think I was trying to tell you?*

All the times I looked at her and felt violent.

All the nights I had to take three or four other women to bed just to numb the need that burned through me.

All the things I said when she had me vulnerable and open.

This is why.

The maid is *our mate.*

And—oh *Christ*—the things I've *said.* The things I've made her *do.* The ways I tried to push her away.

I can never take any of it back.

Self-preservation kicks in. Those desperate, feral instincts that take over when someone's been stabbed or something. Denial floods my system. Arguing that this makes no sense. Can't be possible. She's a beta...

But no.

She *isn't*.

And I know that on a cellular level. Even from across this goddamn ballroom.

Shit. Fuck.

Someone touches my arm and I snap my head to the side, snarling instinctually. Until I see it's Asher. Looking just as pale as I feel.

He curses under his breath, casting Bast and Ivy a quick, strained glance before meeting my wild eyes under this mask.

On the verge of losing my shit, I reach up and rip the stupid thing off. Asher doesn't pause before following suit, shooting me an urgent glare. "You feel it, too?"

If by "it" he means this world-ending crater in my middle?

Then, yeah.

I fucking feel it.

When I open my mouth, though, that self-protective denial comes pouring out. "No. Asher. It can't—that—she—"

Am I *stammering*? I don't think that's ever happened. Not even when my father used to "teach me a lesson."

Asher takes half a second for surprise before frustration pushes down his brows. He looks irritated, but his eyes still roll over me, concerned. When they work their way back to mine, he gives me a long, wry look.

"Are you honestly going to fight this?"

He's truly asking. Trying to gauge how difficult I'll be. And maybe—shit—even determining if he needs to keep me away from the omega.

The beta.

Ivy.

I can't process what's happening. None of it makes *sense*.

Baring my teeth, I bite back a snarl and grit, "Asher, listen to me, that's not—"

His growl is so vicious, I might be proud under different circumstances. It's a true pack leader sound. My body twitches as I maintain eye contact and try to argue again.

Asher's answering bark knocks me back a step. "*Enough*. You do this every time. I'm not going to ignore what my Alpha is saying right now. If you want to stay here, then stay. I'm going to meet her."

If he hadn't silenced me so effectively, I would tell him he already has.

eleven

How can I want something so much and also hate it so fiercely?

I don't know. But every pace across the gold-veined floor is a lesson in extremes.

I can't get there fast enough. I also want nothing more than to return to the way the world was five minutes ago. Before I saw this blonde little omega and my insides *lunged* for her.

Because all I can think, with every step my feet eat up, is *I'm sorry*.

So damn sorry for so many things.

Loving Ivy. Making Ivy leave me. Trying to forget her. Failing at the forgetting. Thinking about her. Even now. While this new woman drags out a part of me I thought I'd already given away.

Should have given away.

I'm sorry, goose.

The fact that I know she would understand only makes this worse. I can practically picture her face—the wide, genuine smile she would give me, even if her eyes watered.

I drag myself across the floor, regret and urgency screaming through me. My heart pounds in my ears, the sound thick and oddly slow.

I've studied enough about anatomy to know that's not right. My pulse should be higher with all this stress. There's only one reason why it would drop into a calmer rhythm at a time like this.

My mate.

This beautiful girl, in her glimmering blue dress, flitting wide-eyed looks at Bast's face and then over at the crowded ballroom. Her lips twitch a couple of times, like she wants to smirk, but she's too nervous.

That sweetness appeals to me.

I hate myself for it.

Bast has his own mask dangling from his left hand. I wonder if there's a specific instinct at play, something in all of us that wants this woman to see our faces.

He must be flirting up a storm because the omega is having hard time keeping herself from laughing. And her *scent*—

It hits me as I step closer. Warmth and sugar and something... comforting. Familiar. A sweet, buttery piece of paradise.

Either way, it sails right through the neutralizers in the air, puncturing my lungs like a well-honed dagger. My center pulls taut as my spine snaps straight. Every cell in my airway vibrates until a low rumble hums out of me.

A purr.

Bloody hell.

Self-loathing and awe jostle one another in my chest. I'm not sure what it does to my scent, but the omega suppresses a quiver.

Bast takes note, too, drawing a step closer as his brows pinch in consternation.

"The air conditioning can be drafty in here with the hot weather outside," he chuckles, playing off her obvious goosebumps with a gentlemanly smile. "I prefer warmer climates for this season. Where do you usually summer?"

Because I'm slightly behind her—fixating on the cool, lustrous waves brushing her bare back—I can't see if her expression matches the awkward pause she allows. Finally, she fumbles, "Oh, I—um. Well. Summer? I usually stay, um, here?"

Confusion settles between Bast's brows, but he keeps his charming grin in place, God love him. "On the continent, you mean? You know, there are some beautiful places right in our own backyard. I should really mention that to His Highness. Although"—he catches my eye and winks—"you might get the chance before I do, lovely."

I live and die and hope and hate every second that it takes for her to *turn around*. But then it's done. And we're face to face.

Years of training serve me well. As she dips into a curtsy, I incline my head and offer a hand. With her chin tilted and the silver-blue mask covering half of her features, I can't see very clearly. But I get the distinct feeling she's gawping at my outstretched palm with disbelief.

I feel my mouth curve, but another gasp of pain pangs into my diaphragm. Because this shy hesitance? Barely-there manners coated in utter earnestness?

It all reminds me of Ivy.

A lot of things about this woman do, actually. Her fine-boned, unmanicured fingers. Her wispy eyebrows. The way her front teeth press into the corner of her lower lip while she sets her hand in mine.

Have I lost my mind?

This couldn't actually be *her*. Because Ivy was a *beta*. And this omega smells like all my wildest dreams and darkest fantasies, dusted in a fine layer of sugar.

She inhales sharply as our palms meet. I understand why when an answering snap of electricity thunders through my veins. Crackling up my arm, right down to the quiet corner where my heart sits.

Covered in ivy.

twelve

One of the doctors at the town's free clinic eventually got sick of me coming in for anxiety-related symptoms and had me download a list of "Medical Anxiety Coping Techniques."

The first one was: "Breathe."

So as my hand slides against Asher's—and a wave of delirious dizziness swallows my insides—I force myself to inhale.

Which... turns out to be a bad move.

Whatever citrusy, caramelized richness is filling the ballroom sends a jagged jolt of *want* right to the aching cramps that squeeze my core. Another wash of giddiness follows, lighting every nerve in my belly and creeping higher. Pinching my lungs until a high-pitched whine builds behind my breasts.

But, *no.* That can't be *right.* Betas don't truly *whine* the way omegas do. And certainly not as some involuntary reaction to—

What?

Them?

Fluttering my lashes, I try to clear the blurred edges of my vision. Working hard to remember *how* I ended up here. Or even *where* "here" *is*...

Something warm and surprisingly gentle squeezes my hand. My eyes finally settle on the face looming over me—all high cheekbones and square tightness. A flexed jaw, worry pulling at a chiseled mouth.

And hazel eyes.

Light brown, green, gold. They flicker, absorbing my gaze. A faint twitch leaves the prince's fingers clasped a bit tighter over my own.

The prince.

That's right. I'm at their party—the masquerade to help them find their mate. I came down the stairs and, for some reason, found Lord Burns waiting for me.

And then I realized he didn't recognize me like this. He was *flirting*. And *staring*. And...

Now Asher is here.

Ash.

I should scold myself for even thinking of the nickname in his ballroom, while he frowns at me. It's sort of hard to do much of anything, though. This deep bergamot scent has my head floating.

Not to mention whatever burned, sugary warmth is making my mouth *water*...

So, yeah.

Breathing does *not* help.

The second thing on that medical anxiety list was a grounding technique. Finding a certain number of things to look at, touch, and smell.

Since that last sense is out, I focus on the feel of the prince's skin. His fingertips, skimming the thin flesh of my wrist. Stroking back down to my palm. Curling my hand over his to bring my knuckles to his lips. That soft brush, the sort of kiss that's really a question.

I don't know what he's asking.

But, for Ash, my answer will always be yes.

My body agrees. The jitters stretched taut between my hips give a shiver and start to *melt*.

It's the strangest sensation—too cold and too hot all at once. When it breaks, a molten trickle of wetness soaks into my panties as a chill streaks up my spine, stiffening my nipples until they peak under the thin silk of my gown.

Sebastian makes a strangled sound behind me, covering it with a cough. I barely notice—too transfixed by the way Asher's eyes *burn*.

His nostrils flare as his fingers spasm around mine again. Chest heaving under his gilded white tuxedo, he tugs me closer. Pain breaks over his face.

"Please," he rasps. "Dance with me."

THIS IS WRONG.

It doesn't really matter what sort of confusion is causing the royal pack not to recognize me or my true designation. Letting the prince think I'm an eligible omega, allowing him to lead me onto the polished dance floor in front of God and all the world...

It's *wrong*. I *know* that.

The fact that I *want* it—*need it*, somehow—makes it worse. More selfish and sinister.

I know who I really am, but he doesn't. And if he did...

Well, it would be bad either way, right?

If he finds out I'm the beta maid he can't stand the sight of, it will be humiliating for him. And, on another level, if he finds out I'm also *me*...

At the end of the summer after I turned sixteen, he asked me to leave the manor. It was too hard for him, he explained. Caring for me and knowing he had to preserve his heart for his mate.

Something I could never be.

It was difficult for him to even say the words. Sometimes, when I close my eyes to sleep at night, I still see his face. The true, deep regret. The longing.

I promised I wouldn't come back. And I didn't... Until I had to.

Working at the manor was the only way to support my family. I couldn't quit and risk not finding another position. Not even when the princes made Maytown their home while they courted every omega in the country.

And quite a few from other countries, too.

I wonder which one this dress belonged to.

Another waft of delicious perfume rises from the fabric as I follow His Highness. The unique scent—tart, sweet, dark, fresh, warm—squeezes my lungs.

The feeling only swells bigger and higher. Blocking my throat as Asher whisks me to the center of the dance floor and arranges us in an all-too-familiar position.

His hand at the top of my hip. Our free fingers clasped at shoulder level. The broad height of his body carefully locked into a proper dance frame.

How To Ballroom Dance For Morons said as much. He was to be the frame—and I the picture. He liked those sorts of metaphors; they helped his rational mind grasp abstracts.

I always loved watching his gears grind when he tried to understand simple things. He could build a nuclear reactor if he wanted to—but learning how to rest his hand on the curve of my waist sent him into a scowling *mood*.

Ash.

Fresh guilt seasons the pain slashing my stomach. *He wouldn't want this with either version of me. The girl he sent away... or the maid he can't stand.*

So why can't I stop him?

I'm so busy thinking about how wrong it is, I forget to worry about how *stupid* it is.

For two reasons. One: Because, of course, dancing requires *closeness*. The heated skin of his throat is just inches from my nose. And somehow, as his touch digs into the curve of my hip with a bit more force than it should, the dark, bitter bergamot turning my panties into a creamy mess gets *stronger*.

He might clear his throat, but I can't be sure. I'm too busy feeling like the room has melted into a watercolor painting, all the hues bleeding into a blur as the orchestra starts up.

A waltz.

I can still hear his voice from years ago, the deep, uneven tone of an almost-grown man. Counting his steps while I tried to hide my smiles.

One, two, three. One, two, three.

He moves exactly the same.

I'm sure I do, too.

Which brings me to the second, perhaps more pressing reason why this is so dumb:

We are still *us*.

And as the violins swell, he sweeps me across the boards, cutting a turn that should be too sharp to follow cleanly.

If I were *anyone* else.

But I'm not.

So I see him coming. And that sudden pivot doesn't trip me up or even throw me off balance. I clip right into it, my hair flying behind me as he stops short. Both his large hands fall to my waist, framing my ribcage as we crash to a halt.

With harsh, visible breaths, he glares down at me in horror. His mouth drops halfway open, one hand automatically flying toward my mask.

I barely manage to shrink back before he touches the silver-trimmed lace. "No," I mouth, almost inaudible. "Please. Don't."

Of course, he listens. His hand drops limply to his side as he stands and stares. Not noticing the way other couples have stopped dancing to watch.

Or not caring.

A strange fervor glows in his eyes. And when he opens his mouth, he only has to say two words. "It's *you*."

I know what he means.

Me—the *real* me.

Ivy, not Addison.

The girl from the garden, not the maid on her hands and knees.

He knows it's *me*. Which means, if I take this mask off and let him see my face... he'll know the girl he rejected is also the one who folds his laundry. And scrubs their toilets.

God, none of this was supposed to happen! I was going to keep my head down, do my job, and help in any way I could while he *finally* found the mate he's been dreaming about since we were teenagers.

It wasn't supposed to be like *this*.

And I'm not even sure what this *is*.

I feel sick and scared and *ecstatic*.

Because he's looking at me. *Seeing* me.

"Finally."

Um.

Was that... a voice? In my... stomach?

Lord, I really have lost my mind. Maybe going to the doctor tomorrow isn't soon enough. Maybe I should have Gracie call an ambulance this time.

Then again, hearing voices isn't exactly a physical emergency. More like a psychological one...

It's definitely there, though. Behind my diaphragm, under my lungs. In a place I can only describe as *the middle* of me.

The voice sounds small and soft. Weak. But it echoes inside

my body the same way thoughts usually reverberate through my mind.

Does he understand? she asks, too pitiful to sound as desperate as I feel. *Does he see me?*

Am I supposed to *answer*? Wouldn't that officially make me a lunatic? But—gosh darn it—I've never been good at ignoring pitiful creatures. Or even *capable* of it, really.

I... I think back, blinking while the room whirls and the prince speaks. A low, humming question I can't answer because I have to reply to—myself?

I don't understand what's happening, I finally manage. *What —what do you want Asher to see?*

Maybe she's a lost spirit. And if I complete her mission, I can release her ghost. She'll go away and I'll go back to being nobody.

No! she cries, more insistent but distinctly less powerful. *No,* she mewls again, crying. *Please. He has to see. He has to know I'm here.*

Here? Like inside of *me*?

I can't think because—*oh*—I can't *breathe*. New hands skim my back. My arm. Flashes of color fill my vision.

Golden blond. Inked fingers.

White, gray, and—black.

Dairragh?

But, yes, that's his hand, with a thorn-torn wildflower tattooed on the back. Cupping my cheek.

Dark, shining beams connect with my gaze. The voice inside me rises, higher and more frantic. *I'm here, I'm here, I'm right here.*

And, this time, *Dair* answers her.

"Hey," he murmurs, low and urgent. "Hey, I see you. It's okay. Stay with me, all right? Stay with me, baby."

This time, I can't contain the whine that tears from my lungs. When it ekes out, the hand petting my back twitches. Bast's, I think. That sugary richness definitely smells like his new cologne—

And is he... purring?

"People are staring," he whispers. Not angry, just... *aware.*

Dair snarls. "I don't give a *fuck*," he growls, menacing. "She's obviously about to pass out. And can't you *smell* her? The fear is making me fucking *sick*."

Strong fingers smooth over the back of my hair. "I don't want her to be embarrassed," Bast replies, gritting the words. "This is a very public place to do this."

Do what?

What am I doing?

I was dancing with—

Asher's gone. I whip my head around, searching the crowd for him. Bast steps closer, until the rattle in his chest rumbles along my bare back. More slick heat slips into my panties, and I whine again, so confused and scared and just—*where is Ash?*

"He'll be right back, angel," Bast breathes. "It's okay. He went to get his parents. We're going to—"

His parents.

Oh God.

Oh *no.*

Whatever this is, they can't know about it. Asher's parents were the main reason he asked me to leave. We knew they would never approve of *me* for their alpha prince. And my mother's job was on the line if they found out how thoroughly I'd broken their rules.

Only now, it's *my* job on the line. And for what? So these poor guys can get their hopes up over nothing?

Because that's what I am.

Nothing. Nobody.

Just the maid and a beta and a silly girl who talks to ducks.

If anyone finds out the princes mistook *me* for their *mate*, The Crown will be humiliated.

An image of Asher from the day we met flies through my mind. Of his face when those boys mocked him. I don't ever want to be the reason he looks like that.

The voice inside me tries to scream, begging me to stay, but she's too weak. And as one group after the next pause their conversations to turn and stare at the princes. At *me*...

Strangling panic spikes, shoving me into motion. I slip from under Bast's hands, away from Dair's. When I see a gap in the crowd, my hindbrain takes over.

And I run.

thirteen

At some point in my life, I took a bullshit biology class about designations.

A lot of it was annoying drivel that made omegas sound helpless. Or painted alphas as slaves to their impulses.

Well, they got one thing right.

Omegas *are* fast.

And Ivy *is* an omega.

I might not know when or how our beta maid changed her designation, but her scent can't lie. And even if it could? The way she darts into a narrow crack in the crowd doesn't.

Grinding out a curse, I yank back the part of me that wants to launch myself after her. Because if everyone sees that, there's no going back. She'll be The Chosen One—and right now, she doesn't even want to be in the room with us.

I don't fucking blame her.

But I forgot one other thing from that bullshit class.

When omegas run?

Alphas chase.

Bast blinks at the blank patch of dance floor where Ivy stood. His pupils blow—and the urge to *protect* rears up inside of me. When he takes off, I'm right on his heels.

Asher meets us at the exit she raced out of, his chest heaving like he's already run a mile—but his face is white as bone.

Cameras flash behind us, but there's no time to worry about that shit.

She's getting away.

And I haven't even told her how sorry I am.

Ivy must truly be quick, though. Because despite Bast and all his athleticism sprinting ahead, she loses us.

Asher and I catch up to him at Maytown Manor's front gate. It's closed—the iron slats sealed with tangled vines—but I still see clusters of paparazzi stationed outside.

If Ivy had flown past them, wouldn't they be after her?

And how the hell did she get through the gate?

Bast is thinking the same thing, turning from left to right and back again, scanning the dark lawn for any trace of her.

Normally, this is when our pack leader would start barking orders. Questioning nearby guards, ordering the security footage be reviewed.

But Asher... drops to his knees.

Right in the middle of the gravel path, in his white tuxedo.

He reaches for a sliver of silver, lifting it by its thin chain. The scent of bergamot and black tea descends into utter darkness. He sets the necklace in his palm and examines it for a long moment.

"It's really her," he says, almost to himself. "*Ivy.*"

Bast's toffee aroma is also burned to crisp. He spins back to us, clutching his hair with both hands, eyes flashing with wild desperation. "Who's Ivy? Our mate? You *know* her?"

Asher closes his fist around the silver heart charm and swallows. His free hand gestures at his chest—where we both know he only has one tattoo.

"The girl," he says. "Her name was Ivy. *Is* Ivy."

"That was *her*?" Bast crows, his eyes somehow even rounder.

"No," I bite out. My eyes drop closed while regret and fear hurtle through me. "*That* was our maid."

fourteen

I'M NOT A VIOLENT ALPHA.

But I might kill these two fuckers.

I pace between the antique sofas in Their Majesties' private sitting room, running my hands through my hair so many times, I swear it will start falling out.

On the coffee table, my phone sits silent. Which would usually be weird—but now, it's unacceptable. Once Dair explained who the omega from the ball really was, we all tried calling the number our housekeeper had on file for her. Until Maman pointed out that our mate probably left her phone behind when she bolted.

"I can't believe this!" I shout, turning from Asher to Dair and back again. "What the fuck?!"

Normally, spitting insults and epithets in his parents' precious presence would at least make Asher glower. But he hasn't looked up from the locket in his hand yet.

His Majesty, Asher Leopold the Fourth—"King Leo"—starts to growl at me, but Maman reaches over and pointedly squeezes his knee, shaking her head slightly.

"*Mon petit chou* is right to be upset, dearest," she tells him. Her pointed gaze snaps back to Dair and Asher. Sharp and full of reproach. "His packmates have let him down."

I could live without being called "little cabbage," but at least she's on my side. I wave a less-than-delicate hand at her and burst, "Exactly! The hell is *wrong* with you, Asher? You knew this girl for *years* and never thought she might be your *mate*?"

He doesn't answer. Hasn't this whole time.

But his dad does.

"That girl was a beta!" he harrumphs, rubbing at the wrinkles around his muddy eyes. "Her mother was a *seamstress*, for Christ's sake. He could hardly *court* her."

Maman frowns fiercely. "Well, clearly, she is *not* a beta. Her mother was also an omega—Ivy must be a late bloomer."

Ivy.

Fucking hell.

I'm still getting used to hearing that name. Because that's the other side to this whole goddamn mess—I've been calling our maid the wrong name for six months. And she is, in fact, Ivy.

Ivy *Addison*. When we met, and Mrs. Kemp introduced her as Miss Addison, I stupidly assumed that was her first name.

I'm a fucking *numpty*.

A now-familiar deluge of shame hits me for the dozenth time in as many minutes. Images of me lounging around on my phone while Ivy—*our mate*—cleared away my breakfast tray or sorted my laundry or balanced on ladders to wash our windows.

God.

I glare at Dair, needing someone else to blame. "And *you*! You've been barking and scowling at her since the day we got here! You didn't think there might be a *reason* she got under your skin?"

If I wasn't about to put my fist through his face, I might be worried about His Grumpiness. I've never seen him so beat-to-shit.

Bent over his own lap, dark hair brushes his forehead while his inked fingers press into his eyes. "I know," he groans. "I didn't—she *had no scent*. I couldn't understand why I—"

He looks up, baring his teeth while he strangles a growl. "You guys don't even understand how badly I've fucked this up. And once I knew she probably hated me, I just—"

Why would he think she *hates* him? Apart from the way he tried to intimidate her?

Dear Lord—is there *more*?

I can't ask him here, in front of Asher's parents. But the way he drops his face to his hands makes me think so.

Maman tsks. "So you thought she didn't like you, and your solution was to scare the poor darling half to death? And parade endless women under her nose?" she scolds, eyeing Dair with her trademark blend of concern and disappointment. "*Cherie*, you know better than that."

Dair shifts, letting his arms fall slack as he nods at the Persian rug and croaks, "I know."

Asher finally moves. Slowly, his fingers curl shut around Ivy's locket.

"I knew, too," he says, agreeing with Dair. "Back then. Every day since. I knew, and I convinced myself it wasn't possible instead of fighting for the truth."

His father's saggy features furrow. "You couldn't have known," he blusters. "You did the right thing, my boy. I would have sent her away, too."

Fire snaps in Asher's eyes. "Yes, that's exactly the *fucking problem*. I did what you expected instead of doing the *right thing*. What I *knew* was right for me *and my mate*."

I don't think I've ever heard him snarl at the king. The whole room goes still, but Asher isn't done. He levels his searching, serious stare at his father. "Is this how you would have wanted to treat Maman? To send her away and make her suffer and let her think she wasn't *good enough*?"

King Leopold clearly isn't used to being called out by anyone who isn't his wife. He frowns mightily, swelling up to shout—until Maman lays her hand on his arm and turns to him. Whatever her expression conveys immediately deflates him.

"You knew back then?" the king grumbles. "Truly? Without a scent? How?"

Asher looks down at her locket, turning the etched silver heart over and rubbing his thumb along its delicate engravings. "She was"—he stops and swallows, his voice breaking—"the most beautiful person I'd ever met. So..."

"Warm."

The word falls out of my mouth, and everyone turns to look at me. That sickening shame squirms in my stomach. I remember running into her in the garden this week. Wasn't she wearing the silver locket that day?

"I think I knew, too," I admit. With a sigh, I collapse onto a nearby chair, exhaling hard enough to expel the tension that kept me on my feet. "What the fuck do we do?"

Leopold slants another disapproving look at me, but Maman sits back with a *harrumph*. "I suppose you'll have to go find her and apologize." She glances at Dair and her son. "*Profusely*."

"She'll need medical care," I realize. "The way she was acting —I don't think she knows she's designating as an omega. She must be so confused."

"And scared," Dair puts in, uncharacteristically quiet.

Maman shrugs. "We have the finest doctors from the palace with us. We can take care of everything she needs."

That reminds me—I put in a request with her mother's

medical group to get some of her bills paid off. Now that we know Addi—*Ivy*—is our mate, though, I can probably figure out some way to get rid of them altogether.

When I mention her mother, everyone turns to gape at me. I look from one face to the next, appalled by how self-absorbed and awful we all are.

"Her mom," I repeat. "She died five months ago, but she was sick for *years*. That's why Ad—*Ivy* had to drop out of college. It's why she works *here*."

The others gape at me. A vicarious wave of anger rises in my chest as I grit, "None of you ever thought it was *odd* that she worked *seven days a week*? She never had a *choice*."

There's a long, taut moment.

Then Dair pushes to his feet and stalks out.

fifteen

I CRACK ONE EYELID OPEN, HOLDING MY BREATH. Waiting.

It's quiet, but my fitful night taught me that temporary silence doesn't mean the voice in my head (or center?) is gone. Every time I managed to block out Aunt Matilda's TV enough to fall asleep, I startled back to consciousness minutes later.

And each time, I would wait, thinking the voice inside me had finally gone...

Then she'd start up again.

Begging in pathetic whimpers I could barely ignore. Asking

me to take her back to the manor. And, more specifically, the princes.

Somewhere around three a.m., I decide she'll get her wish.

Because I don't really have a choice, do I? I have to go to work for the same exact reasons I've forced myself to go every other day, no matter how sick or sad or sullen I felt.

Not to mention—I left my phone, keys, and just about everything else I own in Tanya's room.

Including my mother's locket, which I suspect fell out of my dress when I fled. I'll have to try to retrace my steps later, if I have time... *Hopefully, it isn't lost forever...*

I force down the tightness in my chest while I finish buttoning my work dress and tying my apron. Shaking fingers leave my usual bun sloppy—and I don't even bother considering a layer of makeup.

The goal, I decide, is to look as little like the girl they think they met last night as possible. Then, with any luck, I'll fly under their radar.

It's not like any of them recognized me, really. So what if Asher knew I was the girl he used to dance with and read to and trade secrets with late at night? That didn't mean they would piece together the rest of my identity.

No. Today, I go back to being nobody.

The maid Dair hates and Ash ignores and Bast chats to while he texts other people.

It won't be a big deal.

My stomach seethes all the way through town, empty but too tender for anything more than the slice of toast and half glass of tap water I consumed before I slipped out of the apartment.

By the time I make it through the quiet brick streets of our little village and hit the damp gravel path up to the manor, I regret not forcing down one of my usual protein shakes. It's been almost a full day since I had a meal—and whatever freak-out started last night seems far from over.

My heart hammers. Every other breath snags on whines. I quiver and wobble, but trudge on. Thinking of Mama's bills and my promise to help my aunt. Trying to look around and let the beautiful periwinkle sunrise distract me.

When that doesn't work, I remind myself what all the doctors have said. *This is all in my head. I'm perfectly healthy. I just have a low pain tolerance.*

And now maybe some balance issues, too?

Our all-night tug-of-war must have worn out the voice in my middle because she stays pretty quiet until the vine-covered gray stone of the manor comes into sight. And, even then, she only scrapes out another feeble whimper.

She can't speak at the moment, but I still somehow know who she's after: the princes. Of course.

Will going straight to their chambers encourage her and whatever this madness is? Should I go to Tanya's room first?

Turns out, I don't have time. According to the gorgeous Victorian clock hanging above the keypad where staff members check in, I barely made it to my shift.

I've always liked Maytown Manor on Sunday mornings, particularly if they come after a grand affair like last night's ball. Mrs. Kemp has slept in, leaving me and a couple of kitchen assistants to quietly work around each other while we gather supplies from the storerooms.

Sunday means I need a bucket, rags, a scrub brush, and the special wood cleaner that keeps the manor's ancient floors gleaming. I also manage to place the guys' typical breakfast orders.

Asher will want his tea straight away, along with whatever's left of that banana bread I baked him and a plate of bacon.

Bast likes a green juice—but if he's had too much to drink, he also downs a glass of raw eggs and allows himself *half* a muffin. I giggle every time I order it, knowing the cooks will roll their eyes.

After a big party, Dair always requires fresh sheets and… *rehydration*. Three bottles of Voss water and a plate of fruit with his toast usually does the trick.

"His Highness will want the papers as well," I tell the kitchen apprentice. "All three. Oh, and aspirin, please."

I don't tell them the pills are for me. My head is *pounding*—and the beginnings of breakfast make me even more nauseous.

Luckily, once I get upstairs and into the princes' chambers, that lovely blend of sweet, citrusy tartness fills my senses. It works like magic, silencing my body's upheaval long enough for me to get each of their trays set in front of their bedroom doors.

Next, I nip into the small kitchen attached to their wing and fill my bucket with cleaning fluid and warm water. My pain might be muted by the aspirin, but the dizziness isn't. When I lower myself to the living area floor and start to scrub, I have to concentrate to keep my head from floating away.

That strange new voice in my middle stays quiet. I get the oddest feeling she's… relieved? And too exhausted to explain why.

Every time I try to unriddle the sensation, I get an image of a bedraggled girl washing up on the beach after going overboard. Too depleted to move, but most definitely grateful to be on dry land.

I still don't understand what's happening to me, but the wing's peaceful silence helps. So does the sunrise. Within an hour, the pretty pinks have faded into a bright blue morning and half of the hardwoods are freshly washed.

On the other side of the round room, I hear stirring behind one of the closed doors. My heart stalls while my stomach lurches, the earlier nausea flooding back.

But no.

No.

I am nobody. I have to be.

And I need to act like nothing is wrong or they might get suspicious. Bending closer to the floor, I fix my eyes on the wood grain and keep cleaning. Just like I would have a week ago.

Because I'm here to serve. Not to be seen or known or cared about. I'm not even *me*, here, I'm—

"*Ivy.*"

My real name stops me cold. None of them have ever said it. Except for Asher, years ago, but he usually just called me—

"Goose?"

The word is breathless and hopeful and ever so *pained*. I want to look up at him—the prince, *he's the prince*—but I'm frozen to my core.

Another door flies open. Someone groans. I know it's Lord Burns when he says, "Oh, thank *God*. Dair! She's here!"

Who's here?

...me?!

The shock is enough to snap my head up. Feeling ridiculous, I gape at both Prince Asher and Lord Burns, utterly stunned to find them both *undressed*.

Well, partially. Sebastian has on a pair of silky blue boxers that barely cover the very tops of his thighs. And Asher's wearing a slightly longer, solid gray pair along with a plain white undershirt.

I've never seen him so... undone. Pale and tense. His hands opening and closing as his jaw grinds. Tortoiseshell glasses sit crookedly on his nose, highlighting just how mussed his thick, wavy hair is.

Somehow, no matter how messy he gets working out or riding, Bast always looks like he strolled out of a cologne ad. Right now, he smells that way, too. While Asher stares at me as if he's seeing a ghost, the baron immediately drops to his knees at my side, putting his bare, tanned chest inches away from my shoulder. Reaching out to—to—

His hand, solid and warm, settles on my spine. Stroking.

A high-pitched sound I only recognize from last night rips out of me.

I'm mortified. *Shaking*.

But his face creases, concern mingling with an undeniable sort of... tenderness. "Angel," he whispers, "we've been so worried about you."

...

What?!

But how did they—*when* did they—*who*—

Oh.

Him.

Dair.

The second he appears on his threshold, all wild, black hair and wilder, blacker ink, I see it. I *know*.

He's the one who figured it out.

And now *they all* know who I am.

sixteen

Ivy is more beautiful than I ever could have imagined.

The last time I truly saw her face, she was barely sixteen, covered in freckles, and still very much growing into her features. It didn't matter, back then, that she seemed awkward—I loved *her*.

Her high cheekbones and full, pink mouth used to look as oversized as her clear blue eyes—but now...

She's a woman.

And a gorgeous one.

But there's no color to her face. Her shining gaze is dazed.

And her body quivers so intensely, the brush in her hand clatters to the floor.

It takes me a moment to process that.

She's on her *hands and knees* with a *scrub brush*? Why? Did she honestly think we expected her to go back to work after discovering who she really was?

Who she *is*—because, as I stand in front of her, my Alpha lunges.

I drop to the floor, gathering her hands and guiding her up from her strained position. "Darling," I murmur, "What are you doing on the floor?"

She flutters those glassy eyes again, resting on her bent legs and looking from my face to Dair's doorway, then over to Bast.

"I—I scrub the floors every Sunday."

The horror of that simple statement washes through the room. This—*her*, on her *hands and knees*, scraping *our* dirt off *our* floors—is her reality. Her *life*.

And I allowed it. Because I wouldn't let myself *look* at her. *See* her.

Because I was afraid of wanting anyone who *wasn't* her.

The irony is too tragic. Unacceptable.

Ivy watches my face contort and starts to stammer, "B-but if it doesn't please you, Your Highness, I can—"

Dair's growl rends the air, stilling Bast's hands halfway through his hair and freezing our omega in place. I look at him, torn between wanting to fight him and understanding the bastard all too well.

He hates me for this.

He hates *himself* for this.

And if the way I feel is any indication, hearing her—*our mate*—earnestly use my formal title has just about killed him.

Bast's face confirms it. In all the time I've known him, I've never seen him look so sick.

Because of me.

And her, lying. Feeling like she *had to* lie.

Because. Of. *Me*.

My hands tighten around her wrists.

So fragile. Pale. Weak.

All my fault.

I can't even begin to describe the shame and anguish churning through my body, so I settle on a low bark.

"*Never* call me that again."

Ivy trembles, ducking her head as tears trickle down her face. "I—I'm so sorry, Your—Sir. I should have told you who I was, but I didn't want to lose my job and—"

Bast's arms fly out to wrap around her quivering frame. "Angel," he breathes, sounding as if he's on the verge of breaking down himself. "*Stop*. Please. My fucking heart can't take it. You haven't done anything to apologize for."

I feel a twinge of disagreement—because, God, how could she have been here *every day* and *not told me*?—but it's easy to stifle. Especially when Dair slowly strides over...

...and drops to his knees, too.

seventeen

The duke's tattooed hand shakes as he reaches for—

Me?

I wouldn't believe it if I didn't feel the soft press of his touch, shuddering as he gently grips my jaw and lifts my chin.

Their chamber is as blurry as the ballroom felt last night—but when those dark irises beam at me, my lungs unlock. His eyes bounce between mine, examining closely.

"Ivy," he finally says, thick but soft. "You don't know what's happening, do you?"

It's somehow the exact problem and perfect question all rolled into one. Because, actually, *no*. I *don't* know what's happening to me. Or *them*.

A week ago, I scrubbed this entire room and the kitchen *and* all three of their bathrooms—no one even *noticed*. But now they're all here? Protesting and apologizing? Half—or in Dair's case *mostly*—naked?

This can't be real.

The foggy edges of my vision make it feel like a dream. Or a fantasy that's gotten away from me.

I don't know *what* it is. But based on the heavy, grief-filled gazes trained on my face? They all seem to.

Mortification and fear swoop through my stomach. My chin quivers in his grasp. "A-am I sick? Or... crazy?"

Dair's brows fold together, his gaze softening in an unfamiliar way that somehow looks perfectly right on him. "No, baby," he whispers. "You're not crazy at all. I bet you *hurt*, though." His thumb rasps over the hollow of my cheek as his nostrils flare and his eyes sharpen. "Show me where."

How does he know? My mind swirls. I'm so confused, I can't resist the compelling pull in his eyes. And the answering urge to please him.

My hand finds my lower abdomen, pressing into the cramps twisting between my hips. He snarls quietly but kneels closer. The scent of tart cranberries and torn mint slices into my lungs—sharp and refreshing. Like the exact kind of deep breath I've needed for the last eighteen hours.

He slips his fingers over my clutched hand, stroking my knuckles with intent. Like a lover might. Deep, dark eyes snag mine, more solid than I've ever seen them. "This hurts because you need a knot, omega."

Omega.

The word reverberates through my entire body. Buzzing. *Blaring*. And, finally, connecting directly to that new voice buried in my middle.

I'm here, she says again. So quiet and helpless. *Please. I'm here, alpha.*

She used that word last night, too, didn't she? Not duke. Not prince. Or "my lord."

Alpha.

And he just called me...

"Omega?" I repeat, my lungs shriveling with anxiety. "N-no, Your Grace, I'm a beta. I—they've done *tests.*"

His answering glower is very Dair-like. "I don't care what the damn tests said," he replies, "I'm your alpha. I *feel* it."

Before I can protest, Bast jostles into Dair's side, his navy eyes wide on my face. "Me, too, angel," he agrees.

I don't know what to say. I don't even know what to *think.* But as I blink at Lord Sebastian Burns' oh-so-handsome features, his expression creases. All hope falls from his face, replaced with pleading.

His warm, strong fingers reach for the sudsy hand that held the scrub brush, squeezing carefully as his eyes search mine. His voice drops low. "If I can ever get you to forgive me for being a *complete idiot*, I hope you'll let me show you how much I want to be your alpha."

My alpha.

They all keep saying it. Dair, now Bast. The voice I'm imagining.

Everyone except—

I whip my head to the prince, all but begging him to set this whole mess straight. "Ash," I whisper.

He forbid me to call him that ever again. I need him to tell me the *truth,* though. To tell *them.* "I'm a beta, right? I'm—I'm not —*I can't be your mate.* That's why you wanted me to leave, remember?"

Asher is pale as bone. As pallid as the first day we met when those horrible bullies mocked him and his mother. More colorless than he looked the rainy afternoon he asked me not to come back to the manor, and told me he wouldn't be returning, either.

"I need you to let me go," he'd said, looking so pained. So much

like he does right in this moment. *"I'll never find my mate if you're here."*

But I was a stupid young girl. Too in love and hurt and worried about him to understand. *"Here at the manor?"* I'd asked.

I still had dreams about the way he'd pounded a fist into his chest, only once, and twisted his expression into a snarl. *"No. Here."*

His heart, I realized later—after he had issued his orders and stiffly strode off. Away. *Gone.*

Except he's here now. Watching me with sparkling hazel eyes. *Wet* eyes, actually. And the pale, anguished face that resembles cracked china when his features break.

"No, goose," he says, dragging in torn breaths. "I was *wrong.* So fucking wrong. And I'll never—"

His chest heaves as he shakes his head, grim certainty settling in his gaze. "I'll never be able to tell you how sorry I am," Asher scrapes out.

He keeps speaking, his brows crouching lower and lower. Frowning more deeply as the edges of the room melt, and I miss half his words.

"—an omega."

"—get you help—"

The voice at my center—*my... Omega?*—hates that he feels so upset. She's frantic with guilt, whimpering that this is *her fault.*

Which would make sense, if I really *was* an omega and these truly were my *mates.*

I whine, so confused and overwhelmed that I don't know what else to do. Asher's voice gets more urgent. Dair growls. Bast's perfect chest echoes with a rolling purr.

Gasping, I sway toward that sound. *Needing* it in a way that leaves me reeling. The pain between my thighs tweaks tighter. My lungs squeeze, then squeak.

And the room dissolves.

eighteen

I've never given much thought to what having an omega would be like.

Anyone who's ever met me will tell you: I don't want one. Can't take care of one. And probably shouldn't even try.

Well.

Fuck.

Bast is the one carrying Ivy this time. I walk behind them, my muscles thrumming with the memory of having her body that close to mine.

Jesus. How stupid am I? I had her *in my arms* and couldn't figure out why the hell holding her made my Alpha *feral*.

I sense that same wildness now, lighting my blood. Prowling under skin that feels too tight for my bones.

Holy hell, is this a *rut*?

Now?

Bad fucking timing when we're about to walk into the manor's medical facility and hand Ivy over to a bunch of doctors.

Asher shoves the door open, standing there to hold it. He pauses Bast on the threshold, reaching over and cupping our omega's cheek.

She's unconscious, her eyes shut, and her pretty face smooth. So beautiful when she isn't working or worried.

I bite down on the rage and urgency pounding through me. Telling my Alpha, *no*.

She's more important than whatever bullshit we need.

And, frankly, after what I've put her through? I can go to hell.

Stuffing it all down comes much easier than I expect. For one, we're all on rut-blockers. But, more importantly, anytime my pulse gets too thick or my teeth start to grind, I look at Ivy's face, focusing on the way her body automatically folds itself closer to Bast's purr.

He has her on an exam table, refusing to let go of her. Asher sits lower on the cot, turning so he can press his own purr close.

The truth stings as it sinks in. *They know what to do, and I don't.*

By the time the king and queen's royal physician strolls into the room, I'm sure our scents are burned to shit. I can't tell, though. All I smell is Ivy's buttery, sugared perfection.

So when the asshole doctor swoops in and tries to *touch* her—

A dangerous rumble snags in my throat as I press my hand to his chest, walking him back a step. "I will *end* your life."

The doctor's eyes fly wide, snapping to a place just past my bare shoulder. Hunting for Asher, probably. Wanting him to call off his Rottweiler.

Usually, the prince would sigh and scold me. But, right now? An odd beat of silence swells before he manages, "If you could perform the exam without touching her, that might be best."

Dr. Grant nervously twitches a nod. "Yes, Your Highness. Of course. I'll try."

Despite putting on gloves and taking care not to let anything aside from his instruments touch Ivy, all three of us spend the next ten minutes snarling at him. Even Bast.

When the doctor finally steps back, my blond packmate holds Ivy closer to his purr, stroking her head. My eyes fly to the bun hiding all of her pretty hair, hating it. Wondering if, had she not been forced to wear it every day, Asher might have recognized her sooner.

My instincts urge me closer, until I'm at Bast's other hip, reaching across their bodies to undo the pins. Asher casts me a grateful look I'm not sure I've ever earned before. As soon as I finish letting her hair down, he immediately combs his fingers through the long strands.

They're lovely. The lightest, coolest blonde. Almost silvery, like her ice-blue mask and her locket.

I can tell its texture and color are familiar to Asher—as he massages the place where those cursed pins poked her scalp, his hand visibly shakes. We all pretend we don't hear the quiet, mournful sound that snags in his airway.

The doctor turns to his work counter, dropping one of the swabs he collected into a flask of yellow liquid. Within seconds, it starts to turn green. When he drops a second Q-tip into a glass with clear liquid, nothing happens at all.

Fuck. The anxiety gripping my stomach is—

Not new, I realize.

This restless edginess... I've felt it for months. Since the day we got here.

Near her.

Which means my Alpha has been climbing my goddamn walls for *this woman*. And all those drunken nights, the endless need, the urge to fuck as hard and as much as humanly possible. The *rage*.

My body was trying to tell me something important, and I basically shoved a wad of socks in its mouth and duct-taped it shut.

Shame creeps back into my scent, turning Bast's head. I've never seen our packmate so solemn. When our eyes meet, he doesn't offer any platitudes or try to make excuses. Instead, his toffee essence chars, and he drops his forehead to Ivy's, whispering more apologies. Tucking her closer to his naked chest.

Suddenly, I can't fucking *stand* any of this.

Shh, little dove.

Would you really say no to a duke?

Don't leave me. Please.

All this time, she wasn't planning to use any of it to blackmail me or go viral. She was *protecting* me. Because the Omega lost inside her recognized her *mate*.

I never want to see her in this horrible gray dress again. Turning to the nearest nurse or assistant—who gives a shit?—I bark out, "*You*. Our princess needs new clothes. Bring her some of mine."

The girl starts to stammer a reply. "P-prin—?"

Asher *growls*, "Yes. *Our princess*."

The woman dips into a curtsy and scurries off, returning just minutes later with a pile of clothing. I note with satisfaction that, while she chose our own sweats and shirts for the three of us, the ones for Ivy are, in fact, mine.

The doctor keeps muttering over whatever he has in those damn beakers. I draw the privacy curtain around the bed and turn back to where Bast and Asher are both staring at Ivy. Hesitating.

"Should we call her friend?" Bast murmurs. "Would Ivy want her instead of us?"

Asher swallows thickly. "Which friend?"

I suppress a jealous snarl. "One of our PR managers, Gracie. She's an alpha."

We all tense at the thought, none of us able to stomach another alpha putting their hands on our girl right now. Let alone taking her clothes off.

Asher must hate the idea as much as I do, because he sighs. "You two get your clothes on. I'll undress her."

nineteen

The voice in my middle still sounds weak, despite *glowing* with contentment. I feel warm, but certain places on my body tingle. A swath along my left shoulder, both sides of my neck, my forehead.

And my right hand.

That's where my eyes fall first—to the hand currently tucked into both of Dairragh Vreeland's—as he slowly rubs his stubbled chin over the thin, buzzing skin covering my knuckles.

The duke meets my gaze, black eyes swirling. "Little dove," he rasps. "There you are."

I don't think I've ever seen this man look surprised before. Or maybe that's something else, curving his brows up and parting his lips.

Before I can parse it, the pillow wedged into my side moves. Because it isn't a sack of feathers—it's a *lord*.

"Thank God you're awake," Sebastian practically moans, tucking a bare, muscled arm around my waist like it's the most natural thing in the world. "I've been worried sick, angel."

I blink at the rippling expanse of his bare torso, squirming when his warmth sinks into my skin and the scent of toffee tickles my nose. A second later, that hot-and-cold sensation streaks down my spine, landing in a puddle that soaks my panties.

Sudden, masculine groans surround me. Including one from the prince sitting behind me. Asher's fingers curl in my hair, tugging softly while he drops his chin and breathes over a rumble in his throat.

Against my thigh—which is now covered by a pair of men's sweatpants?—I feel a hard jerk. Heat stings my cheeks when I realize it's Sebastian's *cock*.

I start to rear back, mortified. "I'm *so sorry*, my lord," I gasp, struggling to sit up. "This is so inappropriate."

To my dismay, the baron cringes guiltily, hauling himself upright. "You're right, angel. I should be the one apologizing—it isn't right for me to touch you without your permission."

...um.

What?!

"N-no," I argue, looking at all three of them in turn. Waiting for someone to call me impertinent for accidentally shaming a baron. "Not *that*. I meant it's not appropriate for *me* to be touching *you*." My gaze finally settles on Asher's as I brace for his disapproval. "R-right, Your—?"

Dair's snarl cuts me off. Asher's hazel eyes blaze with pain. "No, darling," he murmurs, sitting forward and collecting the hand not currently clutched in the duke's. "There's nothing wrong with you wanting to touch your alphas."

The sappy, clueless voice in my middle practically *squees* with happiness. My heart aches, and my head spins, trying to make sense of what he's saying. Trying not to *hope—please, God—* because letting myself wish this is real might be the thing that finally breaks me.

Dair, I think desperately. *Dair will be horrible to me and remind me of my place, and then I'll be able to breathe.*

But the cruel duke doesn't have even an ounce of his usual animosity. Only searing regret and a jaw that flexes as he stares back at me.

"Ivy," he finally croaks, "baby..."

Baby?!

I almost laugh at the absurdity of him calling me that, but a middle-aged beta in a white coat clears his throat. We all turn to watch him wring his hands nervously.

"Your... Highnesses," he starts, uneasy. "The test results have been collected and finalized. I'd like to explain them to Miss—*Her Highness*. If that's all right."

Her Highness? As in Princess Ahmad? Or some other princess I don't know about? Why on Earth would this doctor want to explain *my* test results to—

Oh.

OH.

This time, I do laugh.

Because *me*? *"Her Highness?"*

It's *funny*.

I scrub toilets and talk to squirrels and can't apply blush without looking like a clown. I have no graces or title or money or poise. My only jewelry is a now-missing locket and my one pair of shoes has plastic soles. I can't be a *princess*.

I can't even get Starbucks to make my latte with oat milk.

My hysterical giggles grate the silence dangling over the room. Beside me, Bast winces. His warm hand lands on my shoulder. "Ivy, I know this is a lot, but the staff has to call you whatever they call us. Because you're our mate."

Their mate?

Their. Mate????

The start of another crazed laugh dies in my throat when I see the doctor's solemn expression. My voice shrinks. "But I—There's nothing *wrong* with me. I'm not an omega; I just have health anxiety. So I can't be—I'm not—"

Dr. Grant holds out a tablet, as if I have any prayer of reading the charts and notes in his medical program. "Actually, Your Highness, you very well could be their mate because you *are* an omega. Your saliva sample contained no beta signatures, but the solution to detect omega pheromones lit up immediately. I need to order more detailed bloodwork to confirm, but I suspect your levels are akin to those in an emerging omega during adolescence."

But that's *impossible*.

I've been told, over and over, that this is *all in my head*.

Bast glances over and sees whatever my face is doing. He immediately tucks me into his side, sliding his solid arm around my middle to squeeze me reassuringly.

"So Ivy is a late bloomer?"

Dr. Grant grimaces. Dair's chest snags on a new snarl as Asher shifts, his eyes flashing.

The poor man mops his palms on this white coat. "Actually, Ivy's results are more consistent with an omega who's been... *abused*."

Dair's voice is dangerously even. "Abused?"

The murmur in my middle feels frantic at the thought of displeasing him. I start to shake my head, unable to help the whine piercing my lungs.

Bast casts the duke a glare, holding me closer to his side. Asher turns away from the doctor and runs his eyes over my features, his immediately softening. A moment later, a thick wash of alpha dominance floods the area around the bed.

For me, it's soothing. But Dair drops his chin, breathing harder. As if he's somehow been put in his place by the same rush that settled me.

Bast chokes out a sound of reluctant amusement and sets his

chin on my shoulder. "You'll get used to them, angel. I'm just glad I'm not the only sane one around here anymore."

Asher spares him a glower before turning back to the doctor. "Abused?" he repeats.

Dr. Grant nods. "Yes, Your Highness." His nervous eyes run over my face. "Omegas in unsafe environments often designate later or, in extreme cases, not at all. The stress can put undue strain on their bodies."

Another long silence swells around us. I shake my head again, forcing words up my dry throat. "I'm not—I've never been abused."

The doctor looks like he doubts my words, but he doesn't argue. "In that case, there's a very good chance this is all a simple case of bad luck. Many medications and products aren't safe for omegas because they suppress or affect their hormones in other ways.

"Most omegas avoid those substances once their preliminary designation bloodwork flags them as a potential omega during adolescence. If you—*Your Highness'* blood work didn't show any omega potential, you may have inadvertently suppressed what few omega pheromones you had by treating yourself as a beta."

Another growl from Dair has me burrowing into Bast's golden warmth. But this time, the duke pins his death stare on the doctor.

"*Treating herself?*" he demands. "You mean whatever asshat doctors she had when she was a child fucked up her results and essentially guaranteed she would wind up *poisoning* herself?"

The doctor wipes at his damp forehead. "Well, um."

Pity swarms my stomach. I find myself reaching over to touch Dair's black T-shirt, my fingers trembling. When he whips his head around and stabs my gaze with his dark eyes, I flinch. His mouth drops from a scowl into a soft pout.

"It isn't his fault," I whisper, glancing at Asher. "Or any of the other doctors. With all her medical issues, my mother and I could never afford private medicine for me—and the public system is really overwhelmed. I looked like a perfectly healthy beta when they tested me, so that's how they treated me."

Asher's brows snap together behind his glasses. "They should have followed up."

And, God bless him, he really *believes* that. The poor man has no idea how the majority of his subjects live.

"They don't follow up with anyone," I tell him gently. "They're not able to because of the demand for their time and the strain on their resources. Most doctors in our public system work twelve-hour days and make a fourth of what private practice physicians make."

I look back at Dr. Grant. "Right?"

He only hesitates for a second before confirming, "I'm afraid that's correct." The wrinkles in his forehead deepen as he frowns thoughtfully. "Did they have you on any medications, Your Highness?"

It takes me a moment to realize he's still talking to *me*.

I've been on several medicines, all to treat my "nervous disorder"—and always whatever was the least expensive option. As I list the prescriptions, Dr. Grant's expression lapses into pained resignation.

"Most of those weren't safe for an omega," he informs us, turning his attention back to Asher. "And she never ought to have been working as a maid. The chemicals in bleach alone are enough to cause hormone fluctuations if an omega is exposed to them regularly. Let alone whatever else she uses to perform her duties. And the level of energy she likely expends doing so."

Dair spins away, running both hands through his hair as he mutters, "*Health anxiety* my *fucking ass*. We've been *hurting* her."

His harsh growl should scare me—and would have yesterday. But just like last night, the voice in my middle feels *seen* by him in the oddest way. Even when tension pulls taut throughout the room.

Asher is as frozen as a statue, not even blinking as Dr. Grant nervously adds, "I'd like to run more tests and assess how much damage has been done to your princess. We can give her a shot of omega-safe birth control, too. She'll also need to begin an immediate regimen to help regulate her body's needs."

Before I can turn bright red, Bast shifts next to me, the scent of toffee—*his* scent—thickening. "Meaning?"

The doctor pushes his glasses up his nose. "She's never had a proper heat. Heats act as a reset for omegas and their hormones. We'll need to ensure her body is strong enough to work up to a heat and she's well-tended to during it. She's likely in acute touch-starvation, so that will need to be addressed, as well as any heat spikes that occur."

Oh f—

My stomach drops. Bast's solid warmth squeezes me gently. "She was on the verge of one earlier, I think," he murmurs. His deep blue eyes dance with the loveliest softness. "How about now, angel? Do you still have cramps?"

A pinch pulls at the muscles in my lower abdomen, but I don't want to admit it. I need to get back to work—and figure out how I'm going to pay for more tests and different medications. Not to mention a *heat.*

I won't be able to afford a nice clinic with professional volunteers. Besides, the idea of my first heat being in a sterile room full of strangers *terrifies* me.

When Bast's blond brows draw together, I think he's somehow read my frantic thoughts. But then I remember—*Oh. He can scent my fear.*

And probably my need, too.

Asher definitely can. His hazel gaze blazes as it roams over my features for a long moment before he shoots a glare at Dr. Grant and barks, "*Out. Now.*"

twenty

"Where are we taking her?"

Asher absorbs my low, anxious words without breaking stride. Dair charges ahead of us, issuing barks and threatening scowls to every person we pass.

Luckily, Maytown Manor is sleepy this Sunday morning. We only encounter a valet and two members of the housekeeping staff as we stalk from the collection of medical rooms on the first floor back up to our wing.

Ivy protests weakly when we hit the stairs, but the way her cold fingers dig into my shirtless shoulders makes a liar of her. She doesn't want to walk—and she definitely doesn't want any space between us.

I can scent that on her—the lovely, sugared aroma deepening into something golden and buttered. When I nuzzle my cheek against her crown, a shiver races down her spine and slick wets the fabric between her sweet center and my abs.

Holy. God.

Both of my packmates glance over at us, their jaws taut and eyes bright. I fight the urge to bare my teeth at them, gritting my molars. "Hurry."

No matter how much I'm enjoying this angel clinging to me, wetting my skin with her slick... she's in need. Which means she's in *pain*.

I don't recognize myself right now. Normally, I'm the one with a quick joke or an amused observation. But I can't find a smile for anyone aside from the poor omega bundled in my arms.

"I'm so sorry," she whispers into my collarbone. Her dozenth apology in two minutes. "I'm so—"

I rub my cheek over her forehead, deliberately scent-marking her. Fuck, we smell good together. Her fresh-baked goodness and the salty-sweet of toffee. It's like a miracle.

"Shh," I whisper. "You're doing me a favor, angel. If I had to put you down, I'd be in agony."

Her legs tighten around my waist. A quiet whine echoes behind the breasts pressed to my pecs, her nipples hardening through Dair's oversized T-shirt.

I know the feeling. My cock has been at full mast for *hours*.

Ignoring the pulse beating in my knot, I duck into our wing behind Asher, noting the sour tartness emanating from Dair's pores as he holds the door open.

Concern looks odd on him. I'm not sure he's ever made a face quite like this one before—amped up and intense, but soft, too. When he catches me staring, he's barely able to muster a pale shadow of his usual snarl. "Fuck off."

I hide a smile against Ivy's rumpled hair. "Hear that, angel? I think His Grumpiness is *worried* about you."

Ivy chuckles weakly. "I told you that nickname is rude, my lord," she says in a voice reminiscent of her sweet teasing in the garden.

And, just like that day, hearing her call me "my lord" simply because she knows I *don't* want her to...

God, how can I possibly get *harder*?

I remember thinking she was the perfect blend of softness and wit. A good girl, begging me to break the rules. Everything that makes my blood roar.

Now I know why.

She's my *mate*.

I kiss her forehead, turning toward my bedroom. It's the only one left open, and—

Asher barks quietly, freezing us all in our places. "*No. My room.*"

Uh...

No one is allowed in His Highness' bedroom. The guy has serious personal issues with privacy—well-deserved, after a lot of childhood trauma with the paparazzi. I've only seen the inside of his room once or twice and we've been living here for *months*.

Yet, as he stands beside his door, jaw grinding, I think I might understand.

This is different.

She's different.

He *wants* her in his space. Maybe in a way I don't even fully comprehend.

This whole time, was the poor guy's self-imposed exile some sort of penance? Has he kept his room—and his life—empty because he was waiting for *her*?

Damn. I almost never understand Asher, but I *get that*.

Amazed, I tuck my chin to peer at Ivy's face. Her closed eyes, the fan of silver-blonde lashes, and the faded freckles along the bridge of her nose.

It's only been an hour, but she's already bringing our pack closer than we've been in years. Helping me relate to the parts of my packmates that have always baffled me.

I even understand the slight growl vibrating on every breath Dair manages to take. My Alpha is raging, too—and Dair's has always been harder to control than most. The fact that he's trying so hard gives me new respect for the guy.

All because of Ivy.

The missing middle we've been looking for.

"You really are an angel," I murmur against her hair.

She stirs, bleary eyes blinking. They're glassier than they were in the hallway, likely because this place smells like all three of us blended together. I track the way she winces. Her body stiffens as a new cramp hits her.

I don't even have to think about it—on my next breath, a purr springs to life. Ivy startles, her eyes flying up to mine.

It's my turn to cringe. "Do you not like it, princess?"

Her lashes flutter in bewilderment. "I—no, I do. I just... *Why* do I like it?"

We all pause. Asher meets my eyes, then Dair's. And I see the exact moment it sinks in for each of us; our omega has absolutely no experience with *any* of this. It's our job to teach her.

Lucky for Ivy, Asher was born for this shit. He should have been a professor instead of a prince, and now he has a perfect pupil.

"You like it because it means your alphas are here, ready to take care of anything you need, darling," he murmurs. "Our purrs relax your Omega because she knows she's protected."

With a shaky exhale, he reaches over to cup her cheek. "I'll get you some books to read," he adds, then stops himself. Something unspoken passes between them before he amends, "Or I'll read them to you, if you'll let me."

I don't understand what he means, but I hate the way her scent shifts. Not burned by fear or pain... but something saltier.

Sadness?

Asher senses it and flinches, dropping his hand in the process. I follow the instinct to move her further away from him, carrying her quivering body to his bed and carefully lowering her onto the edge.

Dair instantly crowds in beside me, unfamiliar anxiety splashed across his face again. He might not understand what's happening to him, but he understands *her* better than we do. As he tilts Ivy's face in his direction and reads her features, tension pulls tighter at his brow.

"What's wrong, baby?" he mumbles, kneeling beside her legs. Her mouth visibly wobbles, the scent of fear encroaching on her sadness. Dair's eyes burn. "Apart from everything I did, I mean. Is there something else?"

Ivy's hand falls limply to the place above her core, clutching at the spot that aches for an alpha to fill it. "It hurts. And I know I need... I—I need—"

Dair can't quite keep the rumble out of his voice. "To get off. We know, baby. We want to help you."

She pales at that. His nostrils flare as he grinds his teeth, clearly *forcing* himself to offer, "We can leave you alone if you want to take care of this spike alone..."

Desperation lurches up my throat. I feel my eyes bulge with it, and Ivy's drawn expression loosens a bit at the sight. Her lips even flicker into a weak half-smile for a second before she exhales and hangs her head.

"I don't really know what I'm doing on my own. Or with anyone. I—I've only done it a couple of times."

She's... only had sex a couple of times?

Oh dear, sweet *Lord*.

Dismay and awe spiral through me, settling into a bittersweet slurry of absolute *disbelief*. Because... *how*?! She's literally the most beautiful thing I've ever seen. So sweet and warm and kind and—

Loyal.

Dair and I both turn slowly, pinning Asher with accusing

looks. Unnecessary ones, because he's had the same thought and arrived at the same conclusion.

She loved him and he sent her away.

But that doesn't mean she *stopped* loving him.

She probably spent her few years of freedom missing him... and then she had to come back and take care of her mother. Working day and night. Making herself sick from stress and chemicals and all the bullshit we put her through.

Ivy hasn't had a single day for herself. Probably in years. She's been trying to *survive*. Of course she's had no time for *this*. Alone or with a partner.

But it sounds like she didn't have much inclination, anyway, after Asher broke her heart.

God, how old was she when that happened? Sixteen?

And she's just been alone *ever since?*

I'm down on my knees before I finish the thought, winded by it. "Ivy," I whisper, dropping my forehead to her lap. "Angel, I'm *so sorry*."

Ivy's hand lands on the back of my head. "Why, Sebastian? You were always"—she swallows, her voice rasping as her thighs flex—"so kind. Charming and gallant and..."

Her need is getting hard to ignore. The deeper, richer, sugared warmth has my mouth watering, but I have to know what she's about to say. I straighten, finding her azure eyes so she knows I'm listening. "And?"

The sheen in her gaze doesn't seem entirely heat-spike-related. When she replies, emotion clogs her throat.

"My friend," she whispers. "You've tried to be my friend this whole time."

It's true, I have. It made no sense to me why I needed to... but now I get it.

My heart cracks. I fit my fingers around her face, swiping at her tears with my thumb.

"I am your friend, Ivy," I vow. "No matter what else happens, you can count on that."

Horrible, stinging sadness emanates from her as her eyes slide from mine to Asher's.

Which also makes sense. Because everything I'm promising her? Wasn't true for him.

He sent her away and banished her from his entire life so completely, she wasn't even supposed to *work* here. Whatever friendship they had at the beginning of their story died when he decided she couldn't be his queen.

Asher is pale and utterly still—like a statue carved from a block of pure pain.

But, fuck. None of this is about us right now. Ivy *hurts*.

Dair sees the anxious look I slant toward Ivy's clutched hand. His gears spin for a moment before he turns to Asher. And *barks*.

"*Out.*"

A low snarl echoes in the prince's chest, but he manages to keep his tone level. "Pardon me?"

To my shock, Dair stands and steps away, walking back toward our pack leader. "You and I are leaving. Ivy is in pain, and she needs help. But neither of us has even apologized to her yet. Can't you sense how sad she is? Because of *us*. She's more comfortable with Bast right now. So. *Out*."

Well, damn.

Asher processes the command, his expression somewhere between murderous and agonized. Finally, he releases a harsh breath and starts to leave.

Ivy's little whine is weak enough to shatter my heart all over again. "Angel," I whisper, clambering to sit beside her and pull her into my lap. "Come here."

Asher hears her cry and freezes mid-stride. With another softer exhale, he comes back to his bed and runs his fingers down the side of her face, holding her gaze. "I don't want to leave you, darling. But Dair is right. You need to be comfortable right now. We'll wait outside while Bast takes care of you. If you need us, just say our names and we'll come running back to you."

She looks so heartbroken. I hug her closer and start purring again, giving her a little bounce to get her to smile. "Trust me," I rumble, "we won't need them."

twenty-one

The room is starting to go hazy at the edges by the time Asher and Dair shut the doors behind them.

For half a second, I worry it might get awkward, being alone with Bast. Like *this*.

But, of course, he is charm itself, casting a sly look around Asher's bedroom and then giving me a conspiratorial smile. "I've never been left alone in here before," he admits, rueful. "Should we unalphabetize his books? Or run his underwear up the flagpole?"

A trembling giggle tickles my throat. "All this time, I thought *I* was the only one not allowed in here."

His face softens. "No, angel." Another slight smile reveals one dimple. "In fact, I suspect you may be the *only* person allowed in here after today."

The thought does not compute. None of this does, really. The fact that I'm here, in Asher's room. With his packmate. And I'm —I'm—

An omega, the little voice finishes.

Yeah.

That.

Denial tries to rear up every time someone says the word; but the aching, tingly cramps crouched low in my belly stop any doubts before they take hold.

Bast watches me squirm and gives a quiet humming sound. "Let's get more comfortable, okay? Here."

His body is like a cradle of muscle. With one fluid flex, his left arm secures me to his chest while his right keeps us balanced. His strong legs propel us backward in two shoves.

He doesn't even skip a breath, effortlessly maneuvering us to the plush pile of pillows propped against Asher's antique iron headboard. The deep, citrusy musk of the prince's scent mingles with Bast's toffee richness and the traces of cranberry tartness embedded in Dair's T-shirt.

When the baron catches me sniffing the hem of black fabric, his purr deepens with approval. Tenderness mixes with the heat flickering in his blue eyes. "Do you want to leave Dair's shirt on?"

My answering nod is shy. Some deep emotion passes over his face, and he swallows hard. "Okay, angel. How about these sweats?"

They're actually pretty scratchy, which is silly. I know the fabric is soft—but somehow, it feels like sackcloth abrading the overheated skin between my thighs. An involuntary whine trips up my throat while I shimmy restlessly.

His irises flash. "All right," he says, thicker, "I can take those for you, baby."

I know I should be embarrassed, but as he smooths his hands

down my sides, it's all I can do not to moan out loud. His touch feels *incredible*—warm enough to raise goosebumps and soft enough to send tingles racing to my core.

He has callouses from all his hours of rowing. They scrape lightly as he slips his fingers under the loose waistband of Dair's joggers and glides the material off me. The second cool air hits my thighs, I realize they're wet—and not just a little bit.

Slick.

More of it seeps from my center when Bast rests one of his hands over the front of my panties, tracing the plain white waistband.

His fingertips send more aches spiraling through my middle while all the wet muscles inside me squeeze desperately. I whine, panting, and kick my feet free from the fabric pooled around my ankles.

"Shh," Bast soothes. "I know, angel. I'm going to fix it, I promise."

I'm mortified by how eager I am. When I squirm in his lap, I whimper, "I'm so sorry, I—I don't know what's wrong with me."

Bast's free hand floats up to cup my jaw, turning my head. He runs his straight nose down the length of mine and hesitates, hovering there for a long moment before finally pressing the softest, sweetest kiss to my mouth.

His lips rasp against mine. Warm and firm and soft all at once. He makes sure I feel it, then pulls back an inch to catch my gaze. "There's nothing wrong with you at all. You need your alpha to take care of you."

My stomach somersaults as pure *need* blooms through my body. A sweet scent—*my perfume?*—winds into the air. Bast groans, finding my mouth with his again.

This time, he isn't as gentle. His tongue sweeps in, curling against mine until my core contracts. Feeling my spasm, he begins rubbing slow circles over the front of my soaked panties, murmuring praise between lush kisses.

"Perfect omega."

"So gorgeous. So good for me."

"Sweet angel, grinding this slick pussy into my hand."

A haze creeps over my mind, blotting out reality and reason. Until there's just his palm against the fabric covering my clit, salty richness blurring my thoughts, and his hot tongue in my mouth.

My body moves on its own, bucking between his hand and his lap, but he seems to *approve*.

"That's it," he grits. "You've got it. Should I put my fingers inside this sweet pussy next?"

A sharp sound vibrates out of me. The purr rumbling behind his bare chest edges dangerously close to a growl. The hand cupping my face drops to my breast, thumbing my tight nipple through the shirt that smells like another alpha.

Urgent pleasure snaps from the point pinched between his fingers, crackling down into my clenched pussy. Whatever tight, itchy material was covering my core disappears. Warm, perfect pressure slides down my slit, teasing the ring of muscle that desperately spasms at my opening.

I can't remember his name or mine, but I don't care. He's *perfect*, holding me close while his fingers roll my aching nipples one at a time and carefully work themselves into my clutching heat.

The second he slips inside, a ragged groan sloughs out of the alpha. He rests his forehead against mine, rubbing his scent there as his hips pump underneath me in perfect time with the plunge of two thick fingers. Sensation streaks through my limbs as he twists his insistent strokes, pushing into a secret spot that *throbs* and running his thumb along my slick-coated clit at the same time.

Damp warmth seeps into the fabric under me, and my alpha hisses. The sound acts like a tripwire. My awareness evaporates, leaving my brain awash in smoke and glitter.

I don't know anything, except what I need to do. Everything around me flips. Until I'm facing some big, black metal wall and the golden-haired alpha.

His mouth moves, but numb buzzing drowns out the words. My fingers snag on something, yanking a soaked waistband out of the way. So I can get to—to—

That.

Hard girth springs up, smacking the tight lace of muscles shifting under my palm. Brawny hands clutch my hips and I nearly lose my balance, pleasure swarming to my core and pouring out.

A harsh growl breaks through the fog, along with a bark. "*Yes. Take what you need.*"

I move. Broad heat expands under my hands. Solid strength flexes against my inner thighs. Something smooth and round kisses the desperately dripping opening spread over the body under mine.

"So good," the alpha groans, his head falling back. "You gonna fuck me, love? Take this alpha cock?"

A sharp sound slices the air, and my hips follow, pumping straight down. Hot hardness splits my center, pressing part-way into the trembling muscles, screaming for more stretch.

The alpha snarls, gnashing his teeth. For a second, fear freezes me. I can't find the voice in my middle anymore—or maybe *she* can't find *me*, because I have a feeling I'm not the one in control anymore.

Either way, I can't breathe until deep blue beams sink into me, glowing with urgent softness. "It's okay, omega," his deep voice vows, starting a new series of tingles in my core. "I want you to *use me*."

Another bark. One that my body knows exactly what to do with.

It starts with shallow pumps, then plunges lower. And deeper. And *harder*. And—

A ragged, masculine moan cracks up the alpha's throat. He shifts, somehow caressing the aching pulse that the thickness lodged inside me can't quite reach. I chase that sensation, bucking into his hand and his body until the tight throb in my middle *bursts*.

Every internal muscle locks down. Burned-sugar perfection tingles in my lungs when I gasp, crying out. A fierce roar rips from the alpha's lips as his hips drop from mine in a sharp motion that leaves me bereft. My inner walls keep clutching as he tilts forward, his straining cock spraying all over his belly and mine.

The second his release hits my skin, languid heaviness rolls into my arms and legs, pleasure and relief leaving me limp.

The room dips and disappears for a minute… or maybe longer. When I finally manage to blink my eyes open, I'm bundled securely into Bast's tan, muscled perfection as he croons to me over his purr. "So good for me. Shhh. I'm here, angel. Right here."

Reason and reality come rushing back in.

Oh my God.

What have I done?

twenty-two

His Highness doesn't suffer well.

He isn't used to it, the poor bastard. Apparently, no one ever put the future ruler of Crenmore in timeout; let alone anything more brutal.

Asher wasn't bred for this shit. The tedium of waiting for your punishment, the stoicism one cultivates when pain becomes so common, it's *boring*.

He paces while we wait outside his bedroom, restless and visibly agitated. Meanwhile, I've been training my whole life for this moment—my final, most epic fuck up. Feeling resigned, I sit slumped on the floor with my back to the sofa, replaying every cruel thing I've ever said to Ivy.

Our *mate.*

In this case, I'll take the punishment. In fact, I'm going to seek out *more.*

Unlike all the beatings my father liked to dole out, I *deserve* this. And, you know what? I'm going to fucking sit in it.

Shutting my eyes, I let the truth sting me again and again.

She's afraid of me.

I hurt her feelings. Scared her. Made her feel worthless—like an object.

I took advantage of her position.

And I never apologized.

The rest of it is distressing, but that last one? I hate myself most for that. The fact that I knew I'd fucked up and hid from it every day.

That *disgusts* me now.

Maybe it has this whole time. And the loathing I felt whenever she looked at me with trepidation? Maybe that was *me* hating *myself* for not having the balls to give her the amends she deserved.

Jesus. I am way too sober for this.

Asher finally halts on one of his many turns, snapping his attention to me. "How can you just sit there?" he growls. "I'm going out of my goddamned mind!"

I shrug, sighing up at the chandelier. *Did she have to clean that? It looks like a bitch. Would it have killed us to use recessed lighting like normal people?*

"I'm marinating," I tell him.

"In?" he demands.

Remorse. Regret. Resignation.

"Reality."

That takes the wind out of His Highness' sails. His shoulders fall as he exhales hard. "I'm afraid if I start, I'll never stop."

I nod slowly. "That's sort of the point. Do you think anything either of us feels right now compares to whatever she's lived with after you sent her away? Or how she's felt coming to work every day, knowing she would have to see *me*?"

Asher's jaw works. "What did *you* do to her?"

I sense his anger, but there's a sharp bitterness to his bergamot scent, too. Fear, I think. The worry that I've done something we won't be able to come back from.

Which is a feeling I can really fucking relate to right now.

It takes work to swallow. Then I rasp, "I scared her. Badly, I think."

Asher seems so stiff, it's a wonder his joints don't creak as he lowers himself onto the settee across from me. Solemn judgment presses between my shoulders as his heavy gaze locks on mine. "Tell me."

And then I'll decide if you can stay.

He doesn't say that last part, but he doesn't need to. It's unspoken. And exactly what I would say if the tables were turned.

But they aren't. Of course. Because no matter how much Asher may have messed up, I'll always be worse.

It's like a law of nature.

Tipping my head back, I blow a slow breath toward the stupid, perfectly clean chandelier.

"It was maybe a month after we got here," I start. "Right around the time—" I swallow. "The time her mom died. I didn't know that, then, but still. One night, we had one of those fucking disastrous dinners. With that omega Bast sorta liked—Countess Something?"

In my periphery, Asher nods, waiting. My fingers spasm against the Persian rug beneath me. "I ruined it, of course. Made some joke about her father fucking his horse, I think? I don't remember. Either way, you had to face a lecture from His Majesty because of me—and Bast was *pissed*."

I recall being surprised by that. In all the years we'd been a pack, Sebastian had never gotten *angry* with either of us. He got annoyed, sometimes, or exasperated.

It wasn't even about that other omega, really. I think he was just fed up with me starting fires he knew he'd have to put out. And his fury made me feel... *bad*.

Guilty. Full of self-directed rage.

And hopeless, too—because, hell, I *couldn't help myself*.

"I wound up at some crappy bar in town," I admit aloud. I'm fully braced when his scent darkens further—I knew he'd be upset about me getting sloshed in public. It's against basically all of our royal rules.

Which makes this next confession awkward.

"I got in a fight, somehow. I don't even know why. But they kicked me out of the bar when I knocked a table over."

Asher growls quietly. "Christ."

I sigh. "Yeah, I would have been fucked if anyone had taken a video. But after they kicked me out, I wound up sitting in an alley while I waited for my nose to stop bleeding. Someone walking past noticed me... and it was Ivy."

I can still picture her—wide blue eyes and blonde wisps poking out of her bun, catching the glow of the nearest streetlight like a halo. She'd been walking home from another long shift, up to the collection of dodgy apartments at the far side of the village. As soon as she recognized me, she came flying to my side, paying no mind to the street sludge that soaked into her frumpy gray skirt.

Our gazes connected in the darkness, and something in me snapped. Now, it makes sense—but at the time? I couldn't understand why my blood felt thicker and my lungs wouldn't work right.

"Your Grace," she'd said, running her soft little fingers down my sleeve. *"You're hurt."*

I was.

I had been for a long time.

For a second, I thought Ivy had seen through all the ink and anger, to the wreckage hidden in the darkest parts of me. But next, she reached up and touched the edge of some stinging wound slashed across my cheek. When I flinched in pain, my chest heaving as the street melted into a drunken blur, she took pity on me.

Of course she did.

She does the same thing with the mice who live in the basement.

"She could tell I was out of my mind, and I guess she figured that if she left me on my own, someone else would probably see the duke passed out in a gutter. So she walked me back to the manor and snuck me into my room. Tried to help me patch myself up... but I made a pass at her instead."

Shh, little dove.

Would you really say no to a duke?

And when she started to back away, anxious in the face of my pushy attempts to draw her closer: *Don't leave me. Please.*

That last word stopped her. She wavered, not sure if she should walk out on such a pathetic creature. Because that's what I was that night. And what I have been every day since, alternating between ignoring and antagonizing her.

Asher's low snarl brings me back to the present. I sit up and let him see the regret written all over my features. "I didn't hurt her," I tell him. "I don't even think I meant to *scare* her. My Alpha just *wanted* her so damn badly, and she was there, and I was fucked up."

I remember waking up with a mouth full of cotton the next morning, convincing myself it had all been a drunken dream. Until I ran into Ivy Addison, in a clean gray uniform with her same messy bangs, setting a breakfast tray laden with bottled water right in front of my door.

The way she gazed up at me with so much fear and uncertainty... I knew it hadn't been a dream at all.

"She's been skittish around me ever since," I finish. "And I've been a dick every time I've seen her because I hated remembering that night and what I did."

Asher's fingers drum against the side of his leg, his brows snapping low over his glasses. He opens his mouth, probably to lay into me—

But the scent of charred shortbread explodes through the common room.

And we both leap up.

twenty-three

Ivy always liked to hide.

I remember finding her in the garden, tucked between two rows of hedges or under the alcove carved into the side of the manor. Usually with her knees folded up to her chest and dirt smeared along the hem of her skirt.

There were other places she liked, too. The back corner of the estate's library, the extra pantry our cooks never filled. She sewed in there, actually. And she *swore* there weren't any mice in the cellar, but I used to find her down there a lot, too. Typically with snacks...

Why didn't it occur to me that hiding was an omega habit?

It hits me now when Dair and I burst into my room and find Bast slumped on the floor beside my closet. His tight expression doesn't match the smooth purr he's put on for her, but it goes well with his burned-toffee scent. I note the large wet spot on the front of his pajama bottoms before turning to the cracked closet door.

Behind me, Dair swells to his full height and fixes Bast with a murderous glare. "I swear to God, if you hurt her..."

An answering wail echoes in my closet. "No!" Ivy sobs, "He's *perfect*!"

Bast sighs over his rumbling chest, both brawny hands rubbing his face. "Ivy is... embarrassed about her first heat spike," he explains, empathy softening his words. "I told her it's so normal and *healthy*, actually, but she feels really—"

She snorts an audible sniffle.

"—bad," he finishes, wincing.

A new wave of guilt washes over his features. "It's probably my fault. I'm sure I should have explained everything more clearly and put her under the covers, and I obviously didn't do a good expressing how fucking *incredible* she was—"

It wouldn't have mattered. I know this version of Ivy; the girl who cries at even the *thought* of upsetting someone else. And, since this was her first time losing control to her Omega... well, the girl I knew would have been mortified, too.

Damn it. I should have stayed in here. I could have talked her through it. The way I would have if I'd been the one she'd chosen to give this to back then.

But guilt clearly isn't getting us anywhere. Bast looks like he'd rip his own throat out and offer it to her on a platter if it would help calm her down.

She needs something else.

For the first time in my life, I have nothing to offer. No material wealth or favors or titles. I can't give her one goddamn thing in this moment. Except, maybe...

I slip my shirt off and hand it to Dair, hoping no one hears my hard swallow. "Hold this."

He takes it, and Bast moves to the side, ceding space for me to slowly open the closet door. My insides ache when I spot Ivy tucked into the only available bit of space along the edge of the walk-in, between a low bookcase and the door's molding.

Wide, reddened eyes glisten as light seeps in from my bedroom. She squints through her tears, wiping her nose against her wrist and tucking her bare legs closer to her body. The position is so familiar, I can't control myself.

Finally—*finally*—I do what I wanted to every goddamn time I found her huddled in one of her hiding spots during that last, precious summer we spent together:

I reach down and scoop her into my arms.

She's so upset, she doesn't even fight me. *Poor darling*—she's been through more in the last two days than any of us ever have.

My naked skin works like a charm. She inhales my scent and starts to whimper, hunting for the heat of my throat to nuzzle into. I fold her against my chest, slinging her legs around my waist and carrying her back to my rumpled bed.

It looks like she got her panties on before she fled the sheets, but Bast silently ambles over to sheepishly offer her borrowed sweatpants, too. I wave them off and focus on purring for Ivy, cupping the back of her head against my neck to absorb her sobs.

I decide I'm not going to rush her. She can cry if she wants to; I'll be right here. Where I should have been all along.

"I know, darling," I murmur, scent-marking her damp cheek with mine. "This is so much to take in."

The fingers clutching my back scrabble for a tighter hold. "I feel like I don't recognize my body anymore, and it's—" Her voice drops into a whimper. "Ash? Am I going to be okay?"

Ash.

Relief and regret pour through me as I hitch her closer. "Yes, darling," I vow. "I will make sure you're okay from now on. You'll never have to worry about any of this again. Because I'm going to take care of you."

The way she tenses speaks of the truest form of disbelief—not shock or even doubt.

Mistrust.

And I've earned that, haven't I?

Before I can work up a decent apology, Bast slowly steps closer. "Angel, would you feel better in a nest? We don't have one here, but there's one waiting for you in your new suite."

Ivy hiccups, turning her pale, wet face toward him. The wariness soaked into her features softens when she sees how horrible he feels. Her hand stretches for his automatically—because Ivy can't help but try to comfort anyone suffering.

Bast folds her fingers into his with a harsh, grateful exhale. He draws them to his lips and kisses her knuckles as she stammers, "N-new suite?"

Anxiety pinches my lungs, darkening my bitter bergamot scent. Dair's bottomless eyes meet mine, and he sighs in a distinct *fine, asshole, I'll tell her* way.

"In the palace," he mutters, making his displeasure clear. Dair hates the Everdeen Palace almost as much as he hates suits, crowns, and actually *ruling the nation*. "Now that we've found our mate, we're expected to go back."

Ivy blinks, processing that. "So... you'll go back to the capital, and I'll...?"

"Come with us," I interject, nodding once. "That was always our plan once we made a match."

Dair grimaces. "There are a lot of royal traditions around mates and bonding, little dove. I'm sure *Maman* can explain them better than us, since she's been through the process."

I watch her realize he's talking about my mother, the queen—who will be *her* mother, too, in a way. If Ivy will let us court her... and bond with her.

Come to think of it, back when we were teenagers, Ivy seemed to think my parents didn't approve of her at all. Something about the rule my blowhard father made to keep the other kids from interfering with my tutoring.

My hand smooths a line over her spine. "I already spoke with my parents about everything last night," I add, hoping to reassure her. "They're happy we've found our match, and Maman is eager to meet you again."

Bast's blue eyes light with genuine excitement. "You'll love her, angel. Asher's mom is waaaay cooler than him."

I start to smirk, but, as always, Dair is a storm cloud, his expression clapping like thunder over a picnic. "Before we can take you to the palace, you'll have to agree," he tells her, quiet and solemn. "To let us court you."

That was our one stipulation all along—whichever omega we selected had to agree to officially be ours before we brought her back to the capital and introduced her to the world. The Crown can't afford to allow the public to fall for a potential princess only to have her decide she doesn't want us after all.

It's incredible how actually having a mate—and knowing it's *Ivy*—has changed everything for me, though. As I watch her tremble, trying to absorb the choice laid out before her, I realize I don't give a single fuck about public perception.

She can have as little or as much of me as she wants. I'm hers either way.

Her Omega makes her opinion known with a whine. But Ivy's voice quivers, "I don't know if I can just..." She blinks at Dair. "You don't *like* me, remember?"

His face splits, teeth gnashing. "No, little dove. I don't like *me*. It never had anything to do with you—other than how badly my body wanted yours. I was just too fucking stupid to realize it."

Her wispy brows drop in disapproval. "You aren't stupid," she argues. "You were *confused*."

Her tone is so familiar, I almost lose my breath. Like that first day in the garden, when she defended her duckling "friend."

"You aren't daft, are you Bartholomew?" she'd asked the pitiful pile of feathers. *"You're just* lost."

God, maybe the three of us are. Perhaps that's the reason divine providence sent us *this* woman—the girl who couldn't stand up for herself, but found the strength to champion anyone downtrodden.

Dair doesn't accept her forgiveness. I see it in the way his chest stutters. He thinks he needs to suffer to prove he's learned. And he likely has no idea how to court anyone, let alone this sweet omega.

Still, he holds her gaze and rasps, "I was. And I'll spend the rest of my life making that up to you. If you'll let me try."

"Us," Bast corrects, his hopeful eagerness returning as he squeezes Ivy's frail fingers. "If you let *us* try, angel."

But, ultimately, none of this is really their fault. It's *mine.*

Ivy must understand that, because instead of agreeing or spurning them, she turns to me with the same wary hesitation she wore before. Tears well in her eyes as they bounce between mine, reading all the pain I leave plain for her to see. Her scent plummets farther into a salty, melted mess.

"You *left,*" she whispers, "You *told me* to leave. You knew I loved you and how much I cared about you, and you didn't return any of those feelings."

I hate that she believes that—but it's self-loathing, entirely directed at myself. I never said I didn't care about her, but I certainly *acted* like it.

Instead of refuting her, I listen as she sniffles, "Why would it be any different this time, Ash? I'm still the same person I was."

Yes, she is.

And I'll never know why I got so lucky.

Being a prince gives you an odd sense of pride. When your life is full of people doing everything they can to avoid embarrassing you, humiliation is a hard pill to swallow.

But being an alpha who's found his omega makes it *easy* to ignore the way my face burns. *I'm going to show her she's the most important thing in the world. And I'm going to start right now.*

My hand drops from her back, coming around to find the

fingers that aren't currently wrapped in Bast's. I lift them to my chest, pressing her chilled palm to the exposed ink etched into my left pectoral.

Her crystalline gaze drops to the tattoo branded there, the image I got to remind me of her.

A perfect anatomical rendering of my heart, wrapped in delicate vines of ivy.

Our omega gasps. Her burned scent starts to brighten. "A-ash..."

I purr without effort, bending to rub my forehead against hers. "If you're the same girl I knew," I murmur, "then you are the one I've loved and missed every damn day since I made the mistake of letting you go. And that makes you my queen."

twenty-four

"Ivyyyyyyyy!"

Oh boy.

Not today, I beg the universe, wanting nothing more than to bury my head in the pile of mending on the low table beside my mother's sewing machine.

I might have finished it already, but the back of my skull is pounding so hard, I don't think I could even bend over to pick it up. The image of Asher's serious hazel eyes staring me down sails through my throbbing brain. Along with the ultra-soft bark he issued before I stepped out of their car.

"You need to rest. *No work, darling*."

Turns out, disobeying alpha barks can cause a lot more than the guilty wince permanently pulling at my features. My head's been in a world of pain. And the sick squirm my stomach gives every time I reach for a new piece of mending isn't my favorite, either.

Our alphas will be mad, my Omega frets. *They said to rest, eat breakfast, lunch,* and *dinner.*

They just want to court us, I correct gently. *They aren't <u>our</u> alphas.*

She flashes me an image of Bast licking into my mouth while his fingers plunged into my core. Then one of Dair's shoulders *heaving* as he apologized. And Asher's broad, bare chest... with that *tattoo.*

His heart, wrapped in ivy.

My fingers work faster, feeding more fabric into the machine. As if pressing the pedal will somehow help me outrun the riot of emotions that rise to block my throat.

But that's the problem—my whole life, anytime I felt scared or anxious, work has been my outlet.

My Aunt Matilda still doesn't know what happened at the ball or in its wake, but she apparently knows me well enough to shove a mop and some gloves at me the second I walked through the door yesterday. She didn't bother asking why I was in Dair's clothes—nor why my hair was undone or why I had clearly been a crying mess for hours. She only put up a fuss when I told her I'd been given the day off today.

She was so mad about me giving up a long shift, I couldn't tell her that I'd actually given up *every* shift for the rest of... forever, really.

That wasn't my fault, though. Dair wouldn't even hear of me continuing to work, and Asher acted like the idea personally offended him. Bast offered sympathetic squeezes of his warm, strong hands, occasionally rolling his eyes at them while the duke growled and the prince blustered. But the baron also continued to carefully remind me about the doctor's warnings.

The message was clear. My old job—my old *life*—isn't really an option anymore.

I can either find the courage to go back to the city with the princes and let them court me... or I can stay here and find some other omega-approved job. A different way to deal with the heat Dr. Grant warned me about... and perhaps, eventually, some other alphas, too?

But, no.

No.

The thought alone makes me physically sick. I learned that last night after trying to follow Asher's calm, concerned instructions. Aunt Matilda's tomato soup went down well enough, but the longer I sat there, listening to my cousins bicker over the last breadstick and imagining that this would be the rest of my life...

I barely managed to make it to the bathroom before the whole meal came back up. And every meal since, too.

The Google searches I've done while I tend to Mama's mending clients inform me that this is pretty normal. Omegas who find scent-matched alphas are supposed to *stay with them*. Period.

Otherwise, all sorts of horrible things start happening.

I close my eyes, recalling the quiet beeps of my mother's heart-rate monitor. It used to be the only sound in this room, sometimes. The steady rhythm a constant reminder of exactly what happens when omegas lose their mates.

It's more than that, though. Because—*Lord, how pathetic*—I think I *miss* them?

Their tender touches and worried eyes. The way they argued among themselves about how best to please or comfort me.

Even more humiliating? I miss my *work*.

Not the scrubbing and the scraping, but being in their space, inhaling their scents. Listening to Bast sing off-key while he fixes his hair. Sneaking peeks at whatever books Asher leaves around so I know what he's thinking about during the day. Dair's dark gaze gliding across my skin when I least expect it.

If they go back to their *real* home without me, who will bake Asher banana bread when he's had a bad day? Or leave strategic bottles of water around for Dair? And Bast *never* remembers his *keys...*

"IVYYYYY!"

Sickness somersaults in my center as a stab of pain hits between my hips. Panic pinches at my lungs—because, really, what do I *do* if I have another heat spike *here*? Without any space or privacy? Without *them*?

And with my cousin Claire deciding it's perfectly all right for her to waltz into my room...

The light from the short hallway to the kitchen burns my eyes —which is when I realize—*oh, it's dark.*

Nighttime... and I haven't eaten all day or mustered the courage to turn my phone off Do Not Disturb. My Omega trembles with unease, pacing my insides while she mutters that the alphas won't like us anymore. We should obey them, try to please them, check and see if they've called us or—

"Ivy!" Claire snaps, stomping on the sewing machine's cord to rip it from the wall socket. "Jesus, I've been calling you for like five minutes! What the hell is wrong with you? Mom said you didn't even work today!"

Aside from eight hours of mending, two hours cleaning the bathrooms, and another two folding and sorting laundry.

I'm too exhausted to bother arguing. My numb fingers rub at my throbbing temples as I ask, "Did you need something, Claire?"

She throws her hand on her hip, glaring expectantly. "You owe me thirty dollars for the takeout last weekend. And you said you'd fix the strap on my tote bag *two days ago.*"

Now would probably be a good time to point out that charging me thirty dollars for the one slice of pizza they saved me isn't exactly fair. Especially considering I pay our rent and all.

But Claire works, too, in the bar down the block... and I did *eat that one piece...*

With a sigh, I fish for my own beat-up tote bag, noting that it could use repair, too. At least Claire's is fixed. I hand it to her along with all the money in my wallet. I'm five dollars short—and she sneers as she informs me she needs the rest by tomorrow.

She slams my door as she storms out, not bothering to thank me. My shoulders slump, a shooting pain jolting through them.

Great.

Dr. Grant warned me about *that*, too: the physical aches of touch-starvation.

Feeling like I might start to cry, I leave my unplugged sewing machine and wander over to my bed. The mattress squeals while I roll onto my side and bring my pillow to my chest, hugging it as I turn to the window.

I can't see the stars from here because my room faces a brick wall, but I remember gazing up from the kitchen last week, thinking about that day Asher and I wished on the same star.

And the fact that, even days ago, my wish was the same.

That he'd see me the way he used to. That maybe one day...

My wish came true.

So why am I lying here in agony?

The voice in my middle may be even more anxious than I am, but she also seems to know things quicker than I do. She answers easily, her tone sad but resigned, *Because he couldn't see me. And he broke your heart.*

There's a beat of silence before she winces slightly. *Not to mention the wild one.*

Dair's dark, feral eyes flash into my mind. My Omega is right —he's part of the problem, too. I may understand why he was so cruel now, but it doesn't undo months of feeling fear in his presence. I've been conditioned not to trust him... in an entirely different way than I distrust Asher.

And, Lord—*Bast*. He was so wonderful to me in every way. Before the ball. During it. After, too, in Asher's bed.

He probably feels terrible, I think. *Especially if he's tried to contact me. He might think I've ignored him all day because I hated what we did and blame him.*

That's an awful notion. I may not have been prepared to deal with the way I felt afterward, but he didn't do anything wrong. If anything, *I'm* the one with issues.

I need to *tell* him that, at the very least...

With a deep breath for courage, I swipe my phone open and turn off DND. Usually, I might have one or two complaints from my aunt and a text from Gracie—but this time, messages *pour* into my inbox.

I've had the princes' numbers saved for emergencies and errands, but I never expected to see them actually scroll across my screen.

Lord Sebastian Burns.

Duke Dairragh Vreeland.

Prince Asher Everhart.

Sebastian's texted the most. I guess that isn't surprising. He's constantly on his phone—messaging women, I always assumed.

The visceral stab of jealousy that gores into me doesn't last long. Once I start thumbing through his texts, it's vividly clear he hasn't thought of any other girls today.

LORD SEBASTIAN BURNS

Good morning, beautiful.

I missed you so much last night, sleeping was impossible.

I was worried you were cold and wanted to hold you. Please tell me you have an electric blanket or a body pillow or *something* so my Alpha doesn't rip right out of my body and storm over there.

TODAY 12:41PM

Angel, I'm so sorry about yesterday. Next time, we'll go so much slower, ok?

Or fuck me, there doesn't even have to be a next time.

TODAY 2:18PM

Just promise you have the toys and stuff you need. Please?

TODAY 4:03PM

Okay, so, impulse control? Not my strong suit. You might be getting a big box of nesting stuff and alpha substitutes sometime this week… I picked the colors based on that pretty dress you wore to the ball.

I hope you kept that dress, Ivy. It makes you look exactly like the angel you are.

I'm in tears by the time I reach the last message, but the picture of Bast's handsome, coiffed perfection grinning with a squirrel at his feet manages to make me giggle.

TODAY 6:56PM

Nigel and I are fine, btw. I took some cookies out to him after dinner, and we had a nice visit. Lovely chap.

Asher's thread is next. He hasn't written as often, but his texts are *jammed* with details of all the work he's done to try to make this easier on me.

Doctors he's lined up—one set here and another in the capital, "in case I choose to accept their invitation."

A play-by-play of the conversation with his parents, where he essentially told his father they would not be entertaining any more prospective princesses—*ever*.

Another he had with his mother, where she assured him that she learned all the duties her role entailed, once upon a time, and has no doubt I could do the same.

He also spoke to Princess Ahmad, informing her that his pack had found their mate. According to Asher, she was gracious and offered to stay for a while longer to help me learn the ropes if it suited me. Judging by his tone, he seemed surprised by the suggestion but didn't have a preference about my decision either way.

My heart skipped when he messaged a photo of my mother's locket, telling me they'd found it the night of the ball and asking if he could have it cleaned and get the clasp repaired. Since, apparently, falling out of my bra and onto the manor' rocky driveway caused some damage.

There was more—designers and personal shoppers, language tutors, jewelry makers. He'd even opened a brand-new bank account and sent me a digital version of the debit card, requesting that I "please" use it for "any and every expense" I had. Indefinitely.

He must know I won't use it at all. Perhaps that's why he was so quick to give it to me?

My angry headache has become a full-blown migraine by the time I scroll to the final message under his name. A short, simple one.

PRINCE ASHER EVERHART

I know this is all so much more than any of us deserve from you, but we will spend our lives earning it. I've missed you every day, goose. I know I deserve to miss you forever. But if you feel you can't be my princess after all of this, please tell me you'll forgive me before I go.

Oh, Asher.

He always seemed so stoic, even as a boy. I was one of the few to see all the vulnerability under his careful mask. How much he worried and wondered and *wished* his life could be different.

We were alike in that way.

Maybe we still are.

Beep. Beep. Beep.

The memory of Mama's monitor underscores every beat of my restless heart. Highlighting just how fast my pulse races as I realize: *This is it.* Everything I've ever dreamed of. My lost prince. A better life.

I just have to be brave enough to try... and let *them* try.

My phone vibrates in my hand, alerting me to another message. From Dair.

His thread is much less effusive than the others. There are no promises or pleas. Just a series of short, terse lines demanding to know if I'm okay.

DUKE DARRAIGH VREELAND

Have you eaten? And rested?

TODAY 10:21AM

Answer me, omega.

TODAY 3:04PM

None of us have heard from you. Tell me you're all right.

TODAY 7:49PM

Ivy, my Alpha is fucking frantic. Are you sick? Hurt?

And the last one, received seconds ago.

I'm downstairs.

twenty-five

THERE'S SOME FUCKED-UP IRONY IN ME LOITERING ON Ivy's dingy street, trying to hide from the nearest streetlight by standing in an alley.

But I can't be seen.

And I'm sober enough to remember that, this time.

Completely sober, actually. Every time I thought about slugging some of the scotch Asher keeps on the bar cart in our living room, I found myself wondering how often Ivy had to shine those damned crystal tumblers. Then I'd start worrying about why I hadn't heard back from her.

What if she needed me to come get her and I couldn't wait

around for a driver?

I had to have a clear head. In case she needed me.

I know, I know.

I'm a simp.

Shut up.

The creeping chill in the air reminds me of the other issue at play: summer is over. Our six months are more than up.

And we did it. We found our mate.

But now we need to convince her to come with us.

Anxiety buzzes under my skin at the thought of leaving her.

Here? I growl internally. *This is the most dangerous street in the whole damn village. It will be cold soon, too. And icy. She wears those shoes with the thick soles, but she could still slip.*

What will she do when her heat comes? That doctor said she has two months, tops, and the nearest public clinic is three towns away. Will strangers from a different city be the ones tending to her? What if they hurt her?

My Alpha presses at the surface of my skin, urging me toward the crooked stoop at the front of Ivy's building. I grit my teeth, but I can't stop myself from closing the gap between the side street and the scraped-up concrete steps.

It makes sense a moment later when the door cracks open, revealing a slice of pale skin and one light blue eye.

Unable to control myself, I practically rip the damn thing off its hinges. The next thing I know, there's a surprised squeak tickling my ear, and my hands are full of Ivy.

Her body goes rigid as I lift her into mine. I drop my voice to a low murmur. "It doesn't have to mean anything. I know you haven't forgiven me, and I haven't fucking forgiven myself, but if I don't hold you for a minute, I'll lose my shit, okay?"

She needs it, too. I can tell from the way she nods with almost frantic relief.

Some innate part of me also knows she hasn't honored our requests. She's even lighter than she was two days ago, and her skin is so pale, it almost looks translucent under the yellow glow of the nearest streetlight. Gathering her closer, I drop to sit on the top step and lean back to examine her.

Hell.

She looks *exhausted.*

Frayed, actually.

My hand snaps up from her legging-covered ass to cup her chin. Scowling, I demand, "Baby, what the *fuck*? You haven't eaten? Or rested?"

This girl might be good at taking care of *us*, but she's obviously abysmal at looking after *herself.*

Fuck it.

That will be my job now.

Ivy blinks, dazed by my question—and probably the fact that I showed up here like a stalker, too. "Dair? It's so late. How did you get out here without anyone seeing you?"

I arch an eyebrow at her. "You think you're the only one who knows how to sneak out of that place, little dove?"

I've never considered where that nickname came from. Probably her light gray work uniform... and the fragile, flighty quality I've always seen in her. I wince when I think about the first time I said the words; when I was sloppy and drunk out of my mind.

Frowning, I add, "I can be pretty stealthy when I haven't guzzled a snifter of scotch."

Her wispy blonde brows fold doubtfully. "You do that every night."

"Apparently not, now that I have an omega." My shoulders bounce under her forearms, shrugging. "I had to stay alert, in case you needed me. Which, clearly..."

I nod at how her oversized black T-shirt hangs from her frail frame. A bud of warmth blooms in my center when I recognize it. *Mine*. She hasn't removed it since Asher put it on her almost two days ago.

My scent must be fading now. Without thought, I guide her face to the crook of my neck, where I know my aroma is the most potent. My fingers slide to the base of her skull.

She moans softly, and my semi-hard cock kicks to life, throbbing under her gently rounded backside. *Too thin*, I think. *Needs me to feed her and hold her and—*

Goddamn it.

I cast a quick glare down at my impatient dick. Ivy follows my line of sight, her cheeks tinging rose.

I open my mouth to apologize, bracing to move her into a different position—but she swallows visibly... and scoots closer. Shuffling forward until her heated core hovers directly over the hardness pressing into my fly.

Another quivering breath ekes out of Ivy as she casts me a shy look. Something about her uncertainty calls to me on an elemental level, until I find myself bending to rest my forehead against hers, my eyes falling shut.

For the first time in days, my Alpha is *settled*. I'm still hard enough to drive nails, but the impulse to fuck isn't nearly as strong as the need for this: the connection I feel when her gaze locks on mine, close enough for me to trace the silver-blue patterns carved into her irises.

I've never wanted anything as much as I want to kiss her. She seems to be thinking something similar, because her teeth sink into her lower lip as her buttery sweetness deepens.

Shoving the impulse down, I focus on massaging the pulse throbbing at the nape of her neck. She sighs more deeply, nuzzling my forehead as she leans into my body like a good fucking girl.

The best girl.

My purr isn't nearly as smooth as Bast's or as even as Asher's. It's more of a dull roar, really, but I can't strangle it this time. The vibrations melt into Ivy's chest and goosebumps rise on her skin while I wrap my arm around her waist.

Some indistinct instinct floats to the surface of my consciousness. A new understanding of the woman so sweetly snuggling into me as if my affection is everything she's ever dreamed of.

"I'm not angry, sweetheart. I know you didn't mean to

disobey Asher," I murmur, working through the feelings. "You like to please us, don't you, omega?"

Her answering whimper is desperate. Thin arms tighten around my shoulders, and I purr louder.

"Shh," I soothe. "It's okay. I'm here now. I'm here." An image of her panicked eyes sails through my mind—that moment on the dance floor when I looked into her, saw her Omega... And knew, somehow, that no one else ever had.

"I see you," I rasp, remembering how the words had calmed her then. "I see you both, okay?"

Ivy nods against my forehead, rubbing more of her sweet scent there. It reminds me that I haven't marked her since yesterday, which is intolerable. With a gruff hum, I nuzzle both cheeks over hers before tucking her head under my chin. She quivers, perfuming at the sensation of my scent covering her.

Sweet, innocent baby. She probably doesn't even know that's what's happening when her spine snaps straight like that. Or why it makes her so wet.

Damp heat seeps from between her legs and starts to sink into my lap. My knot expands, aching to fill her until neither of us can ever leave.

I bite down on a growl, forcing myself to concentrate. "You like to please us," I repeat, "so why haven't you eaten, baby?"

The way her muscles tremble under my fingers tells me she hasn't rested, either. What has she been doing instead?

"I tried last night," she admits. Her cold nose grazes the sensitive patch beneath my ear. My dick twitches. "But I couldn't."

I hug her harder. "You *couldn't*?"

She shakes her head. "I got sick when I tried. I think—my Omega was really upset I'd left you guys. That's why I didn't sleep very well. She was—"

Embarrassment winds into her scent. I recognize it from the moment Asher pulled her out of his closet.

"Tell me," I demand, tugging her into me as tightly as I can. Wishing I could pull her inside for safe-keeping.

"*Crying*," Ivy finally whispers. "All night."

I've experienced a lot of pain in my life. The physical kind, which started way earlier than it should have. The emotional kind, when I lost all the things that I loved.

Nothing like this, though.

An urgent burn rips through my gut while my lungs snag on the edge of a snarl. My Alpha snaps back to the surface, flattening my logic under his feral need to be with the omega who spent thirty-six hours *crying* for him. *Needing* him.

God, he loves that part. No one's ever *needed* us before. And with good reason.

But now that this sweet, delicate woman does?

He's not fucking that up.

And neither am I.

I pull back just far enough to catch her gaze. My voice is hoarse from the lump jammed in my throat. "I told myself I wouldn't kiss you until you forgave me."

She swallows, her scent turning saltier. Until I sigh, drawing her lips into mine.

"I think I lied."

IVY FREEZES, BUT ONLY FOR A SECOND. THEN, TO MY shock, her mouth quirks up in a small smile.

Unable to wait another moment, I make good on my threat, fitting my lips between hers. Licking the taste of her from the full bottom curve before gliding my tongue into her velvet heat.

If Ivy's touch starvation weren't already obvious, it would be when she moans softly, hips squirming against mine. I growl, deepening our kiss as my hand slips to her ass, guiding the way she moves until she gasps.

There.

We have at least two layers of clothes between us, but I still feel her searing heat as the ridge of my erection finds the outline of her slit. When I tilt her hips forward and down, making sure my fly connects with her clit, her mouth drops open against mine.

I take the opportunity, sucking on her tongue while I urge her to grind faster and try different angles.

I worried her lack of experience would be a hurdle for me. Something I've never had to contend with before, and might not be good at managing.

But it isn't. Instead, knowing she might never have done this before fills me with the deepest sense of satisfaction. Because she's choosing *me* to show her. Letting *me* adjust the slant of her core to demonstrate how different types of pressure affect the sensations we can create together.

There's joy in it, too. Witnessing her awe, having her cling to me while she learns more.

Trying to trust me, I realize.

And goddamn it, I *will* be worthy of that.

My internal vow has me scanning the street over her shoulder, ensuring it's still as empty and dim as it was minutes ago. The way my shirt drowns her helps, too. Anyone walking by wouldn't be able to see how insistently she's working her pussy along my hardness. They'd just see a couple making out a little too passionately in the shadows.

Still, when a fresh burst of her perfect perfume swells around us, I have to suppress the territorial urge to hide her. Instead, I groan into Ivy's mouth and slide her over my covered dick until the top of her clit presses into the knot thickening at the base of my shaft.

"Feel that?" I murmur. "My knot is a picky son-of-a-bitch. I can't remember it *ever* being this hard."

A tremor of pleasure and disbelief rolls down her back, pressing her pebbled nipples into my chest. "R-really?"

I nod, dipping my head to kiss her flawless milk-white throat. Imagining a silvery bond mark branded there is enough for me to swell even wider. "I know you've seen me with a lot of women, but I didn't knot any of them. I usually can't, but I never wanted to, anyway."

Ivy listens, sadness creeping back into her essence. It must have been agony to watch me fuck around like that. If the roles had been reversed, it would have driven me insane.

"I won't take you until I've earned your forgiveness," I promise, my chest aching with determination and a smoldering sort of longing. "But, fuck, I will be dreaming of this pretty pussy *every damn day*."

She draws another gasp at the same second I drag in a loud breath. Her voice shakes. "Do you want me to s-stop?"

I shake my head, gritting my teeth as I work her along my length faster. "You are perfect. Gorgeous and so fucking sweet. I'll always get you off, no matter how much it tortures me. You can have it anytime you want, and I'll fucking *crawl* for the privilege of being the one to take care of you."

I wish I could pretend I said the words to make her come—but, really, I can't stop them once they start. Either way, they shove her to the edge. Until she's pumping her slick core over mine with the sort of intent that can only mean one thing.

"That's it, baby. Come on my knot for me."

Her keen is brief but breathtaking. I swallow it, along with the roar vibrating in my throat. My cock twitches, cum sizzling up my clothed length until it jets out, bursting into the damp fabric between us and the muted pulse of her swollen clit. She feels it and seizes up again, letting her pleasure crest a second time.

God, I'm so *fucking proud*.

The depth of it carves into my middle, winding me. I cup her jaw again, admiring the way the ink branded into my fingers looks against her peachy skin. Kissing her as she whimpers and sighs. Holding her, so she knows I meant every damn word I said.

Ivy burrows into my chest, seeking warmth and the stronger scent pouring from my neck. I soothe her with long passes over her spine and gentle fingers along her arm, barely recognizing myself.

But my relief is undeniable.

Jesus. It's like I've finally inhaled after holding my breath for *months.*

Her fingers stroke the back of my hand. She pulls at my wrist until the tattoo on the back of my hand is under her nose—the wildflower I got for my mother.

Ivy's voice is light and quiet. "This flower has more thorns than petals."

And, damn. That about sums me up, huh?

I chuckle into her hair. "Fitting."

When she giggles, a peaceful languor unfurls in my limbs, settling the beast behind my diaphragm. All from having my omega in my lap, sated and smelling like the sweetest slice of heaven.

"I'm not sure how I'll live without this now that I've had it," I mutter.

Ivy stills for a moment, glancing back at the image inked into my scarred knuckles. Then she releases an unsteady exhale and leans back to find my gaze. "What if you don't have to?"

It's my turn to shake, I guess, because an involuntary tremor bolts down my back. "You mean…?"

Her eyes shine up at me, a small, timid smile playing at her kiss-swollen lips. "I want to go with you. I want to try."

twenty-six

I'M NOT SURE WHY I'M SURPRISED TO LEARN THAT "packing" for the princes means one suitcase each, if that.

Of course they each have a set of clothes here and different ones at their palace. They're *royals*, for crying out loud. Why did I think they'd be stuffing their lives into duffel bags like I have over the past week?

Unease flips my stomach inside out as I glance at the pile of belongings next to me in the backseat of the car Asher sent.

I really hope this isn't a mistake.

Originally, they all insisted on picking me up personally, but we still need to fly under the radar in the village. Aunt Matilda has already given me enough attitude about my sudden change in life plans. The last thing I need is paparazzi at her front door.

Despite Asher's pack making good on their vows to take care of my mother's medical bills, my family still isn't thrilled—even though all of this is technically just temporary, at this point.

I'm not sure what they're so upset about. Especially since, according to Matilda, I'll likely come crawling home within weeks.

This is delusional! You're not an omega; you're a beta. Did you show them all your designation tests? Do they know you can't take their precious knots? Even if you were an omega, do you really think you could be a mate for a pack of princes? And what? Become the queen? It's insanity, Ivy!

I block out the memories of her stinging barbs, trying to settle myself with deep breaths as the car rolls to a stop at the center of Maytown Manor's circular drive. The guys are all outside—and if I get out of the car smelling distressed, it will interrupt their work.

Asher seems especially busy, nodding at a clipboard Mrs. Kemp holds out to him while also directing the valets pulling various vehicles up to the entrance. His phone lights in his hand and he answers it, still scanning whatever document the housekeeper needs him to approve.

Dair leans against the largest of the glossy black sedans—one designed to be a custom limo. Not that he's impressed by it. With his arms crossed and his head tilted back, lips firmly sealed into his signature scowl, the duke looks like the very picture of disdain.

Bast is the only one who seems at ease. He smiles as he shakes hands with staff members who have gathered to see them off. Gracie isn't there—but we said our goodbyes last night when she came to help me get the last of my stuff together.

It wasn't very much. And some precious things—like my mother's urn and her sewing table—were inappropriate to cart to the palace. Especially since my stay there might be very temporary.

Every night, when I finish texting the guys and lay in my

squeaky bed, I try to picture it. Being their omega. Living at Everdeen. *Ruling...*

I suppose it probably isn't a good sign that I still haven't really been able to envision any of it.

Because I'm trying not to smell like a burned biscuit, I don't let myself dwell on that thought for too long. Instead, I shut my eyes and feel my way back to the last night I was alone with any of the guys—when Dair showed up on my doorstep.

Things between us may be a long way from settled or certain, but something about the memory of him relaxing beneath me loosens the tightness surrounding my lungs. I focus on that, along with the squealing excitement my Omega can't contain.

I may be worried I'll never be enough for a pack of royals, but *she's* totally oblivious to anything other than the fact that we're about to be in the back of a car with them, alone, for hours.

As our tires crunch to a halt on the gravel, all three princes immediately freeze, their heads whipping in my direction. Asher's face becomes more severe as he growls at whoever he's speaking to. Dair's posture unwinds—*with relief*? And Bast's face beams with a grin that could rival the sun.

Over the last week, the baron has been in constant contact with me. Texting and calling and generally being the most charming man in existence. The day my box of omega gear arrived, he spent three hours with me on FaceTime, explaining what every single item was for. And biting back chuckles when I got flustered over some of the more... intimate things.

He's the closest to my car—and the moment our eyes connect through the tinted glass, I fly out of my seat. The skirt of my only non-work dress flies up behind me as I dive into his open arms.

Bast catches me with a laugh, effortlessly swinging me into the cradle of his body.

"We've been waiting for you," he murmurs, brushing his lips against my temple. "Princess."

twenty-seven

CALLING IVY "PRINCESS" MIGHT FILL ME WITH satisfaction, but it's going to take a hell of a lot more to help her *feel* like one.

Asher is doing the most, though, immediately pocketing his phone and stepping up to offer his hand. It's a very gentlemanly gesture—his palm outstretched to keep her balanced as she blushes and ducks into our Maybach limousine.

God, she looks so fucking pretty. That seafoam color is miraculous against her milky skin and cool-blonde waves. The way the fabric cups her waist and ruches along the tops of her breasts makes me *salivate.* My fingers itch to unlace the little bow tying her square neckline together. I settle for sliding into the seat beside her and running my palm up her crossed thigh, tracing the little white daisies sprinkled across her skirt.

Ivy flashes me her small smile. My heart flips at the sight. After a week of only seeing her through my phone screen—feeling so close but so fucking far away—the timid curl of her lips is all it takes for me to start purring.

We had to keep our distance to make sure the press wouldn't identify her before we made the move back to the palace. But, clearly, having some time has given her a chance to come to grips with her Omega a bit. Instead of wide-eyed panic, she reacts to the rumbling in my chest with a contented sigh, only casting me the quickest apprehensive look before scooting into my side.

I open my arms for a proper hug, nuzzling the top of her head. "There's my girl."

Her happiness is a sweet, warm breath of heaven. The second it sinks into my lungs, a week's worth of tension melts away. "God, I *missed you*, angel."

It's true. We talked all day, most days, but it wasn't nearly enough. The more texts and calls we exchanged, the more I adored her.

She's the lightest, loveliest person I've ever met. The fact that the universe made her *my mate* seems like it must be a mistake.

What did I ever do to deserve her?

I can't even imagine how Dair and Asher feel, knowing how much they've let her down. Under ordinary circumstances, I'd probably have some sympathy for the bastards—but, lately, their mistakes enrage me in an unfamiliar way.

This is my *mate*.

And they've jeopardized that.

What if we can't convince her to stay with us? What if we get to the palace and she hates it? What if—

Dair's foot kicks my shin in a pointed *hey, asshole* move. He drops onto the bench across from ours and subtly rolls his head toward Ivy.

Oh. Right.

I did this last time. Getting so wrapped up in my reactions and my concern for her, I forgot to actually *talk* to her.

It was easier over the phone, when I couldn't scent her or feel the way her body fits against mine. Now, a wad of anxiety sticks in my throat, blocking all the stupid small talk I would usually make. Leaving me defenseless.

I've never had this issue before. Back in school, when Asher would brood over every social situation and the extent of Dair's game was some combination of teasing and glaring, I was the one who knew how to talk to girls. The social clean-up crew. The packmate with all the witty observations and polite chit-chat.

None of that will work with Ivy.

It's obvious I'm not the only one struggling. While Dair stretches his legs out and eyes our omega like he's searching for signs of wear, Asher slides into the space on her other side. Stiff as a board.

Good Lord.

We are *pathetic.*

I move as casually as I can, jostling Ivy slightly to move her a bit closer to the paralyzed prince. Over her head, he catches my desperate *get your shit together* look.

Knowing Asher, I wouldn't be surprised if he still hasn't figured out how to properly apologize to our girl. I guess he sort of did, that day in his room after he carried her out of his closet, but he probably needs to do it again. With clothes on.

I know he's spoken to her over the past week, arranging things for our impending move—but has he really *connected* with her? Will he be able to work that out before it's too late?

The way his eyes soften when they fall to her face is a good start. After a long moment tracing her profile through his glasses, he reaches over and cups his hands around hers.

Ivy turns, blinking in surprise as he lift her knuckles to his lips and skims a kiss over them. Their gazes connect, his blazing as he murmurs, "Hello, goose."

I'm not sure why he calls her that. But then I realize—this is *exactly* the shit we need to be talking about. To bond.

"Where did our prince get such an illustrious name for our princess?" I ask, squeezing Ivy's knee and adding in a mutter, "Did you try to tame a goose, angel?"

Our omega's sweet little giggle makes the whole car feel lighter. "No," she laughs, skirting her eyes to Asher's again. Her scent somehow darkens and sweetens at once. "I guess *I* sort of picked that name, huh?"

I've never seen Asher like this; his phone sitting abandoned on the seat beside him and his focus so completely aimed at one person. He doesn't look like the formidable leader or dominant alpha he wound up growing into. Right now, with his brows and lips quirked up, he seems... *young*.

Defenseless, but brighter. Carefree and more caring, too, somehow. Like she's accessed a part of him no one else gets to see.

Or maybe the part no one else ever bothered getting to know.

"I'm not sure about that," he hedges in reply. "I think I picked it."

Ivy's eyes glow as she turns to Dair, melting the steel off his face. "Does he like to take credit for other people's hard work, or is that just you, duke?"

Dair's dark eyes flicker as he smirks. "I don't *take* credit. People just *give* it to me."

"Hmm," she hums, looking up at me. A bolt of amazement sticks in my gullet as I absorb her beautiful grin.

"Asher and I were dancing," she explains. "He was trying to learn a Viennese waltz for some big event, and he had this book: *How to Ballroom Dance for Morons*."

"It did not say *Morons*," Asher grumbles, his flushed face betraying him.

"Yes, it did," Ivy chirps, smiling wider. "Anyway, we practiced in the garden. Because I guess I was the only girl he could find."

Asher's mouth quirks up fondly. "Oh sure. *That* was the reason. Nothing to do with you taking pity on me."

"Right." Ivy nods, agreeing with his sarcasm. "And one of the chapters compared the person being led in the waltz to a swan. So when I did a turn correctly, Asher told me I looked like a swan."

Asher moves closer, dipping his head to put them face to face. His voice drops into a quiet tone just for her. "And you said, 'I'm no swan, I'm a *goose*.'"

God, his attention makes her *so happy*. My canines ache from the golden, buttery sweetness leaking into the confined space, my knot pulsing. Dair suppresses a growl, clearing his throat and shifting in his seat.

Asher and Ivy are in their own little world. She arches her neck to tilt her chin up, and his eyes flicker to her lips. The hand not wrapped around hers touches the side of her cheek, lightly grazing her blush until he slides his fingers into her hair.

There's a brooding pause that she recognizes—because she *knows him*. More than I realized. And she knows he's overthinking at a mile a minute right now.

The corners of her mouth flicker, and his eyes flash. I can't help the grin that cracks my features when he finally lowers his lips and softly presses them over her smile.

Hell, even *Dair* is grinning.

He tries to hide it, but I catch the bastard biting back the expression as he slaps the control panel on the door. An opaque panel glides up between the backseat and the driver, sealing the scent of blooming bergamot and Ivy's golden sweetness around us.

Asher pulls back with a quiet groan. Ivy's lips look even more tempting than before, the darker pink striking against her pale skin. Silver-blonde lashes flutter in surprise.

"I can't believe you remember that day," she whispers.

Pain carves lines around the prince's eyes. "I remember everything, goose."

Dair and I might not know exactly what that means, but our omega definitely does.

Or, rather, *her* Omega does.

Ivy's pupils blossom as her scent *explodes*. Asher's chest stutters. Dair *snarls*. And I have to lock every muscle in my body down to stop myself from *lunging* at her.

Instead, *she* launches herself at Asher. He catches her on instinct, the dark center of his eyes edging out his irises. An alpha roar echoes in his chest as he growls and purrs simultaneously.

The sound melts Ivy. She goes limp in his arms, tilting her head in supplication. His for the taking.

I expect him to pause. Consider. Overthink again.

But he immediately takes what she offers, sealing their mouths together while one hand clutches under her breast and the other skims up to band around her throat.

Holy fuck.

She squeaks, but her kisses grow more frantic. She likes that, I realize. And when Dair makes a pained sound, I can tell he's noticed, too.

Our omega better be careful, or she'll end up wearing tattooed hand necklaces every night.

Actually, she may not mind that.

Her perfume is so thick, I can *taste* it in the air. Rich, crumbly, sugared *perfection*.

Goddamn. I could come from that alone.

I did last time.

Dair snags my attention, shooting me a loaded look. We discussed this sort of thing as a pack. One of several group decisions we've made this week. Which is novel for us.

We're determined to do everything we can to encourage Ivy's sexuality. It's all so new for our omega—and we want her to enjoy how it feels to give in to her body's needs instead of feeling shame.

Time to put our money where our mouth is.

Or maybe just put our mouths where she wants them.

Dair has the same thought. He waits for the car to finish coasting around a turn and then drops to his knees. Asher moves the collar of his fingers to the soft place under Ivy's jaw, clearly keeping her kisses for himself as he adjusts their position, pivoting her hips until her ass is flush with his groin.

Ivy moans, and he growls, greedily licking the sound from her lips. His free hand moves back to her breast. This time, he strokes the side of the gentle curve with intent.

Jealousy spikes hot and hard in my middle. I shove Dair to the side, claiming the spot directly between her parted knees.

Our packmate starts to rip me out of the way, but Asher's sudden growl stops us both cold.

Fuck. He taps into his full dominance so rarely, I always forget how *strong* it is.

With Ivy still secure in his grasp, he shoots both of us a glare and allows his expression to melt into fond indulgence before turning back to her stunned, gasping face.

"Don't worry, darling," he whispers. "Your alphas are *gentlemen*. I'm sure they can work out a way to share." He flicks one final warning glance our way and then gazes back into her crystal eyes. His thumb strokes her lower lip. "If that's all right with you, princess."

Our omega whines, a heartrending sound that has me bending to suck softly at the pulse in her wrist. "We can share, angel," I assure her. "Would you like that? Both of us kissing your pretty pussy?"

Ivy's hips buck slightly, a sharp whimper tearing up her throat. Asher soothes her sweetly, running his nose down hers before kissing her again, purring against her back.

My own rolling rumble starts up as Dair eases her legs apart. The sideways look he shoots me would be funny if I weren't two seconds away from strangling him to get to our omega's panties first.

But I won't make the same mistake twice. I'm going slowly this time.

So, instead of rending the soft pink cotton peeking at me, I skim my lips along the inside of her knee.

Ivy draws a sharp breath when Dair mirrors my motions with

a wicked smirk he can't quite swallow. We both kiss the insides of her creamy thighs—me licking and sucking while he nips and scrapes his teeth over her thin, silky skin.

"Oh!" she cries, grinding into the air. "*Oh!*"

Dair laughs darkly. "Baby, we haven't even *started* with you yet."

I hum my agreement. My mind races. There's so much to show her, but she seems to be enjoying this, so I offer, "What if Dair takes those wet panties off and I keep kissing these gorgeous thighs?"

My packmate pauses, surprised. But Ivy nods, the motion desperate. "Dair," she cries, "P-please?"

He snaps into action, filling the space between her legs, opening them as wide as he can. One of his tattooed fingers hooks into the soaked fabric covering her center, pulling it aside.

Oh fuck, she's *beautiful*. Peachy pink and glistening. Visibly trembling with *need*.

Her perfume pours into the air while her opening twitches, begging for one of us to fill her. I groan into her thigh, my teeth biting harder than I intended.

Our omega thrusts her hips forward as she moans—and Dair can't take anymore. His ink-covered hands spread to frame those gorgeous, glimmering lips. With a pained sound, he lowers his face and laps at the cream trickling from her core. Ivy gasps again, spasming in Asher's arms.

"Shhh," the prince murmurs. "Such a good girl, giving your alpha so much slick."

His fingers unlace the bow holding her dress over her breasts, letting the split neckline fall open. As he dips into the strapless bra underneath, Dair teases his teeth over the top of her mound.

Ivy shrieks, leaking more sugary wetness. My impatient snarl pauses Dair's greedy licks. With a grumbling sigh, he leans aside and makes room for me, turning his attention to the leg slung over his right shoulder.

While he mumbles rough praises along her skin, I jolt out of my stupor and move into position, automatically glancing up at her for permission. Her slack features turn tender. "Please, Sebastian," she whispers. "I—I've wanted you so much. All week. I—"

She's about to apologize. *Again*. For being scared and having such a strong reaction the first time I touched her.

But none of that was ever her fault, and I won't let her think it was.

With a low growl, I snap forward.

Good. Holy. Fuckingggggg—

The taste of her renders me completely feral. I inhale the sweet, golden musk coating my tongue as I plunge it directly into her quivering core. Ivy sobs a moan, her hand winding into my hair. She tugs, drawing my gaze up to her wide-eyed, open-mouthed gape.

Asher trails kisses along her jaw, murmuring to her as he frees both breasts from their cups. Her nipples match her perfect pussy—peachy and *tight*. Fucking *hell*.

Her inner walls clamp around my tongue, trying to keep me inside her. I push as deep as I can get, managing to reach the ring of swollen muscle that will stretch to fit our knots.

Slick slips down my chin. I moan my appreciation, hoping it soaks into the collar of my shirt. Into my skin. Into my *soul*.

Yes. More.

It ends much too quickly. Dair grips my bicep hard enough to bruise. I can tell he's riding the same fine line I am—and if either of us lose our shit, we'll scare Ivy.

Dragging in a pant, I let him at her, falling back to watch. Unlike me, he goes right for her clit, rolling and plucking it between his lips.

Her pleasure is glorious. The way her skin glows. Her sparkling eyes and quivering keens. I watch while I try to drag air into my lungs, my hand falling to my throbbing erection, gripping it though my slacks.

Ivy's gaze tracks that motion. Another, more desperate sound flies from her mouth.

She turns to Asher and satisfaction smolders in his eyes. He loves being the one she turns to—her pack alpha.

"I—" she stammers, looking back at me. "I want—"

She may not know, but the prince does. "Bast, darling?" he asks. "You want his cock?"

When our omega nods, whining, I nearly spill in my pants. Her wide gaze drops back to the bulge along the front of my trousers. Her tongue peeks out to wet her lips.

Dair hums his approval. His shoe knocks the side of my leg as he mumbles into her mound. "Our omega wants to suck your dick."

Holy fuck, but she *does*. Her irises shine with eagerness—because that's *exactly* what this sweet girl wants.

My hands fumble with my belt, unfastening everything in her way as I move around Dair and kneel on the edge of the bench seat. Asher slides her lower in his lap while I present her with my straining dick. It juts forward, mere inches away from her parted lips.

We both moan when she slides her mouth around the head. Smooth, wet *heat* surrounds me. My knot instantly twitches fuller, the thick swell growing heavy at the base of my buzzing shaft.

I exhale, shaking, and sift my fingers into her hair. "Ivy, love," I pant. "Fuck, you feel *so good*."

She soaks up my encouragement, gazing at me with the prettiest vulnerability in her eyes. "So good," I repeat, petting her hair. "Perfect for me. I loved the way you tasted so much, I almost came in my pants."

"Again," Asher adds, smiling to himself as he nuzzles the side of her face. I understand why when shock pours through her expression, followed by a tinge of delight.

"I see how it is," I mutter, cocking a brow at her. "Are you going to be a naughty princess?"

Her tongue whispers along the underside of my cock as she pulls back just far enough to answer, "No... my lord."

Beautiful little coquette. She knows I have a love/hate relationship with hearing her call me that. It reminds me of just how proper she can be while also mocking me. The fact that I don't think she'd ever want to tease any of the others this way makes it *our* thing.

My heart swells as my cock thumps. The fingers woven through her hair tense, resisting the urge to fist the blonde strands and tug her back to me. Instead, I offer a grin and guide her back slowly, showing her how to tilt her chin for a better angle.

A hiss escapes as she takes my dick halfway into her mouth, testing how far she can stretch. Dair chooses that moment to go back to work, sucking her clit until she moans around my length.

Asher reaches for her tits, swirling the pads of his fingers over the pert little nipples until she starts to chase Dair's lips, pumping into his face. My head falls back when she naturally finds a rhythm, sliding her lips up and down in time with her hip thrusts.

Just that—the thought of her imagining my cock plunging into her slick-soaked center—sends me over the edge. I try to bumble out a warning, but Asher has to help.

"You want your lord to come in your mouth, darling?" he asks. "You want to taste him?"

Ivy hums sharply, grasping my hips and sinking as deep as she can, her nose grazing beneath my navel. I come instantly, my knot screaming as hot cum rises up my shaft and bursts onto her tongue.

My flavor must be as good for her as hers is for me, because as soon as I finish, she follows me over the edge. Dair practically sobs, his groan ragged and breathless while she strangles his fingers and slicks his face a final time.

"Shit," he gasps. "*Fuck.*"

The tart scent of cranberry winds into the rest toffee-and-shortbread sweetness filling the air as he comes in his pants, clamping his teeth over the top of her pussy while he loses control.

When he's done, he turns his face and finds her lower stomach, pressing his cheek into her softness. Her hand flutters to his hair as those wide, awestruck blue eyes find mine again.

I smile softly, hoping my expression is as reassuring as Asher's murmured praise. I nod down at Dair—who resembles nothing so much as a tamed panther. Sleek, dark-haired danger, all cuddled up and purring against her belly.

"Well angel," I sigh. "That's two of us. Are you going to ruin the prince's boxers next?"

twenty-eight

I've never had a boyfriend before, so you'll have to tell me:

Is meeting the parents *always* this terrifying?

Or is it worse because these "parents" are the *king and queen* of our country… and we happen to be approaching their *palace*?

The fact that I'm still practically comatose from our car ride doesn't help. I expected the guys to put me back in my own seat after we finished, but Dair stayed firmly wedged between my thighs, purring, with his head on my abdomen for the next hour.

Asher held me in his lap the entire way. Even after he fixed my bra and retied my dress, his hands never left me. Idly skimming over my arms, shoulders, and sides while he explained some of the ins and outs of palace life I'll need to get used to.

Bast claimed the seat that used to be mine, sending me eye-rolls and amused grins whenever Asher said something he deemed pompous. He also had a lot of useful information to drop into the conversation; since, apparently, he knows *everyone's* names, life stories, and pet peeves.

Dair, on the other hand, collects secrets. He's also much more aware of the staff than Asher seems to be. While Bast happily chatted about the groundskeeper and the valets, the duke added an occasional grumble of dissent or a begrudging nod of approval.

He only out-and-out disagreed once, growling to inform everyone that one kitchen assistant in particular is *never* allowed to be alone with me. When I asked why, he scent-marked my belly and kissed it softly. "Nothing for you to worry about, baby. I'll take care of it."

Between the deluge of information and, you know, the fact that we're about to walk into a literal *palace*, I'm already nervous by the time we hit the capital.

Driving through the city doesn't help much. Crenmore's capital, Lyledon, is a sprawling metropolis with a population thousands of times larger than Maytown. The streets are a bustling maze—some hodgepodge of cobblestone and new construction, all blended into a tapestry I'll never be able to learn.

Part of me breathes a sigh of relief when we pass right through it, to the opposite edge of the city. Stone walls appear, guarding what appears to be a park. Really, though, the acres of manicured landscaping are a *lawn*.

Their *front yard.*

While the cars surrounding ours have to pause at a security gate, our plush limo sails right past, winding through a thickly forested band. Once the tree line breaks, my eyes bulge.

Oh. My. God.

I'm not sure why I never imagined the palace being... well. A *palace.*

But it is. An *enormous* structure stretching five times as wide as it is high.

And it is *tall.*

Smooth white stone stacked into impossibly large walls, all matching the paved path winding up to equally impressive pillars and an ornate entrance. The front area must serve as some sort of façade, though, because we drive by without stopping. Our car takes a smaller track around the right side of the palatial building instead.

"The central structure faces north," Asher explains. "The wing is staged for visitors and closed off from the residential sections, where we'll be. My parents occupy the western wing; all the common areas, like the kitchens and entertaining spaces, are in the southern wing. Ours is the east wing, here."

He gestures to the endless expanse of large ivory blocks and shining windows blurring outside the car window. About halfway down the side of the palace, we make a sharp turn, darting into an archway tunneled through the first floor. It spits us out into a large circular area with similar paths carved into the south and western walls. A troupe of valets trots forward, swarming the cars around ours.

Asher leans to the side and raps on the privacy partition three times. It's clearly some sort of signal; the engine cuts off, but no one approaches the doors.

Bast cups his hands around my face, grinning with excitement as he scent-marks my forehead. "You're going to love it here."

Is there any other choice? And what happens if I hate it?

I glance out at the endless stretch of pristine lawn. The maze-like "garden." Stables that seem ornamental and far too still. There isn't so much as a squirrel chirring or a duck quacking.

Dair's expression reflects my resignation. He gives a harsh sigh and shoots a baleful look out the window. Asher ignores him, smoothing a hand over the back of my hair to capture my attention.

Swirling hazel eyes plumb my depths for a long moment. His

brows dip behind his glasses. "Are you ready? We can wait here as long as you like."

I want nothing more than to beg him to hold me a little longer. But his parents are waiting... and we're already going to make quite an impression, with all three of them drenched in my perfume.

I bite my lower lip, and Asher makes a soft sound just for me. "Goose, we don't have to go in yet. I'll stay out here with you all day."

My nickname puts a catch in my throat. *He remembered*, I think for the dozenth time, awed by the way he recalled our story without skipping a beat. And how he kissed me afterward... how he held me and touched me.

It was every dream come true.

Things between us have finally taken a turn today. I won't lose whatever progress we've made by causing him undue anxiety now.

I choke down the whine scraping my throat and force a nod. "I'll be fine, Ash."

His nickname brings a quick, dazzling smile to his face. He drops one last kiss on my mouth and slides toward the door.

Ignoring Dair's probing gaze, I move to follow him, repeating the assurance that feels more like a lie.

I'll be fine.

How bad could it be?

twenty-nine

So...

Bad.

Or, really, *good*. *Too* good.

So fantastically incredible that the word "good" sounds like a wet *plop* when compared to the utter splendor around me.

Gold leaf wallpaper. Gilded archways and roof beams. Wood floors and paneling as old as the monarchy itself.

Huge curved staircases, intricate carvings and stonework. Stained glass. Crystal doorknobs. Chandeliers adorned with actual *diamonds*.

Art. Tons of it. Beautiful oil paintings of royals dating back for centuries. Watercolor canvases of the countryside. An entire *hall* of sculptures.

At one point, my eyes start to sting and I realize they've bugged out so far, they're practically rolling on the floor behind me.

The portly man leading us around is named Holden. He's the royal family's butler—a position that's been held by *his* family for *two hundred years*. So it's no wonder he looks at me like I'm something he'll have to scrape out of the carpet later.

I don't blame him. This Persian rug probably costs more than most people's cars.

I haven't said a word during the esteemed man's running monologue, so I'm surprised when Dair suddenly growls and yanks our group to a halt.

Asher's jaw flexes before he calmly tells the butler to go on without us. The man nods, drawls that Their Majesties are waiting in the "throne room"—*the throne room?!*—and makes himself scarce.

Bast sighs at his retreating back. "Fantastic," he mutters, rubbing his neck.

Confused, I turn from one tense face to the next, wondering why they're all so upset. Did I mess up already?

Dair catches my eye and speaks around a scowl. "Your scent, little dove. It's so stressed, I can barely breathe."

Oh.

Figs.

I startle, impulsively moving to correct my faux pas. But how do you turn off your *scent*? And what happens if I can't? Will everyone in the *entire* palace know?

Before I can stammer through any apologies, Dair snaps me into a hug. "Fuck," he breathes, his chest rumbling. "It's okay, baby."

Bast looks at Asher, mumbling, "This is too much. She needs her nest."

The idea of how outrageously beautiful the omega suite meant for a *princess* must be only sends me into a whole new spiral. I've never even *seen* a nest before, let alone *used* one.

Or—oh *no—built* one.

I hadn't thought of *that*! I'm going to have to build a nest worthy of these men?! In their *palace*?!

Desperate to avoid it, I use the way my scent darkens to my advantage. "No," I insist, shaking my head. "I want to meet Ash's parents, like we planned."

The prince frowns, concern clouding his eyes. "Darling, you don't have to—"

"Please?" Panic rising once more, I look to Bast, hoping he'll take pity on me. "Please, my lord?"

My alpha's blue eyes soften. "Of course, angel. As long as you're sure you feel up to it. Of course we'll take you."

When I was a child, I remember thinking of Asher's parents as statues. Perfect, stony figures, chiseled to perfection.

They *loomed,* the way monuments do. Casting shadows, exuding power. The fear of their disapproval, the memory of their influence... it terrified me. Even once I crawled back to Maytown Manor for work, I did everything I could to avoid them.

Lofty, untouchable *royals*.

Imagine my surprise when I find out they're just as human as me.

I expect them to be in their thrones. Because this wide, sky-high hall full of blue stained glass and gilt molding does, in fact, have a pair of periwinkle velvet chairs on a marble dais.

They're empty, though. Just like the rest of the room.... aside from the middle-aged couple standing in its center.

I haven't seen the king for quite some time, but I've certainly *heard* him. At least once a week at the manor, he would have words for Asher and spend an evening shouting them.

The king matches his voice. He's… blustery. Thick salt-and-pepper hair swept back from a high forehead. Barrel-chested, with stormy eyes and a thunderous quality, he inspects us as we approach.

Meanwhile, the queen grins and glows. Her features may match Ash's deep brown hair and hazel eyes, but she somehow seems lighter. Clear happiness shines in her expression when her son winds my arm through his and guides me down the long, cobalt runner.

He stops about a meter away, dipping his head in a mild bow. I remember to curtsy, but my ankles wobble as I lower myself.

Bast and Dair copy Asher. The baron then goes forward with a grin, kissing the hand the queen offers him; while Dair silently slides his fingers against my palm, entwining his right hand with mine and stepping into my back.

"*Maman*," Bast chirps before motioning to the king. "Your Majesty."

King Leopold nods, barely glancing at my blond alpha before pinning his gaze on me. Or, really, *raking* it over me.

"Father," Asher starts, his tone firm. "This is Miss Ivy Addison, our princess."

As soon as he says the "P" word, King Leo's flinty eyes fly to mine. Alpha power rolls off him, crashing onto my head in a mighty wave. My Omega whines, huddling into a ball I wish I could mimic.

I flinch on instinct, but Dair is there. Solid and broad. All dark ink and darker eyes. After giving the king a look that very clearly communicates his thoughts, he completely ignores the monarch, wrapping his free arm around my waist and whispering to me.

"Shh, omega. I'm here." He may not say the words, but I hear them anyway: *no one will touch you as long as I'm around.*

Asher's hand squeezes mine in agreement. He barks, cold and clear. "*Father.*"

The king's mouth twitches in displeasure, but he draws a deep breath and turns to Asher. "Son." When he flicks his gaze back to me, it's markedly less intimidating. "Miss Addison. Lovely to meet you."

Like an *idiot*, I curtsy a *second* time. Which means I have to find a way to speak around a mouthful of mortification when the king's brow draws up, expectant.

"Y-you as well, Your Majesty. Th-thank you so much for—"

Hosting me? Not making me sleep in the dungeon? Letting your son consider bonding with one of your maids?

"—welcoming me."

A distinct twitch at the corner of his mouth tells me he wouldn't classify his feelings as "welcoming." But before I make an even bigger fool of myself, Asher's mother sweeps forward with a serene smile.

My eyes go wide when she doesn't stop, stepping into my personal space and lifting her cool hands to cup my cheeks. I start to panic, but there's something hypnotic about her. So calm and stately.

She gently turns my face from side to side and nods, satisfied. "You *are* very welcome here, Ivy," she announces, as though reading my mind.

The squeeze of Dair's fingers around me tells me he has, too. And he finds the queen's intuition as impressive as I do.

He bends forward, murmuring in my ear with a voice as deep and silky as the devil's. "Don't get any ideas, little dove. *I'm* Maman's favorite."

Queen Selene laughs at that, the sound genuine. "I think *mon petit amour* is my favorite," she muses, smiling at Asher with the sort of maternal affection that puts a lump of grief in my throat.

Oh, *dang it*.

I keep *forgetting* they can sense that.

When my scent gets saltier, Asher drops his formal stance and pivots to open his arms for me. Before I know it, his chest is pressed into my side, one long arm around my waist while his hand turns my head for his appraisal.

Green-gold eyes read the sadness welling behind my features as Dair fully hugs me, paying no mind to wrapping his arms around Asher's. The duke drops his face to my neck and purrs.

Stark compassion covers Queen Selene's face. "Oh, you poor dear. You must miss your own *maman* terribly. I was so sorry to hear she'd passed. She was a rare talent, and I simply adored her. Perhaps, once you're more settled, you'll allow us to host a memorial service?"

Right now, I can't do much more than breathe around the wad in my throat. Bast comes to my other side, ensuring I'm boxed between three broad, purring chests. "We can discuss it, angel," he coaxes. A frown creases his brows. "Though, maybe you'd like to rest first? This has been a big day."

For some reason, I find myself turning to Asher. Believing he'll know what to do. *Trusting* him.

His face softens when our gazes meet. "I'd like to feed you dinner," he admits, "and get you into your nest."

My prince's face brokers no arguments as he regards his father once more. "Ivy is severely touch-starved and expecting her heat soon. She'll need our attention whenever it suits her Omega—and that will be our *top* priority."

To my shock, King Leo doesn't glare. Instead, he blinks, surprise etching its way into his somber features. "Of course," he agrees. "That's understood."

Asher's answering nod feels like a handshake sealing a contract. "Good."

Nerves bubble at the base of my lungs, telling me this isn't right. *I'm going to take them away from their work. What if I need too much or something gets ruined because they had to tend to me? Maybe this isn't—*

There isn't any time to protest. Queen Selene claps her hands, smiling. "You must show our princess her suite!" she exclaims, tossing me a wink. "After all, Ivy's putting up with the likes of us. She ought to get *something* out of it."

thirty

I'VE IMAGINED THIS MOMENT.

When I was teenager, smitten with a girl I thought I could never have, I pictured what I'd do if I had the kind of freedom most people are born with.

How I'd whisk Ivy away from Maytown and bring her to the palace. Parade her around for everyone to see what a gorgeous, good-hearted person she was. And then give her this; the suite reserved for my princess.

Even while we were apart, I held on to that fantasy. Had dreams about it. Added it to the pile of regrets I carried between my shoulder blades.

Last week, when we discovered Ivy's true designation and she agreed to give us a chance to prove ourselves to her, those fantasies became inevitabilities.

I pictured the moment over and over. Bast flinging the creamy double doors open. Revealing the grand, airy space, all trimmed in thin white silks.

There's a lot to see in here. An entire wall of gleaming stained-glass windows in every shade of blue and pink imaginable. The view of the garden maze, our lake, and our stables. A two-story-high ceiling, domed and intricately carved into hundreds of frescos and fleurs-de-lis, all delicately painted in soft shades of sky and lined with gold luster.

The rest of the suite matches those colors. An enormous white-stone fireplace off to the left of the oval floor, framed by tufted light blue sofas. Gold-veined marble floors. Powder-blue window treatments.

And that's just the beginning.

To the right, tucked slightly away from the windows and their sunset vista, there's a large circular platform. Ivy's new bed—with plenty of room for the rest of us—stands at its center. Partially shrouded by an ivory silk canopy... hanging from a second platform that floats several meters above the first.

The nest.

Whoever prepared the suite for our arrival chose to leave it open. Usually, the thick velvet curtains are closed, hiding the enormous mattress built into the cylindrical space. Shining glass encloses the smaller room—designed to let light in, if desired, or not, when the curtains are drawn.

I've been up there once or twice, inspecting how safe it is. But the floating nest is every bit as solid as the two curved staircases bracketing the bed below it. All of it was carved from the same solid marble—one giant piece that could withstand an army, let alone an omega's heat.

I suppose it's rather pretty, too.

The four of us stand on the threshold, silently staring into the suite. Bast shifts, clearly nervous Ivy doesn't like it. Dair is too busy watching her to betray his own anxiety, but his scent sours as seconds tick past.

Explanations and reassurances bubble to my lips. I open my mouth to tell her we can change the whole room. Or choose a different one. Or, hell, *build* a new one.

In all my years of imagining this moment, I thought I'd pictured every possibility. But Ivy turns her head slowly for a final time, blue eyes climbing over every detail they touch. Then she looks away...

And buries her face in my chest.

Baffled, I close my arms around her and start to purr. "Darling? Is something wrong?"

She trembles slightly, shaking her head. "The room is beautiful, Ash," she whispers. "But it doesn't smell like you."

Her nervous gaze flits to my packmates. "*Any* of you."

Awe echoes between the three of us. My heart seizes, spasming behind the secret tattoo I kept covered for years. An ache blooms at the base of my throat.

Any other person might be enamored with the luxury of this room. But not Ivy.

She doesn't really care about any of this. She cares about *us*.

None of us know what to *do* with that. Until Bast blinks once. Twice. "Well, fuck, gorgeous. Let's fix that right now."

He walks into the middle of the room and undresses, flinging pieces of clothing in every direction until Ivy's uncertainty cracks into a tiny smile.

Dair loves it. I've never seen him look at anyone with the soft, warm regard he has for the little curve of her lips.

He doesn't bother walking into the room before kicking his shoes off and following Bast's lead. His black suit pants go flying onto the sofa. His dress shirt to the plush padded bench at the foot of the bed.

The bastard even takes off his underwear—paying no mind to

how Ivy's eyes widen and snag on his half-hard dick while he leverages the waistband like a slingshot and shoots the black briefs right at the chandelier. They catch on one of the cut crystals and dangle there.

Ivy's giggle makes it impossible to feel annoyed. The sound is shy and shaky, but bright and bubbly too. I'll do anything to hear more, so I hug her closer for one last precious moment… and release her with a sigh, rolling my eyes while I start to strip.

It's a good thing I had all the security cameras taken out of here.

Bast's bare arm accidentally jostles mine. He flips me a quick cringe, and I can hear his unspoken apology.

Sorry, bro.

It's not his fault, though. Ivy wanted our scents in her space… and now her Omega wants them in our nest.

If that means the three of us have to stand nude on the platform next to her sacred space… well, here we are.

Dair shifts on his feet. I know being naked doesn't bother him, so I assume his restlessness has more to do with the way Ivy's been standing in the center of the mattress for close to three minutes. Hesitating.

Over the last week, we've collected our worn clothes for exactly this reason. I had them placed in a hamper and brought to the top of the stairs when we arrived. The staff knows better than to enter the nest, though, so Bast dragged the laundry into the rounded glass-and-gilt room.

At first, Ivy picked through them happily. But within minutes, she seemed to get overwhelmed.

I hate that I can't do anything for her. Part of me wants to pluck our shirts out of her frozen fists and reassure her that she doesn't need to build anything for us straight away.

I did a lot of research on this, though. If we storm into the nest without being invited and take over, we risk her Omega rejecting the space entirely. Or, worse, demoralizing her to the point where it won't be possible for Ivy to build a proper nest for her heat.

Bast starts to move but reins himself in. I shoot him a firm, quelling look, my pack leader command clear in the expression.

No.

We wait for Ivy.

My darling blinks an uncertain glance over her shoulder. Her scent darkens, singeing. "I—"

We all hold our breath over purrs. She swallows. "I think I need some help."

Relieve slackens my posture. I step forward, gesturing. "Can we come in?"

She startles and I realize—*she didn't know she* needed *to invite us*. Sadness mingles with the anticipation pinching my lungs.

I can tell she senses it in my scent. Her head falls forward slightly, but she nods. "Please."

We practically trip over each other to get to her. The shame doesn't fade from her scent, but at least her body seems to unwind a bit as soon as we all touch her.

Bast snuggles into her back while Dair twines her fingers in his. Her free hand finds mine, squeezing weakly as she skirts her crystal eyes to mine. "Where do I start?"

The question throws us all. We catch each others' gazes, confirming that, no, none of us have the first clue how to build an omega's nest.

That's the thing, though—her Omega *does* know. She just needs to get better at reaching that new piece of herself.

An idea winds into my mind. I step into her front, framing her face in my hands and lowering my lips to hers. "Let's start here," I murmur.

thirty-one

"There."

Dair nods, his black hair flopping over his forehead as he shoves a pair of boxers into the crack between two pillows.

Bast hums into my nape, his teeth nipping me gently while brawny hands skim up my sides. My thoughts scatter, leaving room for my instincts to rise higher. "I need… a blanket?"

The strong fingers kneading my hips yank me backward. An approving purr hits my ears the same second Bast's hard cock presses into the small of my back. My body reacts before I can, grinding into him.

Dair holds out two blankets—a silky silver one and a velvet

blue piece. I freeze, until Asher approaches. On his knees like the rest of us, the prince promptly settles his own hard heat against my belly, bending to take my lips in another lush kiss.

Of course he's the one who figured out how to fix this for me. I'm sure my prince read about every omega-taming technique under the sun. When he saw me start to melt down over how to make this nest, he stepped in with a less-than-subtle solution:

Turn me on so much that I *can't* think.

I can only *feel.*

As his tongue teases mine and his palms cup my breasts, a whine scales my throat. Bast rubs his erection against my back, and Asher presses into my front. Feeling two throbbing shafts through the thin fabric of my sundress sends me into a dizzy spin.

I fumble to reach Asher's cock, the compulsion to *touch* too strong to ignore. With a low growl, he guides my hands to his thick length, showing me how to stroke with both.

I love the way he feels, the solid, springy texture of his swollen knot. Questing my fingers lower, I find his balls full and tight. Asher hisses, his scent brightening until I can barely gasp for breath.

"Mm," he groans quietly, gently taking one of my wrists and drawing it to the side, guiding my touch to the two blankets. "Which one?"

My fingers curl in the silk instantly. Dair chucks the velvet away, handing my selection to his packmate. Bast wraps it at my waist and holds it there for a moment, making sure it will have both their scents all over it.

Part of me is grateful for the way the thick duvet muffles the perfume pouring from my pussy when Asher's cock ticks higher, visibly straining in my hand.

I'm surprised my clothes aren't bothering me. That day in Asher's bedroom, a simple pair of sweats felt like wearing a sack of needles—but now, my dress's thin cotton material is soothing, somehow.

Probably because I know if I took it off, we'd end up in a tangle. And my Omega *needs* this nest to be finished.

I'm not sure if Dair can tell or if he's just sticking to his promise not to touch me until I can trust him. Either way, his dark eyes are focused—if a tiny bit tight—when he takes the blanket back. "Where do you want it, little dove?"

Bast bites down on my shoulder the same second my brain trips over the question. I moan as an image of a blanket wall slides into my thoughts.

I can see how being bonded would make this whole process much easier. Since Dair can't read my mind, I point to the far portion of the round mattress and peep, "Can we make it... like a wall?"

His expression softens and he drops a kiss to my forehead. "Of course we can, baby."

As soon as he gets the duvet rolled and curved into a soft barrier, the rest of the space falls into place. I fluff pillows and stack them in the strangest ways, but the guys never offer anything apart from the most sincere encouragement. And the occasional love bite.

Finally, I collapse into the central mountain of cushions, exhaustion buzzing in my brain. Bast grins and crawls over, nodding at the spot to my left. When I reach for him, his heart-stopping happiness lights the whole room.

With the baron nestled into one side, Asher carefully lowers himself to the other. My eyes lock on Dair's, and I beckon him closer, but he grimaces.

"Don't trust myself," he mutters, sitting near my feet instead. "Your scent is driving me insane."

"Me too," Bast groans into my shoulder. "It's perfection, angel. And it's soaking into *everything*."

His cock stiffens at the thought, the hard ridge brushing the outside of my thigh where my skirt has ridden up. My Omega whines, wishing we could—could—

Oh. My. God.

No! I tell her, mortification swamping me in response to the image she conjures. *Absolutely not!*

But—damn it all—Dair sees her. He *always* sees her.

"What is it?" he rumbles, dark eyes glinting. The barest edge of a bark puts panty-melting roughness into his command. "*Tell your alphas, baby.*"

My mouth gapes as I grope for an excuse. Asher props himself on his elbow, watching embarrassment stain my cheeks before bending to rub a slow scent-mark along my blush. I perfume, my spine tingling as wetness soaks my underwear.

A familiar haze begins to fog my awareness. I try to push it back, but Dair takes my feet in his big, inked hands and begins kneading the soles just as Bast starts to caress his brawny hand over my belly.

More slick melts from my core as my Omega takes the reins, forcing the words I would sooner die than admit to.

"I want you to... *cover* the nest. With your... scents."

Without Asher's glasses on, I see the confused line between his brows all too clearly. "Haven't our clothes done that, darling? Do you need us to get you more?"

I can tell Bast is closer to my true meaning. His body has locked into stillness, each breath scraping somewhere between a growl and a purr as he blinks his deep blue eyes at me.

But, of course, Dair catches on first. The cocky, crooked grin he tries to hide is enough to make my nipples bead tighter.

"Such a dirty princess," he murmurs, eyes bright. "You want *our cum* in your nest?"

My mouth blubs like a fish's, but nothing comes out. Because I can't *deny* it... but I also can't admit to any more than I already have.

I mean, *seriously*?! Where did this depraved idea even come from? And what kind of *princess* would ask her alphas to—to—

"*Mine.*"

Asher snarls, lunging to lock our lips together. For a second, my blurry brain wonders if he's heard me somehow, but then I realize: this is just his reaction. His true feelings about my insane request.

Relief and shock drag a whimper out of me. Their scents swell and deepen, until every breath is a symphony of citrusy warmth and sugared tartness. I quiver, more perfume and slick pouring into the nest.

Asher kisses me harder, his hand flipping my skirt up, baring my thighs for his hungry hazel eyes before gripping his cock. A spike of outrage pierces my lungs. With a sound I've never made before, I find myself knocking his hand out of my way so *I* can fist his length.

"Fuck." Bast nuzzles the side of my neck, watching me grasp the prince's hot, hard shaft with wild eyes. "This might be the best day of my life."

He always knows how to make me smile, even when I'm half out of my head. Squirming, I reposition so the baron is stretched along my back, letting my skirt bunch around my waist and presenting the baron with my much-abused pink panties.

I slant a pleading look at him. "Please, my lord. Can I—can I have you again?"

Bast groans, his face dropping into my hair. "You want me to fuck you, angel? Pull out and come all over your pretty pussy and this beautiful nest you made for us?"

My chest stutters as my core throbs and my heart melts. Pride and desire mingle with my apprehension, swirling into pieces of me that haven't been allowed to want anything for years. Filling in some of the cracks.

I nod desperately, whining. Bast scrambles to peel my underwear off as my eyes fly to Dair. He's waiting for me, staring with a sort of steadiness I never would have pictured on him.

"I'm going to watch, little dove," he rasps, kneeling to put the way he's stroking his cock on full display. "Make a pretty picture for me."

I'm not sure how he manages to speak directly to my Omega. Like he has some sort of tether to her most basic desires.

She *wants* to be on display for these alphas.

When Asher's fingers find my throat, wrapping securely to hold me in place, Dair's answering growl blots out the last of my logic, leaving me awash in sensation.

The smooth hardness pulsing against my palm, a thin layer of pre-cum wetting our skin. Firm lips on mine. Strong hands tugging at my hips—the warm ridges of tight abdominals, brushing my bare behind before solid girth kisses my clutching pussy. Goosebumps raising over my arms as a pair of dark eyes slowly drink in every piece of me.

I feel them like a caress, tracing along the insides of my thighs as Bast grasps one knee and lifts my bent leg, slinging it over his chiseled hip.

This alpha is a true athlete. His muscles work in fluid rolls that feel effortless, pulsing his cock deeper with every pump. He holds his position and keeps his tight pace, groaning praise into my nape. "Goddamn it, you're so perfect. Missed this sweet pussy so much, angel."

Asher speaks between kisses, adding his own temptation in a velvet murmur, "You're going to make us come all over your nest, aren't you?"

He matches Bast's rhythm, bucking into my fist and taking my mouth for rough kisses, so completely at odds with the gentle way his thumb skims the pulse beneath my ear.

Bast leaves my knee hooked over his thigh, reaching between my body and Asher's to roll my slippery clit between his fingers. I keen, the sound earning a low snarl from the dark-eyed duke watching his packmate thrust into my pussy.

That midnight gaze... how can it tether me to reality and steal my sanity at the same time?

What will I do if he keeps staring at me like this?

How will I live if he stops?

I have a feeling I may never find out. Because as everything inside me squeezes and bursts… and they each go off, filling the nest with their mind-melting scents…

Dair never looks away.

thirty-two

EVERHART PACK GROUP CHAT

IVY

Um... I have a question.

BAST

Is it "how did I get more beautiful since yesterday?"

Because I was wondering the same thing.

DAIR

Kiss ass

ASHER

What's your question, goose?

IVY

Do princesses wear panties?

BAST

I think my heart just stopped

DAIR

Nope.

Never.

ASHER

I can't say I have much firsthand knowledge, but I presume they do.

Why do you ask, darling?

IVY

I can't find any in this closet...

And then I thought maybe that was on purpose

BAST

Well...

Are chairs always this cold?

Or is it worse because I don't have any underwear?

Bast and Dair were delighted, but Asher took pity on me and promised to find some. The thought of that—the crown prince, scrambling to find slick-absorbing panties—has me biting back a giggle as a royal-blue-clad attendant sets a silver tea tray on the table beside me.

"Her Majesty will be along in a moment, Your Highness."

He keeps his head bowed, his face averted. The way I was trained to.

It never struck me as silly until this moment. Why in the world should anyone avoid looking at someone else? At *me*? I couldn't even find my own underwear this morning!

"I'm Ivy," I say, sticking my hand out.

He blinks at it, hesitating like he's about to put his wrist in a bear trap. Still, I suspect he can't really turn down a handshake from the princess.

Me.

"Duncan, Your Highness," he replies, still not looking up from the Oriental rug and its various shades of soft blue.

For a second, I almost insist he use my first name—but then I remember how I used to feel when Bast asked that of me. I don't want to make anyone uncomfortable.

But that doesn't mean I can't be friendly.

"Nice to meet you, Duncan," I tell him. "Thank you for carting this all the way up here."

It couldn't have been easy. This palace is grand and historic, meaning most wings don't have elevators. And the polished tray must weigh thirty pounds on its own, with those thick, intricately carved legs.

Not to mention the priceless china laid on top of it.

And, you know, all the food and tea.

Duncan catches my grimace and offers a kind half-smile. "It's no trouble, Your Highness. Is there anything else I might get for you?"

The faces of my alphas flash through my mind. I wish I could ask for them, but they literally spent the entire afternoon and evening attending to my every whim yesterday. I can't ask them to come running back to me every time I get the least bit anxious...

Can I?

No, I decide. Certainly, that's not proper royal behavior. And today is supposed to help me get a handle on what *is*.

Besides, it's only been a few hours since I woke up with Bast. They decided to ease me into sleeping with all of them, not wanting to bring my heat on too suddenly. For some reason, when they asked who I wanted with me, my Omega chose the baron almost immediately.

I'm still surprised none of them got upset. They genuinely seemed happy that I listened to my instincts, just like they did up in the nest...

Asher slept in his own room, but returned to Omega Suite before we woke up. Bast and I found him reading his papers beside the blazing hearth. A picture that was so familiar, I nearly wept with relief.

At least *something* is normal.

Everything else most definitely isn't. The fact that *Dair* brought *me* a breakfast tray only underscored how much things have changed in such a short amount of time.

Our prince joined me for tea and toast, insisting on holding me in his lap. While we ate, he explained the family crest on all their china. It's a traditionally-shaped heart surrounded by a flaming crown. His voice got a bit gruff when he told me that, should we bond and form our own royal pack, we'll get to design our own emblem, too.

I couldn't breathe then, and the memory leaves me winded now.

Or maybe I'm fooling myself and this tightness boxing my lungs has less to do with becoming a princess and more to do with Asher's mother, the queen.

She invited me to her personal parlor for this "girls only" luncheon. It strikes me as odd to call it a "luncheon" when it's just the two of us; until Duncan retreats and I glance down at the tray again. Noticing its size... and the fact that there are three cups on it.

Three?

Sure enough, a moment later, Queen Selene sweeps into the room.

And she isn't alone.

A wide smile graces Her Majesty's ageless features as she takes in the short, frothy pink dress Bast selected for me this morning. Before I can determine whether she approves—or, God forbid, notices the lack of certain undergarments—Asher's mother turns to the beautiful woman hovering behind her.

"Ivy, *mon amie*," she starts, waving to the glamorous person wrapped in sumptuous red silk. "Meet Princess Ahmad."

thirty-three

I'VE NEVER REALLY UNDERSTOOD THE PHRASE "SHIT fit."

Well.

My Omega definitely does.

As Princess Ahmad's rich white-chocolate scent drifts across the queen's parlor, the floor shifts under my feet. For the first time ever, the voice at my center is *angry*.

She doesn't see an unimaginably elegant princess or her blinding beauty. She sees *competition*.

Another unbonded omega. One with more natural appeal and poise than we have.

The princess floats into the room, her asymmetrical red dress sliding around her legs, revealing a slit that nearly reaches her hip.

Great, my Omega thinks. *So she's sexy, too?!*

I shush her, trying to ignore the way my stomach flips inside out when her sweet scent hits me. It's... a good scent. Have the princes noticed that? Did they like it, too?

I wish I had Asher's poker face right about now. Princess Ahmad flits her deep brown eyes over my entire body, pausing in particular places—my bitten nails, my unpolished toes... and, *oh my God*... the fading bruise Dair left on the inside of my left knee during our limo ride.

Oops.

Didn't notice that this morning.

I could swear this woman knows I have no panties on. Her dark gaze lingers on my hips for a long second as humor flickers on her red-painted lips. Finally, she extends her hand and pins me in place with a frank stare.

"Nice to meet you, Princess...?"

"Ivy," I correct, mostly because I have no idea what my title is. *Surely not "Princess Addison," and we aren't bonded, so I'm not "Princess Everhart" either.* "Just Ivy, please."

She nods, her satin-smooth black hair cascading over one richly tanned shoulder. "Ivy, then. Lovely to make your acquaintance. Selene has told me so much about you."

Selene?

She calls the queen *Selene*?

My Omega wants to snarl, but Princess Ahmad only smirks wider, clearly amused by my shifting scent .

Heavy footsteps distract us for a moment. An enormous alpha wearing all black steps into the room. He silently takes up residence beside the door, folding his hands in front of his broad body and snapping his focus to the princess.

Her sweet scent tweaks higher at the same moment her lips do. "My security," she explains, eyes sparkling while they land on mine. "You understand."

I don't, actually, but a nod seems best. Queen Selene calmly joins us, setting a gentle hand on the puffy sleeve covering my upper arm. "Our Ivy will learn soon enough. I doubt Asher will let her leave this palace without two armored cars full of men."

That image shoves a bolt of panic into my gullet. My answering laugh is a bit too squeaky. "Uh-of course not."

The queen motions to our tea tray, urging us to sit. I slump back into my seat as Princess Ahmad perches herself across from me, perfectly crossing her ankles to the side without missing a beat.

As our hostess, Queen Selene insists on serving the tea. Even that makes me feel inadequate—she doesn't spill one single drop while I can barely hold my saucer with how hard I'm shaking.

Princess Ahmad notices. Her gorgeous face folds into a frown while she watches me try to steady the china.

"Ivy has hardly had half a minute to get situated!" the queen exclaims, smiling kindly. "It's a wonder she hasn't run off for the hills with all the demands we've already put on her."

"Mm." Princess Ahmad nods sagely, her Cheshire Cat grin returning. "Have the princes already started trying for an heir? So soon?"

I choke on my tea, coughing into the cup. The Princess raises a sculpted black brow. "Oh dear. Did I misspeak?"

Queen Selene laughs merrily, patting my knee. "Not at all, but I'm sure they're still... hammering out the details of such... delicate matters. Producing royal heirs can be quite a handful. Especially since I know Sebastian wants his very own polo team."

Oh. Em. Gee.

A whole polo *team*???

Wheezing, I finally manage to get enough air into my lungs to clear the spots covering my vision. The princess regards me quizzically, like I'm a puzzle she can't figure out. "Is it the bonding ceremony, then? I must admit that gave me pause, too. The thought of so many people *watching*. *In the room*."

She shudders, and Queen Selene's grin takes on a brittle quality as my mind races.

The royals bond *in public*? As in... *at a church*? For *everyone* to see?

Surely not?

But the look on the queen's face confirms my worst fears. Clearly, she was subjected to this public bonding tradition and she didn't like it one bit, either.

That doesn't bode well for us, given they've been bonded for close to forty years. Having such an intimate thing on display like that would have been mortifying back then, too... But they didn't have to deal with video apps and live-streaming and *memes*—oh *Lord*—

"Your Majesty?" Duncan reappears, standing on the threshold with his head ducked once more. When the queen nods, he continues, "There's an urgent call for you from His Majesty."

A flare of alarm sparks in my chest, but Asher's mother only rolls her eyes. "He and I have very different definitions of urgent," she mutters to us, throwing in a wink. "I'll be right back, *mon amies.*"

In a swirl of silver and cream, she makes a graceful exit. Duncan follows at her heels, leaving me with Princess Ahmad and the bodyguard she pays no mind to.

Her brown eyes track the way my hands tremble around my teacup and saucer. Something dark creeps into her expression.

"Ivy."

Until she says my name, I don't realize I've been staring at the floor. Keeping my eyes averted. The way servants do.

Our gazes snap together. Hers narrows.

"I am the fourteenth Princess Ahmad, heiress to the Amizi Empire. Daughter of Shah Umar Ahmad the Sixth. My family has been in power three times longer than Asher's—and, unlike this country, ours is an *absolute* monarchy. One that's *five times* larger than Crenmore, with a militia to match. We export oil—one of the most lucrative resources in the world—and have mines of rubies and riches you couldn't begin to dream of."

I feel myself shrinking with each sentence, crushed by the weight of her words. Her *power.*

If this is my competition, I am toast.

But then she sits forward, casting me a conspiratorial smile. "So it might be best if you *look alive*, babe."

When my mouth drops open, she laughs. A genuine sound full of warmth and abandon. "I'm only partly kidding," she goes on, slanting her sparkling eyes back to mine. "There will be *plenty* of bitches trying to tear you down—but I'm one of the most influential omegas your alphas courted. So if you can handle me, you can handle those hoes."

Hoes?

Did the future ruler of Amizi just say "hoes?"

And, Lord—do I like her more because she did?

I can't help the small smile that twists my lips. "Which hoes?"

Princess Ahmad's air is blasé, like all of this is old news. She sets her saucer on the table between us, waving her hands around to indicate our surroundings. "Everyone, basically."

When I blink at her, she takes pity on me with a kinder smile. "Look, I get that you've had about twenty seconds to get yourself together, but we're going to have to work fast if you want to do this."

My brows crease. "Do *what*?"

More sly humor. "The *princes*, honey. Selene says you're their scent-match. So I'm guessing you don't really have a choice."

The thought of *doing* the princes has me smoothing my skirt over my legs. Specifically, Dair's love bite.

Princess Ahmad's mouth curves. She flashes a quick look at her guard, probably to make sure he isn't staring right at her before she bends forward and tugs at the neck of her dress, revealing a series of similar bruises wreathing the top of her right breast.

I gape and she smiles wider with a shrug, bouncing back to

her original stance. "Don't worry about the marks; I have my own from someone back home. It's an alpha thing. You'll learn to hide them. And your princes will learn not to be so painfully obvious."

My face must reveal how dubious that seems. She gives another shrug. "Or maybe they won't. That could be fun, too. More ways for you to mark your territory."

I can't understand what she's saying. What she's doing—talking to me like this. Like... she wants to help? Or support me?

Princess Ahmad somehow manages to look even lovelier when her face softens. "I've heard about your mother," she adds. "My mother died when I was very young; becoming an omega without her guidance was... difficult. I wondered if you knew any other omegas. If anyone had helped you or answered any of your questions."

Gracie tried, but she's an alpha, just like the guys. And aside from the queen—who I absolutely *cannot* ask—I realize Princess Ahmad has a point.

But can I trust her?

Why is she still here if she has no intention of going after the princes for herself?

She watches my face for a long moment and sighs, her smile resigned. "Might as well ask me and get it over with. "

I remember what she just told me—there are dozens of pretty, polished, titled omegas like her. All vying for *my* alphas. The thought has me squaring my shoulders and raising my gaze directly to hers.

"Do you want them?" I ask. "Is that why you're still here?"

Something like approval streaks through her eyes. "No. I don't want the princes. I never have—but my father wants them for me. And that *will not* happen."

Understanding and relief wash over me. She doesn't want us to be friends—or, rather, if she does, it isn't just out of the kindness of her heart.

For some reason, that settles my doubts better than pure intentions would. She has a stake in this, too.

"You need this to work out to save yourself from being married off?"

"Something like that," she admits, settling into a much more casual stance. "Besides, *you're* their mate, not me. Now that they've found you, they'd be miserable without you. So it's pretty important for everyone involved that we get you sorted out and turn you into a proper princess." Her eyes glint. "Or at least a perfectly *improper* one."

I can't quite help the dubious way I squint at her. "And you're going to help me?"

She smiles widely, as if pleased I'm finally showing some spirit. "No. You're going to help *yourself.*"

I might not be royalty, but I like to think I'm not a complete moron. And even if she's just trying to trick me or use me... wouldn't it be better if she thought I was oblivious?

So I smile. "All right, Princess Ahmad. You have a deal."

The gorgeous future empress grins. "In that case, you should probably call me Jasmine."

"I DON'T KNOW IF I CAN DO THIS."

My lips move in the reflection staring back at me. Forming the words I've been thinking all day. The ones I don't have the courage to say to anyone else.

But it's the truth.

Can I do this?

Do I *want* to?

The sky darkens outside, twilight peering through a strip of windows high above the Omega Suite's grand whirlpool tub. Any minute now, the guys will come back from their busy days.

I have to find my bearings. I promised I would try. Let *them* try...

But after ten minutes of staring at my own face, searching for any trace of worthiness, I feel more lost than ever. Sighing, I turn back for the double doors to the suite...

Only to find a darkly-clad figure leaning against the doorjamb. A dangerous alpha, covered in inky muscle, with bad ideas in his eyes.

Dair.

He rolls that bottomless gaze up to mine, seeing *everything*. Reaching out to me. "Let's get out of here."

thirty-four

Asher's going to have my balls for this.

Sort of worth it, though, for the wide-eyed excitement on Ivy's face.

Okay. *Totally* worth it.

Grinning behind my face shield, I swing my leg over my Ducati and turn to unbuckle her helmet. I ordered it after our night on her front porch, unable to get the image of her clinging to my back as we raced through Lyledon out of my mind.

It lived up to the hype in a way few things do. Sneaking down the back stairwell with her little hand tucked into mine... watching her stammer and grimace while I explained how to hold on to me... hearing her yelp when I started the engine... leaning into the wind while she clung to my back, her breathless giggles blurring into our wake.

And, best of all, Everdeen shrinking away into nothing.

She needed that as much as I did. I felt it in her posture, her muscles loosening as she sank closer and closer to my back.

I fucking loved it.

On the other side of the city, I pulled onto a quiet side street. It's a Monday night and the pubs lining the sidewalk seem sleepy. I was counting on that. After we introduce Ivy to the world, she won't be able to go anywhere without people noticing her—but for now, this should be fine.

I wore street clothes for the same reason. Asher is far too famous to ever go incognito, and Bast's good looks are equally well-known. I can usually fly under the radar, though, as long as I wear the right outfit.

Ivy doesn't comment on my black jeans or the hoodie I threw over my T-shirt. She changed into one of her pairs of threadbare leggings and a T-shirt after her shower; I unzip my jacket and wrap it around her body without thought.

She blinks in surprise, and I cock a rueful smirk. *Welcome to the club, baby.*

Two weeks ago, if you'd told me I would be so down bad I'd resort to *chivalry*...

I would have stabbed myself.

At least my disgust amuses Ivy. She snorts a quiet laugh at my expression, shaking her head. "If I didn't know any better," she teases, "I'd think you liked me."

Ha. I *wish* I liked her.

That might be manageable. Unlike whatever the hell *this* is.

And, yes, I *know* what it is.

Shut up.

"Yeah, yeah," I grouse, grinning. "This happens to have nothing to do with you, little dove. I need cheese fries."

That isn't strictly true. More like my Alpha needs *her* to eat some cheese fries. Because my mate is wasting away, and last night I had to sit and watch her push fancy food around her plate.

She follows the wave of my hand, her eyes lighting when they reach the truck parked between two bars. Then her brows pinch.

"You mean cheesy *chips*?"

With an eye-roll, I sling my arm around her shoulders and kiss her crown, muttering, "Whatever. In America, they're cheese fries."

Relief bleeds through my chest when my omega wraps her thin arm around my waist and leans closer. "You moved there when you were a kid?"

A reflexive bolt of rage snaps down my spine. "Yes."

My tone doesn't invite any more questions, and Ivy takes the hint. We approach the food truck, and my muscles tick tighter, preparing to be recognized. It doesn't happen, though. To the vendor, we're just a random couple. The way he throws two gloopy batches of fries together proves it.

I drop some cash and take our food. Ivy follows meekly, sitting beside me when I drop down to the curb, handing her the paper carton of fried potatoes and melty cheese with a grunt.

Shit. I really suck at this. Bast would have some witty observation and a charming smile; Asher's manners and class could send most women swooning, too.

But me?

Ivy blinks down at her "cheesy chips." Surprise lifts her features once again. "They don't have any bacon."

She must not have heard me tell the guy to hold the pork. Probably too busy trying to figure out why I went from zero to dickhead in two seconds flat.

I scoot closer and wrap my arm back around her in silent apology. "You're a vegetarian."

Ivy smiles slightly. "I don't think I ever told you that. Stalker."

Her little jokes always catch me off guard. And delight me in the craziest way. A grin cracks my bad mood instantly. "*Stalker*?

No, I just sent that charcuterie tray up the day you passed out and noticed you didn't touch any of the meat."

She smiles wider. "Only stalkers hang around to see what people leave on their plates, Your Grace."

I really hate it when she calls me that. But that cursed title is the whole reason I'm here. The whole reason... I found her.

Fuck me.

I'm going to have to tell her, aren't I?

"I think I prefer 'Stalker.'" I mutter. "Or just 'Dair.'"

She looks over at me, seeing far too much. Understanding softens her frown. "Okay. I-I'm sorry."

I nuzzle my forehead into her temple, scent-marking her. "Nothing for you to be sorry for, baby. I just... hate being what I am."

Nervous blue irises flash up at me. "Any particular reason?"

Waiting for my answer, Ivy pops a fry in her mouth. As she chews, something in my center unclenches. The relief unlocks my lungs enough for me to answer, "Well, my father was the last Duke of McAffry—and I hated *him*, so."

This is how she gets to me, I realize. Most people would ask why. Or launch into a reply. But this is *my mate*. And some innate part of her knows me in a way I may not even know myself.

Instead of speaking, she scoots closer and leans her head against my shoulder. Just... there. *Here*. Not judging or fixing or even reacting, apart from offering the reassurance that I haven't offended her.

Which is sort of a miracle. Hearing I hate my wealthy, well-connected father and the title that's gotten me everything I've ever (or *never*) wanted usually pisses people off.

Somehow, knowing she doesn't expect an explanation makes it easier to offer one. I set my takeaway tray on the curb and sigh, balling my fists and pressing my elbows into my knees.

"Did anyone ever tell you why my mom and I went to America?"

Ivy eats another fry. "No. I don't think so."

That's no shock. Only a handful of people know the real reason. I swallow the wad in my throat and stare unseeingly across the dark street.

"I was only two, so I don't remember it. But my mom told me she had to leave for me. That my father wasn't a nice man and hadn't been nice to her. She married him because they were scent-matched. She thought she could withstand all of his bullshit, because she loved him. But when he started slapping *me* around, she couldn't take it. So we left."

Ivy's scent has burned to ash by the time I find it in me to go on. "He had a lot of influence here, so we went to America, which is where I grew up. I knew I'd have to come back eventually—he didn't have any other heirs, and by default, that made me the next duke."

Shame swells in my stomach, recalling the way I secretly *wanted* to return. After a decade, my mother's stories about my father's cruelty faded into background noise. And I was a teenage idiot—one who wanted all the money and power my name could give me.

I never expected my mom to *die*.

Or to be sent back here to *live* with *him*.

As I say the words, I feel Ivy's sharp, shaky inhale. My Alpha doesn't know whether he should purr or rage. He doesn't like me upsetting his mate. But he wants her closeness now more than ever.

Her comfort and goodness... she's everything we're not.

Especially right now.

"My mom wasn't exaggerating," I remember, growling slightly. "She said he was a cruel bastard... if anything, she down-played just how bad he was. And I was a perfect target, of course. Powerless and stupid. Plus, he always had a built-in excuse, because I sucked at being a duke pretty much the same way I suck at being a prince."

She starts to swell up slightly, ready to rush my defense, but I shoot her a wry look. "It's okay," I assure. "I do it on purpose, mostly. Once I realized I'd never live up to my father's standards, I went out of my way to piss him off. The tattoos, the smoking, the drinking, and sleeping around. If I had to be the Duke of McAffry, I wanted to make damn sure that title became a *joke*."

And, fuck, I *suffered* for it. The first time I came home with a tattoo, he beat me so hard, I couldn't see my ink for a week. It just blended into the bruises.

I flex my right hand, remembering. Staring at the tattoo I have there for my mom.

Ivy's pale, unmarked fingers stroke the barbed curves. Her observation floats through my mind. *This flower has more thorns than petals.*

I'm not sure anyone could sum me up better than that.

"I still didn't like the fact that he'd gotten what he wanted—an heir. Another *alpha* to pass his title to," I admit. "When he sent me away to boarding school and I met Asher and Bast... I came up with a solution."

Sadness salts Ivy's sweetness and fills her sparkling eyes. "You decided to join their pack and become a *prince* instead."

Hearing her say the words... for the first time, it occurs to me that they're *hurtful*. To Asher.

I used him. His name, his title.

And if Ivy figured it out in five seconds, he must know it, too. Probably has from the very start, the brilliant bastard that he is.

Why didn't he call me out?

Why didn't I ever apologize? Or at least explain?

I sigh, deflating. "Yeah. The laws of succession in Crenmore force any titled alphas who officially join the royal pack to give up their original titles when they bond."

Ivy still isn't judging me. I don't know how; I'm judging the fuck out of myself.

Especially when she peeps, "So... if we bond..."

Fuck, my heart. It *aches*. "Yeah," I husk again. "If we bond, I won't be a duke anymore. I'll be a Crown Prince."

Ivy's face is as pale as her nod is solemn. "And then a king."

A stone sinks into my center. "Yes."

She stares at me for a long moment, then nods again slowly.

Now she knows just how much I've fucked this up. If she thought my self-imposed celibacy was only a punishment for the way I treated her at the manor...

It's always been more than that.

Because, really, I'm not just using Asher, am I?

Ivy sets her food aside and ducks her head. "I think I'm ready to go h—"

But she doesn't have a home. We took her away from that. Brought her here, where she doesn't fit in. And, God willing, never will.

I don't want her to change. The thought is fucking agony.

"—back to the palace," she finally fumbles. "Please?"

I agree, unable to blame her. I've lost my appetite, too.

thirty-five

BAST & IVY (NO GRUMPS ALLOWED)

BAST

On my way to get you, love

IVY

Oh thank goodness

Queen Selene brought knotting diagrams today

I've been bright red for an hour

BAST

Diagrams, hmm?

I might need to review those...

IVY

Oh, and Jasmine said I should ask you what "queening" is?

??

Bast?

BAST

Sorry, angel.

Had to stop and remember how to breathe for a second

IVY

Is queening… something bad?

BAST

Oh no.

Not at all.

But, actually, I think we should let Asher explain that one.

Ivy's laughter has become my very favorite sound.

She giggles as I stagger behind her, keeping my hands over her eyes while I lead her through the garden at the back of the palace. As she mentioned the other day when she looked out her suite's window—the hedges look more like a maze than a pretty place to grow beautiful things. Nothing like the wilder, softer gardens she loved at Maytown Manor.

Which got me thinking…

"How much farther?" she asks, breathless from all her squeals and laughter.

I nuzzle the back of her head. "Excuse me, this is *my* official gift for *my* omega. I'll take as long as I like."

Another giggle bubbles into the late-afternoon summer sunshine. "It only took you three days to find it," she argues. "How official could it be?"

I growl softly, nipping at her exposed shoulder. Running my hands over the sides of her pastel-blue day dress. Wondering, idly, if I should have asked her to change into trousers for this... or at least checked to make sure she's found her underwear.

Judging from the thick, buttery sweetness filling the air, I'd guess maybe not. The thought—along with the perfection of her perfume—has me hard as a rock when I stumble us to a halt.

"Okay, here we are."

Nerves simmer in my stomach. I pull my hands away, watching her blink against the golden light and take in the creature waiting for us.

My latest acquisition.

Riding horses has always been a hobby of mine—but I love the beautiful animals almost as much as I enjoy putting them through their paces.

Unlike most of the horses in our palace stables, the white filly covered in silvery speckles isn't a thoroughbred. When I bought her a couple of months ago, I didn't understand why I was so drawn to the sweet creature, aside from her unusual markings and calm temperament.

Now, I know. She's *perfect* for Ivy.

Our omega looks and smells much happier today than she did earlier this week. Her resilience puts a pinch in my lungs—admiration and adoration and some guilt, too. I wish I could make all of this easier for her. Maybe the rest of my gift will help.

Ivy gasps as her eyes land on her horse. "Oh, Bast, she's *gorgeous*. Is she yours? Or Asher's? I can't picture Dair riding a horse."

I smirk at the image, shaking my head while I wrap an arm around her waist. "No, angel. She's *yours*."

Wide crystal eyes beam up at me as her mouth drops open. "M-mine?"

I nod, smiling wider. "She's a very sweet, pretty girl. I figured you two would get along."

True joy lights Ivy's beautiful features. "Really?" she squeals. "I get to take care of her?"

I can't help but pull her closer. Of course my angel wants to care for her horse on her own. I never expected anything different. "As much as you wish, love."

Kissing her temple, I murmur the rest of my reasoning. "I want you to have a friend to visit with. In case there are days I'm not here, and you need to talk."

Softness melds into her gaze. She stretches up and brushes her mouth against mine. "You truly are Prince Charming, you know that?"

I grin against her lips, setting my hands on her hips and aligning our bodies. "Only for you, angel."

I did my best to prove as much when I whisked her out of the queen's clutches earlier. Princess Ahmad was also there—which panicked me for a moment. Just weeks ago, Ivy had to watch me rush off to tea with the future empress; I worried that might make my sweet omega feel intimidated or unsure.

But Ivy's subtle confidence surprised me. She came right to my side, accepting the scent-mark I left along her cheek with a glowing blush.

I still got her out of there as quickly as I could. The other princess' scent used to be mildly tolerable, but now? I could barely stand to inhale it without my Alpha snarling in disgust.

He only wants Ivy.

And so do I.

Our princess drifts closer to her speckle-flanked filly. As I suspected, the horse is perfectly docile while Ivy gently offers a hand for her to sniff before smoothing her other palm over the silver-white mane.

"She looks like a star," Ivy whispers with wonder while the creature lowers her muzzle and looks right into Ivy's eyes.

"Asher told us you love wishing on stars," I tease, stepping into her back. "Maybe we ought to name her after a constellation. We can brainstorm while we ride."

Ivy casts a suspicious look over her shoulder. "Ride?"

I gesture at the brand-new saddle I picked out for her—a deep, rich navy, perfect for my angel's cool-blonde beauty and her filly's silver-white hair.

Ivy bites her bottom lip. "I don't know how to ride..." Her eyes darken as they take on a mischievous quality. "*...my lord.*"

God help me. How am I supposed to sit in a saddle with a boner?

"I can teach you," I murmur, dropping my face to skim my lips along her unmarked throat. Rubbing my cock against her soft backside with intent. "From what I recall, you're a natural."

IVY MOST DEFINITELY DID *NOT* FIND ANY PANTIES THIS week.

I bask in her bare skin as I settle her onto the saddle and arrange her limbs. She squeaks when the sun-warmed leather presses between her thighs. I bite back a grin, swinging up into the spot behind her.

I'm really not in any position to tease her. She might be pantiless, but I'm the one nudging an erection against the small of her back.

Ivy doesn't mind, snuggling into my embrace and handing me the reins. I go over a few basics—showing her how to balance and how I use my heels to signal different speeds to her mount. Within a few minutes, we're trotting away from Everdeen.

My omega laughs and glows the whole way across the property. She alternates between complimenting me on my handling and telling her horse how lovely she is. I might be crazy, but I swear the filly seems to understand her praise, holding her head higher by the time I bring us to a halt near the willow trees clustered at the edge of our lake.

I tie the silver-white beauty to a low branch before lifting my blonde one down to the ground. Ivy grins, patting the horse's flank.

"Andromeda," she announces. "That's her name. Andi for short."

It's perfect. Our omega has a knack for naming all her creatures. Calling me "my lord." And shortening the prince's name to "Ash."

I wonder what she calls Dair.

Probably not "dickhead" like Asher and I do.

Whatever it is, it's having quite the effect on His Grumpiness. Last night, he slept in the hallway outside her room. Didn't say a word about it, either. No complaining or bitching to try to get her to let him into the suite—or her bed.

Nope. The Duke of McAffry just helped himself to a slice of hardwood. I found him there this morning after sleeping with my face in Ivy's hair and waking early enough to lay out a dress for her.

When I caught him, he didn't put up a fuss or act like an ass about it. Instead, he growled a terse "good morning" and stalked off to get Ivy's breakfast.

I'd call him a simp, but, uh...

"Bast!" Ivy stops short between two groups of swaying trees. "This is *beautiful*."

I suppose I *may* have gone a bit overboard on the picnic. We probably don't need *eighteen* pillows. Or a solar-powered champagne fridge. Or *three* duvets—

Not to mention the food. Dair pointed out her eating habits, so I didn't include any meat, but there's tons of fruit, various cheeses and breads, spiced nuts, little lemon cakes, chocolate-covered strawberries...

I lead her over to the arrangement, falling to the cushions and reaching up to pull her on top of me. Ivy shrieks with laughter—a high, musical sound I can't help but echo with a bass harmony.

Her legs part, resting over mine while she tucks her face into my throat, leaving the last of her chuckles against my skin. Moving with her feels as natural as breathing—without thought, my hand finds the back of her head, stroking her scalp as I shift under her weight, leaning back to give her more space.

For perhaps the first time I can recall, I don't feel I need to say anything. Most people expect me to be "on" all the time. Lord Sebastian Burns, the life of the party. The one who smooths ruffled feathers and always has something witty to say.

Ivy isn't expecting small talk or jokes, though. As she snuggles closer, sliding her arms around my torso, she just wants *this*. Affection. Intimacy. A moment of connection.

With me.

It's so sweet, I almost forget my *actual* gift for her.

Until it makes itself known with a chorus of *quack*s.

Ivy and I both turn to the lake as a family of ducklings paddle toward the shore. Their mama leads them away just as quickly, not trusting us or our setup.

My omega turns an accusatory look at me. "Asher said there weren't any animals on the property other than the horses!"

I can't help but grin, shrugging. "But you love animals."

Understanding lights her crystal irises. "So you—you brought these ducks here? As like..."

"Your gift." I nod. "I found a wildlife rescue and rehabilitation center and offered our grounds for healed animals in need of a new home. This morning, they brought a couple of duck families they had saved from a polluted pond. A hawk with only one eye. A few owls. And a *bunch* of squirrels."

Too many, actually. But whatever. We won't tell Asher.

Ivy blinks, turning back to the pond. Across the water, two geese glide around some lily pads.

Oh yeah. "Forgot about those. I figured this might go down better with the prince if one of the animals is an ode to his nickname for you. But it seemed mean to only get *one* goose and leave it all by itself. They mate for life, you know, so I thought—"

My angel tackles me with a kiss, pressing her softness into the planes of my body. I hum against her lips, gathering her closer.

"Thank you," she breathes, tears clinging to her voice. "Thank you, Bast."

Hugging her with all my strength, I brush a kiss over her temple. "My pleasure, love."

It truly is. Surprising her is the most fun I've had in months.

Her tastes play a big part in that. Turns out, buying perfume and pearls isn't nearly as much fun as choosing duck families.

It's almost ironic how little she cares for wealth or glamour. The dress she's wearing cost thousands of dollars, but I doubt she even knows. She has her first public event tomorrow, and the clothes for that are even more expensive—but when I showed her the ensemble this morning, she simply beamed up at me and thanked me for my help.

My *help*—not the Chanel dress or its matching $10,000 purse. She barely even *looked* at those. But the fact that I went out of my way to take time selecting them... *that* made her smile.

I honestly don't know who's luckier to have *her* for a princess —our pack or our country.

Now, we just need her to believe that.

I frame her face with my hands, brushing her bangs and loose waves back so I can look her in the eye. "How are you, love? Feeling ready for tomorrow?"

Her first outing as a potential princess is a big deal. None of us have lied to her by downplaying it, but I can tell Asher and Dair are miserable about the whole thing. Our prince thinks forcing her into this role is the height of selfishness; while the duke detests these events in general. I suspect putting Ivy in the path of paparazzi and rooms full of strangers is only adding to his usual angst.

Our omega tilts her head back to look me in the eye. Her fingertips dance along the patch of grass beside us as she bites her lip, thinking.

"I don't want to let you all down," she finally whispers. "Especially Asher. I know he thought I couldn't do this... back then... What if he's right, Bast?"

I'm starting to think this is one of the reasons finding an omega means creating bonds between alphas. Because in this moment? I could strangle our pack leader. It would be convenient to be able to send him a mental middle finger.

Or, you know, show him her face and tell him he needs to sort shit out with our girl.

Punching him is still very much an option, too...

"Asher's dad clearly thinks I can't do this," she goes on, her hushed voice full of hurt. "And his mother was telling me about the public bonding ceremony and designing a new crest and making *heirs*—"

Oh fuck. Did I just start purring when she mentioned *babies*? *Shit.*

The rumble behind my sternum cuts her off. She blinks at it and swings her wide-eyed stare up to my face. A slight wince creases her brow.

I fumble for an explanation, blurting out an overshare, "I... don't have any siblings, and I hated it. Playing by myself all the time, going to big events and boarding schools alone. I've wanted a big family of my own ever since I was a kid."

Ivy listens with the purest sort of empathy, her whole face softening. "I used to wish I had siblings, too. And a bigger family," she whispers back. A dash of fear streaks through her sky-blue irises. "I just never imagined *needing* to have children. To... *produce heirs.*"

I can't deny the thought of making a small army of pretty blonde babies with my angel appeals to me on a cellular level. But I would never want her to do anything she wasn't one hundred percent comfortable with.

And besides, having her here? Making her happy? If the rest of my days end like this, I'll be perfectly happy with no heirs at all.

"It's whatever *you* want, love," I vow, impressing my certainty into every word. "You're our center. Whatever you decide is right for us is all that matters. That goes for everything. Babies, the bonding ceremony. *You* decide."

Ivy bites her lower lip again. "Y-you guys won't be disappointed? You promise?"

Her pained features pinch my heart. I draw in a deep breath, cupping her cheek in my palm as I frown back at her, keeping my face entirely solemn as I raise my other hand and offer my smallest finger. "Pinky promise."

It works—she cracks the loveliest smile, laughing quietly as she wraps her little finger around mine. "Okay then. I guess... I'll try my best to figure all this out."

Our connected hands fall to my abdomen as a less urgent sort of uncertainty winds into her scent. My purr kicks up a notch as I stare at her, considering.

Jokes and charm are my comfort zone—she usually likes that, but maybe she needs sincerity right now.

"I know this place is intimidating," I murmur, stroking a thumb over her cheek. "And the expectations of possibly becoming a queen are... a lot. But, Ivy, we don't want you to feel like you have to be anything other than yourself to be ours. Because you're *exquisite* exactly as you are."

Her eyes glimmer. "Bast..."

It hurts to watch her tears spill over, but I keep staring into her, hoping to prove how fucking sure I am. "Your heart is a thing of *beauty*, Ivy. If that means we have a queen who talks to ducks, we'll all be better for it."

I can see how much she *wants* to believe me. The teeth pressed into her bottom lip bear down, blanching the peachy curve. "When I decided to come here with you guys, I thought I would do everything I could to make myself the sort of omega everyone expects for the princes' pack... but it's been a week and I don't think that will work. I can wear the right clothes and learn correct etiquette from the queen, but I can't change who *I am*, Bast."

I bend to press my mouth over hers, freeing that abused lower lip. "That's my whole point, angel. The fact that you can't change who you are? Might just make us the luckiest men on the planet."

thirty-six

Look, I know I spout a lot of bullshit.

But if anyone lays a hand on my omega, there will be *blood*.

Our Maybach rolls to a stop at the front of The Crown's latest pet project—a hospital of some kind. I sneer up at all eight stories of blue glass and modern architecture, hating the whole damn building on principle.

"Is everyone familiar with the plan?"

Asher tugs his sleeves as he speaks, scowling down at the cuffs of his tweed suit jacket. I refused to wear one, opting to cover my white button-down with a black vest and nothing else.

Half my shirt is untucked. Bast glowers at it, but knows better than to complain. They're lucky I even have a damn collar on.

Our prettiest packmate is wearing some insane white blazer, of course. Along with a navy shirt and trousers to match the Burns family crest emblazoned on the suit's left breast.

It's sort of insane that he won't be able to wear stuff like that anymore, if we bond with Ivy and become a real pack. Giving up my name won't be a sacrifice for me, but it will be for Lord Sebastian Burns.

I wonder how Ivy feels about her name. I know it was her father's, the alpha who died when she was young. And her mother's, by extension. She might not want to part with it...

I eye her across the back of the limo, raking my gaze over her elegant outfit. It's a cream suit—feminine and fitted, with pink trim and a blush ruffle along the skirt's hem. Her hair is as lovely as ever, the cool-blonde waves styled with pearl-encrusted combs.

She's *gorgeous*.

And *terrified*.

The scent of her stress has been turning my stomach since we attempted breakfast two hours ago. I was lucky I got my coffee down, especially after she announced she was "full" after two bites of a waffle and half a cup of tea.

Asher might hate this shit as much as I do. He's been all frowns and bitter bergamot, holding her body against his like he's absorbing the last of her.

He might be.

There's a chance she'll run screaming from all of this before the day is done.

I know, deep down, Asher's been dreading this moment. Thrusting his beloved girl into the limelight. Subjecting her to scrutiny and ridicule. Forcing her to fit into our box... or fail him.

Bast is the only one in the car who doesn't seem nauseous. He sits forward with a clap. "Show off our gorgeous girl to these fine photographers, head inside so Asher can cut a giant ribbon, then go upstairs for a formal tour of the pediatric wing."

He winks at Ivy. "Easy peasy, angel."

If only.

Smothering a growl, I flex my fingers in and out of balled fists. "We don't have to go in, Ivy." I bore my gaze into hers. "Seriously. I'll leave with you."

Asher cuts me a severe look. "Of course *you* will."

I guess because he doesn't have any choice about being here. And I'm normally the first one to break from the team. Still, the bastard has some nerve to criticize me when *he's* the one putting our omega through this whole mess.

I start to snarl, but Ivy catches my eye again, shaking her head. "P-please don't fight. I—My—" She presses a dainty hand over her middle as her voice drops to a hush. "She hates it."

Well. Fuck.

That shuts us all up.

Ivy is still coming to terms with her Omega and her body's needs. Given how bad her health anxiety must be when we're about to walk into a hospital... and all these rabid reporters outside...

Swallowing, Ivy's light eyes scan the tinted glass behind me, absorbing the crowd of media leeches waiting for us. With a slight nod, she drops her gaze and answers Asher's earlier inquiry, "It's a good plan, Ash."

Asher sighs, abandoning our argument to brush a kiss over Ivy's knuckles. "You don't have to do anything but be yourself," he vows, staring hard over his glasses. "And tell us immediately if you feel overwhelmed or want to leave."

As soon as he has her agreement, Asher heaves out a deep breath. I watch him slam a mask of indifference over his features, going from the guy we know to the man the world sees when they turn on the news.

He raps twice on the door. It promptly flies open, revealing a raucous rabble of paparazzi and flashing cameras.

Bast turns on the charm, visibly pasting a grin onto his face before stepping out first. I hear him managing some of the rowdier photographers with a few well-placed barbs. Always charming and likable—even when he's telling people to back the fuck off.

Asher goes next, squeezing Ivy's knee before sliding out of the car. I catch our omega's wide eyes from across the backseat, silently offering to bust her out of here one final time.

Her fear shatters into exasperation as she huffs, "Can't you use that evil mind for good? Just the once?"

I shrug. "Best I can do is inappropriate flirting. Maybe a little light recon if someone seems shady."

She's adorable when she pouts. Even more so when she wags a finger at me. "*Behave*, Stalker."

Which is how, for the first time ever, I find myself *smiling* when I slouch out of a damn limo.

It takes Ivy twenty minutes to put me to shame.

She's just... *enchanting*.

Her glowing little smile, the honest shyness in her eyes. The way she makes a point to stop and shake hands with every person who steps up to meet her—including about fifteen nurses, ten doctors, and a few janitors to boot.

She asks questions, too. Following along as the president of the board gives his tour, pausing to inquire about everything from new equipment to how they fund community outreach projects.

All sorts of shit that probably should have occurred to me.

Okay. Shit that *has* occurred to me, but I've chosen to ignore.

Just like I'm choosing to ignore the way one doctor is staring at my omega's chest. Because we may be in a hospital, but strangling someone half to death would probably still be frowned upon.

The sweet woman slanting her bright blue gaze up at me definitely wouldn't approve.

I bend close so no one will overhear me. "All good, baby?"

She nods absently, her brows furrowing as she glances at the pamphlet someone handed her. It's their philanthropy bullshit—details on how much healthcare and aid they give away to communities in need.

"I was just wondering," she murmurs back, casting a nervous look at Bast and Asher as they charge ahead of us, locked in a conversation about an upcoming insurance initiative in Parliament. "Are there any rules about how much private hospitals are required to write off?"

She's too smart for me, I swear. It takes a moment for me to follow her train of thought. "As in...?"

"Like, a certain percentage of their profits, maybe? Because I researched this hospital group before today, and the figures in the pamphlet *look* like a lot of money... but it's really less than one percent of their profits."

She's earnestly confused. Thinking she's made a mistake. When, in reality, I have a sinking feeling she's *exactly* right.

And no, I don't think there is a rule to ensure places like this aren't hoarding profits and turning away those who can't pay.

Which is fucked up, considering how many people need decent healthcare and can't afford it.

People... like my mate.

If she had come to a place like this instead of whatever shitty public clinic she had to use, would she have discovered her designation at the proper time? Might she have been spared from accidentally suppressing her hormones and harming her Omega?

Would we have found her sooner? Before I had the chance to hurt her?

And—for that matter—why the hell is our government-funded low-income medicine so crap anyway?

Can't we do better?

Why haven't I ever tried?

thirty-seven

"ARE YOU *REALLY* A PRINCESS?"

It's the question I've dreaded all day, delivered in the most adorable way possible.

The little boy squinting up at me can't be more than four years old. Or perhaps a bit older, since he's missing his front teeth. It's hard to tell, up on this floor of the hospital—most of these poor kids aren't as hardy as they should be because they're battling chronic illnesses.

Though pale and partially toothless, this kid is undeniably precious. With messy brown hair, round glasses, and a dubious expression that reminds me of Asher when he was young. Always a scientist at heart.

The boy looks at me the same way the prince used to. Like I'm a riddle of some sort.

I can't help but smile down at him, casting my gaze around the sixth-floor's nurses' station to make sure no one is watching me. Our tour ended moments ago and the guys were instantly swept into a conversation with a few board members, as well as the mayor.

I've already met everyone and posed for the photos we needed. As nervous as I was, that part wound up being fairly easy. A smile, a well-placed nod. Some handshakes.

It's *this* sort of thing that daunts me—being left to my own devices and having to act... *royal*. Whatever that means.

When I see that even Dair is frowning in concentration, absorbed in their conversation, I lower myself into a crouch to put the boy and me at eye level.

"No," I confess, taking in his earnest surprise and biting back a chuckle. "I'm *not* a princess. I'm just Ivy."

It feels good to say it out loud. Offering him my hand, I'm overjoyed when he shakes it, looking relieved. "I *knew* you weren't really a princess. That's just *crazy*."

He isn't wrong. All this media attention. The security. My overpriced clothes and the three royals who have kept an eye on me the *whole* time they've worked...the fact that I'm somehow doing okay? I think?

I have to giggle, nodding my agreement. "It *would* be crazy, right?"

"Mmhmm," he agrees. "My name is Piper, and my sister is Gemma. She's in the playroom—do you want to see the tower we're making?"

"I—" My heart lurches at the hope shining all over his pasty face. *When's the last time this little guy got to go outside? Or just... run?*

Chest aching, I glance over to the princes again. Surely, no one will notice if I play with building blocks for two minutes...

"I'd love to," I finally finish. "Lead the way."

Piper practically jumps, whirling into motion. I follow with another quiet laugh, pleasantly surprised when the floor's playroom is only a few steps from the central hub.

Inside, rainbow colors reflect the midday sun from a large picture window. A couple of nurses hover over various patients, checking vitals and adjusting IVs while the children play like this is any other day. For them, I suppose it is.

The pain in my chest carves deeper. I do my best to smile around it as Piper tugs at my hem, paying no mind to the skirt's price tag... which I've been doing my best to forget.

Oh well. If he didn't mess it up, I'm sure I would have eventually.

"Gemma, look!"

Piper pulls me over to a low table surrounded by pint-sized chairs. There's a blonde curly-haired toddler in one and a woman a bit older than me in another. She must be a parent—her clothes seem rumpled, and her face looks drawn with exhaustion.

When she looks up from the papers clutched in her left hand, her mouth immediately falls open.

Oops.

I forgot people know my face now.

"Gemma," Piper starts again, ignoring his mom to focus on his sister. "This is Ivy. She wants to see our tower."

The little girl blinks up at me, then over to her stack of magnetic tiles. With utter solemnity, she points and repeats, "Tow-a."

I laugh some more. "It's lovely!"

My voice seems to snap the woman out of her stupor. She immediately straightens, her face horrified as she hisses, "Piper! What are you doing? This is—"

Nervous that others will overhear and look up from their own playtime, I offer my hand without thought. "Just Ivy, please," I beg. "And I hope you don't mind; Piper and I met in the hallway. He wanted me to see his tower."

Embarrassment stains her cheeks, but Piper whispers loudly at her, "*Mama*—she was all *alone*. She needed a *friend*. You told me to invite new friends to play when they're all alone!"

"Well, yes," his mother answers, "but, Piper—"

I call upon years of experience with being a mere mortal surrounded by royalty, remembering how much more at ease I felt when Bast would put himself on my level. I point to an empty chair. "May I, ma'am?"

She jerks upright again, nodding fervently. "Oh dear! Yes! Of course! I—I'm sorry, Your—"

"Ivy," I repeat, smiling as I lower myself into the seat. The woman starts frantically gathering the pages spread out in front of her, adding them to those in her hand. In her haste, she accidentally flashes the document my way. I wince when I see the lines of itemized charges, amounting to one grand total.

I have visceral memories of receiving statements like these. The phantom sensation gores into my stomach while I watch her hide them in her purse.

It takes more effort than I expect to find a new smile, but I manage for Piper and Gemma's sake. Within minutes, they have me stacking tiles with them, building a new tower. Showing me, in Piper's words, "where a real princess would live."

I'm giggling, listening to his confused version of the Princess and the Frog, when the woman sitting much too still across from me suddenly leaps to her feet. "Your Highness!"

Uh-oh.

I repress a guilty cringe, knowing I'll find Asher behind me when I turn around.

It's worse than that, though.

The doorway clearly frames *all three* of my alphas. And the board. And *two* photographers.

Figs.

I stand automatically, barely stopping myself from launching into a bow of my own. My Omega squirms, searching the room for any trace of their disapproval or anger.

But they seem... happy?

Bast grins widely, leaning against the doorjamb like he could hang out and watch all day long. Asher stands beside him with a softer smile and a certain glow in his gaze. And Dair...

He's there, right behind them both. Staring so intensely, tingles shiver down my back.

The prince reaches a hand out to me. "There you are, darling. Making some new friends?"

Relieved and grateful for his lifeline, I step toward him and place my fingers in his. "Yes! This is Piper and his sister Gemma. Piper, Gemma, this is Prince Asher Everhart."

Piper peers up at Ash with the same narrow-eyed wariness he gave me. "Are you *really* a prince?"

Asher's brows bounce high, but Bast and I can't contain our laughter. The baron moves to stand at my other side, sliding his arm around my waist. "I'm afraid he is, little guy. Makes things *dreadfully* dull for the rest of us."

To my delight, Asher chuckles. "That's true, I suppose."

Never one to leave a stone unturned, Bast soon knows the name of every person in the room. While he puts Piper's mother at ease with a few well-placed jokes, I turn to Asher and Dair, looking back and forth between them.

"I... think I have a question."

Ash brings my hand to his lips, kissing the back of it reverently. A camera flashes, but I barely notice with his eyes so soft on mine. "Anything."

I lower my voice so no one will hear. "That account you gave me... can I use it to help other people? Do I have to spend it on myself?"

Dair's brows snap together. "Why? What do you want to do?"

I touch the lump sitting low in my throat, toying with the strand of pearls Bast clasped there this morning. "I'd like to help some of these families with their bills if I can. I used to worry about Mama's medical expenses endlessly. I can't imagine if I had to worry about a sick child, too. Or *children*."

Anxiety swarms my chest and flips my stomach. My scent burns. Asher's expression gets even more tender. He opens his mouth to console me—

But *Dair* answers, "I'll take care of it."

We both swivel to him, gaping. "W-what?"

Dair stares back at me, his gaze so unfathomably sincere, I have no choice but to believe every word he says. "These kids. Their bills. I'll make sure they're paid in full."

I blink. "Y-you will?"

Asher seems even more surprised. "Seriously?" he echoes. "I mean, we can do it, but we have a few other philanthropies on our docket this week, and I need to—"

Dair shakes his head. "No. I said *I'll* do it. You don't have to worry, Asher. I've got this one."

My dark-eyed alpha squeezes my free hand, tossing me a wink. "Excuse me, baby."

Asher and I watch him storm over to the board members, already barking a low string of orders. My prince looks absolutely stunned—and so does Bast when he ambles back over.

"Holy shit," he smirks. "It's a miracle."

thirty-eight

NO KNOTS ALLOWED (PRINCESSES ONLY)

JASMINE

Heard a rumor that *someone* convinced the heartless Duke of McAffry to find funding for a whole children's hospital?

That's some iconic pussy power, babe.

IVY

Did you honestly just type the words "pussy power"?

JASMINE

Did *you* honestly just fuck the monarchy into spending $52 million?

IVY

I mean…

Technically no?

JASMINE

So you're saying the duke's doing this without even getting laid?

Like I said.

Iconic.

An itch beats in my blood like its own separate pulse.

My shoulders twitch, tweaking higher. Outside, each raindrop that hits my study's window feels like an individual distraction.

The spreadsheets laid out in front of me are important. If for no other reason than because *Dair* made them. *Himself*.

Ever since Ivy blew us away during our first public appearance, he's been a man on a mission. Last night, after Bast and I purred Ivy to sleep, Dair spent thirty minutes pacing at the foot of the bed, whisper-shouting about how "terminally fucked" our healthcare system is.

He had a point. And when I asked him what he thought we should do, he tossed me a look that somehow managed to be indolent and determined at once.

"We change it," he'd said. *"Obviously."*

That's where he's been all day—meeting with some of The Crown's biggest financial supporters, trying to make good on his promise to our omega about getting the children's wing funded on his own.

I know Bast is supposed to be having dinner with her and keeping her company while I work, but I can't stop the tingling sensation that streaks up my spine every time Ivy's scent rises off my collar. I haven't seen my princess since breakfast, but I have a feeling the strength of her mark doesn't matter much. I'm pretty sure her scent would still be obvious to me, even if I wore this shirt into the downpour currently sweeping across Lyledon.

I'll have to get used to living on traces of her. It's been almost two weeks since we brought Ivy to the palace, and here I am: alone. At dinnertime. In my study. Working.

It's been this way most nights, which is actually pretty normal for us. The guys and I have never observed formal mealtimes together—and I usually work into the night.

Having Ivy here makes it depressing, though. I wish I could leave and go find her. Take her up into her nest and help her rearrange it for the millionth time. Hold her and kiss her. Maybe slide a bit closer to that line we haven't crossed yet.

Part of me loves the waiting. Rolling around until neither of us can breathe, then tucking her safely into my side. It feels right in the strangest way—exactly what we would have been doing as teenagers... if I hadn't been such an idiot.

Mornings have become our designated time for that. Bast leaps right up at dawn, off to work out and lay out our omega's clothes. Dair refuses to sleep inside the suite for some self-loathing reason he's only vaguely explained, so he usually slogs off to get some actual rest once we're awake and Ivy's fed. Leaving me to soak up a few precious moments with our mate before I have to get ready.

Sometimes, she lets me feed and dress her. The attention makes her a little skittish, but I plan to wear her down. There's no better way to start the day than making sure she's taken care of. I only wish I could end our evenings the same way.

We're all still adjusting, but our omega has settled into life here as seamlessly as I could have hoped. She spends her days under Maman's tutelage and has even made friends with Princess

Ahmad. If she's not with the ladies, we usually find her walking the grounds, tending to the menagerie Bast talked me into allowing.

After the press dubbed yesterday's outing an unmitigated success, I know Ivy also plans to visit a number of other charities next week. That's the sort of thing she loves; caring for others. The people and animals without anywhere else to go.

I should have known that would make her a fantastic future queen. The fact that I ever spent a moment doubting whether she could handle life as a royal shames me.

I woke up to dozens of articles heralding our mate as a "princess for the people." The photos of her playing with sick children are an internet sensation. It seems everyone loves her guileless kindness and her genuine desire to connect with others.

Which means I wasn't just wrong about her being a beta; I was also wrong about her ability to live with this role.

When I sent Ivy away, part of me did it to protect the girl I loved. She seemed so soft and innocent. I worried she'd be miserable in the face of all the pressures and injustices we manage. I thought joining me and taking on the power she never wanted would either crush her... or make her into a stranger.

I knew I'd never be able to live with myself either way.

But I was *wrong*. So wrong.

If yesterday proved anything, it's how Ivy being Ivy might just be exactly what my people need. A queen who understands their struggles and sits with them. Someone to empathize and take my hand and explain what needs to be done for those who can't help themselves.

And if the papers in front of me are any indication, she isn't just bolstering our subjects. She's helping *us*. Bringing our pack together; inspiring the best in everyone. Even Dair.

I hate myself for ever questioning her.

When I close my eyes, I can see Ivy's face in my bedroom at Maytown Manor. I can hear her broken sobs, repeating all the doubts I planted in her head ages ago.

God.

The apology I gave her wasn't even close to sufficient, but I still haven't found a way to talk to her the way I need to. Alone. With humility. And the right words.

If I'm honest, that last part is the real problem. Or, rather, the fact that I truly haven't had thirty damn minutes to myself since we got back.

I wanted to wait until my official gift for her was finished. But is that an excuse? Am I really just keeping myself busy to distract from feeling *sick to my core* about what I did to my mate?

I look down at the mounds of paper scattered over my desk and realize, *Maybe.*

Probably.

Outside, rain pelts the palace. Each droplet a reminder of another rainy afternoon. And all the mistakes I made that day.

Definitely.

I spin my leather desk chair, pivoting to face the arched window built into my study's stone wall. My eyes track the raindrops, watching them roll down the glass.

It's a proper storm. Not the weak, drizzly sort of weather we had the day I made the biggest mistake of my life and sent Ivy away. More of a true downpour. Like the afternoon I knew I was in love with her and gave our omega her first kiss.

She had always been a pretty girl, but that was the first time I realized she was *beautiful*, too. The way she tipped her face back and laughed into the rain. The water soaking into her white shirt, molding it to her body. Her graceful, spinning circles.

There wasn't a single ray of sunshine in the whole sky, but her face *glowed*. It took me years to figure out; all that light came from *her*.

The silver locket in my pocket feels a bit like a hot coal, burning a hole against my hip. Ever since I found it, I've carried it with me every single day. Unable to let go of the proof that my lost mate somehow, miraculously came back to me.

It's another thing I need to apologize for. I'm sure she's

missed her locket—if only since it appears to be the one piece of jewelry she owned before we brought her here. I need to return it, eventually. *I just want to make a slight addition first...*

A quiet knock taps at the thick oak office door. I sigh and toss my reading glasses onto the desk, rubbing my eyes.

I don't particularly want to deal with Holden and his chronic scowl. He's probably brought me a dinner tray, though.

"Yes?"

There's a long beat of hesitation, which isn't like the butler at all. I sit forward, frowning. *Is it my father?* He normally just barges wherever he pleases.

But, no. As the heavy door swings open, the scent of shortbread winds into the air.

Ivy.

She hovers on the threshold, biting her lip. Looking small and soft and lovely in a white summer dress. The garment is about as casual as her wardrobe allows—loose, billowing sleeves and long, floaty skirt, all thin cotton. I notice her feet are bare, and my mouth automatically quirks up.

She used to run around the manor without shoes on. I love that she feels comfortable enough to do that here.

Warmth expands in my lungs, coloring my voice. "Hello, darling. I was just thinking about you." Ivy's cheeks turn pink, but she hesitates. I frown. "Is everything okay?"

Our princess nods shyly, taking a few careful steps forward. "I brought you something," she peeps, holding up a brown paper bag. "Can I come in?"

Always. Forever. Anywhere.

"Of course you can," I tell her, impressing how much I mean my next statement with a steely beat of alpha determination. "You can come in here and any other room whenever you want. This is your home, too. I'm your alpha. You can always come to me."

Her scent sweetens, even as she blinks in shock. "But what if you're in a meeting, or negotiating a big treaty, or about to be on the news—"

"Doesn't matter." I shake my head, opening my arms in invitation.

Ivy doesn't even glance around at the pomp of my study. The carved bookcases and priceless art don't interest her. She comes right to me instead, sliding into my lap and setting her paper bag on the desk.

"You're my princess," I whisper. "You belong anywhere I am."

She clearly doesn't believe that. Or *can't*, probably. My voice drops lower, melding with the quiet purr in my chest. "If we were to bond, you'd always be with me. All the time." I feel my brows furrow. "Would you hate that?"

It's impossible to ignore the way apprehension fills her features any time the subject of bonding arises. I know she has doubts about being here—being ours—but we've never talked about this part. Now, I wonder how much she even knows about the process, given she grew up thinking she was a beta.

Ivy shakes her head slowly. "I actually think that would be my favorite part. Never feeling alone. Never..."

I trace the lines of her face with my gaze. "Never...?"

She swallows, pink sweeping over her cheeks. "Never losing you again."

Fuck.

Fuck.

My throat tightens, shame and devastation strangling me. I force myself to breathe around them, gazing into her while I vow, "That won't ever happen again. No matter what you decide."

The wariness lurking in her eyes carves deep gashes into my middle. *I* put that look there. And I'm going to take it—take the pain—because those are my crosses to bear. Not hers.

So I let her search my depths, looking for the insincerity she won't find. If I need to, I'll sit here and let her examine me for any traces of doubt every damn day.

"I do... have questions," she finally says. "About bonding."

My cock jerks as images fly through my mind. I barely manage not to shoot my groin an annoyed look, but Ivy scents my arousal and the answering irritation. Her soft pink mouth quirks into a cute smirk.

"I'm pretty clear on that part," she tells me, looking at my trousers. "Jasmine was fairly thorough with her explanation. Not that she would know from personal experience..."

There are few things I want to discuss less than another omega. Now that we have Ivy, I find it hard to remember that other women even *exist*. To me, they never really have. Even before I got Ivy back.

It was always, only her.

Wrapping my heart in ivy.

Sighing, I settle back and snuggle her in my lap. "Well, if you want us to bond, the whole thing is actually pretty simple. I'm the pack alpha, so I would bite you first. Then you could either get bites from the guys next or bite me back to complete our circuit. It works either way."

She nods, but the motion has a tight, breathless quality. Her voice squeaks slightly. "And you'll all be able to hear me? Inside?"

I nod into her crown, dropping a kiss there. "Yes. You'll hear us, too. But there are internal curtains for everyone. We'll each be able to close our sections of the bond if we ever need a break. And we will *all* understand if you need to do that sometimes, darling. Having three mates is a lot. We respect how much work that will be for you."

She slants a teasing look up at me. "Even Bast?"

Her wry tone has me chuckling. I can picture my packmate's exuberant ass pouting whenever she wants peace and quiet. Clearly, my mate knows him well.

"Yes, even Bast," I assure her, flexing a solid bit of dominance. "He doesn't have to *like* you taking time for yourself, but he *will* respect it."

Ivy's perfume swells, her lips falling halfway open on a quiet inhale. *Turned on*, I realize. She likes it when I flex my power.

And, God, I *want* her.

But I owe her a real apology first.

To distract myself, I look down at my desk. When I raise a brow at the paper bag she set there, Ivy smiles shyly. "Banana bread. I know it's your favorite."

Surprise and a thick wash of emotion fill my throat. "Is that why I suddenly started finding it on my breakfast tray when we moved into the manor? Were you having the cooks make it?"

She shakes her head, her easy expression revealing how oblivious she is to the way her next statement strikes me. "Oh. No. I made that at home and brought it in for you. But this time, I had to use the fancy kitchen, so it might taste a little—*mmmph.*"

A purr and a growl tangle in my lungs as I find her lips and part them with my tongue. Unable to stop myself.

It was the silliest, smallest thing. But those treats—which always seemed to appear on the days I woke up questioning how much longer I could hold myself together—were one of the only things I looked forward to.

Before I found *her* again.

Desperate regret and soul-deep gratitude suck all the air from my chest, leaving my heart a burning, sinking star. How will I ever tell her what she means to me? Will she truly stay and be mine? The way we were always meant to be?

Ivy giggles quietly and breaks our kiss, giving me an amused look. Relief bleeds through my chest as she cuddles close, rubbing her face against my collar. Marking me. I tighten my arms around her, brushing another kiss onto her crown and turning us back to face the window.

"I need to talk to you," I murmur, swallowing the lump in my gullet. "I've been meaning to for weeks."

Ivy's buttery sweetness darkens as she leans back to study my face. "Ash," she whispers. "You don't have to keep feeling guilty forever. You didn't *know*. None of us did."

I shake my head. "It doesn't matter. I shouldn't have *cared* either way. And I'll never forgive myself for hurting you. And for doubting you. For putting us in this situation where you'll always wonder if I only want you because of your designation."

Her full lips turn down as she places her cool fingers over my chest, spreading them against the tattoo hidden there. "I don't wonder about that," she whispers. "I—I always knew you only sent me away because you thought you had to, Ash."

But how is that possible? When I did everything I could to convince her—and *myself*—that I didn't love her or want her?

Ivy's crystal eyes shine as she reads the doubt in my expression. "No matter what," she adds, "I've always known *you*. I still do."

Her meaning hits like an arrow to my abdomen. Because I *believe* her. From the second we met, she's seen me in a way no one else can. And she remembers that pure, un-princely version.

All these years and everything I put her through. The mantle I've had to put on. The titles and duties and airs.

She still sees *me* in here. Underneath it all.

It will be the same for her, I realize. No matter where this takes us—if she's our queen, the mother of our children, producing heirs for an entire *kingdom*...

She will always be Ivy to me.

The girl spinning circles in the rain and wishing on stars.

Twined around my heart. Part of me.

Is it the same for her? If it is, I never want her to lose that version of me. I want her to keep him. Me. Forever.

My voice is hoarse when I finally manage, "Will you make sure I don't forget? Who I really am?"

Her gaze shimmers. "I'll remind you," she promises. "Every chance I get."

I have the same duty to her now. She might be our princess. My queen. But I want to make sure she gets to be Ivy, too.

Sudden inspiration strikes. I shove to my feet, holding her against my chest as she gasps a laugh. "Ash! What are you doing?"

I smile despite the ache at the very center of me, striding out of the study. "Taking you somewhere only you and I know."

thirty-nine

MOST PEOPLE WOULDN'T RECOGNIZE THIS MAN.

Storming through the corridors of his palace, holding a giggling woman as he charges toward the southern wing's exit. Ignoring the curious glances we garner—and outright *growling* at any disapproving glares.

They might find his power familiar. Or his serious expression.

But the version of Asher who gets to the double doors and simply strides into the storm?

That's *my* Asher.

I squeal as rain soaks us both, the downpour drenching our clothes within the space of ten steps. "Ash!"

He laughs, the sound a perfect blend of my masculine alpha and the playmate I used to adore. "Hold on to me," he directs. "We have a bit of a walk."

I cling to his neck, and he picks up speed, carting me toward the garden maze. I've walked past it a dozen times, always eyeing the hedges dubiously. They look like the sort of shadowy place that's made for getting lost, but Asher doesn't even pause. He winds through the walls of shrubbery so quickly, I'm breathless from laughter by the time he sets me on my feet.

Blinking rain out of my eyes, I peer into the mist shrouding the center of the maze. There are cobblestones on the ground, along with a marble structure that seems about three-fourths of the way finished. An archway, I realize.

Nearly identical to the alcoves carved into the side of Maytown Manor.

Where Asher and I used to hide.

And read.

And talk.

Where he kissed me for the first time.

When I whip my head around to face him, I know he's remembering precisely that moment. Hazel eyes flit to my lips before meeting my gaze. Waiting. Hoping I understand.

Did he... make us a hiding place?

"Asher," I say, barely able to inhale around the squeeze in my lungs. "What is this?"

"It isn't finished yet," he says instead of answering. "I had them start it as soon as you agreed to court us. I was going to wait to give it to you until it was done, but—"

I get it. This moment, the rain. It's *perfect.*

And he knew I would want him to give it to me now instead of waiting for it to be sunny. Because he knows *me.* Because he—

Asher looks right into my eyes, ignoring the raindrops falling from his brows. "I love you, Ivy."

The words sink into my center. He says them again, closer. Our lips brush as he presses his forehead against mine. "I have loved you since the day I met you. And I think you may be the only person in the world who's ever known me well enough to love me back. So, even though I don't deserve it, I hope, one day, you will."

Pain burns in his golden eyes as I shake my head, the motion slow. I swallow hard. "That won't happen," I whisper. "Because I already love you. I never—I never stopped, Ash."

My prince stares at me for a long second, his chest rattling on a series of ragged pants. All his hesitation and overthinking are reduced to a sliver between breaths. His gaze burns brighter, hands snapping out to grip my nape and tug my hips flush to his body.

His mouth devours mine, kissing deeper and harder than he ever has before. Backing me into the partial cover of the unfinished arch. The place we'll have if we want to hide together.

My heart feels like it's bursting through a cage I didn't even know I was trapped in. Pure joy and adoration and need flow from the cracks. A shiver streaks down my spine and into my core, hot slick slips into my panties as cool rain pelts my back.

Asher growls with all the might of a true alpha, but his next gasp sounds desperate. His hands soften and smooth over my body, his lips chasing mine with a dizzy sort of desire that matches the need smoldering between my hips.

Lost. My prince is lost. In *me*.

Something in my center clicks. My Omega nudges me. *Now*.

I pull back long enough to catch the love and lust blurring his irises. Our gazes snap together, years falling away. Washed clean by the rain.

"Take me to our nest."

forty

By the time Asher bursts into the Omega Suite, my fingertips ache from clinging to him instead of tearing his clothes off the way I want to. He sets me down before the doors even swing shut, as intent on undressing me as I am to strip him.

My Omega pokes at me, but I can't register anything other than the way Asher's hands feel as they glide up my sides, lifting my sopping dress to my breasts before whipping the whole thing off. It hits the marble floor with a wet *thwack*.

His soggy shirt follows, then his pants. Until I'm shivering in my panties and he's completely nude.

We've been undressed around one another before, but never

like this. Never alone. With *intent.* And time for me to fully *appreciate* him.

My mouth falls open, eyes roaming to absorb the cut perfection of his tall, lean form. All pale muscles and burning eyes. And one tattoo.

His heart... wrapped in ivy.

I whine at the sight of it, practically leaping into his arms. He hauls me off my feet, stringing kisses along my cold skin, burying his face against my shoulder.

He turns for the stairs to the nest. My insides somersault.

My Omega seems completely set on having her alpha in her nest. She seems to have forgotten that I have no idea what I'm doing.

What if I mess this up somehow? What if the tests are wrong and he doesn't fit? Or if the tests were right, but I'm malformed, somehow, and I can't—

Asher feels me shaking and hugs me closer. "Are you sure?" he murmurs. "There's no rush, Ivy. I can put you in your nest and spend the rest of the night with my head between your legs. We don't have to do anything... new."

His meaning is so obvious, a blush scalds my cheeks. So far, Asher and I haven't done anything outside of him getting me off. Dair has exiled himself from my bed. And Bast has had me a dozen times, but he insisted on saving this for Asher, knowing I've never taken a knot.

Jasmine said I would know when I was ready, which seemed trite... until this moment. Because she's right—I *know* this is the right time.

My alpha seems to know, too. He reads my pause and answers with a bone-melting purr. His teeth slowly scrape at the side of my throat like he's marking his spot. Slick slips out of my bare pussy.

"We'll take our time," he promises. "I want to be in you all night. As long as you're sure."

I cling tighter, unable to put into words what I feel so keenly.

It *needs* to be Asher. It has to be *now*. For my Omega, but also for me.

"Okay, darling," he soothes, quelling the desperate sound scaling my throat. "I'm here. I have you."

He rounds the landing at the top of the carved stairway. I hold my breath, remembering the last time we came up here. The shining glass, the thin gossamer curtains, and thicker, powder-blue ones.

It's different this time. For one, the shades are drawn, enclosing the circular platform in a bubble of icy velvet. They're clearly high-end blackout drapes—and they work perfectly. The only light in the nest spills through cracks between the panels.

Asher pulls one of the shades aside and steps into the darkened cave. Our rumple of perfectly scented sheets are still piled on the round, recessed mattress, the walls I built entirely untouched. The pillows have moved, though.

That strikes me as odd for a few seconds—*none of us have been back up here, right?*—before I'm distracted.

The tart freshness of Dair and Bast's warm, rich toffee hit me hard enough to steal my breath. A knowing chuckle warms Asher's expression as he picks his way over my carefully arranged blankets and takes me to the stack of silky cushions where their scents are the strongest.

He lowers me with enough care to bring tears to my eyes. Diffused light fills the planes of his body, highlighting how tall and strong he is while he kneels between my legs.

The erection straining toward me is just as impressive—but nowhere near as mind-boggling as the thick swell at its base. Growing wider and fuller by the second.

Oh Lord.

How am I going to—

My prince smiles fondly, cupping a hand around my cheek. "It will fit," he promises, eyes molten with want and tenderness. "My queen."

Heart bursting, I reach for his forearms and pull him over me.

Some foreign feeling snags in my throat. When I try to breathe around it, the tiniest omega purr escapes.

He groans softly, lowering his face to nuzzle the noise. Looking so vulnerable in his bliss.

"I don't need to be your queen," I whisper, wanting him to understand. "I just want to be your..."

Mate? Partner? Best friend?

Sincerity fills his features as he bends to skim his nose along mine. "Everything," he finishes, settling his weight between my thighs. "You're everything, Ivy."

Asher's mouth melds into mine as he moves, carefully pressing the full length of hard heat along my pussy. Gently shifting his hips until the swollen head rubs at the top of my clit and I gasp.

"There you are," he whispers, scent-marking my forehead. His arm stretches alongside my head, his hand finding my damp bangs and sifting them back. "I'm going to go slowly. Enjoy every second of you."

I nod, the motion a bit too fast to be casual. His stern lips crack into another smile. "Not too slowly," he adds, casting a heated look at my breasts. Then lower, to where he slides his cock against my spread lips. Not teasing, the way Bast would—but genuinely wanting me to feel every inch. Showing me how *he* feels.

Scorching. Long and wide. With that knot swelling more on every roll of his hips.

He isn't like Dair, either. There's no demand—no edge of impatience. Asher moves like he's treasuring every single moment, skimming his hands along my curves, panting as he watches my reactions to each little action.

We kiss until the nest swirls into a dizzy blur, and a puddle of slick pools under me, dripping from my slit and his pulsing knot. Even then, when he starts to lose control, Asher only hangs his head against my shoulder and breathes through his lust, exhaling rough praises into my collarbone.

"Jesus, Ivy, you're so beautiful."

"Good omega. I can feel your pussy getting ready for me."

"Sweet darling, slicking our nest. Such a perfect girl."

My fingernails scrabble against his broad back, marking the rain-cooled skin. He takes my lips with a serrated groan. His arms bundle me closer, and he lowers his body over mine. Every hard line melts against my soft smallness.

Hips churning, I wrap my legs over his thighs, squeezing. Asking without asking. Because even though I've done this part dozens of times with Bast, and I know Asher wants me as much as I want him, some part of me will always be the starstruck sixteen-year-old who can't quite believe he would ever *want me.*

Asher reads my face and hums, the sound a soft reassurance. "I'm right here." He rubs his nose over mine in the sweetest gesture. Hazel eyes burn with entreaty. "Can I have you, now?"

He doesn't need to ask again, but this is Asher. He probably knows, somehow, that hearing him beg helps raze the last of the self-doubt rooted in my belly. The thorny weed curls into dust as he shudders through another plea. "Please, darling?"

The moment feels *cosmic.* Like the second Asher's body lines up to push into mine, every star aligns, too.

The feel of the silky blue sheets cocooning us, the gold swaths of light streaming over my prince. My friend and first love and tormentor.

And, now, just... mine.

Ours.

Because as his cock gently presses past the muscles clamped at my core, my Omega writhes. Elated and relieved and finally *whole.* He's her missing piece. Or she's his.

Maybe both.

I blink up at his face. The handsome, regal features set in fierce lines, green-gold eyes glowing with emotion. He pushes all the way into me, pausing with the throbbing heat of his knot pulsing against my pussy's opening. Letting me feel it—or perhaps just giving me a final chance to prepare.

It doesn't help. Couldn't help. Because nothing on Earth could possibly ready me for how it feels when he bears down, seamlessly popping his body into its rightful place.

The world splits into strands. Sensation, sound, color, feelings. Fullness, pressing into every screaming nerve sizzling in the slick muscles of my center. A bellowing alpha roar, climbing up to the canopy with a high-pitched omega keen. Blue and gold, swallowed by a sudden burst of sparkling white.

How can I feel so complete and so *desperate* at the same time?

How can I possibly have *everything* and need *more*?

"Ivy," Asher snarls into my throat, working his hips in shallow circles and sudden, scorching plunges. Stretching me, rubbing each aching tingle as his cock carves so *deep*, I swear I feel it low in my belly. "*Goddamn it.* You're *perfect*."

That last word is nearly a sob; one I mimic when he tilts his hips and somehow manages to hit the bottom of my clit. Just barely grazing it.

A sharp rush of pleasure impales the tension pulling at my depths, unraveling it. I thrash and shriek, almost *afraid* of how good this feels.

Asher growls, eyes flashing darker as he presses his knot into a spot that vibrates for more, giving my body the perfect counterpoint for its clutching. The tender muscles sing, slick gushing from my slit as I tip over the edge and fall.

"Fuck, Ivy. *Yes*." Asher bucks and groans, finding the side of my neck with his teeth as his cock erupts. Thick washes of molten cum glaze the deepest parts of me, his warmth somehow soothing the tingling spasms echoing there. Melting them into a sort of euphoria I've never felt before.

I try to inhale, but air catches on the lump in my throat as fresh tears dribble down to my temples.

Asher huddles over me, his body locked within mine. He licks at the indentations his near-bite left behind, whispering, "Shh, my love. I know. I'm here."

He is. Sealed with me.

Mine.

He somehow hears the thought, gathering me into his arms and turning us onto our sides. I cuddle against his broad chest, my cheek rubbing over his tattoo. “Yes,” he agrees. “Only, always yours.”

forty-one

BAST

How long do you think we have to wait until we go into the nest?

DAIR

They've been up there for like 12 hours

Fuck it. She needs to eat.

Bringing breakfast.

BAST

Brilliant excuse you glorious bastard

I’ve never been more grateful for a Sunday morning.

Sleeping under the nest? Listening to Asher pleasure our princess all night? Inhaling her perfect perfume and maybe—*accidentally*—jacking off three or four times?

Torture.

If I had to wake up and run off to accomplish anything, I’d be in misery.

This is better, though.

“Don’t *touch* that.”

It’s Dair, hissing and glaring at me from across the nest. He’s never whispered at me before, which makes the fact that he’s bent out of shape about me touching a specific blanket even more hilarious.

I pinch the soft silver silk and hold it up. “This?”

“Yes,” he snaps, leaving our breakfast tray on the lip of the recessed mattress so he can snatch the fabric out of my hands. “It’s her favorite.”

My eyes widen. I glance over at Ivy—or, rather, what little I can see of her at the moment. Asher is still knotted, his front pressed to her back, his limbs and a fluffy duvet wrapped around her body. Covering everything apart from the side of her face and her dainty feet.

“When did she tell you that?” I ask, carefully sitting back

against the low wall of blankets our omega created. "Did you two sneak back up here at some point?"

Dair glowers at me like that's some sort of absurd impossibility. As if he didn't steal her off into the night last week.

That was over a week ago, though, and I haven't really seen him touch her since. My gaze narrows. "Dair... what did you do?"

Rage flits through his dark eyes. "The fuck are you implying? You think I would *hurt* our omega?"

He has a point. Of the three of us, he's proven the most zealous about her safety. I thought he would have a coronary the day I took her for her first riding lesson and she almost fell off Andromeda. He must have laid into me for a full half-hour afterward.

I reach over and snag a grape from our platter, chewing thoughtfully. "So... you won't sleep in bed with her or, you know, fuck her... but you somehow know which blanket is her favorite? And you're telling me nothing weird happened?"

Dair grumbles an insult under his breath, but doesn't give me the death glare I expect. Instead, he keeps his eyes trained on his tattooed hands, flexing his fingers. "Fuck off," he says without heat.

I keep watching him, waiting for a real answer. When our eyes finally meet, he sighs. "Fine. We went out and talked and... I don't know. I'm trying to figure out how to make this up to her. The way I treated her. All my other bullshit."

He shifts, bending his right leg so the erection tenting his joggers is a little less obvious. "It's not that I don't want her. Obviously. It's that I don't fucking *deserve* her, and I can't figure out a way to fix that."

I can't exactly argue with him. Looking over at Ivy, it strikes me that no one could ever possibly *deserve* her. She's too good and kind and beautiful. I understand why Dair feels particularly unworthy, though, given how he acted in Maytown.

"She'd probably like it if you slept in the bed with us," I mumble, careful to keep my tone casual. "It's not like Asher and I are willing to share her, anyway. You can sleep on the other side of me or something."

A grimace of true pain splits his drawn features. "Not a good idea," he mutters. "Trust me. I still have—" He cuts himself off with a shake of his head and changes direction. "I wouldn't be able to control myself. I'm barely doing it now, and our pack leader is still *locked inside her*."

Asher looses a low snarl. "Would you two *shut up*? Ivy and I didn't sleep at all."

I can vouch for that. Still, it's ironic. Just a month ago, Dair was the one trying to sleep in after a night of non-stop fucking. And Asher was the one dragging his sorry ass out of bed.

"Oh, how the tables have turned," I chuckle, lightly kicking our alpha's leg. "Get up and share, *Your Highness*. Our omega needs to eat something. Regain her strength."

My jab is ironic. Because, at the moment? I've never seen Asher look *less* like a prince.

He shoots me an irritated glance and sighs, turning to nuzzle at Ivy's nape. "Good morning, goose." The arm at her waist tightens. "How do you feel?"

Ivy stretches, moaning quietly before snuggling back into his embrace. "Ash," she hums sleepily. "Mm. You're so warm."

God, the way he *smiles*. I've never seen him so *happy*. Is that what I look like these days?

It's how I feel. Even now, watching my angel gaze over her shoulder and kiss Asher... I've never been more content.

The harsh lines on Dair's face soften, too. Without a word, he twists to grab the breakfast tray, setting it on its ornate silver feet in the center of the nest.

For a dickhead with an attitude problem, he definitely knows how to put together a decent spread—omelets, fruit, scones, tea *and* coffee. I wonder how many times he's done this in the past.

Ivy seems to have the same thought. Her eyes are shy as they skirt up to Dair's face and down to the food. The last of his anger dissipates, leaving only exhausted defeat.

His lip quirks up in a bleak half-smile. "Hope it's up to your standards, little dove. I've never done breakfast in bed before."

That dulls the salty edge of her scent. She swallows, dragging the duvet up to the base of her throat. "It's great. Thank you."

She slants a much more spirited look at me. "And you, *my lord*."

I grin, lunging forward to steal a kiss. Asher growls low, but Ivy giggles, leaning back to beam at me. "They're so grumpy," she stage-whispers.

Laughing, I brush our lips together, relishing her sweetness with a low purr. "Thank God we're here."

Asher's dominance swells, knocking me back to my prior position. I smile crookedly at him. "This is fun. You're usually impossible to goad."

The prince pulls our omega straight into his lap, dropping his face to her neck. He clamps his teeth over her shoulder for a long second, inhaling deeply before kissing one of a dozen love bites littering her neck. "Sorry," he murmurs to her.

With a brief glance in my direction, he adds, "You too, Bast. I'm... ah..."

I shrug, plucking a bowl of berries from our tray. "You're the pack alpha buried in our omega for the first time. I think you've been shockingly polite. The first time I knot her, I'll probably bite your hand off if you try to touch her."

Ivy's cheeks flush peachy pink as her perfume sweeps into the air. My canines ache, but I keep smiling as Asher curses, hiding his face in the crook of her neck. Beside me, Dair twitches into utter stillness, his scent sharpening.

The duke's voice comes out wooden and a little too rough. "Eat," he demands, nearly barking as he snaps up an omelet and sets the plate in her lap.

Asher and I give him matching glares, but Ivy's features melt slightly. She picks up a fork, nodding. "Yes, alpha. Thank you; I'm really hungry."

That knocks the blade off Dair's essence, but he still seems stiff to me. Instead of pressing him, I grab my own plate of eggs and potatoes, tossing Asher a shit-eating grin. "Want me to feed you, Your Highness?"

He actually laughs that time. "They're *jealous*," he tells Ivy. "Can't say I blame them."

Our omega shakes her head, silently scolding each of us. I notice she's downed half of her plate in two minutes and bite back another grin. Clearly, going at it all night is a good way to get her to stop eating like a damn bird. We're going to need to stock up on snacks for her heat.

If she's staying...

At this moment, with all of us in her nest? It feels impossible that she could ever *leave*.

She belongs here. With us.

Ours.

How the hell do we *show* her that?

Dair is mildly appeased by her healthy appetite. Still scowling, he shovels down his breakfast, eyes flickering to the half-moons branded along her bare skin.

Yeah, those are hot.

I'm not wearing any pants, but if I were, they'd be uncomfortable.

Ivy smirks at the bulge pressing into my boxers. "You must really like omelets."

Asher chokes, and Dair snorts, both sounds every bit as funny as her joke. A loud laugh bubbles out of me. I shake my head in mock disapproval. "Such a naughty princess."

Asher's eyes turn adoring as he regards the side of her face. "Mm," he muses, giving me a wry look. "*My* princess is perfectly behaved. You must be a bad influence."

The conspiratorial wink Ivy sends my way is everything. I grin broadly, knowing I must appear just as lovesick as our prince.

Because I definitely am. Ever since our picnic, it's been killing me to keep the words in. To avoid giving her any more obligations to us than she already has.

"I don't know..." I tease, narrowing my gaze. "I think we should show the prince how you *usually* behave for me. Maybe put him in his place."

Asher sips from his tea, scoffing. "*Excuse* me?"

Ivy catches my eye, her expression pinking. "Bast!"

I shrug. "I told you, angel. The prince should really be the one who explains 'queening.'"

Dair's head falls back on a plaintive groan. "Oh my *God*. Are you guys trying to *kill* me?"

Our pack alpha's hazel eyes gleam, examining the mortification staining our omega's cheeks... and probably taking stock of the way she squirms over him, too.

"If my princess needs a lesson," he decides, "*I'll* be the one to teach it."

Dair's mouth drops open as the prince works Ivy free from his half-full knot. She squeaks as he lifts her onto her knees and abruptly moves to put his face under her leaking pussy, guiding her hands to balance on his abdomen. I hand the breakfast tray to Dair, who turns and sets it outside the nest, his dark eyes never leaving our mate's thighs, spread over our pack alpha's face.

"This," he murmurs darkly, "Is queening. Riding our faces until you get off. Any way you want."

Sugared perfume blooms into the air as Ivy's legs tremble. "But I-I'll—you—Ash, don't you want me to shower first or—"

His snarl is just feral enough to silence her doubts. Instead of answering, he grips her hips and tugs her straight down onto his open mouth. The growl morphs into a groan as a mixture of his cum and her slick gushes over his working jaw.

Ivy cries out, her blunt nails scraping at his abs. The scent of bergamot spikes in the air, the bitter citrus a perfect complement to the golden sweetness seeping from her slit. Our omega's pupils blow when she senses the combination, a whine eeking out of her as her hazy gaze flies to the way my cock has hardened—so stiff it's poking out of the bottom of my boxers.

I scramble to my knees, shucking the tight navy fabric in one shove. Dair starts to protest, likely wanting Ivy to be the center of attention, but her next whimper cuts him off… especially when she reaches one hand toward him, silently begging.

The duke pants, gripping himself through his sweats with white-knuckle force. "Fuck, baby," he roughs out. "Don't look at me like that. You know my rule."

Asher hums, delving his tongue deeper. The stimulation has our girl keening, her eyes flashing with need. "Please, alpha," she begs. "I want to taste you."

Oh fuck.

Dair might be a crazy bastard, but even he isn't insane or masochistic enough to turn *that* down. His dark eyes trace her desperate expression, softening with tenderness. "Are you sure? You know I don't deserve one goddamn thing from you."

Asher's next moan is quieter and almost pained. As if he's somehow agreeing while he has his face between her legs.

These fuckers, I swear.

No game.

I stroke my fist over my cock, shooting Ivy a brief conspiratorial look before casting Dair a glower. "Either you take our princess' generous offer, or I will."

Ivy *licks her lips—Jeeeeesus*—and… yep. That does it.

Dair snaps forward, settling his knees on either side of Asher's left leg, pushing at his black joggers until his cock bobs out. He's so hard, it carves a slightly curved line all the way past his navel.

Delicious *greed* lights Ivy's eyes. He sees it and snaps his hand out, cupping her jaw with his tattooed fingers. Meeting her eyes with the sort of indolent lust that only he can pull off.

"You want to taste my cum, little dove?"

A breathy, beseeching noise catches in her throat just before he fills it, giving her exactly what she wants in one punishing stroke. Her eyes fly wide, and his crease slightly, the expression pained.

"Sorry. I told you I was rough, baby," he mutters. "But I'll—"

And—honest to God—she *bites* him.

Not hard. Not *much*. But enough to immediately cut off his apology and leave two little nips at the top of his swelling knot.

If he could hear me, I'd tell him, *Insulting a queen while she's on her throne. Not smart.*

Before I can say it out loud, Dair growls. The serrated sound rattles the nest's glass walls, but feral delight glimmers in his black eyes. Ivy doubles down, working her slick pussy against Asher's mouth faster while she hollows her cheeks around the duke's girth, refusing to drop her gaze from his.

Pride swarms my chest. She really does know how to handle each of us perfectly. Effortlessly.

Like she was always meant to be at the center of this.

As if sensing my thought, Ivy puts her left hand back on Asher's abs, balancing on it so she can reach up with the right and run a teasing finger along the bottom of my shaft.

Fuck. Yes.

My cock jumps toward her, aching for the squeeze of her dainty fingers. When she retreats to dip her hand between her legs, bringing a slick palm back to my member, I almost come right then and there.

That juices Asher's knot, too. His hips buck as he hardens, coming back to life in a series of hard jerks. Ivy's eyes snag on the rigid jut of his erection, a whine echoing through her chest.

Goddamn it, she's so hot. Wanting all of us. Needing to get us off together. Not having enough hands to get all the cock she wants at once.

Desperate need simmers in her irises when she suddenly pulls back far enough to speak around the veins throbbing up Dair's length. "Please, my lord," she pants, glancing at Asher's groin. "*Please.*"

Well, fuck.

What did I say about insulting a queen on her throne?

Asher's ragged groan confirms the prince is down for *anything* his princess desires. And if she wants to watch one of her alphas jack another off?

It's a good thing I'm so coordinated.

Spreading my legs slightly for balance, I manage to keep myself inside Ivy's hot little hand while I wrap mine around her prince. He's still glossy from spending the night inside her. I use that to my advantage, immediately going hard.

Asher muffles his shout against her pussy, lapping at her clit. Ivy takes Dair back into her mouth, but her eyes never leave mine. Shining with gratitude and affection that put a hoarse lump in my throat.

"So beautiful and good for us," I praise, my free hand stroking her hair. "So fucking perfect."

"Yes," Dair agrees, pumping his cock between her lips faster. His head drops back. "Ivy, God. *Yes*. Just like that."

Ivy suddenly wails, her body jolting as Dair fills her mouth. Slick bursts from her pussy as Asher sucks her clit, dousing his face. The sight has my own balls drawing tight, my hand working his knot harder and faster and—

"Fuuuuuuuuck."

We both explode in a round of simultaneous volleys, jets of cum covering Ivy's chest, her hand her arm. My hand, Asher's stomach, his thighs, the nest around us.

Holyyyy shit.

It smells like a fucking *miracle* in here. All of us blurred together—golden sugar, dark crisp cranberry, bitter bergamot, and bubbling, melted toffee. Dair takes two breaths and basically collapses, falling onto the nearest pile of cushions with a breathless moan. Asher finishes devouring every last drop of our omega's sweetness before following suit, sloughing out a satisfied sigh as he relaxes, his eyes falling shut.

I pull Ivy into my arms, kissing her deeply. Tasting Asher and Dair and not caring one bit because it's her. Us. Our pack. Our mate.

The way she nuzzles her face into my neck speaks of the deepest adoration. I sit back against the edge of her nest, petting her hair and purring for her. The others start their own rumbles, until the whole nest is a muddle of blissed-out vibrations and the best scents imaginable.

If I weren't already madly in love with her, I would be a second later when Ivy flicks a sly look at her two incapacitated alphas and then smirks at me. "They seem less grumpy now, huh?"

forty-two

"You have *got* to be joking."

Jasmine's face looks a lot less appealing when she's scowling. Over the last couple of weeks, I've started taking a perverse sort of pleasure in that fact.

Whenever the princess scrunches her nose in disapproval or glowers at me like I've lost my mind... well, at least she's just a little less beautiful?

It's more than that, though. Ever since the afternoon Asher claimed me, I've felt different. Changed. But also more like myself than ever before.

As unfit as it might make me, I'm beginning to believe the guys truly want me to be myself. Sometimes, it even seems like they *need* that.

One thing at a time, I coach internally, remembering the advice my mother used to give me. *When you don't know what to do, just do the next right thing*.

Being a queen? Ruling a country? Maybe not. But this? Choosing a space for the pack's "official sitting room"? Simple enough... right?

A flutter of warmth tingles in my belly as I turn and look around the derelict drawing room. I nod once, certain. "Yep. This is it."

Queen Selene glides forward with a serene smile. The wide legs of her blush suit pants float around her legs, sending a new flurry of dust motes drifting into the golden air.

Jasmine's disapproval isn't so shocking. This room hasn't been used for *quite* some time. As in, centuries. But that feels fitting, somehow.

Asher, Bast, and Dair will be the first *group* to ascend to the throne in generations. Even without me, they stand a chance to become the first bonded pack to rule Crenmore in *two hundred years...*

During one of our many lessons on the Everhart lineage and the history of Everdeen Palace, Selene explained that the princes' wing is actually the oldest. Designed specifically for a pack of rulers instead of a single monarch.

There's even a separate *throne room* on the first floor, shrouded in tarps—designed with enough space for four or five thrones instead of two.

This particular parlor is just down the hall from the Omega Suite. A cozy pocket with a wall of windows that matches the one in my room.

It's clear no one has used it in eons. If the dancing dust particles swarming the air weren't enough of a clue, the decor would be a dead giveaway. Half the room is missing furniture, but the pieces left behind are clearly decades, if not centuries, old.

I turn in a semi-circle, clapping my hands excitedly. "It's perfect, I think. Just the right size. And I love that chair."

I point to a particularly elegant chaise lounge upholstered with an ice-blue damask pattern. Queen Selene nods, exuding pure approval as she sets a hand on my shoulder. "If this is the room you feel is right to host your private engagements, then this is the room we will use! I'll get the maids in here this afternoon."

My stomach twists. "I can clean it up. Really. There's no need to—"

Jasmine shoots me an exasperated look. "Ivy. Not *this* again."

Selene casts our guest a soft, quelling glance. "It must be hard," she says to me. "Going from being the one called to tidy up after us to feeling like you're making someone else do it."

In truth, it's been one of the more difficult parts of this change. I expected to hate dressing up, but Bast has made that a fun bonding activity for us. And I thought for sure I would *mortify* Asher in public, but he's only proven, time and again, that my natural instincts and reactions are precious to him.

And Dair...

I have a feeling he would personally *gut* anyone who made me feel out of place. The first few times the butler sniffed at me, the duke snarled so viciously I thought we'd be calling the maids in to mop up actual *blood*.

Which would have been a lot worse than dusting off old pieces of furniture and shaking out some drapes.

I know, on some level, that the Everharts pay their staff very well and treat them graciously. Everyone I've encountered since arriving at Everdeen likes working here. They consider it an honor and remark regularly on what fine leaders Asher and his father are.

Even back at Maytown Manor—everyone adored the royal family. They all liked their jobs and performed them happily.

I was the miserable one.

Gazing after Asher, wishing against all hope that he would

finally turn around and *see* me. Feeling my insides tweak from longing whenever Bast graced me with his perfect, dimpled grin.

Really, as employers, they were perfectly good to me.

It was His Grumpiness who made my job hell. Barking, snarling, scowling, sneering. And *staring*. Always. Burning those hot-coal irises into my profile at the most unexpected times.

Now I know he couldn't help it. I've forgiven him for not understanding—I didn't get it, either. I wish he would make amends with Asher for the reasons he originally joined their pack... but I hate that he's punishing himself by denying his Alpha's needs.

If anything, *I* should be the one suffering.

My body played tricks on us, not his.

Still, I would be lying if I said it didn't hurt to remember how cruel he was. All the women he paraded around. His mortifying errands.

I'm just not sure his self-imposed exile is *helping*. I almost feel worse about our situation now than I did when we got here, apart from what happened in the nest the other day.

So maybe more of the physical stuff would help bridge some of these gaps?

He has a hard time communicating with others, but he always tries to talk to me. The night he showed up at Aunt Matilda's... The time he stole me away on his bike... Swooping in at the hospital and taking on a *huge* project because of a mere *suggestion* I made.

He's *trying*.

But this avoidance... not touching me, sleeping apart from us... There may be some twisted nobility in it, but it feels like it would be too easy for this to become permanent.

Easier for *him*, even. To keep avoiding. Punishing himself. Feeling like he has no one because he doesn't deserve us.

Or maybe I'm just not enough to sufficiently tempt him.

The self-conscious thought dies when a sudden current of urgency snaps under my skin, drawing my spine straight.

Our alpha, my Omega interrupts, as if she's been listening to my train of thought for a long time and waiting for an opening. *We need to go to him.*

Jasmine notes my sudden rigidity. Her tweezed brows arch. "Hmm. I know that look."

Queen Selene frowns in consternation. "Yes, dearest, you've gone quite pale. Should I call for one of the doctors? *Mon petite amour* is in Lyledon at the opening of the new education center. I believe Sebastian is with him, but we can call—"

It's sweet of her to explain, but I know where the guys are at all times, these days. They take extra care to fill me in every morning, then send updates throughout the day. Never wanting me to feel alone, I suppose.

Bast is actually at a separate function by now. Something for a climate preservation philanthropy. He mumbled about it while choosing his tie, joking that he should probably wear green.

The memory of such a normal moment with one of my alphas settles my stomach a bit. *See?* I explain to my Omega. *Everything is fine. They were totally normal this morning.*

Ever since she got her strength back, the voice in my middle has developed a bit of an attitude. Or maybe she's just learning from Jasmine. If my Omega had a face, it feels like she would be giving me the same *c'mon, babe* look I'm getting from Princess Ahmad.

I fly back through the events of the morning, remembering. I woke up to Asher's mouth at my neck, making sure his hickey would live to see another day. Bast then jokingly snatched me off him and rolled on top of me.

They took turns "stealing" me from one another until Bast ended their scuffle by claiming me with his cock. I thought Ash would watch, but he wound up kissing his way down my body instead, then wrapped his tongue around my clit until I came all over his packmate. Three times.

All of that seemed... well, maybe not *normal*. But good. Not worrisome.

Asher fed me breakfast in his lap while I read him headlines from his three newspapers. I loved the way his eyebrows wrinkled behind his glasses while he listened, completely focused on my voice as he cut my veggie omelet into bite-sized pieces.

Then Bast and I got dressed, him joking and pausing to whine about how pretty I looked in today's jade sundress, pouting that he'd have to wait far too long to remove it. At which point, Asher chimed in with that no-nonsense, pack-alpha, world-leader, *literal-king* energy of his, simply stating that Bast had had his turn and the prince himself would be the one to undress me tonight.

See? I say again. *Nothing.*

But my Omega sends me another image. One of their faces when they realized Dair wasn't in his usual spot outside my door.

He's been sleeping out there for a week—but at least I finally convinced him to use a chair. Or, rather, I had Duncan put one across from the double doors in the hope my stubborn alpha would give in when no one was watching.

Some mornings, he's gone before any of us wake up. Others, he's waiting with our food. Sometimes, he leaves to get ready and comes back down to do a quick check-in before he disappears for the day.

None of those things happened this morning, though. He was just... gone.

And then... my Omega prompts, showing me another mental picture. One of Asher and Bast both bent over their phones. The prince scowling. Bast wincing.

They were just about to race off for their days, so I didn't press either of them about whatever diplomatic issue had gotten their attention. But there was a moment, right before he left, when Asher paused to cup my face in his hand.

He asked what my plans were for the day, confirmed that I wouldn't be "wandering upstairs," and left with Bast, the two of them arguing lowly while they clipped to the elevators.

It didn't register as anything to be concerned about at the

time. Clearly, it had nothing to do with me... and they've both been so attentive today. Checking on me *constantly*.

...maybe a little too much?

My eyes meet Jasmine's through the dusty air, her earlier sentiment echoing through both me and my Omega.

Uh oh.

forty-three

Since Asher asked me if I planned to "wander upstairs," that seems like as good a place to start as any.

After all, if Dair is *gone*... if he *left*...

My gut cramps as tears prick my eyes. It's been hard, pretending that his desire to maintain a certain distance doesn't feel exactly the same as rejection. I've done my best, but the idea that he would actually *leave* never crossed my mind.

Have I brought out the worst in him yet again?

Even if I have—this doesn't feel like the duke. Dairragh Vreeland doesn't *flee*. And he's faced a lot more pain than most people.

My Omega frantically urges me down the corridor on the top floor of the east wing. Plush, midnight-blue carpet sinks beneath my slight "training heels," as Jasmine calls them. I still have to focus to keep from wobbling when I walk, but the added speed from my anxiety seems to help.

I sail around the curve, peering at each door I pass. I haven't been in this part of the palace since my original tour. For the most part, the guys have made my space into *our* space, so there really wasn't a need to trudge up the stairs.

Besides, their rooms are nearly identical to the ones I spent months tidying at the manor. Bast's door hangs open. Asher's is closed, hiding walls of books. And the last one at the very end of the hall...

Has Duncan in front of it?

Um...

I was *not* expecting that.

The attendant is stationed there as if guarding the portal. As soon as I see him, I stop short, and he snaps to attention.

...blushing?

His balding head falls forward on a bow. "Your Highness."

"Ivy," I correct absentmindedly. "I was—I just came up to visit the duke. Is he... in?"

The air seems to crystallize around me. Duncan grimaces. "I'm afraid—I'm afraid His Grace is *indisposed* at the moment."

Indisposed?

I hear a growl and something squeaky. A bed frame, maybe?

Dread chills my middle. "Is he... alone?"

Could he be with someone else?

Jasmine warned me that many women are jockeying for position with these men. And apart from the time he gave in, Dair has been denying himself for almost a whole *month*. After the way he used to carry on before, that must be taking a toll...

Surprise slackens Duncan's features. "Of course he's alone, Princess. He's just—"

This time, there's a *roar*. One that sends a skitter down my back and slick dribbling into my panties.

Duncan pales, concluding, "—not himself."

Confused, I drift closer. Until a familiar scent *slams* into me.

It's cranberry and mint and everything I love... but so achingly *sharp*, it slices the breath right out of my body. I hiss, my teeth rattling as pure alpha *need* curls in my lungs.

A *rut*.

It has to be. Nothing else would possibly do *this*.

My Omega whines, desperate to get to our alpha. She wants to help him, but I also have the distinct sense she's scrambling. Clueless, just like me.

Figures. Just when I was starting to think maybe I could actually do this...

I clear my throat over a whine, looking at the poor beta attendant. "I suppose I ought to..." My head lolls toward the door. A twinge tightens my pussy at the same moment that a prick of apprehension stings my stomach.

Duncan winces. "I'm afraid not, Your Highness. His Grace is quite volatile in this state and—"

He continues, but I can't hear him over the memory of Asher murmuring to me this morning. Essentially warning me to stay away. And, obviously, *somebody* made this poor man stand guard out here.

"The others were worried he would hurt me?" I demand, throwing my hand on my hip in a gesture that betrays my Omega's outrage. Because, sure, she doesn't really *know* what to do—but how dare her alphas *imply* that?

Duncan stammers. I plant my feet, indignation flowing through me. "Did Asher and Bast make you promise to keep him *locked away*?"

Bless this man's heart. His eyes bulge so dramatically, it looks like they're trying to escape his skull. "No, Your Highness! No, of course not!"

Is he lying? If he is, I am going to call Asher right now and give him a piece of my mind.

Dair may not like that he needs me, but he *does*. And I'll be damned if anyone is going to *lock him up* over it.

I've never felt *rage* before. Vaguely, I wonder if this is what my duke experiences every time he loses his cool and orders people to stop touching me. Or threatens their lives because they already *have...*

All right, so he's a bit violent on a good day. And he's warned me that during sex, he can get... rough.

Perhaps the others reacting to his rut like this has something to do with *that*? But it still makes my blood boil.

They sent him up here to be imprisoned in his bedroom, alone?! As if he's some sort of beast! A literal monster they have to chain up and—

Duncan's panicked expression cracks. "It wasn't Prince Asher or Lord Burns," he blurts. "It was *him*. The duke himself. He... he is worried for your safety and asked me to make sure you didn't happen upon him."

Dair.

After everything his father put him through, all the violent punishments and confinement... my alpha locked *himself* in his room and gave someone else the key?

To keep me safe? Or was it actually because he didn't want me?

I think of his eyes, burning into mine from across any and every room.

And *I know*.

He's doing this *for me*.

But aren't ruts horribly painful for alphas without their omegas? Especially scent-matched ones. And no matter how much Dair may try to avoid it, *we are mates*.

As if agreeing with that unbearable thought, a pained groan echoes from behind the door. Steel spreads through my stomach and straightens my spine. "Duncan, open the door, please."

He freezes. "Y-Your Highness—"

"Duncan," I say again, insistent. "Please open the duke's door."

Our attendant visibly cringes, sputtering more denials. All the urgency buzzing in my middle suddenly snaps like lightning. A thundering crack that sends an unfamiliar voice swerving up my throat.

"*The door. Now.*"

Oh dear.

Was that a *bark*?

Jasmine told me omegas can make them, too, but usually only if one of their alphas or children are in danger. She also explained that they're actually more potent than alpha barks, because they work on alphas *and* betas. Instantly.

I guess she was right. Before I can sheepishly drop my chin and mumble out a "please," Duncan scrambles with the key and unlocks the door.

Dair's room goes suddenly, deafeningly silent.

I gather what little air I have left in my body and muster one more bark, even though the words tremble.

"Leave us."

Some vague part of my brain registers that I won't have to worry about Dair hiding in his own room anymore.

Because it's in *pieces*.

I don't see my alpha at all. Instead, my focus flickers over the carnage he's created while I attempt to get my bearings.

Torn curtains hang from a broken rod. A slumped mattress on a frame that's now missing a footboard. The hunk of polished wood got thrown against a wall, apparently, where it splintered and shattered a mirror into hundreds of razor-sharp shards.

Dair's scent—so sharp and *needy*—collides with me again. Slick instantly gushes from my body, perfume swelling off my chest as my nipples bead into tight points.

I gasp, staggering back a step. When glass crunches under my heel, my mind restarts.

Where is he? Is he hurt?

A low snarl comes as my answer. Nothing rabid or full of rage, like his earlier sounds. This is more like the noise a cornered animal would make.

I whip my head toward the bathroom and find him there, in the shadows of the unlit ensuite. My heart cracks.

He's fully nude, his tattoos mixed with reddened abrasions, scratch marks, and cuts. His dark hair hangs limply over his forehead, partially covering his eyes as he gnashes his teeth in a menacing expression.

I was right earlier when I thought he might be gone. Because, in a way, he is. If I'd gotten to him sooner, before the pain took over, I might have been able to help him keep a bit of lucidity.

Now, though? He's...

Feral.

I do my best to ignore the way his scent makes my entire body quiver, raising my hands as slowly and steadily as I can. Showing him my palms. "Dair? It's—it's just me."

He growls loud enough to rattle my teeth. I swallow an answering whine, trepidation taking root in my middle. *Oh God.*

"D-do you want to c-come out?"

Dair goes unnaturally still, until his head cocks to one side and his chin tilts up a bit. *Smelling the air*, I realize. Because, at this moment, he's basically an animal.

I'm not afraid of that. I've always had a particular love for damaged, lost creatures. My duke is no different—so where is this *fear* coming from?

When another whine tears up my throat, I trace it. Not into the pit of uncertainty teeming where my stomach should be... but much higher. To the ache in my chest.

Rejection.

He's not coming for me, my Omega whispers, heartbroken. *Why doesn't he want me? He's not supposed to be able to resist me when he's like this...*

Because that's what he's doing. Gripping the doorframe with all his might, chest heaving while he gouges track marks into the wood as if it's nothing more than soft clay.

He's holding himself off.

And it *hurts.*

I see it in the tense lines pulling at his vacant eyes. The desperate throb of his breath. And, lower... his cock is so hard, it's purple. Leaking fluid in a visible pool between his bloody feet.

I blink at the sight—dark wood floor, pale skin smeared with crimson, a thick puddle of white cum—and something inside me snaps.

But it isn't snapping in half. It's snapping *together.*

Pieces slotting themselves into an instinct that actually makes *sense.*

Run, it says. *Run fast.*

forty-four

I RUN.

So fast, my shoes fly off behind me, and I barely even notice. Fast enough to have my hair bouncing in a blur of blonde, my stomach cramping as I race down the last flight of stairs and make a hard left, flinging my body out of the stairwell and into the second floor's central corridor.

I can't hear anyone behind me, but that doesn't mean anything. At the moment, the only sound echoing in my ears is my own heartbeat.

Nest, nest, nest.

My Omega chants the directive. She might not know what the

hell we're doing, but that's the one thing she's certain of. The nest will be soft enough for our rutting alpha not to hurt himself any more... and if he isn't following the way she wants him to, she'll want to curl up there to *die*.

Are all Omegas a bit on the dramatic side, or is it just mine?

The doors to my suite are unlocked. I burst through them and do a quick scan, making sure there are no staffers innocently going about their business. Because if anyone saw Dair like this other than me...

Yep, my Omega says, *Death.*

She is *definitely* a drama queen.

Resounding silence greets me, but it doesn't last. Within seconds, a bone-shattering *roar* rips into the room.

Dair's body collides with mine before I can blink. Hard, sweaty muscle and flesh that's nearly too hot to touch. His frame jostles me just as his scent slices a burning path down my throat. I cry out, falling forward, but his arm hooks around my front, punching the air from my lungs.

When my shriek dies, the alpha rips me right off my feet, his hands frantic and much too rough as he flips me around.

Panic flares inside me. He's so strong and desperate—and there's not even a speck of the man I know in those bleary black eyes.

If I want him back, I'm going to have to be the one to bring him out of this. Maybe then he'll finally see how much I care about him. That I've forgiven him. And I can handle anything he throws at me.

Can I, though?

I have no idea what I'm *doing*. I've barely gotten used to regular sex and knotting, let alone a rutting alpha who will want to lock us together again and again...

He could really hurt me. *Or himself.*

It doesn't help that he's currently *strangling* me against his chest.

Staring into his unseeing eyes, I scrabble for something—

anything—I can *do*. Should I act seductive or try to find another bark? Maybe if I feign confidence...

But every time I've tried to be something I'm not, it ends horribly. That's how I started this whole mess, anyway, pretending to be Addison...

Being myself has been enough for Asher and Bast so far. Is it possible it will work for Dair, too?

If I show him how out of my depth I am, will it make matters better or worse?

And do I even have a choice?

I'm running out of air.

I manage a squeaky whine, letting fear show on my face. Dair's snarling features freeze, then crumple, his hold loosening.

Air fills my chest, sharpening my mind. I raise a shaking hand to touch the only place I can reach with his arms banded so tightly around me, grazing fingertips over his side.

"Hi," I whisper. "Hi, Dair."

The duke responds to my gentle touch with a ragged exhale. Pain pulls at his eyes again, his teeth flashing as one hand fists my dress.

"Shh," I soothe. "It must hurt so much, alpha. I'm so sorry. I didn't know, or I would have come to you sooner."

A choked growl scrapes up his throat as my second hand joins the first, both stroking down the sweat-misted planes of his lower back.

I lean forward to kiss his chest. "I'm here now, okay? I have no idea what to do, but I'm here, and you and I will figure it out together."

The moment my words register, I'm off my feet. Dair hauls me over his shoulder, his motions coarse, but not painful. Especially when I hear the rumble spring to life in his chest.

Purring.

It's deeper than the few times I've heard it before. More instinctual, perhaps. Not muted by any inhibitions.

The dull roar relaxes my body, leaving me limp as the alpha

carries me to the nearest surface. It's the bed, not the nest. But at least it's soft?

Before I can make any suggestions, Dair lowers me onto the fluffy blue duvet and tears my dress off. In one tug, both thin straps snap, and the green fabric goes flying behind him.

He doesn't hesitate at all, bending to rub his face all over my torso. Marking me with his sweat and scent, those tattooed hands flying to my hips and ripping my lace briefs to shreds.

Dair nips at my hip bone, and I gasp, realizing—*oh, he could bite me.*

"N-no," I quiver. "We can't do that, Dair. Anything else you want, but no biting."

He answers with another growl, though this one is a little more grumbly than his others. It reminds me of my grumpy, reluctant Stalker and all his mulishness. An involuntary smile twitches over my lips.

Amusement must do something to my scent because he groans. A deeply pained, masculine sound that sloughs out of his mouth as he crumbles to his knees, rubbing his lips along my mound.

When I perfume, he snaps out a snarl and dives between my thighs.

Oh!

The way Dair eats me is nothing like the skillful finesse he showed in the limo. This is raw, animalistic *need*. Teeth scraping at my pussy lips, tongue delving in shameless plunges. He's so focused on lapping up my slick, his full lips only hit my clit by accident—but when I cry out, he answers with a tortured moan and nuzzles his whole face into me.

I come more from his need—his hoarse growls and shaking fingers and his *scent*, oh *God*—than anything else. Slick coats his face and dribbles down to his chest. He rubs an absent hand over it, smearing my essence all over his torso, straight down to rub it on his cock.

Oh. My. GOD.

Satisfied, my alpha rises to his feet, panting down at me. His eyes are still empty, and that sends a slight pang to my heart, but there's barely time to feel it.

"*Present.*"

His bark flips my stomach, lurching me into motion. I start to move, but then I realize...

Oh no.

I taste the salt of my own scent as I shiver. Dair doesn't like it. His whole face pulls into a tighter, scarier expression. "*Present,*" he barks again.

I cringe into the covers, knowing he won't understand if I explain. I try anyway, unsure what else to do. "I—I don't know how to."

In all of our nights together, neither Bast nor Asher have ever asked me to present. It was such a non-issue, I forgot this is something omegas are supposed to do for their alphas. If I'd remembered, I could have asked Jasmine or one of the other guys to explain. Now it's too late.

The savage look on Dair's face melts into another pained expression. A shudder wracks his body, unclasping his hands from around my thighs.

For a horrible second, I think he'll walk away. But he slides his touch under my backside instead, maneuvering us to the middle of the mattress and then suddenly flipping me over.

Oof.

I sprawl face-down on the duvet, startled and on the verge of hopeless laughter. Until I feel him climb behind me, the burning skin of his thighs sliding against mine. He hooks an arm under my hips and yanks them upright, putting my ass on display. His free hand flies to the back of my neck and takes hold of my nape.

Rough indeed...

So why am I *gushing* slick?

Dair's throbbing hardness settles against my clutching pussy, the heat of it searing. I gasp, thinking he'll ram right in. Scared I've already ruined this because I'm so out of my depth.

But he doesn't shove inside. Instead, my alpha curls over my back and hides his face in my hair. "Omega," he moans, desperate and raspy. His fingers flex around my throat. "*Mine.*"

I nod, turning my face to his. "Yes," I agree, kissing his sharp cheekbone. "Yours."

I watch the word register, his blank eyes lighting. My heart lurches when I realize—*he's been waiting for permission*. For me to say "yes."

This sweet, wonderful man who has *no idea* he can even *be* sweet. Or wonderful.

I arch into him as he rumbles with a growly purr, canting his hips back and then forward. His cock pierces me in one long glide. My slick pussy grabs at it, tugging his thickness deeper.

Dair chokes and roars, balancing on his knees with one hand banded at my throat and the other gripping my hip, bruising in the most deliciously possessive way. I moan as he drives in and out of my body, his snarls fraying into ragged groans.

After hours of painful priming, it only takes moments for him to come. He sprays out a searing flood, his cum every bit as hot as his feverish skin when it lashes the deepest parts of me.

Another snarl tangles in his throat, tripping over his purr. As I start to turn and look at him, the strong fingers around my neck tighten. "More," he demands.

But the way he pants says something else: *Please. I need you.*

I reposition, moving back to the stance he tried to teach me through his haze. "Yes, al—"

Dair's hips kick back into motion before I even finish calling him 'alpha.' This time, he pounds me in fast, shallow plunges before shocking me into a second orgasm by gliding as deep as he can, popping his knot into place.

The wide, hot swell fills the slick muscles singing for more stretch. Weight and pressure press along my wet, tingling walls, sending them into a series of spasms that white out my vision.

Dair's breathing stutters. A pained moan splits the air as he comes again, somehow hotter and thicker than before.

"Ivy," he sobs, releasing his hold on my neck to fall against my back. Purring and panting. His voice both rough alpha and velvet gratitude. Half Dair and half the part he can't control. "*Omega.* Need you."

I find his tattooed hand sprawled next to mine. That wild bloom, covered in thorns. I lace our fingers, bringing them into the warmth of my body. Wishing he could hear me inside, even as I say the words out loud.

"You have me."

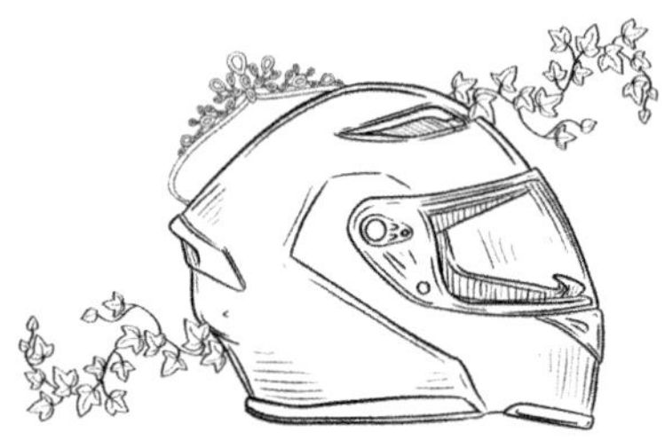

forty-five

When I blink and find my omega sprawled in front of me, my insides heave and twist.

Fuck.

Ivy is in a *heap.* Pale limbs littered with bruises and teeth marks. Thighs smeared with cum and slick.

Holy fuck, I'm a monster.

Her muscles tremble, even in sleep. At least, I *hope* she's asleep and not passed out, or—

"Ivy," I husk, my voice shredded. I shake her limp form, huddling into her back. Bending to bury my face into her shoulder and scent her.

She smells… good? Happy, actually. And *really* turned on…

When my cock twitches involuntarily, her slippery walls flutter around it.

I'm still inside her?

Because it wasn't enough for me to *rut her into next year*?!

Wincing, I slide from her body and haul my sorry ass out of the bed. Forcing myself to breathe, shoving both hands through my sweaty hair until I'm calm enough to hobble to her bathroom.

The soles of my feet definitely have a few cuts. I absorb the sting, wanting to feel it. Knowing I probably deserve way worse.

God knows what I did to her while I was out of my mind like that. I could've—she might've—

Washcloth, my Alpha grunts. *My omega needs attention.*

If I could reach in a strangle this bastard, I swear…

With a sigh, I flip the light switch in the bathroom on, pausing to look around. *This suite used to feel so dead.*

I came to look at it more often than I'd admit, but it never felt like more than a pretty shell. Now, with Ivy's baubles strewn over the cream marble countertop, her muddy boots from yesterday's afternoon walk with Bast sitting beside the tub…

I swallow a lump and start the faucet. As water splashes into the gold basin, memories come rushing back to me. The way I woke up this morning and instantly felt the rut creeping under my skin. How I tried to stay away, keep her from bearing the brunt of my need.

She found me anyway. And *ran*…

Goddamn it, I chased her down. Forced her to present. Rammed into her—

Fucking FUCK.

My limbs fill with lead as I run a white cloth under the hot water, thinking of all the hundreds of times I've hurt Ivy.

Snapping at her. Scaring her. Humiliating her with errands and other women, and now our first time together was this rough, terrifying *madness—*

With robotic movements, I scrub dried blood and sweat from

my hands, feet, and face. Ruining another pristine thing with my bullshit.

There's slick smeared on my skin, too, but I can't bring myself to wash it off yet. Instead, I bring a fresh rag out to the bedroom, carefully cleansing my scent from Ivy's pale skin, counting the bruises I left behind in my desperation.

Thank fuck she didn't get any cuts when she came into my room. It could have happened so easily. All that broken glass and splintered wood—

"I'm so fucking sorry," I whisper, pressure building in my throat with every half-breath. "Ivy, baby, I'm *so sorry.*"

Her face pinches, full, bitten lips frowning. She flops her hand out, feeling around blindly...

Until she finds mine.

There are more thorns on this flower than petals.

She takes my tattooed hand in hers and pulls it right to her face, nuzzling a sleepy scent-mark into my palm. Pleasurable tingles skate up my arm and fizzle through my chest. My thumb automatically rubs at her cheekbone. Utter contentment slackens her features.

Fuuuuck.

The moisture welling in my eyes has me gritting my teeth. I swallow hard, looking around for something—*anything*—I can do for her.

A silver-handled hairbrush sits innocently on her nightstand. I snatch it up.

Leaving my hand under her cheek, I move to the head of the bed and gather her body between my legs. She snuggles against my left thigh, humming softly. It might make me smile, if I weren't on the edge of a breakdown.

I've ruined it. My plan to hold myself back, make myself wait until she had completely forgiven me. It didn't work.

Now she's seen... everything. How rough I am. Worse than I normally would've been.

Misery swarms my soul as I force down the lump in my

throat. With careful fingers, I start to smooth the brush through her cool blonde hair, gently working out the tangles I created.

"I wasn't going to do it like this," I grumble to the silent room. "I had a whole plan. A surprise gift for you. It's ready and everything. Just waiting for *us* to be ready..."

Ivy hums, cuddling closer. I sigh, petting her hair back again. "It isn't nearly enough for you, little dove. But I'm starting to think nothing ever will be. Every day, I wake up and think I'll do better. Be better."

It helps, actually. Having her to look forward to. Knowing the sort of man she deserves. It's made me more attentive to our work and our pack.

She doesn't know it yet, but Ivy's entire project for that children's hospital is fully funded. Fifty-two million dollars. It's taken dozens of meetings—not to mention all those threats I made.

Turns out all the wealthy, titled assholes I've been watching from the shadows will pay big money to keep their secrets under wraps. And, you know, a write-off's a write-off.

"I think I have been, actually," I tell her. "Better. What did you call it? Using my evil for good? I'm *trying*, baby. I swear. And I keep thinking I'll come home and tell you all about it. But somehow, every night, when I get back here and see your face... it's not enough."

Another breath sloughs out of me, and I slump forward. "Why is it so much easier to talk to you when you're asleep? This is *bullshit*."

Her lips twitch. Just the smallest bit—but the bare hint of a smile sends my stomach sinking and soaring.

Has she been awake this *whole time*?

I see the answer before she opens her big blue eyes. They blink up at me, bleary but full of so much softness, my throat starts to fill all over again.

The shy version of her smile graces her mouth. "You're *you*." She reaches for my hand again, tucking it under her chin again. "I missed *you*."

Christ. Is she trying to make me blubber like a little bitch?

The wad in my throat stings my eyes. "Didn't like my alter-ego?" I ask, my tone as bleak as the humorless smile I give her.

She makes a noncommittal sound. "Pretty sure I liked him a bit too much, given how sore I am now."

The glimmer of hope I felt at the beginning of her sentence abruptly burns to ash. *Sore. Because of me.*

I would *end the life* of anyone who hurt her.

But it was *me. I did this.*

Swallowing hard, I cup her face in my palm. "I'm *so sorry*. I never would have—If I had—"

I did everything I could to keep myself locked away and preserve her safety. My brows crease as I realize she somehow got past my guard. I assume her Omega must have sensed my rut, somehow, but—

"How did you get in?"

Ivy's cheeks pink adorably. "I sort of... barked at Duncan."

Well, damn. I must be even more twisted than I thought, because the idea of this sweet, soft little omega *barking* to get to me sends a bolt of arousal down to my spent dick.

It twitches beside her cheek, and she casts it a dry look. As if asking, *Seriously?*

I tug at her hair gently, recapturing her attention. "You barked to get to me?"

Ivy nods, biting her lower lip. Pride and gratitude wash over the chagrin shifting in my middle, warmth melting off its edges.

I'd bark to get her to her, too. Hell, if it were the only way to give her what she needed, I'd burn the whole world to a smoking heap.

Our gazes lock. Understanding sifts through her blue irises. The moment reminds me of one we shared out on the curb in Lyledon, her first night here. The feeling that perhaps we have more in common than I thought.

"But when I got in there," she goes on, "it seemed like you were trying to resist coming with me?"

Her question is implied, written all over her wistful expression. I cup my hand around her cheek and stroke at the hollow beneath her blush.

"Your scent," I murmur, heart twisting. "Ruts are rare for me, with the blockers we take, but when I have them, I usually black out. The second I scented you—and how afraid you were—my Alpha almost… backed down a bit? He didn't want to scare your Omega. But then you *ran*, and—" I shake my head, dropping into a rough rasp. "I had to chase you."

Ivy sighs before she moves, sitting up between my bent legs. "Is it wrong that I'm sort of glad?" she murmurs. "I would have been heartbroken if you'd truly hurt yourself."

Bast is right. She *is* an angel. And no one could deserve her less than I do.

Emotion swarms my chest, seizing control of my body. I snap her into my lap, one hand reaching over to grip her chin between my thumb and forefinger, staring hard into her eyes. "*I* would have been *completely* broken if I'd hurt *you*."

She blinks, her face earnest and so damn beautiful. "Then maybe… no more holding back?"

The heartfelt plea in her eyes undoes me. Even if that didn't seal my fate, her request is too sound for me to deny. She's right—the longer I hold out, the worse my need for her will be when my Alpha snaps the reins away again.

We need her, whether we deserve her or not.

I hang my head, swallowing past a dry lump. "No more," I agree.

Salty sadness touches her scent at the same moment a luscious sweetness perfumes the air. The mix has my chest vibrating on a deep purr. Ivy leans her head against my pec, shyly looking up at me. "You shouldn't do anything you don't want to, Dair."

Shit. The guys warned me she would start to feel rejected. Why are they always *right*?

I fold Ivy into my arms. "It isn't that at all, baby. Trust me, I fucking *live* for the thought of having you. I just want to make sure it's the best thing for you, too. Because that's what matters."

A steely glint glazes her gaze, offering a glimpse of the girl who fought her way to me. For me. "*You* matter, Dair."

Those three simple words hit me like a bullet to the heart. Pain explodes where the pounding organ twists, squirming away from that...

Impossibility.

What I want hasn't mattered to *anyone*, including me, for a long time. My life has been about all the things I *didn't* want—and how to stick it to the people who pushed them on me anyway.

Even joining this pack was a means of escaping my title and my dad's bullshit. A path to screwing him over. Then, I spent years taking a perverse sort of pleasure in making Asher and Bast's lives harder, rebelling against everything our positions demanded because I hated that I'd been "forced" into choosing between this life and my old one.

Backed into this corner because what I wanted for my life and who I wanted to be *didn't* matter. Not as much as titles and money and power.

Not to Ivy, though.

The truth of that is written all over her lovely face. Beaming at me. Offering... a choice.

Do I want her? This? Us?

The answer beats in the shredded husk of my heart, pounding into all my pulse points.

Yes. Yes. *Yes.*

I take her mouth without warning or apology, plunging my tongue against hers and swallowing the whimper she offers in return. Sugared perfume swirls around us. My canines ache, and I groan, eating at her faster and harder.

The way she softens, accepting all my sharpness, heals something deep inside me. By the time I pull back, she's breathless. And I'm more certain than I've ever been.

"No more holding back," I repeat, staring into her eyes so she can see the promise etched in mine.

Ivy's answering smile steals the air right out of my lungs. She glows with joy, throwing her arms around my neck and hugging me. I take advantage, gathering her into my torso and scooting to the edge of the mattress.

"Where are we going?" she giggles.

I slap her ass lightly. "Hush. I'm surprising you."

Her laughter rises up the stairs as I start the climb to her nest. *Our* nest.

I know they all think I pass out in the hallway, but I've been sleeping up here for *weeks*—waiting for them to leave in the mornings before I sneak up the marble steps and crash in sheets that smell like Ivy. It's helped, but I felt guilty every time. Like I didn't belong there.

I'm starting to realize I've had that feeling since the day I decided to join this pack. Festering at the back of my mind—the uncanny sensation that I'm an impostor. A fake prince who was only there to use the title as a refuge from his own.

Now, I'm not so sure it was ever that simple.

If Ivy is my mate... and she's also Asher's... and Bast's...

That means we were always *meant* to be a pack. And, in all likelihood, we would have wound up getting our shit together one day, regardless of my scheming.

I still feel like a piece of shit for using Asher, but the realization helps with the rest of it. I can apologize for being an opportunist dick a whole lot easier than I could for ruining his "real pack."

Because, well—

I guess I'm it.

We really are a pack now. Me and Bast and Asher. We all belong together, because we all belong with *her*.

Stepping into the nest feels different this time. More like I'm exactly where I should be. The shades are drawn, blocking out the sunset spilling into Ivy's—*our*—suite.

It still smells like our omega and our pack alpha, their scents embedded in the sheets from the day and night they spent up here. I brace for jealousy or annoyance, but instead, that deep, consuming pride rears up again.

How fucking perfect is our girl?

God. I love her.

That undeniable fact swirls through my thoughts as I kneel in the center of the mattress, carefully lowering us onto her mountain of silver satin cushions. Laughing blue eyes gaze up at me as I stretch alongside her, propping myself on an elbow and reaching behind us to fumble for the remote I left hidden under all the pillows.

Ivy snuggles closer to my purr, and I drop my forehead to hers, nuzzling a scent-mark there. "You ready?"

She nods, shortbread sweetness brightening with excitement that has me hiding a grin against her crown. I press a button on the small remote, illuminating the constellations I installed above us.

It took hours to get that shit right. I spent two afternoons sitting up here with a map of the stars laid out in front of me, carefully adhering pinprick LEDs in the correct patterns. Now, our girl has an exact replica of the night sky in her nest.

Ivy gazes up at the lights in awe. A choked cry catches in her throat. "Dair! It's beautiful! How—why did you—"

I silence her stammers with a soft kiss, settling into a more comfortable position and turning back up to the constellations spread above us.

"This way, you always have a star handy. I figured my girl deserves as many wishes as she can make."

forty-six

It takes everything in me not to sprint to the Omega Suite before Duncan finishes his explanation.

Bast and I arrive back from Lyledon to find the nervous attendant waiting by the carport, wringing his hands. He launches into his story without delay, and we manage to listen...

Until he says, "It's been about four hours since anyone has seen either of them, Your Highness."

Then I'm gone.

Bast and I rush into the east wing, running up the back stairs that spit us closest to Ivy's double doors. They're firmly shut but unlocked.

I stand on the threshold, chest heaving. The room looks fine, apart from an unmade bed and a few pillows strewn on the floor. The sun has set, leaving the space dark except for the dimmed chandelier overhead... and the nest?

Where someone is *purring*.

Bast and I glance at each other and simultaneously lunge for the stairs. He's faster, of course, and beats me to the landing at the top. When he freezes, blinking in shock instead of snarling, I feel marginally better.

"Uh, hey?" he says.

Dair's voice hisses from the cocoon of velvet curtains and gilded glass. "*Shh*. She's *sleeping*."

Bast's stunned expression makes sense when I step around him. Dair is naked, sprawled in the nest with Ivy bundled into his side, resting peacefully across his purring chest.

Bast cracks a grin, kicking his shoes off to wade in. "I see you two worked your shit out."

I'm not so optimistic. Removing my own Oxfords, I cast Dair a long, examining look. One he would normally return with a growl or at least a glare.

This time, he only stares back, his features solemn but calm. "She busted in on me and ran," he admits. "I chased her down here, but she—we figured it out."

She looks normal, but unease shifts in my chest anyhow. I shuffle forward on my knees, noting the way Dair has to smother a growl when I get close enough to bend over Ivy and scent her. He lets me do it, holding his vicious Alpha in check so I can see for myself.

Ivy smells like heaven. Warm, sugared gold. I nuzzle her bare shoulder with my nose and brush a light kiss there before retreating, tension leaving my lungs. "Seems perfect," I comment. "She wasn't scared?"

Dair swallows loud enough for me to hear. "She was," he mumbles, "But that almost made my Alpha calmer, somehow? It activated his protective side, I guess."

Pride warms my center as my eyes roam over my gorgeous darling's profile. Of course she didn't hide her fear or act like she knew what to do—my guileless girl. The fact that her softness brings out the best in each of us is exactly why we need her.

It seems Dair is finally ready to admit that.

"She's like a special key that opens all three doors," he murmurs, waving a hand at us. "I didn't think that would be possible, because of the way I started out in this pack. I thought I'd fucked up your chances of finding your true mate—or, if you did, I was convinced she'd be wrong for me.

"But from the first time I scented her, I knew. She's mine. And she's yours. Which means all the selfish reasons why I joined this pack didn't fuck everything up, after all."

If I was already surprised, now I'm *shocked*. A feeling that only doubles as he continues, meeting my eye with a determined stare.

"I owe you an apology," he states, certainty radiating from his voice and expression. "It was messed up, approaching you when I knew you needed help with bullies, pretending I wanted all this. Worming my way in to serve my own interests. I'm sorry I did that."

He turns to Bast next. "And I'm sorry you got shoved in the middle. You had to do a lot of work to keep everything together."

A crease mars his forehead as his dark brows draw together, betraying how hard he has to work for his final statement. "Thank you for doing that," he says to Bast, then faces me again. "And thank you for not... giving up. On me. I want us to figure out how to get Ivy to feel like she belongs here, because now I know I do, too."

Gruff emotion scrapes the inside of my chest. My throat works as I swallow past it, nodding. Speechless.

I should have known Bast wouldn't be.

A grin bursts across his face, and he lunges forward. "Awww, DAIR!"

He doesn't care that our packmate and omega are naked. He

goes right in for a bear hug, squeezing them despite Dair's protective growl and Ivy's sudden squeak of surprise.

"You woke her up!" Dair grouses.

But Ivy giggles before she even gets her eyes all the way open, turning to find Bast's face for a kiss. "I'm sure he had a good reason, right, my lord?"

Bast's buttery toffee scent deepens as he rubs his nose over hers, pure happiness lighting his features. "Correct, angel. Your duke was just being *nice*. To *us*."

Dair uses the hand not clutching Ivy to pinch the bridge of his nose, leaning his head back with a groan. "I was not *nice*."

Bast grins wider, and Ivy joins him. Always partners in crime, those two.

"Yes, he was," Bast mouths, earning a scathing glower from Dair. Luckily, Ivy captures the duke's attention a moment later. His entire face relaxes the second their eyes meet, melting into a look of fond concern.

"You good?" he murmurs. "Still feeling okay?"

As her sweetness thickens, Ivy snuggles closer and nods into his tattooed chest. He sets his chin on her crown, and Bast moves to her other side, flopping into the pillows with that same exuberant smile.

Something warm aches behind my ribs, stretching to fill my whole chest. Pride, I think.

I picked these guys. And they're everything Ivy needs.

Except for me.

She makes that clear with a quiet whine. Her dainty fingers float up and wiggle, beckoning me closer with a hushed, "Please, Ash?"

I move to join them, falling on the other side of Dair.

After all, you don't say no to a queen.

forty-seven

PRINCESS IVY'S KNOTS

BAST

I have an...indelicate question

ASHER

Is it about my princess?

Don't make me strangle you.

DAIR

Your princess?

You mean the one who had my hand around her throat an hour ago?

BAST

If Asher says, "off with your head," will he mean your actual head?

Or your 

ASHER

Jesus Christ

What's your question Bast?

Might as well ask while I'm already having the guillotine sharpened.

BAST

Okay

So

Have any of us prepped Ivy for the 🍑 part of her heat?

Dair?

DAIR

What?

Am I the ass expert?

BAST

Um, yeah

ASHER

Thought that was obvious.

BAST

One of us should ask her how she *feels* about it first.

DAIR

Say fucking less.

BAST

I wasn't suggesting you *do* anything, I was just *saying*

DAIR

Already on my way.

BAST

Do you really think you can run faster than me?

"You shouldn't linger."

Ivy's whispered warning puts a huge grin on my face. I do my best to keep my steps silent, sneaking up behind her as she kneels on the patio of her newly furnished sitting room.

She looks every bit like my perfect angel. Lustrous blonde waves fanned down her back. Her face glowing with a peachy blush and painted pink lips.

Of course, she pays no mind to the gown I picked out for tonight. The full, iridescent pink skirt is half-folded under her knees, pressed into a patch of grass as she leans forward and exchanges more words with...

A mouse?

Oh boy.

We won't tell Asher.

"Go on now," she urges softly, placing a shred of bread on the ground. "Back to the stables."

The little critter takes his meal and scampers off. I shake my head, grinning. Sometimes, I swear these animals actually understand her.

"We have mice in the stables, huh?"

Ivy startles, whirling with adorably wide eyes. "Oh my God! Bast!"

I love how easily she says my name these days. Not too long ago, it was a struggle to get her to *consider* it. But now? Over the last few days? We have her "forgetting" panties on a regular basis, wearing Dair's tattooed fingers like a necklace every night, and taking our very eager instructions on ass play.

So... princess lessons are going well, I guess?

Fond warmth fills my center as she reads my dirty thoughts and flashes me a scolding look. I chuckle an apology, holding out a hand to help her up.

The skirt of her dress isn't visibly dirty, at least. The thin, diaphanous material floats around her legs, making for the exact type of angelic silhouette I was aiming for.

Mindful of the clear heels strapped to her ankles, I sweep her into my arms and bend to plant a careful kiss on her mouth.

"You're beautiful," I say, staring into her eyes.

Her cheeks flush a deeper rose. "You just have good taste in dresses."

I shake my head. "I just have good taste in *mates.*"

For a moment, joy shines clear in her gaze. Then, a cloud passes over her visage. "Bast... these are really important people tonight, right? What if I say the wrong thing or embarrass His Majesty or—"

"Ivy?"

It's Dair, stalking out of the house with his newfound (borderline-feral) intensity. He scans the patio for a threat, clipping right to our omega and cupping her face with no mind for how close we're standing.

"What is it, little dove? I can scent your stress."

He really is the master when it comes to that. Until he mentions it, I don't notice the faint edge of anxiety browning the corners of her shortbread essence. But I see he's caught on to something deeper when Ivy bites her lip instead of brushing him off. "I don't want to mess up."

He hums, his chest hitching into a purr immediately.

Like the big, gooey softy he's become.

Asher and I might make fun of him if we weren't just as marshmallowy over our omega.

My lungs echo his rumbling. Some of the tension fades from

Ivy's posture, and she sways up onto her tiptoes to kiss his flexing jaw.

It works. The tight lines around his mouth vanish, and he dips to kiss her back, not giving a shit if he smudges her makeup.

Dair might be *evolving*, but he's definitely still *Dair*.

Asher strides out next, fidgeting with his cuff link and scowling behind his glasses. "Bast, we need to remember to talk to the Shah about that education initiative for young women in—"

"I got it," Dair grunts, not bothering to look up from Ivy.

Asher and I glance at one another. "Uh," I laugh, "*What?*"

Dair shrugs, turning his dark eyes on us. "I *'accidentally'* ran into him in the carport this morning when he arrived and reminded him about it. He agreed to fund his end as promised."

Asher blinks. "Just like that?"

Dair's mouth twitches up. "I may have *also* reminded him of the PR issues for Amizi, trying to marry Princess Ahmad off to a bunch of packs she hated, against her will. Plus, it's a good cause, and he'd already pledged the funding. He caved in." Seeing our open-mouthed gapes, his shoulders bounce again. "Whatever, it was easy. Took, like, three minutes."

Ivy grins, smacking another kiss on his lips. "Putting your stalking skills to good use for once," she teases. "I'm so proud."

Dair rolls his eyes, but his purr gets more insistent. "Yeah, yeah."

Asher smiles, clapping Dair on the back. "Thank you. I hate reminding people about philanthropic debts over hors d'oeuvres."

I wink at Ivy. "Much more suitable for dessert conversation."

My sweet angel nods with complete earnestness, as if she's actually filing that bit of nonsense away for future events. I grin into her hair, leaving a scent-mark on her forehead.

"We better give His Highness a turn," I grumble, noting the way Asher's fingers flex. "Or he'll lock us both in the dungeon."

Asher glowers in my direction, reaching over to pluck Ivy from my arms. "No," he mutters to her, "but I do have something special for you, goose. If you'd like to see it."

She agrees, wearing the shy smile that melts the three of us instantly. Ever a gentleman, our prince helps her navigate her way over the marble patio, leading her back into her sitting room.

Our omega really picked a diamond in the rough. This room was tarped and dusty for literal centuries, but with a bit of Ivy's nostalgia and optimism, it's been transformed back to its former glory.

I love that she matched the decor to her suite and our nest—all shining crystal, gold and silver trims, soft icy blues, and thin ivory silks. The chandelier is off, but golden sunset light seeps through the windows, illuminating frescos carved into the white stone ceiling and its gilded edges.

The place is gorgeous. But it's nothing compared to the girl who abruptly trips to a halt in the middle of it all, her hand flying up to cover her mouth.

"Ash..."

On the low table between Ivy's antique couches, I spy our gleaming silver box. It's open, with the lid popped up to reveal the tiara nestled inside.

Asher moves slowly, bringing the delicate crown to Ivy. Our omega quivers, gazing at the diamonds and white gold as if in a trance.

Our pack alpha shoots Dair and me a hasty, heavy glance. My throat tightens, and Dair's jaw grinds.

At first, we weren't going to press the issue at all. But this week, Ivy's perfume has steadily gotten more come-in-your-pants *incredible* with each passing day. None of us want to alarm her, but she's started exhibiting some other pre-heat behaviors, too.

Like being overly nervous about tonight's state dinner after attending three of them in the past month. Or nearly tearing up the other day when she accidentally stepped on my foot during our afternoon walk.

The real kicker came after we all got in bed last night. Normally, our omega is a bit inhibited about asking for affection, but she practically *pounced* on me the second I hit the mattress. Four orgasms were *barely* enough to lull her to sleep...

Which is how we wound up spending an hour whispering over her head, wondering if this was a step too far, too fast.

We want to be there for her heat and, hopefully, bond with her as soon as Maman can get the big, official ceremony together. But we're all too cognizant of the fact that Ivy has never promised to *stay*. Or be ours.

She only agreed to come here and let us court her. We've been doing our best—and so has our girl.

This is the next step...

But we're very fucking aware that this tiara isn't just another bauble.

It's a *question*.

Will she wear this and walk into a room full of world leaders dressed as our future princess? Or will she turn it down and do everything she can to maintain her freedom?

I don't know.

I'm not even sure what I *want* her to do. On one hand, of course, I want her to be ours. On the other... I need her to be herself. My earth-bound angel. Our mate.

She has to do whatever feels right to her.

And I have to love her, no matter what.

forty-eight

A shooting pain streaks down my neck as I turn my head, straining to keep the tiara balanced.

As uncomfortable as I am, I can't deny, the guys seem enamored with the sight of it on my head. Every time I glance across the smallest of Everdeen's reception halls, I find one of them staring back at me. Dair with that about-to-take-a-bullet-for-me intensity, Bast with a flirty grin, and Asher with the sort of pride that mists my eyes.

I... love them.

It's why I have this tiara on. I may not have a speck of certainty about becoming a future queen, bearing royal heirs, or bonding in front of the entire universe... but *I love them.* How could I see the hope and fear filling each of their beloved faces and say no?

Do I *want* to say no?

I don't think I do. Not really. I only doubt if I *should* be saying yes. If I might somehow fail them.

Truly, I can't think of anything worse than that—and neither can my Omega.

Queen Selene smiles at me, her expression full of the sort of maternal warmth that still makes my throat sticky. I miss my mother terribly, especially on nights like these, watching Asher's parents glow with pride over the prince.

And, now, over me too.

"Ivy has done so splendidly!" Selene boasts, grinning at her husband and Jasmine's father, Shah Ahmad, in turn.

The Shah eyes me shrewdly, his dark eyes so like his daughter's —lively and mysterious. "Jasmine has told me she makes a lovely princess. So far, I must agree."

Selene nods soundly, adding her own agreement while King Leopold stares at my profile. His expression is unyielding, but he has the same calculating gaze my prince gets sometimes. When his wife escorts the Shah to a group of new arrivals, the king doesn't budge.

"That tiara was my mother's," he tells me, taking a slow sip from the tumbler in his right hand, flashing a gold ring inlaid with the Everhart's signature sapphires. "And her grandmother's before that."

Oh, figs.

I open my mouth to apologize, but the king suddenly pins his golden gaze on mine. "I'm honored for you to wear it, Ivy."

I—

He's—

What?!

King Leopold sighs. For the first time, he doesn't seem

imposing and untouchable—for a moment, he actually looks like a normal man. A tired one.

"I know I was doubtful about all this," he goes on. "I apologize if I ever made you feel less welcome here. I only... I know better than anyone how hard this job is. And I want my son to have a partner who will make it bearable for him the way my Selene has for me."

It's impossible to miss how his eyes soften when he says her name. Another expression he and his son have in common—one the prince reserves for *me*.

"Over the last month, I've seen how hard he's worked. I thought you might be a distraction, but you've only made him more determined than ever to be a good ruler." The king nearly smiles. "That's what mates do. They make us better. Braver. Whole."

Have I, though? Or is that just my incredible alphas coming into their own?

I shake my head, refusing the credit he offers. "No, Your Majesty, they've always been amazing men, I just—"

He raises a brow in another familiar face. "Even Dairragh?"

Well... I wince, remembering his mocking orders and burning glares. "He's always had so much potential," I finally manage.

That time, the king actually laughs. "I see my wife's diplomacy lessons have been put to good use," he chuckles. "That's very good. You'll need that sort of tact around here. Much sooner than you think."

My mouth moves to fall open, but I pause mid-gape. "S-sooner?"

Despite the layers of polite descenter covering me, Dair still stiffens the second my insides squirm. His dark eyes snap to mine from across the room. I watch him mutter an excuse before he starts clipping his way to me.

Kind Leopold goes on, oblivious. "Well, with the four of you doing so well, I assume you'll have your bonding ceremony before your first heat or just after it. And once you're bonded, I don't see any reason why Asher and his pack can't take over for me right away. With you by their sides, they'll make fine kings. And you'll be queen by the end of the year!"

He pats me on the back, offering another of his stern smiles before walking away. I stand in a daze, blinking at the blank space beside me as I replay his words.

Queen. By the end of the year?

"Ivy." Dair's low voice hums near my left ear. "I swear to God, if the bastard's insulted you—"

I shake my head slowly, noting that Bast is also on his way over. He stops to exchange a few words with the king and queen, who both smile and wave him my way. Asher also begins shaking hands with his latest group of admirers, turning toward us.

My blond, gorgeously athletic alpha grins as he approaches, sweeping me off my feet and into a swirl. "Perfect angel," he praises, blue eyes shining. "Asher's parents *love* you. I can't wait for you to meet my folks, too. They're abroad for the summer, but they'll be back before the holidays, and Selene was telling me she wants to do our ceremony before Christmas, so I thought—"

He cuts himself off when my eyes fill, setting me on my feet and stepping up to block out the rest of the room. "Love? What's wrong?"

I'm not sure. I only know that my insides are juddering like a washing machine full of rocks. Asher finally reaches my side, his tone low and urgent. "Do you guys feel this?"

Dair nods, scanning the room to make sure no one is watching me tremble in Bast's arms. "Is it her heat?" he mutters, keeping his face blank.

Asher cups my cheek, hazel eyes examining me behind their tortoiseshell frames. "Do you think this is your heat, darling? You don't feel very warm, but it could be a spike."

I open my mouth to tell him that it's actually, in all likelihood, just a boring old panic attack. Courtesy of the walloping notion of me being *a queen* within *the next few months*.

But then I feel it.

The stab between my hips, striking hard and twisting viciously.

No, I tell my Omega. *Not now. Please.*

Her only reply is a hard nudge that sends me into Asher's chest. I bury my face against the base of his throat, and he purrs quietly.

"I-I'm sorry," I mumble. "I'm supposed to be *helping,* not dragging you away from all of your duties and—" I tuck myself tighter against Asher's torso. "I don't want to let you all down."

"You won't, goose," the prince vows, leaning back to capture my face in his palm and staring hard into my eyes. "You *aren't.*"

All my anxieties bubble over, boiling the base of my lungs until I feel like they're melting and I'll never be able to inhale again. And the horrible question I've been thinking for *weeks*—my biggest fear and greatest suspicion in one—finally scrapes up my throat.

"What if I can't do this, Ash?" I whisper, "What if I'm not supposed to be a queen?"

forty-nine

Ivy's words swirl through my mind, replaying in a loop.

"What if I'm not supposed to be a queen?"

Unlike the first time she confessed feelings that broke my heart, this time, I absorb every word.

Because this is the last time I'll ever let her think them.

All the days I've spent worrying and wavering only drive me forward faster. The second our group slipped out the side door of the reception hall, I bent and gathered Ivy off the ground, wordlessly storming down the passage leading to my ultimate destination.

I feel her anxious curiosity and the guys' too. But just like the day I stormed into the rain with my omega in my arms—in this moment, I know exactly who I am and what I'm about. I don't need to analyze it or pick it apart.

Striding without pause, I carry Ivy down the wide marble hallway. When I drop my gaze to her face, an ache rebounds through my chest.

She doubts herself—but, more importantly, some part of her still doubts *us*. And I hate how much sense that makes after the way we started out.

It's time to show her just how committed we are. That she owns us, body and soul.

Even if we had a picture-perfect fairytale, I think believing in this might still be hard on Ivy. It's fine to *want* a different life.... But despite all of her wishes and daydreams, my mate struggles to *believe* she can actually *have* good things.

Or, moreover, that she's *worthy* of them.

But she does. No one in the world could deserve more than Ivy. And no one else could possibly bring this pack together the way she has.

My girl. My mate.

Kind. Quietly dazzling. Unfailingly selfless.

Our queen.

If we can convince her.

Her scent deepens with every step. The warm sweetness of it beats in my blood by the time we round our last corner and approach a set of double doors.

I've had guards stationed here for weeks. Ever since we gave Ivy the tour of Everdeen and she seemed particularly enamored with the old throne room and all its pack-focused glory.

She doesn't know I've had it restored for us. To turn it into the sort of space our omega will *love*.

I nod at the men flanking the entrance, waving them off. "Go. Now. And keep everyone out of this corridor."

They react to the dominance rolling off me in thunderous

waves, breaking rank and racing up the hall to follow my orders. Bast shoves the double doors, pushing them in to reveal the moon-drenched room beyond.

Silvery light streams through glass stained in every imaginable shade of blue. Filtering moonbeams that cast long, watery shadows over the carved ceiling.

Instead of dust and tarped antiques, fresh paint and clean carpet greet us. Particularly the long, pale blue runner I selected to go with the only piece of furniture left in the room.

A throne.

Built for four.

The design took a while to figure out. I looked at separate seats for each of us, but then...

"I had that made," I tell Ivy, absorbing her wide-eyed blink. "For us." Lifting my head, I look at Bast and Dair, too. "All of us."

My mate's teeth sink into her lower lip, the expression so familiar and beloved, I bend to kiss it right off her face. She responds instinctually, fisting my lapels and tugging me closer.

Yes, I think, wishing she could hear me. Willing her to. *Take me. Use me.*

The rush of perfect perfume that explodes into the stillness has us all growling and groaning. My feet move, carrying us closer to the dais at the head of the chamber.

Instead of sitting on the ornate, oversized loveseat, I set Ivy at its center and step back. Dair starts to swoop toward her, but I hold up my hands, halting the guys on either side of me. Needing Ivy's full attention.

"Why do you think I selected this design for our throne?"

She swallows, nervous azure eyes flitting to the creamy fabric beneath her. "I—I don't know? Shouldn't there be three chairs? One for each of you?"

My hand snaps up to my tie, ripping it loose. Ivy's gaze tracks the impatient motion, her gaze glazing as her perfume rises in a fresh tidal wave of sugared gold.

I shake my head. "Couldn't do that," I say simply, shrugging off my jacket and stepping out of my shoes. "Do you know why?"

Beside me, Bast catches on and starts quietly removing his clothes while Dair stares, his focus narrowing on my profile like a laser. Ivy bites her lip again, stammering when I start unbuttoning my shirt.

"B-Because... none of you wanted to be in the middle?"

I might smile if my insides weren't a churn of molten urgency —climbing hotter, burning higher—and love so deep, it carves canyons in my soul.

She *needs* to understand this. She needs to *believe.*

My pants come off last, boxers and all. Until I'm completely naked, standing at her altar.

And—no. Fuck all of this to hell.

I'm going to *kneel* at her altar.

She gasps when I go to my knees, placing both hands over hers. Slowly pushing her skirt up her thighs while I gaze into her depths.

"Because if we had four chairs, only two of us would be next to you," I tell her. "And none of us is willing to be the one who doesn't get to sit by your side."

Silence engulfs the throne room. So still, I can sense Dair breathing harder behind me.

Bast is undressed, too. He looms to my right, still standing and reaching out to cup her porcelain cheek. "This way, no one will be left out," he adds, so very gentle with her. "And we can always be together."

Dair approaches last, his steps heavy and slow. He waits for her wide eyes to shift to his before he finishes, "It was always supposed to be like this, Ivy. Because *I* belong here. And that means *you* do, too."

I'd be lying if I said his words didn't hit somewhere deep and unhealed, smoothing the torn edges of an old wound. When my scent shifts, Dair's forearm knocks my shoulder in a gesture of camaraderie.

"I know," he mutters to me and Bast. "Took me long enough."

Smirking, I turn back to Ivy, letting her take in the look on my face. The way my scent has brightened. Showing her, again, that she's done this.

Brought us together. Made us into a real pack.

She's the reason the thought of taking this throne doesn't fill me with dread anymore. She's the reason Dair believes he has a place here now. She's the reason Bast finally has somebody to care for him the way he's cared for everyone else.

Two months ago, I'd never noticed how much my packmate did to keep this unit from falling apart. Now, with Ivy at our center, his effort is so obvious. Just like Dair's self-deprecation.

She helps us understand each other.

It's our turn to help her understand her value. Her*self*.

There's a zipper along the side of her bodice. I unfasten it and rear up, peeling the iridescent material off her. Bast takes it from me without a word, carefully laying it over the low gold railing enclosing the sides of the dais.

The way an attendant would treat his queen's gown.

She watches him come back to her side and drop to his knees next to me. Bending to kiss her hand, but keeping his head bowed, closing his eyes.

He loves her, too. It's clear in every line on his face—Bast knows exactly how it feels when she flutters her lashes and turns her hazy eyes to mine. Her focus dips to the ink etched over my heart. The organ that bleeds and burns just for her.

Ivy saves Dair for last, slowly lifting her chin to look up at him. He stares back, brows folding low. Something unspoken passes between them, sharpening his scent and salting hers.

I'm surprised how easy it is for me to read them. Now that I know he never thought he belonged here... And she doesn't believe she does, either.

They truly do understand each other.

Dair traces a thumb over her cheek, his stark black ink so

striking against her peachy skin. His chest rattles with a purr that loosens her bare shoulders. She shivers, and I wrap my arms around her hips, parting her legs as I pull her to the edge of the throne. Her silk panties slide over the velvet cushion, eliciting another quiet gasp.

Still locked in their gaze, Dair starts stripping with his free hand, making quick work of his vest and shirt. Ivy's gaze trails over his tattoos, her perfume deepening.

Bast cracks a smile at her reaction, nuzzling his grin into her palm. "Mm. I think our princess is needy."

I *know* she is. My Alpha has snapped to the surface, snarling at the sight of the growing damp spot between her thighs.

Bast truly dresses Ivy like she's a gift to be unwrapped. I hook my fingers into the bows tying her panties at her hips, tugging them free as Dair steps out of the last of his clothes.

And joins us on our knees.

fifty

THERE ARE THREE MEN—THREE *PRINCES*—ON THEIR knees.

For *me*.

And—*oh lord*—I don't think I'm going to be able to protest.

They're all so beautiful. Dair's pale skin bathed in silver light, splattered with black ink. Bast's golden glow and perfect face, so full of longing that my heart stutters. And Asher's strong, regal features, the fire in his hazel eyes as he sets his glasses under my seat.

Under... *my* throne?

No, my Omega says. *Ours. Our pack's.*

That makes it a bit easier to inhale. I've been asking myself for weeks if I can do this... but, really, it isn't just *me*, is it? It's *us*.

I'm not alone in this. I might have been on my own for most of the big, scary things that happened before fate handed me these men—but I don't think I have to be anymore.

If I say yes and we bond... I'll quite literally never be alone again.

But I'd have to find the courage to choose this. *Them*.

Is it really even a *choice*, though? It's not as if I'm weighing up options, trying to determine what's best for me. So why can't I just say yes?

My Omega is quiet, her uncertainty mirroring mine. Asher sighs, his eyes turning tender as they take in my expression. "Goose," he murmurs. "We aren't going to disappear. You won't wake up from your dream this time. It's safe to believe."

He understands me unlike anyone else. Because as he says the words, staring steadily into my eyes, they sail straight to the ache in my center, stabbing the fear twisting my stomach. I lose my breath and can't get it back, replaying his words to myself. Trying to force them to sink into my heart.

It's safe to believe.

Has it ever been, though?

When have I ever gotten anything good that I could keep?

And... how does he know I won't wake up in my own bed, back in Maytown, tomorrow?

This—*he*—was my dream. Every wish on every star. All the secret hopes of my heart.

How could it possibly be *safe* to believe in *that*?

My scent is already so potent, I can sense the salt my sadness sprinkles over it. Pain cracks through Dair's features. His purr sharpens along with his essence, edging toward a growl.

"Fuck, baby," he pants softly, burying his face against my left hand. "Is *that* what you think? That this isn't *real*?"

Bast's toffee aroma gets nearly as salty as mine when he's

upset. The shift tickles my nose, turning me in his direction just in time to see him gulp.

Hurt hits my heart as guilt swamps my stomach. This beautiful alpha has never done anything but treat me with kindness and try to fulfill his duties to his pack. He doesn't deserve to be doubted.

I open my mouth to babble an apology, but his scent suddenly recovers, turning back to the rich, nutty sweetness that makes my core slick. A handsome half-smile reveals the dimple I love so much.

"You know what helps me?" he murmurs. "When I can't wake up from a dream?"

God, he's always so kind. So good to me, even when I don't deserve it. My throat thickens, turning my voice into a whisper. "What?"

His blue eyes flash. "A little jolt."

Before his lips finish forming the words, Dair's teeth nip at the thin skin of my wrist. I gasp, tingles skating down my spine and spreading through my pussy. It clenches, visibly gushing slick onto the blue velvet beneath me.

I don't have time to be embarrassed—they all groan at the sight, their broad shoulders colliding as all three alphas try to get to my center first.

Tension pulls taut through the big, airy chamber as they eye one another. Asher's the first to snap his gaze back to mine. "I know I said we were gentlemen," he roughs out. "But I don't think we can take turns this time."

fifty-one

DAIR'S ANSWERING RUMBLE SOUNDS DANGEROUS. When my eyes leap to his, he cocks a dark brow. "Trust me, little dove?"

Weeks ago, I would have lied. Or said, "Heck no." Now?

My fervent nod takes a bit of the edge off his scent. His chest drops back into a deep purr. "That's my girl. C'mere."

Three sets of strong hands grasp my bare body, turning me... to the side? I automatically reach out with my right hand, gripping the solid frame of the throne as Asher slings my knee over his left shoulder.

Putting his face right between my thighs.

He doesn't wait even half a breath before diving for me with a snarl that sends slick dribbling down his chin. The prince moans, lapping it off my spread lips and tracing it to the source. He flicks his tongue against the trembling muscles pulsing for more, eliciting a cry that echoes through the huge room.

"*Louder.*"

Dair's command is the last word he snaps out before he joins Asher between my legs, gently scraping his teeth over the very bottom of my ass until I shiver, drenching our pack leader again.

Bast watches with sparkling eyes, stretching out to offer his shoulder for my other hand. I grip his warm, chiseled flesh, moaning when his mouth meets mine.

He bites at my lips, sucking my tongue. Kissing me so deeply, I don't notice what Dair is up to until—

Ah!

Slippery heat rims the tight hole between my cheeks, mimicking the sensation lapping at my pussy. When they both plunge into me simultaneously, I gasp around Bast's savage kisses.

He purrs louder, his cut chest vibrating against my nipples. More slick pours out of my body, earning a hungry growl from my prince and a ragged groan from my duke. My clit throbs, begging for relief from their onslaught.

"It's not a dream," Bast murmurs, our lips still brushing. "Or a wish. We're *here*, Ivy. All yours. Do you feel it?"

Half-replies stammer out of me, all incoherent. Dair pauses to nip one of the round curves in his hands, leaving a bruise behind before he goes back to *consuming* me. Bast's hand slides from my cheek down to my chest, pressing between my breasts. His gaze flickers, determination steeling his ocean irises as his mouth quirks up.

"Oh, princess," he sighs. "You might want to hold on to your throne."

My fingers tighten on the frame as he slips back to his knees... angling his face near my belly and—

Oh God!

Paying no mind to how close he and Asher get, Bast seals his mouth over the throbbing bundle at the top of my slit. His tongue loops in slow circles, hunting for the spot that makes me shake. He finds it, then sucks at the rough patch there. Muscles low in my abdomen clench along with my thighs.

"Bast! Ah! Please!"

He hums, smug but sweet. Giving me more. The prince snarls, but the possessive sound only spreads the fire licking at my blood.

Never one to be outdone, Dair adds his finger to my ass, sliding it into me until he bumps the new spot they've been teaching me about. Another pleasure center that will want attention during my heat.

He nudges it in languid circles that match Bast's. Asher lets them go slowly, picking up his pace so the plunges of his tongue glide in and out of my core faster, curling up into the place that aches for a knot on every pass.

The motion is almost demanding. *That's right*, it says. *Use me harder*.

When my hips start to churn, he moans his approval, the veins in his hands bulging as he grips my body and encourages its desperate rolls. Bast adds his own brawny hands, each of them urging me on until I'm riding all three of their mouths at once.

My jaw drops as I gaze down at them, memorizing the sight of the three most powerful men in the palace on their knees. Letting me use them. Ride them. Drown them in my slick and need until —until—

A dizzy rush flutters over my body. Every nerve crackles and pops, release bursting through me in a series of spasms.

All three of them growl against my slippery skin. Rough and desperate and proud.

That last one—their pure, absolute masculine *pride*—is what does me in. Their approval and delight sink into my center.

And I hear myself make a *demand*.

"*More*."

Asher *lunges*.

Lifting me off the seat I'm half-kneeling on and whirling us around. The room blots into a cosmic blur of pastel blue and silver moonlight. His skin matches that celestial paleness, shimmering when a beam slants over his body as it sprawls underneath mine.

The way he balances me in his lap is new for us. We've tried a bunch of different positions, but I normally wind up cocooned in his arms, gazing up at his beloved face.

Now, I'm straddling his powerful thighs with his cock carving into the space in front of my pussy. He's sitting on the throne, but his posture is loose, his legs kicked out straight.

He doesn't look like a ruler. He looks… like he's waiting. For orders.

Bast rubs a reassuring hand down my back while Dair stays on his knees, kissing a path up my right leg to gently bite at my hip.

Fresh slick bathes the prince's lap. His hazel eyes gleam as he reaches up and touches my hair.

No—my *crown*.

I'd forgotten about the priceless tiara fastened into my hairdo. But Asher gazes at it—at *me*, wearing it—like he's never seen anything so beautiful.

His touch trails over my temple, down to my lips. Asher frees the lower one from my teeth, pausing to stroke his thumb along the bitten curve until I tremble. He gives me that small, secret smile I know no one else has ever gotten.

Pure love saturates Ash's face, beaming from his eyes to mine as he finally says the words I've imagined this whole time.

"Use me," he husks. "My queen."

Dair steps closer to my back, his crisp scent tickling my lungs as his hands clasp my hips, lifting me into position.

Asher's so long, my knees nearly leave the velvet cushion when Dair cants my hips slightly. Bast guides my hands to Asher's wide shoulders. The first inch of his cock sinks into my heat, spreading my slick opening around his girth.

I keen, my head dropping back to Dair's chest. He purrs, rubbing his own hardness against my bare ass. My legs quiver, lowering me onto Asher as he groans.

Feeling him stretch the muscles screaming for a knot nearly makes me come again. When Bast's delicious sweetness thickens from the sound that scrapes out of me, I whine his name without thought.

They don't let me feel embarrassed. Bast rounds the throne to face me, and Dair slides his hand around my neck, squeezing tenderly. His voice is somehow rough and soft at once as he praises, "Good fucking girl, telling us what you need."

He trails his inked fingers down my spine before reaching lower, gathering wetness from the place that gushes around Asher. "You gonna get slick all over this damn throne? Use your alpha to get off?"

I nod, moaning louder. Riding Asher faster. Turning to Bast for—

He sees the way I eye his straining cock. A growl melds with his purr. "It's yours," he tells me, stepping as close as he can. Flashing the pure, true grin I can't resist. "I'll keep your crown balanced for you, princess."

The teasing edge of his tone does me in. I lurch forward, sucking his smooth hardness into my mouth. Bast chokes, but keeps his word, easing his fingers into my hair and keeping the tiara in place as I start sliding my lips up and down his shaft, pumping my hips into Asher's at the same pace.

My prince grits his teeth, doing everything he can to hold himself in check while I ride his pulsing cock, teasing the top of his knot with every plunge. Using it to rub the bottom of my clit.

Dair hovers behind me, skating his right hand around my body to tease the throbbing nub grinding on Asher's swollen skin. Never touching directly, just making sure I keep pouring slick all over his packmate's lap. The cushion of the throne. And Dair's *other* hand...

Oh!

It makes sense when he suddenly rims two wet fingers along my back hole. Gliding them in. Rubbing at the thin wall separating their heat from Asher's.

We both shout—my voice climbing higher while the prince's bottoms into a bellow.

Dair's answering chuckle is a dark, wicked sound. His free hand finds my throat, teasing Bast's length, too. My blond alpha pants, trying to slow his thrusts into my mouth.

I don't let him, chasing the taste of his pre-cum like I'll starve without it. The flavor lights up every receptor in my brain, all of them chanting for more. More. *More.*

Dair bends forward to whisper in my ear, reading my greedy thoughts. "You want all of us? I'll fill this tight ass and let you use my cock too, baby. All you have to do is tell me—"

"Now," I beg, pulling off Bast to snap out the word. "*Now!*"

Dair answers with a snarl so salacious, my pussy flutters around Asher. He moans, letting his body buck into mine faster.

Bast copies his pace, and Dair coats his cock with my slick, gathering extra from my soaked thighs and making sure there's no friction between us as he starts to take me where no one ever has.

If I could think, I'm sure I'd be surprised by how unconcerned I am. My Omega and I both know this alpha would never hurt us. We both—

Dair's voice is low and reverent. Marveling. "You trust me, don't you, baby?" he asks, nuzzling the back of my head. "Fuck, I love that. Tell me if this is too much, okay?"

Lord, he's *scorching*.

A pulsing shaft of heat massages the secret spot he found in slow slides. I ride Asher harder, pounding his thickness into all the aching need pulling my pussy tighter and tighter.

Bast's fingers tug at the roots of my hair, his chest rumbling on a deep groan. "*Ivyyyyy*. Can I come for you, princess? *Please*?"

I nod so hard I nearly gag, swallowing as much of his length as I can. Dair's thumb strokes at the pulse in my throat, helping me suck the cum out of Bast with rhythmic squeezes of his fingers.

Sebastian shouts, jetting warm, thick washes of his perfect flavor into my throat. All over my tongue.

The taste of him starts a chain reaction. My core clamps around Asher. He roars at the ceiling, his back arching as he releases a gushing torrent as deep as he can get. Dair feels it and snaps his hips harder, burying his cock in my body and his teeth along the curve of my shoulder, drawing me back with the tattooed hand at my throat.

The world blurs into pure gold. Molten and shining to watch the way my nerves sing, then sigh as I sob.

The duke pulls out slowly, his touch softening as he frames my hips and gently guides them in a circle. With a firm push, he pops Asher's knot into me. The prince and I both cry out, his arms flying up to crush me to his heaving chest while we both come again, our initial climaxes bleeding into seconds.

Panting, Ash purrs deeply; the sound edged with the purest satisfaction. He kisses my forehead and rests his cheek there, closing his eyes in contentment.

Once again, making his point.

I just *had him* on his *throne*. I made *demands*, took whatever I wanted, and decided when we were done. I soaked slick all over the crown prince and the literal seat of his power.

And he loved it.

He loves *me*.

The others haven't told me yet, but right now, it feels like they do. Especially when Bast pets my hair into place, adjusting the crown he made sure I didn't lose.

Dair rests his hands on my shoulders, carefully working the muscles that just had all their strength sapped. "Stay," he rasps, the plea so stark and simple, it turns my head.

Dark eyes glitter in the shadows. "Stay," he says again, making the offer they've been hinting at all evening. "Be our mate. Bond with us."

"Please," Asher adds, so quiet I know the word is just for me.

Bast continues stroking my hair, his blue eyes burning with

entreaty. "We can do it any way you want," he says, speaking in a rush. "Big bonding ceremony. Privately, in your nest. Here and now. Next year. We'll do whatever feels right to you. Because *you're* what feels right to *us*. We don't make sense without you. We never did. So..."

He blows out a deep breath. "So *stay*," he begs. "I know all this seems like a dream to you. And maybe it is, but... you deserve the dream, Ivy."

Tears gather in my eyes as he swallows. Dair steps in, boring those dark eyes into mine. "Just stay here with me, baby," he beseeches. "Keep forgiving me and trusting me. Let me keep earning both."

My heart aches, emotion finally spilling down my face when Asher cups my chin and turns me to face him.

"Be our queen," he whispers. "Because you've always been the center of my whole damn universe. But now you're the center of *ours*."

fifty-two

Where the hell is our mate?

For the first time in a month, I woke up without a soft, blonde omega tucked into my side. I checked the bathroom, our balcony, and her sitting room before I finally gave up and called in the bloodhound—a.k.a. Dair.

I've never seen the fucker get dressed so fast.

"Did either of you hear her get out of bed?" he demands, turning to Asher as the prince hastily shrugs on today's suit jacket. Black. Fitting for the way the sky has darkened.

I choose gray, myself. Dair doesn't bother with more than a white button-down and last night's suit pants before shoving his feet into matching loafers. He stomps to the suite's door and looks back at us like, *you numb nuts coming?*

With a huff, I follow him out. Asher falls into step behind, making calls to the palace security detail and asking who last had their eyes on our princess. When he abruptly stops at the fork between two perpendicular hallways, my heart drops to my shoes.

Oh shit.

"She left."

The words dangle over our heads. A cleaver, slipping lower on every half-breath. Finally, Dair repeats. "Left?"

Asher scowls at his phone screen. "According to the front gate, she walked out early this morning and got in a cab."

My esophagus tangles, blocking my swallow. "In a *cab*? As in, she drove off without any security?"

We all glance at one another—and then we're running. Within seconds, we burst into the morning gloom, barreling into a carport shrouded by cool mist. Asher begins barking orders, demanding a car, a security detail, the latest video footage.

Five steps ahead of everyone else, logically, as always. I'm still trying to remember how to fucking *breathe*.

Dair looks closer to my mindset than the prince's. But as moments slip past with valets and security buzzing around us, trying to follow impromptu orders using protocols designed for *days* of notice, the duke cracks.

"Fuck this," he growls. "I'm taking my bike."

He starts to charge toward the garage, but I shout after him, "Your *bike*? You don't even know where she is!"

"She only has one place to go," he yells back, picking up speed.

Maytown.

"On it," Asher mutters, already typing.

"Gracie," I remind him. "And her aunt."

He nods fervently, jabbing his thumbs at his screen faster. "Yes. Good."

Dair's motorcycle rips out of the garage, the engine tearing the cloudy morning in two. I watch him disappear, the disquiet in my middle expanding.

If we don't find our girl—or, worse, if she's decided she *isn't* our girl—I'm not sure Dair will come back.

A graceful figure approaches through the fog, dressed in riding gear. I recognize Jasmine when she tosses her long black braid from one shoulder to the other. Thick white-chocolate sweetness smothers the air. My teeth sting like they've developed spontaneous cavities.

Ugh, God. No.

The princess notes my grimace with a smirk, pausing between Asher and me. Her dark eyes flick from me to the prince, then back again. She throws her hands on her hips, pointed features snapping into a mighty scowl.

"*Now* what?"

I open my mouth to reply, but she points a sharpened fingernail in my face, halting me. "You *better* not have fucked this up, blondie. Do you have any idea how perfect that woman is for you sorry lot?"

Asher answers before I can, pocketing his phone and casting a murderous look at the nearest valet before meeting her eyes, drawing into the posture of a prince. "We're *aware*. Now, if you'll excuse us—"

"No," Jasmine scoffs. "I will *not* excuse you. What's going on? Where is Ivy?"

Telling silence sweeps between us. Jasmine staggers back a step, her eyes bulging. "Are you fucking kidding me? Did you seriously *lose* her?"

I press my hand over my stomach, wishing I could reach in and stop its restless churning. "So it would seem."

Jasmine blinks, then fixes each of us with our very own glares. "Unbelievable!" she explodes, waving her hands over her head. "I swear to God, I did everything but hog-tie the girl and have her wheeled into your suite on a room-service cart! How the hell did you manage to screw this up? I couldn't have made it *any simpler*!"

Wait.

What?

Asher's jaw flexes, his alpha energy climbing to a fever pitch. To her credit, Jasmine doesn't flinch as he stares her down, demanding, "What are you talking about, Princess Ahmad?"

Our car pulls up behind her, but Jasmine isn't deterred. She slaps her thighs with both hands, expression exasperated. "You guys seriously never wondered why the king suddenly decided that staff would be invited to your masquerade ball? Has he *ever* done *anything* like that before?!"

Another unsettling beat of quiet betrays our reply. The princess rolls her eyes. "And the dresses 'donated by an anonymous royal'? Did you look into *that*?"

I *did* think it was *odd*, when I heard about it, but now...

"I *donated* my dresses *specifically* to make sure Ivy would have one! *I* asked the king to include the staff and implied it was an Amizi custom. And who do you think has been explaining all this omega nonsense to the poor girl?!"

Another strange decision that never made sense to me. I wondered why Jasmine chose to stay here and help Ivy after essentially being rejected by us. Not that she ever seemed all that interested in our courtship in the first place. Her father clearly forced her make an effort with us... and she mostly did...

Until I had that picnic with her.

The day I happened upon Ivy in the garden.

"You saw us," I realize. "That day."

Jasmine huffs out a deep sigh, as if exhausted by my general existence. "*Yes*," she snaps. "And it was painfully obvious to anyone with *eyes* that she was clearly your *mate*. Between that and the way *you* avoided so much as glancing at her." She points at Asher, rolling her eyes again.

"When I asked around and found out she was supposedly a beta, I didn't buy it for a second. I figured her Omega just needed an opportunity to come around. Which is why I gave her friend a dress that absolutely *reeked* of your pack. The one I'd worn the first night we met, when each of you had to dance with me."

Oh God, she's right. I didn't recognize the gown when our omega wore it because—well, Ivy dazzled me. Blinded me to literally anyone that wasn't *her*. Exactly as Jasmine intended.

Asher's brows are halfway to his hairline as I sputter, "So—she—you—"

Jasmine fists her hands on her hips. "I'm basically your Fairy Frickin' Godmother!"

Holy shit.

She really is.

We should probably *thank* her, but before we can gather the pieces of our skulls, she harrumphs and waves at the idling Maybach. "Well? What are you waiting for? I'm fresh out of wishes to grant, and you assholes don't have a pumpkin."

fifty-three

THE COOL AIR MAKES IT CLEAR—SUMMER IS OVER. AND, so far, autumn is a dreary, colorless thing.

I feel the chill unlike ever before, my bones rattling as I stand at the stoop of Aunt Matilda's building, staring up.

Bracing myself.

Knowing, with every step up the stairs, what awaits the second my family sees my face.

We told you so.

They'll be delighted, thinking I failed. I'm not sure why I never saw that before—how they seemed to take some sort of pleasure from my pain. And always looked for ways to heap more misery on my head.

Did Matilda do the same thing to Mama?

I know I'm too emotional for all of this today. After last night, my Omega wants nothing more than to spend the entire day in our nest, perfecting every square inch.

I thought I might struggle to recognize the signs, but I can actually *feel* my heat barreling toward me. Which is why I felt like I had to come back here now.

I'm out of time to make decisions.

It's time to live with them.

I try knocking, but no one answers. With reluctance, I pull the key out of my tote bag, fitting it into the scratched-up deadbolt on the peeling front door.

Behind it, the apartment is in shambles. Dirty dishes overflowing from the sink, a stain on the entry rug. Trash piled around the overfull can.

I stand on the threshold, taking in the silence. It's after ten—are they still asleep? Did they do this every day while I toiled at the manor to pay our bills?

Why didn't I ever notice or care? Didn't it ever occur to me that I might deserve more?

I swallow the angry lump blocking my throat, forcing myself forward. I know what I came to do—and as soon as I finish, I never have to return.

I'm not sure what naive part of my brain thought my family would leave my bedroom the way it was. The moment I open the door, I see that Caitlin's commandeered it. She must have slept at a guy's place last night, but her stuff is *everywhere*—including the closet that used to hold the last of my meager belongings. Blinking, I stand in front of it, reality sinking in.

They got rid of everything else I had. Mama's sewing table... and the urn that used to be on the dresser.

Frantic fear claws at my gut. Whirling, I nearly run back to the main living area, turning in half circles, eyes climbing over every piece of furniture in the apartment.

It's no use, though. The sewing table is gone. And so is my mother.

I know it—I *understand* it—but I can't *accept* it. My brain stumbles over the information while my body flies into motion, staggering to the cabinets and flinging them open. As if my aunt would put an urn in the pantry next to a bag of flour or a bottle of dish soap.

It isn't there, of course. But my hands scramble through everything they can, anyway, knocking bottles and boxes out of their way. Shoving things aside without concern for mess or noise.

Until—

Until—

Oh my God.

Pill bottles. *Dozens* of them. Half-full, empty, and brand new. All labeled with my name. Or Mama's.

My head spins, the edges of my vision blurring. I barely feel the stab of pain between my hips or the nausea that follows. I'm too busy trying to stay upright. Trying to read the names of unfamiliar medications... things I've never been prescribed.

Except... I have. They're here, and pills are missing, and—

"You didn't really think you were a late bloomer, did you?"

Aunt Matilda's voice is cool and even, floating over my shoulder from the threshold of the apartment's single hallway. I jump, my hand flying to cover my heart as I twirl toward her with a shriek.

She regards me with a sneer, her skin as pallid as her gray eyes and the streaks of silver shot through her dirty-blonde bob. Her cold gaze flickers over my outfit, snagging on the hoodie enveloping my upper half.

It's the one Dair gave me the night he took me for our ride. I've been keeping it in my nest, but I wanted something that smelled like all of us to wear here today. Plus, I thought it was casual enough to help me blend in, the way it did for him on the streets of Lyledon.

Matilda clearly knows it belongs to one of my alphas—and that detail is enough to draw a scrape of humorless laughter from her thin lips. "Have they given up on you already? Is that why you came back?"

The insults I dreaded bounce right off me. I ignore her questions, clutching the bottles in my hands tighter. "What are these?"

A cruel gleam flickers in her eyes. "Just some of your mother's old prescriptions."

That's a lie, though. And for the first time ever, I won't let her get away with it. My head shakes slowly. "N-no. These have *my* name on them. What—what are they?"

Austin Matilda's mouth twists into a gruesome mockery of a smile. "Hormones, mostly."

I think back to what the royal family's doctor said when he examined me. About my Omega being *abused*. It made sense, with how weak the voice inside me felt the first days I could hear her, but I never imagined...

"You... drugged me? To make me think I was a beta?"

Matilda scoffs. "So dramatic. Your designation bloodwork was *borderline,* and your mother was too pitiful to even shuttle you in for the follow-up exam. *I* went to get your paperwork instead. And when I saw that you were barely registering as a potential omega, I realized how easy it would be to let you both believe you weren't one."

The room tilts and swirls, the colors at the edges of my vision blotting into an ugly, brackish watercolor. "But *why*?" I burst, scraping in shallow breaths. "*Why* would *anyone* do something like that?"

All traces of amusement drop from her face, leaving the angles sharp and unforgiving as she suddenly stalks closer. "Because your *stupid* mother told me about the *prince*. How you had met and become *friends*. How he was an alpha and seemed so very 'taken with you.' Idiot. Did she honestly think I would be *happy* for you? After what she put us through when she lost your useless father?"

I cringe backward, trying to get away from the horrible rage contorting her features. She reaches out and snatches my arm, twisting it with bruising force. A cry tumbles up my throat when an answering pain rips through my lower abdomen. I stagger, my knees wobbling until they give out.

Our alphas, my Omega pleads. *We need our alphas now. Where are they?*

I thought I could slip away and take care of fetching my mother's things—that by the time they noticed I'd left, I'd already be back. Moved into the palace permanently. I pictured Dair's proud half-smile when he realized I'd devised a way to sneak off. And Bast's shining grin when he heard me confirm what they all hoped for.

I knew Asher would be mad, but only because he loves me. My desperate, hormone-crazed Omega sort of liked the idea of him fussing over us, actually. She was looking forward to a stern lecture while he tucked us into his arms and rubbed his scent all over—

Ah!

Another stab burrows and twists, the visceral pain stealing my breath. When she hears my gasp, Matilda snorts.

"See? So weak. I did you a favor all these years. Letting you go to school. Letting you *work*."

More like *making* me work. To support the whole household while she "took care" of my mother. But, really, what was she doing? Siphoning my mother's omega-suppressing medications over to me? Trying to gaslight me into believing I had health anxiety?

"H-how did you—"

Matilda twists my arm tighter, cutting me off. "Stupid girl. The smoothies. The soups. You ate anything I made for you, and you never even *asked* what was in it. Same thing with those anxiety meds you were on all those years."

She switched the pills. That must be how she kept me on her regimen while I was away at school. Only a few semesters passed before she called me home to help manage Mama—was it possible she felt she was losing control and needed me back here to stop me from designating?

All so she wouldn't have to support herself or her girls?

Or was it all really just to *keep me from my mate*?

New horror washes through me as one final question floats to the top of my bleary brain: *why on earth is she telling me all this? Doesn't she know I'll tell the princes the second I see them?*

She must understand that.

Unless... she doesn't intend to let me leave?

My mind stumbles, trying to understand—the way she's exposing my wrist, why her eyes keep flitting to the knife block on the counter beside us.

She could slash me open. Make it look like an act of desperation or delusion.

"It's a shame," she goes on, confirming the fear flooding my body, "that the pressures of becoming a potential princess finally shattered your fragile mental state."

Because that's what *everyone* would think. What my alphas would think.

That it was their fault. That I left them on purpose.

The thought is enough to finally break through my haze, shooting molten steel into my veins. My limp body comes alive with adrenaline, pulsing with the strength to throw my weight into my aunt's body and topple her to the floor.

Her gray eyes widen with shock when she finds me standing over her and hears me snarl, "Haven't you heard? I'm *not* a princess. I'm their *queen*."

fifty-four

Muscle memory is the only thing that keeps me from dropping my bike to the curb. I turn it off, shove it onto its stand, rip my helmet off, and leap over the seat.

I don't need an apartment number to know where my little dove is, either. I can scent her—the luscious, sugared warmth that's melted into a muck of burning fear and...

Anger?

I'm not sure I've ever sensed that from her before.

Is it *us*? Is she pissed we asked her to bond with us? Or about the upholstery on the throne? I *told* her I'd get that shit *cleaned*—

Someone screams. I double my pace, jumping up three stairs at a time to get to the second-floor landing.

"*Ivy!*" I bark. "*Answer me.*"

There's a commotion behind the door at the end of the hallway. When I hear a whine—*Ivy's* whine—I lunge for it.

I used to think a lot about how traumatic moments turn into memories. The things that stick with you—the stupid details you recall when everything else about a moment becomes a blur.

Bruises as dark as the ink on my arms.

Asher's fingers closing around a silver heart.

And now, the flash of blonde hair that flies across my field of vision the moment this dingy apartment door flies open.

Ivy, sailing toward the floor. Falling—until she's not.

Because I'm here.

The sound that tears from my body is inhuman. A roar that sends the middle-aged woman who just shoved my omega falling onto her ass.

She scrabbles backward, but I barely see her. It feels a bit like catching a priceless piece of art while a cockroach scurries out of the way.

Who the fuck cares if this bitch gets crushed under my heel?

I'm going to kill her anyway.

At the moment, my Alpha and I have other priorities. Namely, the bone-pale omega wilting in my arms.

"Ivy," I mutter, low and urgent. Her head lolls against my chest, lashes fluttering over her blown pupils. And—*shit*. Her skin is *hot*.

"Baby, say something." I frame her face with my hand, too scared to breathe deeply enough to form a purr. "Ivy? Come on, little dove, it's me. I'm here. You're safe now."

The woman on the ground starts trying to crawl around me, and I scoop Ivy into my arms, side-stepping to place my feet right in her path. "*Do not move again,* or I swear to God, I'll—"

This must be Ivy's aunt, the beta. My command shouldn't

work on her, but it does. Or maybe she just knows a losing battle when she sees one.

There's not a chance in hell she'll escape me. Nowhere on this whole damn planet for her to hide.

Shoving *my* omega? Traumatizing *my* mate to the point where she's nearly unconscious? And—oh *fuck* no—are these *bruises* on Ivy's arm?

My mate trembles as I examine her wrist, growling at the marks. She fights to open her eyelids, mumbling to me in a dazed whisper, "D-Dair? I—I think my—my heat... I don't feel so well."

I might be murderous and confused and mad as hell that she left without telling us this morning, but somehow, I end up softly brushing my lips along her brow. "Why didn't you wake me, huh?" I ask, squeezing her tighter. "I would have snuck out with you."

"I—I know," she warbles. "B-but I needed to fit my mom's sewing table in the back of a car with me, and I was trying t-to—" Pain creases her forehead. "—surprise Bast. Get Asher's approval. Make *you*..."

I scent-mark her cheek with my own, murmuring against her temple. "Make me...?"

"Proud," she croaks, almost too quiet to hear.

Fuck. Her heat's about to start, and all she wanted was our approval. Our... love. She snuck out to *surprise* us, not to leave us behind.

My heart *cracks*, the strength of my purr nearly forceful enough to break a rib. "You *do*, little dove. And you did today." I offer a weak smile. "Fighting this bitch off? C'mon. That's *my* omega."

Ivy's scent sweetens, and she nuzzles her face into my neck. A ragged inhale turns into another whine.

"I know, baby," I soothe. "We're going to take care of you, okay? The guys are right behind me."

The woman on the floor squawks, "You mean the *prince* is coming *here*?"

I bare my teeth at her, making a sound that abruptly drains the color from her face. "*I am* the prince," I tell her, "because of Ivy."

fifty-five

"IVY!"

The room is a blur of bellows and running footsteps. My mind feels farther and farther away, like I have to peer down a long tunnel to see what's happening. But a much deeper, stronger part knows without sight—*they're all here.*

My alphas came for me.

The burned, bitter scents swirling around the apartment are sort of a giveaway. Even without those, I have a feeling my Omega would know they were here; the way some piece of my soul seemed to snap to attention every time Dair stared at me. Or when Asher would walk past. Or if Bast smiled at someone else.

My baron isn't smiling *at all* now. It isn't the first time I've seen him so serious, but he's never radiated pure *fear* before.

"Ivy," Bast gasps, practically ripping me from Dair's arms. I expect my duke to snap, but he chooses to direct his rage at Matilda, growling a low explanation to the others while he snarls at her.

I blink, my brain bumbling through the motions. Recognizing Sebastian. Cataloging his expression. Then Dair's fierce face, all harsh lines and the feral gleam of protectiveness. Before it moves on to Asher, who's directing his security to drag my aunt off the floor...

I barely care. All I can think is that they're really *here*. And as that sinks in, I start sobbing.

Bast hums, tucking my body into his and dropping onto the nearest chair, rocking us. "Sweet angel, it's okay. I have you."

Lord. His *voice* is enough to have me squirming in his lap—the place between my thighs throbbing. When I whine, he presses his lips to my forehead for a long second.

"You're hot," he mutters.

A delusional giggle bubbles under my tears. "You, too."

That only draws deeper lines across his expression. His ocean eyes gloss with tears. "Fucking hell," he whispers. "I've never been so scared, angel. I thought you'd gone. And all I could think was—"

He swallows, weak cloud-filtered light catching in his golden hair as he shakes his head. "I thought I'd never get to tell you how much I love you."

Tears blaze paths down my cheeks. "Y-you do?"

His smile is somehow even more breathtaking with pain pulling at his eyes. The hurt underlines just how heart-stopping his happiness is.

"Not sure I've ever loved anything quite like this," he confesses, an adorable beat of bewilderment evaporating some of the worry furrowing his brow.

I try to smile, but it just sends new droplets down my face. "I love you, too, Bast. You're my—" I pant around a stabbing cramp. "—best friend."

His entire face glows, beaming back at me. He leans close and steals a soft kiss, murmuring, "Shh. We won't tell Asher."

"I heard that."

The prince's dry mutter interrupts as he falls to his knees beside Bast's feet. His bitter bergamot scent does nothing to discourage the wetness seeping into my panties despite the intense frown on his face.

Ash brushes my bangs back with careful fingers, so gentle that fresh tears rise to my eyes. "Goose," he breathes. "*Never* scare me like that again. You can go anywhere you want, but you have to *tell me* so I can keep you *safe*."

Dair glares at the open door. Where—*oh*—I guess they just hauled Matilda out. He keeps his murderous gaze on the exit as he replies, "Ivy wanted to surprise us. She was trying to get the last of her stuff and bring it home."

Bast's bone-melting purr deepens, and he hugs me. Another tingly shiver wracks my body. Slick slides out of me, wetting his lap, but he only hums, scent-marking me with his cheek against my crown.

"*Home*," Asher repeats, his hazel eyes glowing. "Is that right, omega?"

I nod against his palm. "I want to bond," I beg him. "P-please alpha. I want us to be bonded, but I—I don't think I want to wait. I'd rather do it with just the four of us, in private."

When he keeps gazing at me, I ramble, "I know it isn't what your parents were hoping for, and I'm so sor—"

He kisses me suddenly, cutting off the apology. When he pulls back, he whispers, "My queen doesn't apologize to me. Especially not for this."

He flicks a look up at Bast. "You're right." Then, to me, "You're too warm, Ivy. We need to get you out of here and back to your nest. We can bond at the end of your heat—that's the best time for your Omega, though I'm not sure if I'll be able to wait that long."

His wry half-smile does crazy things to my heart. I can feel it sealing itself back together, the new cracks filled with pure gold. I sob another watery laugh, nodding my fervent agreement.

Asher's eyes soften with pure adoration. "Let's go home," he murmurs. "Did you get what you need to take with us?"

I shake my head, voice trembling with more tears. "They got rid of my mother's things. And her ashes... I can't find them."

Dair growls low and abruptly stalks off. Bast watches him with exasperation, but Asher only scowls mildly, bending to pluck up one of the pill bottles I dropped when Matilda grabbed me.

"Th-those aren't mine," I explain as he scans the label. "Sh-she was... drugging me. And my mother. Since I was sixteen."

"*What*?" Bast hisses.

Asher reels back, a bolt of pure rage cracking across his gaze like lightning. "*Why*?"

I do my best to muddle through an explanation, but honestly? I don't understand it much myself.

I get that Matilda didn't appreciate having to take care of Mama after my father died... and I think I can empathize with being a beta and wishing I could have mates like an omega would.

But even that... is an excuse.

These men didn't fall for me *because* I'm an omega. They all knew me before—they all *liked* me before. Even Dair, in his own dark way—letting me take care of him that night in the alleyway, all his vulnerable rambling and begging me not to leave.

After months of courting every eligible omega in the universe, none of them *ever* wanted those women the way they desire me. Because how the guys love me has nothing to do with *what* I am.

It's *who* I am.

I'm what they love.

I'm what's made them *whole*.

And that's the last coherent thought I have before hazy darkness closes in.

fifty-six

It's the age-old question—what would you grab if your house was on fire?

Well, turns out, if the palace full of treasures I've called my home for my entire life went up in flames...

I would take my mate's favorite blanket.

We only had three minutes to get ourselves together before we raced after her, and in that time, the silver silk duvet Ivy's become so attached to was the only thing I told Duncan to pack for us.

In retrospect, perhaps that was an instinct. Maybe my Alpha knew how close his mate's heat was, even though I didn't.

Way too close.

Or, rather, *we're* too *far*.

Her nest is over an hour away and Ivy simply isn't going to last that long without one of us soothing her. By the time we get into the Maybach, she's whimpering and barely conscious.

After his short quest to rip the apartment apart, Dair returns empty-handed, with a down-right homicidal gleam in his eyes. I suspect avoiding a murder is half the reason he demands Bast hand Ivy back to him.

He carries our omega out, flipping his motorcycle a dismissive scoff. "Fuck it," he decides. "I'm not leaving her."

I clap his shoulder, pride warming my chest. "We'll send someone."

Two months ago, Dair would have cut off his left hand before leaving his Ducati behind. Now, he truly doesn't seem to care, gazing at our princess like he has the entire world in his lap. Which, I suppose, he does.

Bast flips his phone in his palm. "I've already texted Gracie. She's unlocking the gates and our suite at Maytown, but she doesn't want to get her scent on anything in case it upsets Ivy's Omega. She can send someone to get the bike, though."

Brilliant bastard.

"The manor," I realize, relief rushing my lungs. "Perfect. Great idea, Bast."

He slides closer to Dair, petting Ivy's hair. "I'm worried she may not even make it there. Her *scent* is—"

Earth-shattering. So sweet and deliciously toasted, I feel like I'm breathing gold pixie dust. Or maybe some sort of drug—my vision is sharper with every aching pulse that echoes in my canines.

Dair's fingers twitch, his purr melding with a low growl. "Don't," he grits. "I'm barely keeping our fucking clothes on right now."

I swallow a thick wash of saliva, meeting his eyes. Checking to make sure I don't need to snatch her away. I'm surprised by how steady he seems, though. Not because he's unaffected, but because he's *fighting* for control with every breath.

"You should have seen how scared she was," he mumbles, squeezing his eyes shut and letting his head drop back against the headrest. Distracting himself, I suspect.

"When this is over," I intone, putting a pulse of power behind every word. "I need you to show me."

So I can carry her fear with me. Until hopefully, one day, she won't need to anymore. I hope she'll let me take that burden—and all the other ones her family left her with.

The doctor's words from the day she designated come rushing back to me. *Ivy's results are more consistent with an omega who's been abused.*

Because she *was*. And I missed it.

MAYTOWN MANOR IS FULL OF SHADOWS.

In all the years my family spent summers here, I never returned after the season. I don't have time to notice much, now, apart from how quiet and empty it feels. Ivy is in pain—and every whine from her lungs scrapes the inside of my skull.

The words swirling through my thoughts aren't helpful. The whole ride over, Bast and I mumbled about the pill bottles Ivy found, sending information to Dr. Grant. He said her Omega will either thrive under our attention or go into a traumatized state once her haze kicks in and Ivy can't calm herself down.

I wish I could feel optimistic, but as we sweep into our chambers and chilled silence greets us...

Ivy has barely moved since she passed out in that horrid apartment. What if all of this has been too much for her? If she comes to and she's too scared to let us touch her, she'll *suffer*.

The fact that we don't even have a *nest* for her...

"*Goddamn it*," Dair rasps, clutching his hair with both hands and spinning in a half circle. "Where do we take her?"

The only nest in the manor belongs to my parents. Obviously, that will need to be removed and completely replaced if we ever want our princess to have another heat here.

I'm not prepared. We didn't know this would happen—and there's no time to change anything.

My mind spins, trying to remember everything she asked for in her nest back home. We have her favorite blanket tucked around her small, still body. But the main thing our omega loved was hoarding our *scents*. Having us *cover* everything...

"Our mattresses," I realize. "They've probably washed the sheets and towels by now, but our mattresses will have our scents embedded deep."

Bast and Dair take off. My blond packmate mutters as he goes, "We should bring them to Asher's room. It's the only one we've all been in together. Her Omega might be able to remember that."

I agree with a brusque nod. The guys drag the heavy foam pads out of their rooms and across the round living room, cursing and muttering at each other while they try to get them both through my doors. I mentally record the whole production, hoping Ivy might find some humor in it later...

If her Omega accepts this. And still wants to bond here.

In short order, we have all three mattresses on my bedroom floor, shoved together like a makeshift island. They push my iron bed frame to the far side of the room, against the bookshelves.

Wanting to keep anything pointed or hard well away from our omega's safe space.

It still doesn't look very nest-like. I note the grimace on Bast's face and search the depths of my memories for *something*—*any*thing...

My eyes land on my armoire. "Here."

I hand our dozing princess to Dair. With a few brisk steps and a hard yank, I tug a set of deep blue sheets from the bottom drawer of the antique. When I shake them loose, my scent sours with a distinct edge of chagrin.

"Stars?" Bast asks, half-grinning at the pattern. "Seriously?"

They're clearly sheets for a kid, leftover from my many summers here as an adolescent. When I see their quizzical looks, I clear my throat. "I had these when I was young. One of the housekeepers tried to get rid of them when I got older, but... the stars reminded me of Ivy and how she liked to make wishes. I couldn't seem to get rid of them."

Bast's shit-eating grin has me glowering. He snorts, "Oh, come on. That's cute as hell."

The Dair we've spent ten years dealing with *definitely* would have had some ball-busting comments—but this version? The duke who can't keep his eyes off the small blonde lying limp in his arms?

"She'll like them," he murmurs. "You want to put them on one of the beds or something?"

I fight off a smirk and fail, flinging my focus up to the ceiling eaves.

"Not exactly."

fifty-seven

I WAKE UP UNDER A SAPPHIRE CURTAIN OF STARS.

The sight is soothing and oddly familiar, somehow.

Which seems impossible, because I don't know where I am. Or *who* I am.

All I know is burning, tingling *pain*. Spreading over my skin, licking high between my hips. Engulfing my lungs until a high-pitched keen tears up my raw throat.

"Ivy?"

It's my alpha—the one with gold, worried eyes. He appears in my line of sight, his dark brown hair blurring with the deep blue surrounding us. His face is masculine perfection, but I can't remember his *name*.

Will he be mad?

Will he leave?

Another painful noise sloughs out of my burning body. His features fold. "Darling, I'm here. Your alpha is here. I'll make it feel better for you, all right?"

Relief can't rise into my chest with this thick slab of fear blanketing my belly. Because there's something—someone—oh God, what am I *forgetting*?

Not what—*who*.

Because a second later, two more faces appear. One square and golden, topped with messy blond hair. The other lean and sculpted, with dark eyes that stab right into my breathless need.

A hand covered in pretty patterns snaps up and touches my head. The gentle brush of fingers through my hair has my eyes rolling back and my hips churning. "P-please," I whimper pitifully. "A-alpha, *please*."

The ache between my thighs feels hot and slick. I don't understand it, but the alpha does. He immediately moves, hoisting me into his arms and spreading my legs around his bare body.

"You can have any damn thing you want," he growls. "Starting with this knot."

A *knot*.

Oh my *God*.

My body moves, bouncing, tears streaming down my face at the thought of having this powerful man stuff me and knot me and lock us together and sink his teeth into my neck and—

Three groans fill the room, warm satin skin and tight muscles pressing into me from all sides. Soothing vibrations sink into my bones, rattling them gently until they start to gel. More wetness seeps from my center in a rush I can't control.

The alpha holding me hums, dark eyes smoldering. "That's my perfect girl," he rasps, running his hands over my sides.

Chasing the shiver that shakes my spine and leaving blissful tingles in his wake.

And his *skin*—the way it *feels* against the insides of my thighs. I dive forward, and he catches me, purring loud enough to drown out the fear searing my lungs. Those dark, burning beacons lock on my eyes again. "Baby, I see you. I'm here. Not ever leaving you. I *love* you, Ivy. So goddamn much."

I'm only lucid enough to feel the faintest sparkle of surprise. The vaguest sort of euphoria. And the tiny voice inside me that shouts back to him, telling him she loves him, too? I realize that it's *me*. *I'm* the smallest, weakest part of myself now. And my *Omega* is in control.

It should probably be terrifying. I know she was scared, being trapped inside me. Forgotten or lost or locked away.

But all I see is the dark alpha's eyes. And all I hear are his words. Now. Echoing through time.

A memory. A promise.

I see you. Stay with me.

And sometime before, in a darker place and time. *Don't leave me, please.*

I want to tell him that I'm not. That I *won't*.

Somehow, though, I don't need to. Because part of me knows that he understands—this? This isn't me leaving them. It's me coming *home*.

They all know. I feel it in their hands, the depth of their roaring purrs. The brush of lips over my crown and my shoulder. All three of my mates are here to catch me and hold me and make me theirs.

Just like I wished for.

fifty-eight

THE LAST SHRED OF OUR ANGELIC MATE VANISHES INTO a wild-eyed omega. I watch her consciousness blink offline, the last band of blue around her blown pupils blurring into the darkness.

My Alpha snaps forward, practically pawing the ground. This is *his* mate—and he *wants* her.

The second Ivy hears my low purr stutter into a growl, sparks ignite in her unfocused gaze. She scrambles from Dair's lap, kneeling between his knees, spreading her legs, and whining sharply as she reaches toward our pack alpha.

Asher moves immediately, shuffling across the mattress. We were all so worried about how Ivy would feel in the makeshift nest, but she doesn't seem to mind it very much. Or even notice. Any concerns I had evaporate when she opens her mouth.

"Alpha, *now*!"

A beat of shock ripples through the room. Asher recovers quickly, presenting her with his hard cock and knot, raising an eyebrow. "Hmm. Is this what you want, princess?"

Ivy *snarls*. The sound connects with the desperate desire pulsing through my veins, kicking my blood up to a boil. When my scent reaches her, she moans and tosses her hair back, pivoting to show me her fluttering pussy and the glorious slick pouring from it.

Holy fuck—is she *presenting*? For *me*?

It's typically the privilege of the pack alpha to decide who knots an omega first during their heat. But I barely manage to hold myself back long enough to flick a look at Asher.

He half-smirks, the expression split between amusement and impatience. "It's fine. It's *good*," he grits. "She wants you first, Bast. And she gets whatever she wants."

Really, Asher has always been this sort of leader—selfless and completely lacking in ego. He shares his power so readily, never hoarding any of it or asserting himself over the rest of us.

The fact that he still isn't doing that now, here?

We're goddamn lucky to have him at the head of our pack.

The prince hums to Ivy, cupping her chin and bringing his cock to her lips. She sucks it into her mouth like she *needs* the taste of him to live. He sloughs out a breath, tipping his head back.

The sight of him touching her, our omega's scent, and her starved moan... My hips snap forward, plunging me straight into her sweet pussy.

Good. Holy. *God*.

Her body gels and tightens at the same time. Slippery,

smooth, and snug enough to strangle. The heat of her envelopes my cock, the fluttering depths tugging at my swollen head with every pulse.

A high-pitched sound vibrates around Asher's cock, and he groans. Her perfume brightens—so sweet and heavenly, my mind blurs into a haze.

I rut her harder, and she lifts her ass higher, an answering whine begging for more. My balls slap at her clit until they're dripping. She grinds herself into my knot, gliding her lips up Asher's dick and plummeting back onto it with every thrust of my body into hers.

Dair kneels at her side, fisting her hair and skimming his other hand over her spine. "You look so pretty when you're taking two cocks, little dove. Are you going to take their cum, too? Swallow every last drop your alpha gives you? Let Bast blast this gorgeous cunt?"

Ivy moans over Asher while her pussy clamps around my cock. We both snarl. Our omega reaches a hand back, grasping Dair's forearm and trying to maneuver him.

Asher's eyes gleam with understanding. "She wants to suck you off, too," he rasps, shifting to make room for our packmate. "Give her your cock so she can take both."

Dair obeys with a vicious curse, kneeling beside Asher and holding his cock out for Ivy. Pure delight fills her face as she lunges for it. Rapture replaces her excitement when his flavor hits her tongue.

His fingers weave deeper into her light hair, guiding her. "Fuck, baby. You like the way my cock tastes? Is it as good as Asher's?"

Her body answers before she does, squeezing me in wet spasms that tear a ragged groan out of my chest. Dair's dark gaze glitters. "Yeah? How about having us in your mouth at the same time?"

Fucking *hell*, the *sound* she makes. Her *perfume*.

Jesus.

I might not live through this.

I could already be dead, for all I know. This is basically heaven.

Ivy opens her mouth, tossing each of the guys an expectant, exasperated look that would definitely make me laugh under ordinary circumstances. As it is, the demanding edge to her expression has my balls tingling.

I remember how scared her Omega seemed the first time I eased her through a spike. But now? Gazing up at Prince Asher Everhart with all sorts of *"well? I'm waiting"* in her foggy eyes...

Who knew I had the ability to be insanely proud while *fighting for my fucking life*?

Asher brings himself back to her mouth. She hums, pussy clamping around my cock while she laps at both of them in turn. They hold still, letting her tongue slip between their heads.

After a moment, she gets frustrated, trying to taste them both at the same time, bucking back into my steady drives with a new sort of urgency. Her perfume takes on a distinct edge of desperation.

Another cramp. I purr, churning my hips in circles so she can feel the thickness inside her rub all the quivering muscles clutching me.

Asher strokes her cheek in a comforting gesture. Dair's dark eyes soften into smoldering coals. He uses the hair at her nape to guide her head back, his free hand—*oh, shit*—grabbing both their cocks, lining the first third of each up and shoving them into her waiting mouth.

Ivy gasps and whines, the sound muffled in her throat as Asher's touch slides down to her neck. He's more gentle than Dair, but the effect is the same. Our girl clenches around me in earth-shattering squeezes. Milking my cock the same way Dair works the two cocks she's sucking.

Ivy's hazy eyes zero in on Dair and Asher's knots. She reaches for the prince's first, kneading with her fingers before rebalancing her weight and lifting her other hand to Dair's.

Someone groans, and someone else growls. Drool and slick

dribble onto her favorite blanket, her scent bursting through the room in a golden deluge of pure sugar.

Fuck.

FUCK.

"Gonna come so hard in this gorgeous cunt," I pant. "Fill this sweet pussy with everything I have and give you my knot."

She keens as her body responds, tugging me deeper. Until my knot finally—*finally*—pops into the buzzing ring of muscle spasming for the swell.

"Ivy—*shit*—"

She screams as she flies over the edge, clamping around me in a slick vise of pure ecstasy. Pleasure snaps down my spine, burrowing into my lower abdomen and bottoming out in the knot that expands to fill her. Hot liquid shoots up my shaft, the flood jetting into the whirlpool of wet perfection cradling my cock.

I come with a roar that echoes back at me as the guys go off. They overfill her mouth, sending a mixture of pearly seed dripping down her chin. Asher murmurs to her in a soothing tone, tenderly gathering the excess on his fingers and bringing it up to her lips. Ivy hums, content to lap them clean.

I bend to drop kisses along her spine, wrapping an arm around her waist when I feel her tremble. The shivers send a new wave of tingles over my cock and knot. "You feel so fucking perfect, angel," I gasp. "Such a good omega, taking all that alpha cum."

Ivy arches into my praise. I bury my face against her nape, arranging us in a spooning position before tipping onto our sides.

Later, when her heat has passed, there will be time for me to cuddle her and stay knotted all night. But an alpha's biology responds to omegas in heat with certain changes. Right now, my knot will only hold us together for a couple of minutes to keep her pain at bay. Then, when she needs more, everything will unlock.

My chest hurts at the thought, but Ivy whimpers, nestling back into my warmth. I close my eyes and nuzzle her bare shoulder, telling her how much I love her. How beautiful she is. That I've never felt anything better or truer than I do right now.

fifty-nine

If I ever had any doubts that Ivy was my omega...

I mean, I *didn't* doubt it.

But still. If I *had*... There's no denying she's perfect for me, now.

I glower at Ivy's bratty expression, gripping her hairbrush in my left hand while my right holds her jaw. "Baby. Behave."

Sparks fly in her darkened eyes. Heat radiates off her body as she slowly rubs her slick cunt over my thigh.

And damn. It almost works.

Clearing my throat, I toss her a smirk. "Clever, omega. But

nothing is going to get you fucked until you've let me brush your hair."

Ivy's cool-blonde locks hang in wet ribbons around her naked shoulders. It's a good thing Asher and I have Bast here. Because before this week? Neither of us knew you were supposed to comb conditioner into long hair.

So far, Bast has taken the majority of her hygiene tasks because he genuinely enjoys them. Some days, his nightly bathing ritual—knotting her in the bathtub and lulling her with purrs to let him wash her up—and Asher's strict mealtimes are the only "breaks" we take.

Our omega has been deliciously needy, often working through all of us two or three times before she passes out. Her sleep stretches have gotten a bit longer since Sunday, but not by much.

Which is fine by me.

Hell, bury me here.

Ivy senses my scent deepening when her perfume enters my thoughts. Her blown pupils glitter. She pouts, whining while she works herself over my quad with more insistent glides. Fresh slick coats my skin, reminding me that I need another shower.

My Alpha hates that idea almost as much as our girl's Omega loathes being wiped clean. I chuff at us both, shaking my head.

Drama queens.

Asher finishes his dinner and leaves the empty plate on the tray beside his rumpled mattress. He crawls over, bringing Ivy her beloved blanket. For a moment, I think he's cracked the code. Ivy snuggles her face into the silk and relaxes into his purring chest long enough for me to brush half of her hair.

Before he can switch sides to give me access to the rest, though, our omega squeaks. Slicing, desperate perfume swells through the room. Bast's fork clatters to his own plate.

He curses quietly under his breath, gasping, "God, how does it keep getting *better*?"

"I know," Asher murmurs, stroking her cheek with his knuckles. Some of her attitude fades when he looks right at her.

Our baby's Omega has a different nature with each of us. For me, she's an abominable brat, demanding and spoiled. To Bast, she's playful and teasing. But our pack alpha gets this softer, more vulnerable version.

"Hello, darling," he whispers as the purest, truest adoration fills her face. "I see you in there."

I'm not a romantic, but even I have to admit that watching the two of them is sweet. I might have seen Ivy's Omega buried inside her before the others, but *Asher* sees his girl hidden in this Omega.

We all love her no matter which temperament we're getting—but I miss *our* Ivy more and more by the hour. That shy smile. Her little quips and giggles. The never-ending empathy she has for every creature under the sun...

Bast puts his sprinting skills to good use, sneaking out with our empty dinner trays and returning within seconds. For the first couple of days, anytime one of us left the nest, our omega panicked. She still doesn't like it, but she seems more securely attached, only whimpering for a split second before he reappears at her side and plants a dozen kisses on her face.

"I know, love. I'm here, I'm *here*."

Asher purrs louder, nodding at the hairbrush. Bast slips his hand down her front, cupping her soaked slit and grazing his thumb over her clit in slow circles while I work through the other half of her hair.

Sharp gold sugar spirals into the air, thickening it. We all half-choke, our cocks stiffening instantly. Asher grits his teeth and adjusts his knot, muttering, "I think *this* is her real heat perfume. Whatever she had at the beginning wasn't at full strength—possibly because she was so upset."

Holy fuck. If the way I'm two breaths away from going absolute feral—after *four days* of fucking her *nonstop*—is any indication, I might not have been able to make it to the manor, let alone build our almost-nest, if she'd had *this* sort of perfume.

Her warm sweetness curls in my lungs. The hairbrush goes flying as a growl tears up my throat. I grip her hips, lifting her fully into my lap. "Come here, baby."

Bast soothes her when she whines, bucking her hips in a frantic attempt to get me inside her faster. I pick her up and sink her onto my throbbing shaft.

Oh *God*. She's scorching hot and *pulsing*. *Fuck meeeeee.*

"How do you always feel so *perfect*?" I groan, my chest already heaving.

Bast's eyes are almost as dark as mine, but his lips quirk into a wicked smile. "Maybe we should reward her. Give our omega her new favorite thing."

Ivy and I moan that time. Because her new favorite is also mine.

"Yeah?" I ask, thrusting into her slippery warmth. "You want both your holes filled, baby? Alpha cock in your pussy and your tight little ass at the same time?"

Bast is being an ass, trying to ruin my stamina on purpose. When Ivy kicks into a faster pace, I catch his smirk before my eyes roll back into my head.

Our omega is so slick, it doesn't take much for Bast to coat his cock and line it up with her back entrance. Asher moves to her side, stroking her naked hip. "You're so beautiful, darling," he tells her. "So pretty and well-behaved, taking two of your alphas. Always my good girl."

She's so soft for him, even now. With a quiet whine, she lurches in his direction—and I love that it doesn't even occur to her to worry that I won't keep her upright.

Her trust is everything to me. Moments where she displays it subconsciously are what I live for.

Asher helps catch her, too, slinging an arm around her back and capturing her cry with his lips when Bast starts pushing his way into her impossibly tight ass.

He fills her completely—a solid ridge pressed into the underside of my dick through her thin, heated skin. When he pulls out and shoves back in, the head of his cock traces the bottom of mine. My balls draw up, my knot tingling.

A serrated sound tears from my lungs, melding with Ivy's whimpers and Bast's low snarl, "Yes, angel. Take this dick. Fuck yourself with it."

Ivy obeys, pounding onto my cock and his, thrusting her hips back and down and back and down and—

Asher grunts when her hand starts to tug at his cock, smearing the pre-cum seeping from the tip at her waist. His eyes flash when he catches on.

"You want me to coat you in my cum, princess?" he asks. "Put my scent all over you?"

And—good *God*—she really does. Just as badly as she wants mine in her pussy and Bast's all over her ass.

Asher squeezes his knot while Ivy strokes his shaft. When he finds a rhythm to match ours and starts thrusting into her fist, her cunt tweaks tighter. Collapsing around my cock in hungry convulsions, pressing Bast's hardness into mine and milking us both.

"Fucking *hell*, Dair," Bast roughs out, his knot swelling until it bumps my own. Ivy's slick slips between the hot swells of flesh, letting them glide and grind against one another as we both fight to get deeper.

I drop my hand from Ivy's throat to her spread pussy lips, rubbing the pulsing bud there with two fingers. She gasps and screams, gorgeous ecstasy filling her features as she comes all over both our cocks.

Those wet spasms do me in. My vision goes white as I lift my hips from the mattress and knot her rippling pussy. Hot lashes of cum burst from my cock, painting her depths.

Bast groans and pulls out, coating her entire backside with a thick wash of white. Asher hisses at the sight, releasing his own gushing torrent over her side.

And—oh.
Shit.
Where the hell did I put that hairbrush?

sixty

"She has a scar here."

Dair touches Ivy's wrist, a question lifting his brow.

I'm pretty certain, if I could hear him, he'd be asking, *Who do I have to kill?*

I nuzzle Ivy's neck, hiding a smile against her nape. "It's from a swan. She tried to make friends with it."

Bast practically whines, "I *miss* her. And I swear to God, if she begs me to bite her *one more time*, I might lose it."

He has a point. Ivy has been just lucid enough to start pleading with us over the last twelve hours. I'm optimistic that means her heat is about to break, but resisting her gets more impossible by the minute.

The truth is, I miss her, too. Desperately. But I also love this time with her—caring for her every need, with nothing to do but touch her and make her feel good. I suspect it's been healing for all of us after the way this started.

Dair sighs, but the sound is more pensive than impatient. "I've been thinking... about the coronation..." He flips his gaze up to mine. "Do you think we could wait? Just a little while... until she feels more ready... and *I* feel more ready?"

The urge to blink in shock is overwhelming. In ten years, I don't know if my packmate has ever *asked* me for *anything*. He's complained and insulted and bailed on promises, but I'm fairly sure Dair's never felt he had the right to make any *requests.*

Bast clears his throat. "I've actually been wondering the same thing. It's enough for me that Ivy doesn't feel ready, but if you don't either, Dair..." He meets my gaze. "Can we wait, Asher? Enjoy some time being newly bonded?"

For once, I don't feel the need to analyze or overthink. Instead, I nod, deciding, "If that's what's best for our pack, that's what we'll do."

I've been bred to be king, but as relief darts across Dair's face and Bast flashes an approving grin, I've never felt more like a true leader. Part of me believed I was ready and thought I'd make a decent ruler.

But now I *know* I will be.

We will be.

It's Ivy. She's the one who's brought us together—to the point where not being bonded to these guys is almost as painful as not being connected to *her*.

My lips graze her shoulder. I feel how cool her skin has gotten and tuck her closer, soaking in her sweet scent and how she snuggles back into my embrace.

Our mate gives a sleepy hum, rubbing her cheek over my biceps. "Mmm, Ash."

We all freeze. Bast and Dair's eyes leap to one another's faces, then over to mine. Our blond packmate rolls closer, putting himself right in her line of sight.

"Ivy? Angel?"

She makes another quiet thrumming sound. The hand tucked near her chin reaches for him, but the other goes for Dair's. When she kisses the flower inked on the back of his knuckles, hope swoops through my chest.

That feeling explodes in a burst of true joy when her eyes manage to connect with mine, and a soft, hesitant smile curves her mouth.

"Alpha," she says, then blinks as if correcting herself. "*Ash.*"

"Both, darling. Always your alpha. And always your Ash." I kiss her temple, scent-marking her there. She whimpers quietly, her belly contracting against the arm I have banded across it.

Fresh perfume and slick fill the space between us as she whimpers, "Want you. Want the bonds."

Bast shushes her sweetly, bending to run his nose along hers. His blue eyes snap to mine, full of optimism and eagerness. "Can we? Is it time?"

I read about omega heats extensively to prepare for this. Some of it helped—knowing when and how to bark to keep my packmates on track, using my omega's desire for approval to get her to eat and help keep her clean. But as much as I learned about knowing the right time to bite her and seal our bonds… none of it could have helped.

This feeling? It's indescribable and undeniable.

And there's no science in the world that could possibly make sense of it.

This whisper in my soul. The same one I heard all those years ago when I found a girl in a garden. The silence of the world falling away. Until there's only her and this and us.

"Yes, it's time."

sixty-one

IT'S PEACEFUL IN MY FOGGY MIND.

My first thought is a calm note of surprise. After years of being told I had "medical anxiety," I expected to wake up panicking. And in pain. Instead, I'm... warm?

Safe and tucked into supple strength that smells like the best sort of bitter black tea—the kind that goes with rainy afternoons and crisp newspaper and the reverent musk of a well-loved hiding place.

A name floats to the surface of my placid thoughts, an answering wash of adoration pouring through me.

Ash.

I've done something right, apparently, because the heavenly aroma surrounding me gets even more delicious. Two others join, the three strands of perfection curling down my throat.

My lungs tingle. A high-pitched sound ekes out, and three deep purrs reply.

Cramps are still tweaking my middle, but there isn't an accompanying lurch of fear. My Omega hardly notices the discomfort, too busy whining over the empty place behind my diaphragm to worry about my empty pussy.

When my pack alpha scent-marks me, I can't contain the needy sound. "Want you," I whine, "Want the bonds. Please, alpha."

I barely recognize my own voice, but my alphas do. One nuzzles his nose against mine while the other pets my hair, his essence sharpening.

My usual inhibitions seem to slide right down my back, dissipating before they even touch me. I fling myself toward the fresh scent and land in a cradle of inky muscle.

"Hi, baby," he chuckles, amused and wicked. He kisses me between my brows, reassuring, "I see you. You good?"

He barely finishes his question before I scrabble closer, kissing him with another desperate sound. He moves his mouth with mine, licking and biting as his purr deepens into a low growl. Fingers twist in my hair and tug, revealing my throat. As his tongue glides up the column, slick douses his lap, and a name sails across my mind like a shooting star.

Dair.

A masculine moan carves into my consciousness, turning my head. I find my light-haired, bright-eyed alpha kneeling beside us. His broad chest throbs on labored breaths as hope fills his face.

Something about that vulnerable expression clicks into my center. A light flicks on inside my soul.

Sebastian.

His forehead presses into mine, fervor lining his square features. "I can't wait to be in you," he husks, lungs rumbling in a steady rattle. "You want us to bite you, love? Make you ours?"

My relief must be palpable because the alpha under me shudders. His tattooed hands soften. One strokes down my side while the other massages my nape. Satisfaction echoes in his deep voice. "How does our girl want us?"

Instinct has me whipping my head to the pack leader. Hazel green glints in the muted light—and I realize I have no idea where we are or what time it is. The whole world has been reduced to this. *Us*. Here, under a shower of stars, in a cocoon of deep blue.

"It's whatever you want, darling," Ash vows. "We can take turns... Or we can all put our marks on you at the same time."

The certainty I feel is *powerful*. There's no moment of self-doubt or the sense that perhaps I'm being dramatic. As I look from one of them to the next, the deepest, truest part of me knows exactly what they need. How to bring them together.

"All of you," I tell them, surprised by my own steadiness. "It has to be all of you."

Our pack leader smiles, pure pride radiating from his rare, beautiful grin. "That sounds perfect, omega."

Bast exhales shakily, pressing another kiss to my shoulder. "God, yes," he quivers. "Anything you want, angel."

Dair's purr drops into something even more delicious, full of approval and gratitude. A wicked gleam touches his gaze. "Then you'll have all of us, baby."

Fire snaps through my blond alpha's eyes. "I know where I want to bite you, love, but you're going to have to ride your other alphas while I do it."

My core clamps on air, the desperate squeeze enough to have me whining again. Dair grunts at the sound, meeting our leader's eyes over my shoulder.

"Pack alpha goes first," he grits, clearly working overtime to hold himself back.

Instead of snatching me away, Asher starts stroking his cock, working the dripping head in and out of his fist. When the knot at his base twitches fuller, my perfume swells.

"I have an idea," Asher tosses out, rubbing himself harder. "Let's make sure our princess is *completely* full. Then we can give her our bites."

I bounce in Dair's lap, begging in wordless sobs while he groans his agreement. Bast hums, cupping my face and kissing me deeply. His tongue plunges hot and thick against mine as my other alphas shift below me.

Dair lies back, sprawling his legs in a V and holding his cock up straight. Asher raises a wry brow but smirks, lying in the opposite direction and—

Oh.

OH—

Yes!

The prince arranges his thighs over Dair's hips, lining their throbbing shafts up. Dair's is longer and roped in veins, but Ash has more girth… and pre-cum oozing from his head. Their knots both fill as their balls brush.

Dair pulls his lower lip between his teeth, grunting, "You want to try this, baby? It's been your very favorite, but we've never knotted you in this position at the same time."

I nod so hard, blonde waves tumble over my shoulders. Bast lifts me easily, turning my body so my legs bracket his packmates' hips.

Slick pours out, coating both cocks until they're shiny. Bumping one another while they both strain higher, trying to reach my core.

Dair slides straight into my pussy while Asher works his way into my ass much slower. Pulling grunts out of his packmate every time his rigid cock presses harder into the thin wall separating them.

The fullness is a shock to my system. Urgency snaps through

my blood and clamps my core around both of them. Dair groans, his head tilting back. Asher gives a final shove to fill me, then pushes himself upright, balancing on one hand and using his other to gently cup my neck, pressing his chest to my back.

The new position completely exposes the throbbing bud at the top of my slit. Cool air rushes over it, and I cry out, searching for Bast.

"Please, alpha," I whine, leaning back into Asher's languid thrusts while Dair's batter me hard and fast. Bast groans, immediately lowering his face to lap at my clit.

Wild satisfaction streaks up my spine, sweetening my scent. Sensation spirals into my limbs, the tightness pulling taut between my hips. Smoldering and melting. Dousing my alphas.

"That's right," Dair rasps, fucking me even faster. "You were built for our knots. Come on these cocks and then Asher fill you up and bite you."

Bast moans, the vibration spreading tingles from my throbbing nub to the ring of muscle inside me that begs to be satisfied. Asher pants, his lips sweeping my shoulder. "We'll both knot you," he promises, deep and delicious. "Fill you so much you can't move while we sink our teeth into your perfect skin."

Nothing has ever sounded more *right*. Frantic need swerves through my middle, soaking them with more slick. They all groan, the chorus of masculine pleasure reminding me why we're here.

I'm going to bring them together.

The thought sails through my blurry mind, pure bliss sparkling into my veins. A shimmering rush froths over the empty place at the very center of me, leaving absolute certainty behind.

"Please," I whimper, turning to sink my gaze into my pack alpha's. "*Please.*"

Asher's breath stutters, but his answering nod looks a lot like a bow. Steady and reverent.

"*Now,*" he orders, barking softly.

Before I finish my elated gasp, the prince strikes. His teeth find the place where my shoulder knits into my neck, his jaw opened wide to leave a large, perfect mark where his teeth sink through my skin.

Asher.

There's no pain—only *heat.* The warmth of his cock spurting into my backside, his very essence burning a path to that secret place at the heart of me. Quiet and sacred—perfect for our new hiding spot.

Asher pours himself into it, filling the space underneath my lungs so that every breath brushes the piece of his soul he leaves behind.

A tether appears, glowing like the sun behind the clouds. Soft and ethereal.

Waiting for me.

All this time, he's been waiting for me.

I feel it now. Our rope isn't connected yet, but even without the bridge between us, I *know.* This piece of him? It was only ever mine.

Tears well in my eyes as he moans against my skin, gently moving to pop his knot into me. Bast circles his tongue over the top of my clit, sending me into another climax as Dair lunges upright with a roar. He licks the side of my throat, skimming his teeth there with a savage sound.

I clench around him, crying out when he follows suit, locking inside me. Filling the muscles that flutter and gush around his knot. Stuffing me more than they ever have before.

And *surely*, this will kill me—this much raw, pulsing *pleasure—*

My nerves tingle from the rough scrape of his canines along the column of my throat. He groans my name, emptying hot seed into my depths.

I expect him to tear into my neck, but instead, he takes my right hand and brings it up to his mouth. Nuzzling so gently, I feel his breath shaking. His bite is just as tender, wreathed from the thickest part of my palm all the way around my thumb.

Dair.

The second he breaks my skin, a muddle of joy and pain shoots into my veins. But that's Dair—a study in contradictions.

His light is so much brighter because it's surrounded by so much darkness. Like lightning—so brilliant against his thunderous backdrop.

His love, his trust. Striking the deepest piece of my soul, electrifying it. Giving me pain and heat and joy and wonder before blinking back to a dark velvet night.

I might have been afraid of it before. But now, his midnight is the safest place I can imagine.

Tears well in my eyes, spilling over as white teeth flash at my hip, sinking into the bare skin there. I barrel into another climax, automatically reaching down to put my unmarked hand in Bast's hair, tugging as he follows me over the edge. The scent of melted sugar explodes as hot washes of cum coat the side of my thigh.

Blinding warmth glows into my bloodstream, zipping to my core like a pinball. Bouncing with joy, hitting every aching, doubtful place and leaving complete elation behind.

Sebastian.

He's... goodness.

Color and humor and heart.

Earnest care and teasing lightness—the opposites somehow woven into a single strand that coils loose at my center. So eager. *Waiting.*

They all are.

Asher's knot releases and Dair's follows, their bodies reacting as my scent deepens. I scramble in a half-circle, nearly sobbing with relief when my gaze lands on my mark—the place where I'll claim Prince Asher Everhart.

He catches me in his arms, alpha power tingling off him in waves. Hazel eyes snap with fire, blazing as I sink myself back onto his cock and clamp my teeth over the tattoo branded across his pectoral. He shouts, instantly releasing another load into my body as our tether pulls taut and blinks on.

The pleasure may be violent, but the way he feels couldn't be more peaceful. Asher is the patter of quiet rain. The whisper of well-loved pages. The warmth of a mug of tea on a misty afternoon.

His arms lock around my body, pulling me into his chest just like his soul seems to reach for mine, bringing it into his own for safekeeping. For a moment, there's just blurry bliss. And then, the space where they overlap doesn't truly belong to either of us anymore.

Instead, there's a little alcove. A secret place that reminds me of the one we used to hunker down in together. Behind him, I sense a gate. A straight path to him. And another at my back.

But now, we're both here. In this magic hiding spot *we* made.

There you are, he thinks, full of raw emotion. *It feels like I've been missing you forever.*

He latches his mouth over his bite, sucking it until a new wave of release washes through me. I lap at his claim mark, whimpering as he holds me and purrs against my lips.

I love you, goose. My heart has always belonged to you—but now my soul does, too.

His complete sincerity sinks into my bones. Happiness vibrates beneath my lungs, tickling them until they give their own weak rumble.

Bast groans at my small purr, a zing of urgent want flaring into me. Asher feels it and smiles, pride glowing in the curve of his mouth. "Go get the rest of our pack, darling. I'll be right here."

Hot liquid coats my thighs as I rise to my knees and spin for the baron. Climbing his broad, muscled body to reach the front of his throat.

I'm not sure why, but my Omega needs our claim *right there*. Where every single person he meets will see it and know—he's *mine*.

Bast loves that idea as much as I do. When I lick his Adam's apple, he chokes on a moan, gathering my naked curves in his brawny hands. "Yes, Ivy, love. *Please.*"

I spread my jaw as wide as I can, biting him hard right above the base of his throat. Bast growls and grunts, shoving his throbbing cock straight into me. Locking himself in deep as he comes.

The strand stretched between our souls erupts with color. Jubilant and heartfelt and *true*. Light refracting, throwing rainbow sparks.

Sebastian is everything good. Sprinkles on ice cream, the giddiness of an inside joke. And underneath all that? His loyalty is *fierce*. And nothing—*nothing*—matters to him more than this pack.

Than *me*.

The salted sweetness of his scent matches the taste of our tears. His mouth finds mine, and he presses them together, smearing dampness across my lips. Impressing how much he adores me with every ragged breath.

Happy memories beam into the bond, flooding the secret alcove Asher and I made with golden rays of light. Our pack leader's answering joy bounces back at Bast. The alpha in my arms laughs breathlessly, kissing every part of my face.

You did it, angel, he exults. *My perfect girl*.

His heart is so full of happiness, it's impossible for me to contain my own giggle. He steals the sound from my lips with one final press, his knot releasing me even as his soul clasps tight to mine.

It's a beautiful feeling. One that leaves me sniffling as I turn to the last alpha in the room.

My Dairragh.

I can see how carefully he's held himself in check, waiting his turn. His dark eyes burn, begging me to come closer, while the rest of him strains for stillness.

I fully expect him to sweep me into his lap and sink himself inside my pussy, but he surprises me again. Trembling, he remains motionless, swallowing thickly when I reach his side.

He's scared, I realize.

It doesn't make sense... until vulnerability cracks across his features. His scent slices sharper as he raises his arm and holds out his hand.

Asking me to bite him *there*. Over the tattoo. On top of all his thorns.

I *lunge*, snapping his hand between mine and closing my teeth right over the thicket etched below his wrist. The thin skin breaks immediately. Dair's tether tugs taut, slowly flickering to life.

Boundless passion and the darkest depths carve into my soul. Indelible. Impossible. Perfect.

All the times I looked at him and saw indolent apathy seem laughable now. It was all an act. A coping mechanism. Because he cares *so much*, it crushes him. *So much*, he has to find ways to turn it off. Stuff it down. Talk himself out of it.

Except now he *can't*.

Now, he *loves* me. And it's shifted the very foundation of his being.

She knows I love her, right? Please, God. She has to know.

I hear him and start to cry, whining as I fling my arms around his neck. *I hear you,* I tell him, and then repeat the one thing he's always said for me. *I see you. Do you feel how much I love you, too?*

For a moment, he only feels breathless. But then it finally hits him, winding into his chest like a single headlight on a dark road.

Or maybe like a star, drifting through space.

Warm and bright, changing the darkness around it.

With a ragged inhale, Dair bundles me into his shaking arms. Every fiber of him begging me to sink onto the throbbing length that's already spurting hot and thick between my thighs.

I take it.

I take *him*.

Pouring all my devotion into our bond, showing him that it's safe here. We care about him. He's *ours*.

"Ivy," he whispers, pressing his forehead into mine. "How are you this *beautiful*?"

He has his eyes closed, but even if he didn't, I'd know he isn't talking about the way I look. None of them are as their complete and total agreement swarms the bond.

Dair's mouth quirks, his smile soft as he scent-marks my face. Exhaustion winds its way into my body. *Rest, now, darling*, Asher says, his pride and adoration warming me.

Yeah, baby, Dair agrees. *We're here.*

We'll always be here, angel, Bast adds. *Forever.*

sixty-two

Once upon a time, there was a lonely prince.

The image is so clear. A pond and a willow tree. Fog rolling across still water.

And a boy with a book, pretending to look busy as he reads all alone.

I'm not sure how I know he's just pretending, but the way it feels to have to act like a kid who doesn't want friends… the pain of that curls tight in my lungs, coiling right in the spot that squeezes tears into my throat.

Just as the story's narrator drops off, another, deeper voice picks up. *Which was sort of a problem,* it says, *because this story also has one very pissed-off duke.*

The picture ripples, darkening at the edges. Turning into a dusky mansion with despair piled in its shadowy corners. And then there's the young duke—with wild eyes, black hair, and bruises on his wrists that are so deep purple, they rival the ink painted up his forearms.

I watch him flex his fingers, those dangerous eyes glinting with determination. The sentiment echoes in my stomach—a scorching smolder of resolve. He *will* get out. He *will* find a way to make sure this cursed house ends up in a heap of ash. Even if he has to burn it down himself.

At first, I think the pride that swells in my chest is my own—the reaction to his staggering inner strength. But then, the first narrator speaks again, more solemn.

The two misfits somehow ended up forming their own pack, thanks to help from their friend.

A third, much more amused voice cuts in *—who was much better looking, infinitely charming, and a world-class athlete... but still, against all odds, equally lonely.*

The image glimmers into a new one. This time, the fancy house in the backdrop is a clean, happy place. But the young man throwing a squash ball against its white-brick walls—while gorgeous, blond, and built—is decidedly alone.

A dozen more clips just like it follow, memories from when the light-haired boy was younger. Opening Christmas gifts on his own, kicking a soccer ball against a tree, watching his parents drive away, knowing they'd be back but also knowing, while they were gone, he was on his own.

The first voice fades back in, explaining a new picture of the three men as young adults, sitting around a dinner table. *For years,* it says, *they tried their best to make their own family. But as time wore on, they found themselves feeling just as alone, even with one another.*

The next round of mental video clips is hard to take. My eyes are closed, I think, but I still feel the twitching sensation of a would-be wince when the angry, older faces of the three alphas flood my mind.

They needed something to bind them together. A mate, the most serious voice tells me. *But the lonely prince was already in love with a girl he once knew. The only person who had ever made him feel less alone.*

The roughest one interrupts, *And the duke had a similar problem, since he was obsessed with a woman who pieced him back together in an alleyway. Someone so kind and good, she did everything she could to heal him even when he tried to break her apart.*

Breathless pain accompanies that thought, followed by a deep river of regret. The third one adds, *Meanwhile, the handsome baron had no idea he'd accidentally fallen for the gorgeous woman who talked to squirrels and folded their laundry.*

All three storytellers flash their own images of the women they describe.

Except it isn't three different women.

It's just one.

It's just... *me*.

...

Oh *no*.

Am I *dreaming*?

Has all of this been *a dream*?!

Panic bolts upright inside me, my brain staggering to process everything through the lens of reality. Those men weren't royals from a fairytale; they were Asher, Dair, and Bast. And they were —they—

Did I make all of this up?

A beat of surprise thuds behind my sternum, followed by an overwhelming rush of tenderness.

No, darling, the first voice—*Asher's*—speaks in my center. *It wasn't a dream. Just us. Our story.*

I told you guys we should wake her up, Bast groans, full of restless worry.

Dair answers, his tone grumpy in a wry sort of way, *You told us to wake her up with a cunnilingus competition. Which I thought had merit, but the prince wanted to be romantic.*

Asher laughs at his packmate's internal eye-roll. The warm sound echoes internally and somewhere outside my consciousness, too. *We're all princes now, technically.*

The last time I had a brand-new voice in my middle, it wound up being a *whole thing*. So this? *Three* of them?

It takes me a second to remember how to inhale… and open my eyes.

Asher's beautiful face looms over me, his eyes warm with affection and a touch of concern. *Hello.*

I don't think I'll ever get over how adorable he is when he's acting shy. An involuntary grin breaks over my face. *Hi.*

Soft lips brush the claim mark branded into my palm, Dair's rough-edged rumble entering my mind. *I told them I'd punch anyone who woke you up.*

But he won't, Bast chirps. *Because he loves us.*

Shut up, Dair answers, but his mouth curves against my skin. And, behind him, Bast grins bright enough to rival the sun. His sky-blue eyes find mine, full of pride and gratitude.

That one look is what finally forces it all to sink in.

I did it. We're all bonded.

We're also… outside? My head lolls, and I see we're lying on a palette of blankets, including my very favorite silver one. It's seen better days, frankly, but the scents embedded in the satin have every receptor in my brain pumping out geysers of pleasure.

Overhead, the branches of a weeping willow whisper back and forth on a breeze. The air is cool, with the distinct crispness of autumn. When I turn to the left, I see Maytown Manor's small lake, dotted with lily pads.

Bast crawls to my side, bending to scent-mark my cheek, my chest, my shoulder. Which is right around the time I notice we're all totally naked. And we've left the makeshift nest they built for me.

My blond alpha seems to read my mind, his eyes creasing in chagrin. "Are you upset that we're outside, angel? We were going to stay in the bedroom, but then my Alpha kept shoving at me to get you out here."

The old Dair might have let Bast take the fall for the decision, but *my mate*? He shakes his head and admits, "I thought it was a good plan, too."

Asher's soft hazel gaze traces my face. "You were dreaming about the gardens. And the lake."

Dair's smirk smooths into something much more genuine. "It was nice," he murmurs. "I like your dreams, little dove."

I like this, he adds through our bond. *You and me. All of us.*

He doesn't just like it, though. He loves it.

I can feel that—his overwhelming gratitude, with glimmering edges of awe. Bast adds his own burst of appreciative amazement, putting on a cocky grin. "See? Told you he loves us."

Dair huffs, grumbling a "yeah, yeah" while he lowers his face to my belly and nuzzles. I run my fingers through his unruly hair, sending him a tentative beat of thanks. Trying to get used to the feeling of sharing my feelings this way. He nestles closer, pressing a kiss to my bare skin as his eyes close and his purr kicks up.

Asher shifts, propping us both up and sitting behind me. His fingers start working through my waves, unraveling tangles while Bast updates me on everything I missed.

It warms my heart that the very first thing he does is fish out his phone and swipe through dozens of pictures of all my Everdeen creatures. My ducklings, squirrels, birds, and Andromeda. He's gotten daily reports from the groundskeepers and stable hands, ensuring all my animals have their usual food and attention.

I was in my haze for six days. And during that time, their team managed to get Matilda detained without bail, find the pawn shop she sold Mama's sewing table to, and discover that her ashes were still at the apartment. She pawned the urn, apparently—and I feel all three of my alphas brace at that, waiting for me to spiral. But I only feel relief.

"Can we... there's a plot for her beside my father's, but I couldn't afford the burial and the grounds fees..."

Bast looks mildly horrified that he never thought to ask. Dair snarls softly, huddling closer, apologies and protective promises funneling from his section of our bond. Asher simply tucks me back into his body, his voice solemn. "Consider it done, darling. Whenever you're ready."

The others both nod fervently. I smile at Bast, not wanting him to feel bad. "What else, my lord?"

Toffee sweetness deepens as his lungs expand, his smile returning. "Well, we told Maman we won't be having a bonding ceremony. Or, rather, *I* told her."

Asher shrugs, hiding a smirk against my shoulder, right beside his bond mark. "You were already her least favorite, little cabbage."

Dair outright laughs, his eyes full of surprised approval he directs at Ash. "That was a good one."

I roll my eyes at them, reaching out for Bast's hands. Squeezing them as I give a pointed look. "I think what we all mean to say is *thank you*. Right, guys?"

Asher's smile widens, and he nods. "Yes, thank you Bast."

Dair mutters his agreement, showing us his true appreciation inside. I have a feeling there will be a lot of that—outward grousing while only our pack gets to see the real him. Somehow, I can't imagine anything better.

Soaking in my utter contentment, I stare out at the pond. Watching the water and listening to a nearby sparrow. A sudden beat of anticipation and nervousness stretches between the three of them. Asher snuggles me closer before I can ask why.

"We have a gift for you, goose."

His nickname has me grinning, recalling what Bast told me that day at Everdeen. As Dair sits up and the former baron hunts for whatever present they've gotten me, I meet Ash's eyes and whisper just to him, *Geese mate for life, did you know that?*

Absolute adoration swells inside him and smolders in his eyes. *Yes. You said you picked that nickname, but I think I decided to keep calling you that because part of me always knew you were mine. At the very least, it was wishful thinking.*

Wishes and dreams. So many secret hopes that have come true. Asher hears my amazement and presses his mouth to my bite mark. His claim. Shivery tingles roll down my back as I perfume.

Dair's intensity hasn't diminished one bit. If anything, he looks even more feral for my scent and pleasure than he was before. As Bast produces a periwinkle velvet pouch, my wild alpha stalks over on his hands and knees, stealing my lips for a lush kiss.

He pulls back when I'm gasping and cocks a dark brow at me. My favorite crooked grin graces his features. *Later, Your Highness.*

Sebastian kneels at my other side, presenting their gift. "We hope this is okay..."

Dair nods, his eyes bouncing between mine. "I know Maman explained that our pack will need a new crest now that we're bonded. I took a shot at sketching something, and the guys liked it... but if you don't..."

I reach for him automatically, laying his claim mark on my palm over the one I left on the back of his hand. Squeezing, I smile at him and Bast in turn. "Show me!"

Bast fishes out a delicate strand of silver. It takes me a moment to realize—it's my locket. The one that fell off the night I ran from the ball. My face whips to Asher, who smiles wryly. "I told you I'd have it cleaned and get the clasp fixed..."

With shaking fingers, I take the small heart charm from Bast. It looks beautiful—polished to perfection, on a brand-new chain that doesn't have any bent links. "It's *perfect*," I breathe. "Can I put it on?"

Asher nods, taking the necklace from our packmate and draping it around my throat. He fastens it slowly, then runs his fingertips over the sides of my neck, remembering the day he untangled this same piece of jewelry from my hair… and gave me my first kiss.

He gives me another one. A soft brush of his lips along mine.

I pull back to sniffle, immediately plucking the locket up and lifting it for a closer look.

"Open it," Dair murmurs, pressing my palm to his cheek. Watching me with an adorable pinch of nervousness between his brows.

I snap the small heart open, revealing a brand new plate of silver, carefully crafted to fit where a photo might. The sliver of precious metal is engraved. Etched with the image of—of—

Our new crest, Asher supplies.

Dair's design is perfect. Unlike the current Everheart crest, ours has an anatomical rendering of a heart at its center. One surrounded by a bright halo, with thorns wrapped artfully at its base.

It's… the three of them.

Asher as the heart, Bast as the flare of light, and Dair—the thorns poised to protect us.

And surrounding all of it?

A delicate drape of ivy.

epilogue

SEVEN MONTHS LATER

I DON'T THINK I'LL EVER GET USED TO WAKING UP NEXT to Ivy.

I *know* I'll never get used to Dair's snoring.

On the other side of our soon-to-be queen, Asher sighs. I feel his pang of annoyance through our bond and answer with a thud of dry amusement, *Still have the guillotine around here somewhere?*

Asher smirks. *Not sure it would help. Pretty sure his head would just keep on snoring.*

I slant my gaze over to Ivy's sleeping face, bathed in the soft light from the early winter morning. Dair's snore hitches, and our bride snuggles closer to his chest, scent-marking his inked pectoral in her sleep. *Look how happy he makes her.*

Asher's adoration swells to match my own as he watches our omega. *He's not a total pain in the ass*, he thinks. *He handled the healthcare overhaul by himself.*

He did manage to push that through Parliament with shocking ease. And well before our post-bonding ceremony last month... and today's event.

True, I muse. *I only got like eighteen blackmail complaints?*

Asher chuckles out loud. *We'll take it.*

Groggy awareness creeps into the bond, along with Dair's raspy internal voice. *It was sixteen, assholes.*

I can't help my grin. This camaraderie? It's the reason I always wanted a pack.

I'm not the only one fighting to hold us together anymore. Now, they work alongside me. And we all do our best to build the strongest family we can for our girl every day.

Ivy's giggle tells us she's likely been awake this whole time, listening to us without making a peep. She likes to do that, my naughty little angel. Still eavesdropping on us like a maid with a crush.

Except now, she's officially ours in every way.

Our princess. Our mate. And our *wife*.

The four-carat oval diamond on her finger glitters in the early-morning sunlight. She slants her big crystal eyes up at Asher. I see the knowing look in them and grin—our girl has finally learned that the prince lives to fulfill her requests.

"Ash," she says, smiling sweetly. "Can you open the shades?"

Asher drops a kiss to her forehead, hauling himself upright immediately. "Of course, darling."

We all feel how happy doing something so simple makes him. Dair nuzzles a smile into the crook of our mate's neck, kissing the fingertip bruises he left there last night. "You okay, baby? Feeling good?"

Got give it to the former duke. He may be the roughest of us by a mile, but his aftercare is unparalleled. It always extends well into the following morning. Sometimes, it lasts for days.

I have a feeling our post-coronation vacation will be one long cycle of him fucking her every chance and way he gets, followed by him doting on her endlessly.

I send Ivy that thought and she gives me my favorite look—half innocent angel, half witty tease. *Oh dear*, she replies. *Whatever will I do?*

I hide my smirk in her hair, stretching over to balance my forearm on her pillow and steal her lips briefly. When I let her go, she beams up at me but strokes Dair's hair, answering him, "I feel perfect today."

Asher pulls the shades, revealing the misty garden Ivy's remodeled around her gift from him. Their alcove is barely visible through all the dormant flowering plants and our Crenmore fog—but that's the way they like it. A perfect little hiding spot.

When the almost-king collapses back into bed, he chooses the place between Ivy's legs instead of demanding I give his spot back.

Smart bastard. I should have done that.

Asher flashes a rare grin over at me, then drops his face to our wife's thigh. He bites the creamy skin, sucking his own mark over the one I left there during our last round.

"Rude!" I huff.

Ivy titters, turning to kiss my bare chest. "You can make a new one anywhere you want, my lord."

My gaze softens when it catches hers. I can't help the way that happens whenever I look at her—and she loves it. Joy flutters from her body to mine, the warm tingles spreading through my veins.

I hope you never stop calling me that, I tell her, keeping the admission between us. *Even after the coronation today.*

Her smile turns into the shy, true one we all adore. *I'll never stop*, she vows. *Promise, my lord.*

I offer her my pinky, and she wraps hers around it, bouncing back to the grin that steals my breath. Her pretty eyes take on my favorite sly quality. *Think we can get the grumps to let us have coronation cake for breakfast?*

I've been a baron, a sex symbol, a prince, and, soon, a king.

But being Ivy's partner-in-crime will always be my favorite role.

I've got a plan, I tell her. *But you're going to have to take off those panties...*

I DON'T THINK I'LL EVER GET USED TO LETTING A STRIP of fabric garrote me.

It's called a tie, Dair, Asher's calm, wry voice chimes.

Scowling, I yank the square knot at my collar, muttering as I train my eyes on the horizon. It's a nice day for all of this, and I guess I'm glad. Our girl deserves a nice day.

For all her eavesdropping, Ivy is absolutely terrible at sneaking up on me. Even if I couldn't feel her through our bond, the swish of her skirts is a dead giveaway. I'm grinning to myself by the time her hands slide around my waist.

When I don't flinch, she sighs. "You heard me *again*?"

I chuckle darkly. "I always know where you are, baby."

"Mm. Guess I can't be surprised. You *are* a stalker."

I start to flash her a smile, but I can't even turn my head with this noose around my neck. When my face drops into a glower, she smirks, quirking those petal-pink lips to the side.

"This thing giving you trouble?" she guesses, smoothing a hand over the black-and-silver stripes.

I grumble, tugging at the starchy shirt underneath. "Little fucker is trying to strangle me."

Her eyes are so incredibly blue. And so *smart*. It blows me away, how brilliant our mate is. So fucking good and kind and full of love and just *beautiful—*

The curve of her lips softens when she senses the bent of my thoughts. Her scent sweetens, and some of the tension falls off my shoulders. With a deep exhale, I lean my forehead against hers. Letting her in. The way I did the first time I told her I loved her, through our bond.

I'm fucking terrified.

She hums, stepping into my body and winding her arms around my waist. *Why?*

It's a good question. We've known this day was coming for more than a decade. I never *liked* the idea, but it didn't scare me.

Lately, though, whenever I think about taking this mantel... becoming a *king*... I can't breathe.

Why?

Images flit through my mind. Bast and Ivy laughing while she chases him through the yard. Asher curled up with her on the couch, reading the papers to her each morning. Our mate gazing over at me from across every room, feeling my eyes and finally knowing she's allowed to stare back.

A true *family*.

I don't want to screw this up, I realize. *I want to be... good at this. All of it.*

The king stuff, the pack. It's all so goddamn important to me now. Because *she* is.

Ivy looks into my eyes, reading all my half-baked thoughts and fully formed feelings. Her arms hug me closer as trepidation fills her features. *I... really understand.*

I know she does. Bast and Asher were bred for this shit. Ivy and I weren't. As her heart thrums against my chest, though, I get an odd inkling she isn't talking about the crown or the coronation.

But I think, she adds, a pulse of excited determination rushing through her, *we need to get used to the idea. Especially now.*

I wait for her to show me what she means because somehow I know—*I know*—she isn't talking about some throne. An instinctual jolt of concern flares inside me, but she answers it with a soft, trembly smile.

And when she shows me a mental picture, it isn't anything like I imagined. *It's—it's—*

"Yours," she whispers.

In her mind, there's a small monitor. Black and white whoosh in patterns I don't understand until... I hear a rhythm.

A beat.

A *heart*beat.

"Ivy," I breathe, blinking down at her face. "Baby, what—"

She steps back and catches my hand, pressing the palm to her belly. "I mean, obviously, it will be all of ours," she goes on, blushing, "but I'm almost certain it's yours. Dr. Grant seems to think it happened right after my last heat, when Bast caught the flu... Asher was called away for that summit in Prague... and you and I..."

It was the first warm week of spring, so I took her out for a ride on my bike and brought her home to her starry nest. We wound up staying in there for two days, having food brought up. I told the guys I was trying to keep her from catching whatever Bast had, but really, it was like our own little honeymoon.

And it made—we made—

"Our baby," she whispers. Azure eyes swim as they scan my face. "I-is that okay?"

My chest feels like it will cave in and overflow all at once. "Okay?" I repeat, my fingers cupping her belly with more purpose. "Ivy, it's fucking *everything*."

I kiss her until we're both breathless, panting against one another's lips. Ivy smiles shyly, her eyes spilling over. "You're really happy?" she whispers. "I wasn't sure how you'd feel about producing the first royal heir."

Goddamn, she's *right*. This baby will be our pack's first. So it will also be...

The next king or queen, she finishes internally—and I feel her holding the air in her lungs, waiting for me to react. *After today, the next coronation will be... theirs.*

It's somehow everything I ever feared, yet exactly what I need to hear.

I might never feel like I was meant to be a king... but I love Ivy and the guys. If being a good ruler means keeping the seat warm for our children? Shaping a better world for them to inherit?

"I can do this," I realize out loud. A shocked jolt of laughter tumbles out of me. "Ivy—I really think I can do this."

Our omega giggles, too. A watery, wonderful sound that I file away, wanting to remember it—and her gorgeous tear-stained face—forever. "I know you can, Dair," she tells me.

The princess looks down at my hand, spread across her stomach. At the wildflower with too many thorns. The place she claimed for her own.

She puts her palm over it, pressing her bond mark to mine. Holding me and our baby. Offering one final gift when she amends, "I know you *will*."

I don't think I'll ever get used to not caring.

I've spent my whole life smothered by expectations. Duties. And all the dread that came along with them.

Yet today, as I stood in full royal regalia, about to take my father's crown...

And I didn't care about anyone other than the three people next to me.

It didn't matter what the press said or how the scads of titled observers felt. I couldn't even bring myself to look over at the crowd. As they placed the Everhart crown on top of my head and handed me a scepter that's older than the country itself, Ivy's glowing eyes were all I saw.

It's the same an hour later as we gather on the second-story balcony at Everdeen. The front gates are open to allow the public to celebrate our coronation. Thousands anxiously await our official presentation, teeming below the bower of spring wildflowers strung along the front of the palace.

Despite dozens of attendants and advisers milling about the "presentation suite," I still only have eyes for Ivy. Remembering the words she whispered to me last night before we fell asleep.

"You know what I think?" she'd murmured, glancing at Bast and Dair and then to me.

I'd tucked her hair behind her ear with a hum. *"Hmm?"*

"I think this couldn't have happened any other way," she told me. *"If we'd figured out what we were meant to be back then, you might never have formed a pack with Bast and Dair. You might have just bonded with me alone, like your parents."*

The simple truth of that sank in, and my awe brought her shy smile to the fore, the soft curve warming my chest as her joy sparkled into the bond. *"So maybe we had to lose each other,"* she whispered. *"To find them."*

Bast and Dair still, listening to me replay the memory. Thick emotion wells in the middle of our pack bond as we all turn to watch our omega.

My mother fusses over the royal-blue sash pinned across our

new queen's cream gown, smiling as she adjusts the gold-dusted lace demurely draped off Ivy's shoulders. They whisper and laugh, which warms my heart even further and puts a lump in Dair's throat.

My darling girl feels us watching. When she slants her focus across the room and meets my gaze, the pride and softness buried in her blue irises match the emotions she pours into our bond.

Normally, we're evenly matched. But today? She could never compete with the strength of my joy. With the way it feels to look at her and know she's carrying the next heir to our kingdom. Bringing us together in yet another way that only she could.

Beside me, Bast is doing everything he can not to give in to the tears tingling behind the bridge of his nose. I don't blame him—we barely got ourselves together after Ivy's news this morning.

Ivy hears that thought, sending me another burst of affection as she squeezes Maman's hand and crosses the room to me. Midday sunshine glows around her, filling the hollows under her peachy cheekbones and her lovely silver-blonde hair. Her new crown sparkles—brilliant diamonds, sapphires, and aquamarines set in the lightest gold.

When she gets over to us, we all grin at one another, practically bursting with the secret we've decided not to share just yet. Ivy wants to wait a while before word gets out, and—just like we had no trouble waiting several extra months before today's celebrations to let her get her bearings—we're all committed to making sure that happens.

Still, I can't help but bend to kiss her softly. The rest of the room be damned.

Because I don't care what anyone thinks except for my queen. And my packmates.

Bast smiles at the adviser who approaches. "Is it time for our big moment?" he teases, smirking at us. Dair grumbles under his breath, but stands up straighter, casting Ivy a quick eye-roll for good measure.

The grin that spreads over our omega's face is utter perfection.

I sweep her into one more kiss, pulling back to meet her eyes. Sliding into our own little bubble. "Ready, goose?"

She nods, her smile turning tremulous in the best way. "As I'll ever be."

Dair skirts his hand at her hip a bit lower, surreptitiously grazing it along her barely-there bump. He quickly nips his bond mark and mumbles something in her ear that leaves her perfuming as he smiles crookedly.

Bast snorts at him, framing Ivy's cheeks and scent-marking her forehead. "You look gorgeous, angel. Let's go wave to your adoring fans."

He always knows how to bloom her little smirks into full-blown grins. I send him a beat of gratitude that he returns with a clap to my back. "Come on, *Your Majesty,*" he chips. "Move your ass."

We're all still laughing when we emerge onto the wide stone balcony. The crowd below erupts in raucous cheers, the noise deafening. Luckily, we can still hear each other inside the bond.

They love you, baby, Dair says to Ivy.

Best queen ever, Bast agrees, as if it's obvious. To us, it is.

But Ivy giggles. *I've been the queen for about forty-five minutes.*

Yeah, Bast replies, *and they're <u>already</u> cheering for you. Iconic.*

Ignoring the flash of cameras, I step into Ivy's back and wrap an arm around her waist. Gesturing with my other hand. "Go on," I murmur directly into your ear. "You're the one they all want to see."

It's true. The people adore Ivy—a fact that's undeniable as she floats to the flower-wrapped railing and waves. The crowd goes wild, chanting, "Long live the queen."

Ivy smiles demurely, but her sly voice sneaks into the bond. *I wonder if they'd still approve if they knew I'm not wearing any panties.*

We all freeze. And I'm sure the guys' eyes drop to her backside at the same moment mine do. Ivy shoots us a grin. More cameras snap photos. And the thought of them capturing *this* moment—our mate, teasing us, *here. Now.* All of us *gaping*...

I laugh out loud, shaking my head.

This was always going to be the biggest day of my life.

But now, because of her, it's also the happiest.

I DON'T THINK I'LL EVER GET USED TO RECEIVING presents for every single occasion.

But I'm definitely not complaining.

A construction crew started working on this coronation day gift three weeks ago—and Dair's been breathing down their necks each day to ensure it was finished for tonight.

The balcony is a lovely addition to our suite and an ideal spot for my second favorite gift, which arrived this morning, from Jasmine:

A pumpkin vine in a big gold trough. Along with a note that said, *Just in case, babe.*

I smirk at the seedling, shaking my head. I'm pretty sure I won't need a runaway carriage anytime soon, but it will be fun to make the guys get their hands dirty in the garden when it's time to plant it. In the meantime, I think it will do well out here in the sun.

The balcony will also be a special place for Asher and I to have our breakfasts, me and Bast to keep an eye on our animal friends, and the ideal star-gazing spot to share with Dair.

Dair is one of your daddies, I tell the little life inside me. *He's the one who will make sure you're always safe.*

That's what my inked-up alpha is doing right now, actually. Walking the corridors in our wing one final time, ensuring all the security is in place while he makes his way back to our suite. I tune in to his mental checklist for a moment, smiling to myself.

The grin only grows when Bast's thoughts intrude. Always the loudest, of course, and most colorful. He's firing off a string of internal curses at the moment. Annoyed that Asher beat him at chess. Again.

Sebastian will be the fun one, I go on. *He'll have you outside, running and swimming and rowing and riding horses. I bet if we team up, we can even get another pony out of this.*

The thrill of Asher's victory fades quickly from his mind. He starts to think of his mile-long to-do list but actively halts himself and re-centers, choosing instead to focus on his mild impatience. It matches the others'—they're all anxious for me to come inside so we can get in bed and celebrate our monumental day.

They'd probably be even more worked up if they knew about my third favorite coronation gift—a very on-brand pair of pearl-trimmed panties from Gracie and Tanya. Which are currently hiding under this gown...

But I know my alphas will wait as long as they need to. For me.

For both of us, I whisper to our baby. *Your other daddy, Asher, will move heaven and earth for you. He'll be the most thoughtful, patient person you know. And he's the best listener there is.*

My king proves my point when his warm voice winds into my body. *Are you talking about us, goose?*

The suite's door clicks open as Dair returns, adding his own beat of fond amusement. *Spilling all our secrets already?*

What 'secrets?' Bast asks. *As if me getting our prince or princess a pony was <u>ever</u> in question.*

Laughing, I wave them all off. *Leave me be! I'll come inside in a minute.*

They all grumble, turning their attention to getting out of their suits and unmaking our bed. I smile and spin back to the balcony's rail, leaning over it and gazing upward.

My mother taught me to wish on stars, I finally say, promising, *I'll teach you, too, little one.*

The first star I see winks low on the horizon. And I could swear it's the same one I glimpsed from the apartment window so many months ago.

My hand automatically floats up to grasp my locket, fisting it tightly. I close my eyes, searching through all my joy and gratitude and hope.

Plucking up another wish to whisper to the universe.

want more?

coming fall 2025 from

ARI WRIGHT

Bound to the Beasts

a why-choose

dark & sweet

fairytale reimagining

pre-order now!

coming soon!

KNOT HER Catch

A WHY-CHOOSE BASEBALL omegaverse romance

ARI WRIGHT

acknowledgments

It is my fervent hope that every person finds the sort of best friend who listens to their insane ideas and loves them anyway. Basically: everybody needs a Kelly! Thank you for always being there to listen (and come up with all the cutest names!). This has been the craziest ride and I love you for being on it with me!

To my Katie, who listens to thousands of unhinged voice notes, takes sobbing phone calls, and never says no to, "Okay, but hear me out..." I could never do this without you! Thank you for helping me make this magic and give it to our readers. The universe answered a wish I never knew I made when it sent you to me.

For all of the people behind the scenes cheering me on, especially Amanda, JL, Eliza, and Kendra. I have so much gratitude for each of you! Thank you for being my unhinged enablers!

A big thanks to Nikki for stepping in and helping me get this one over the finish line! I appreciate you!

Lastly, to my husband: thank you for keeping the plants (and the kids lol) alive for the last two months. I owe you, babe.

about the author

Ari Wright was once entirely sane, but then she realized sanity is overrated and decided to write swoony Omegaverse smut.

Because life is short, you know?

When she isn't writing unhinged romances, she enjoys drinking coffee to the point of excess, kitchen experiments, raising her littles, and trying to keep her plants alive (just kidding, her husband does that).

She loves really embarrassing music, moody weather, and any story where the bad guy gets the girl—because what's Happily Ever After without a little (or a lot of) spice?

You can follow her works in progress, favorite reads, and very pink aesthetic on Instagram!

Printed in Great Britain
by Amazon

59680483R00249